ALSO BY CATHRYN GRANT

THE WOMAN IN THE HOTEL

A PSYCHOLOGICAL SUSPENSE NOVEL

ALEXANDRA MALLORY
BOOK FOURTEEN

CATHRYN GRANT

ISBN: 978-1-943142-74-3

This book is a work of fiction. References to real people, events, establishments, organizations, or locales are intended only to provide a sense of authenticity, and are used fictitiously. All other characters, and incidents and dialogue, are drawn from the author's imagination and are not to be construed as real.

Visit Cathryn online at CathrynGrant.com

Cover design by Lydia Mullins Copyright © 2023

CHAPTER 1

 ew York

* * *

I wasn't in the habit of talking to anyone about anything going on inside my head.

But Damien wasn't anyone. Talking to him was different because he would never repeat the secrets I told him. Not verbatim, anyway. He would pick up a phrase here and there, he might choose an appealing word and repeat it over and over, telling everyone who came into the apartment what was on my mind, but they wouldn't understand because he would keep the critical details locked inside his tiny brain.

When I spoke to him, his eyes peered back at me as if he knew more than he was saying.

I was careful to keep the names and identifying details of other people to myself, of course. If I named names, he might give away more than he should.

But I really liked talking out loud, going over the things that were spinning viciously inside my mind until I felt as if four life-threatening blades were positioned inside my skull, a blender turning the flesh and blood vessels and nerves of my brain to pulp.

"I don't know what he knows," I said. And inside my mind, I whispered his name—*Ned*. Lately, he was always in my apartment, even though he didn't belong there. My agreement with Eileen had been that the two of us would live together. But Ned had become a constantly hovering presence.

"He acts as if he knows something, as if he knows *everything*. I'm almost certain he doesn't know anything at all, but I can't be sure. He looks me right in the eye, and that's unsettling. Do you know what I mean? Not many people can do that and lie at the same time."

Damien cocked his head and looked directly into my eyes with his beady, black ones.

I nodded at him. "You know."

He gave a single nod in return.

"He wants me to ask what he knows. He wants me to be upset. He wants me to think he's figured me out. He knows there's something different about me, and his instincts aren't wrong."

Delicious mango!

"I know he can't begin to guess the truth, but I really don't like that he's talking to … well, I know who I mean." I smiled at Damien.

He bobbed up and down. *Guess the truth!*

It startled me when he squawked out those words. I hadn't heard him speak them before. He was listening more closely than I'd realized. Usually, he limited himself to two-word phrases. Maybe I should be more careful with what I was telling him. I laughed, considering how that thought would sound if I spoke it to another human being.

"Even if he knows nothing at all, even if he doesn't think there's anything scary or worrisome about me, I don't like that he keeps poking at me. It's annoying. Is it just a game to show me he has the upper hand? Maybe all he wants is to make me uncomfortable and he thinks that will do it. Who knows? He's strange. But I can't assume that, can I?"

Damien bobbed his head. He turned and began walking around the living room, looking for the rest of the food pellets I'd hidden for him. He was obviously tired of my circular speculation.

I continued talking in a softer voice. I needed to listen for the sound of a key in the lock, so it was better not to talk quite so loudly.

"There's also …" I finished the sentence in my mind—Diana. "She's going to keep thinking and talking and asking questions. There's no way she would ever think … you know. People just don't think that way. They don't assume someone they know could ever do something like that."

I stopped talking as Damien's crown rose higher. Maybe I was upsetting him.

But it was true. People don't ever think someone they know is a killer. Even when they find out someone they know actually did commit murder, they never want to believe it. So there's not a lot of risk. Despite that, she was going to keep asking the same questions and thinking about the unsolved murder of James. She might have suspicions she would tell the police. And the police are the opposite of normal people. They think everyone they know is a criminal.

Damien returned to searching for food.

"And then there's …" I sighed. "He's a problem I created all by myself. A problem that's not really a problem, and one that I don't want to cut out of my life. How did I manage that?" I laughed. I picked up my iced latte and took a sip. I'd left it too long, and the drink was watery. I put it on the coaster, leaned against the back of the couch, tilted my face toward the ceiling, and closed my eyes.

Even thinking about Hunter made me feel the sensation of his hand on my thigh. I felt the resonance of his voice traveling through my bones. The sound of it made them vibrate as if his voice was the perfect pitch for my body. I couldn't explain it in a way that didn't sound like something out of a fantasy story. As if I were creating a fairy tale.

Hunter wanted to know everything about me, and I wanted to

know everything about him. At the same time, I wanted to tell him absolutely nothing about me and everything.

It was like a Rubik's cube, which was actually a Rubik's octagon. Absolutely impossible to solve.

This was why my thoughts were spinning like they were caught in a blender. Without Hunter always at the back of my mind, I could manage Ned. And I would hardly be thinking about Diana and her dead employee slash former one-night stand at all. Hunter was the one who had knocked me entirely off balance.

CHAPTER 2

*A*s I'd been anticipating, I heard the sound of Eileen's key in the lock. The apartment door opened and with it, Damien's yellow crown rose to a ninety-degree angle. He waddled toward the door. I didn't like using that word to describe his walk. It seemed degrading, but it was the best way to describe it. Walking birds look silly, their majesty lost. When they eat, they look awkward and anxious as they try to grab food with no hands to assist, no matter how expert their clawed feet are at picking up and tearing apart tasty morsels. It looks stressful.

Eileen closed the door, then immediately leaned against it to pull off her four-inch heels. She sighed as if she'd just stepped into a warm bath. "My poor feet. I adore these shoes, but such torture when I walk too far."

Torture!

She glared at Damien. She had reached a truce of sorts with him, but she hated it when he mimicked her. She never found it amusing and was never impressed by his vocabulary or his ability to quickly pick up new words. Not even his sometimes eerily accurate context nudged her to admire his intelligence.

"I hope he didn't drop any—"

"He's fine," I said. "He's eating."

"But they sh—"

"He's *fine*. I'm watching him."

She moved toward the couch, leaving her shoes by the door. She dropped her purse and the bag with her make-up and other supplies on the floor. She sat down and lifted one foot onto her opposite knee, massaging the arch with her thumbs.

"Don't you usually bring walking shoes with you?"

"I was late. I forgot."

I stood and went to the far end of the couch. I reached around the side and retrieved the piece of mango I'd hidden for Damien's dessert.

"That's disgusting, leaving fruit on the carpet," Eileen said.

I held up the small paper plate it had been sitting on.

She rolled her eyes. "How much longer did you say he'll be here?"

"I didn't." I went to the kitchen and placed the mango on the floor. Damien moved so quickly it reminded me of watching a windup toy race across the room. He chortled and began eating.

"Are you locking him up after this?"

"Yes."

She leaned back against the couch. "You and I have an unfinished conversation that's been hanging out there a long time," she said. "I thought about it all the way home today and I really want to talk about it. I feel terrible that I haven't been as supportive as I should have been. But I also feel you've left me a little in the dark."

I had a good idea what was coming, and I'd had some time to manufacture an answer for her. I hoped it wasn't a lie that would trip me up later, which some of them seemed to be doing lately.

"Your ex," she said. "The stalking. The violence. The—"

"There wasn't any violence."

"You made it sound like you were afraid of him. I had the impression he hurt you. Physically."

I settled in a cross-legged position on the kitchen floor and studied Damien's fierce beak as he gobbled the mango. I wondered how much damage that beak could inflict on a human body if Damien was upset, if he felt threatened.

"Can't you put him away?" Eileen asked. "I'm trying to talk to you."

Put him away! Put him away!

He already had that phrase integrated into his repertoire. He'd heard Ned say it every time he was in our apartment.. And he'd heard Eileen repeat it countless times already. I was getting a little tired of it.

"Are you enjoying your mango, Damien?" I asked.

Delicious mango!

"He doesn't know what he's saying. You sound bird-brained yourself when you talk to him like he's a human being. Do you know that?"

"I'm just having fun. It doesn't mean anything."

"You sound like you take it seriously. It's a bird. It's *parroting* you. That's all. You can't carry on a conversation with it."

"With *him*."

"Whatever."

"He's a better conversationalist than some human beings," I said.

"Like me? Is that what you're saying?"

"No."

"Why do you talk to him? Is it because you're afraid to have a real conversation with me? That's what Ned thinks."

"I'm not interested in what Ned thinks."

She let out a painful sounding sigh. "Why do you hate him so much?" She lifted her foot off her knee and switched to the other foot, massaging it as if she were rubbing a crystal ball that might provide the answer to her question if I didn't.

"I don't hate him."

"It feels like you do."

"He's constantly trying to pick a fight with me. It's tiring. And irritating."

"No he isn't. He's just looking out for me. And when you act like this, he worries about me. You can see why that is, can't you?"

"How do I act?"

"Talking to a bird. Dodging questions. Refusing to open up."

"We're not required to answer other people's questions."

"That's not very friendly. It's a weird way to look at things. It sounds like you don't trust anyone."

"Don't read too much into it," I said.

"He's just trying to get to know you. And when you don't answer questions directly, it sounds like you're maybe not being totally honest, or hiding something. Like you might be lying. That makes him worry."

"What's he worried about?"

Delicious mango!

The fruit was gone. I stood, toying with the idea of cutting him another piece, but Tess had been firm that I shouldn't over-indulge him, no matter how much he repeated one of his favorite phrases in an effort to get another treat.

I held out my forearm. He lowered his crown and cocked his head to the side, clearly hoping I would relent and give him another piece of fruit. "Time to go back in your cage, Damien. Let's go." He climbed on. I pushed myself carefully to my feet and walked slowly to my room. He made quiet chattering sounds, studying my face as I walked. When I reached the open cage door, he stepped inside without resisting. I closed and latched the door. I returned to the kitchen, cut a piece of mango, went into my room and put it through the opening into his dish.

Delicious mango!

I could have sworn his tone changed, that he wanted me to know he appreciated me breaking the rules. But I wouldn't tell Eileen that.

CHAPTER 3

*E*ileen was right—it would have been more entertaining to continue my conversation with Damien. Just a few short months ago, I'd had quite a few good times with Eileen. We'd spent hours talking about clothes and our careers, food and men. Now, all she did was complain that I didn't share enough secrets with her or spend enough time hanging out. I needed to figure out a way to reverse the trajectory of our relationship.

I sat on the living room floor, stretching my legs out in front of me. I picked up my water bottle that had been sitting under the coffee table out of Damien's way. I took a long swallow.

"Thank you for putting him away," she said.

I took another sip of water. "Just to be clear, my ex wasn't violent. And I'm not afraid of him."

"But you said—"

"He stalked me for a while, and when you and I were getting ready to sign the lease for this apartment, I had a knee-jerk reaction. I wanted to make sure he couldn't find out where I'd gone. Since he works in IT, he's good at crawling through electronic drawers and closets and finding out things about people. It's a hobby for him—

gathering data just to have it. Then, he can taunt people and let them know he knows things about them."

As the words came out of my mouth, forming themselves before my brain had time to consider where this story was going, I felt them growing more solid. I heard how I was shaping another story that would probably be more difficult to dismantle than the sketchy one I'd told her to keep my name off the lease. The more specific the lie, the more difficult it was to adjust it. Soon, it would be impossible to change the elaborate lie at all. The thing would take on the form of an Egyptian pyramid, a perfect shape that was essentially indestructible.

"I didn't intend to make it sound like a massive trauma," I said. "I'm not sure why you interpreted it that way. It was just the easiest thing to do—keep my name off the lease. It wasn't a big deal, and I didn't mean to leave you with all the responsibility."

"That's not how I remember it. You seemed scared. I had the definite impression you were really afraid of him. That's why I was so happy to do it."

I gave her a look of absolute confusion. "I don't understand why you thought that."

"Because that's what you *told* me!"

"I'm sure I didn't."

"Don't gaslight me," she said.

I laughed. "I'm not gaslighting you. I don't get scared, so I never would have said that."

"But you *acted* that way. You said he was angry."

I stood and flipped up the top of my water bottle. I took several large gulps. "Please don't worry about me. I'm not scared. I just don't like him snooping around, trying to get information about me. You can understand that, can't you?"

"Of course. It would scare me, too."

I smiled. "I told you, I'm not scared. He's harmless. He's just a constant annoyance."

"You sound really defensive. And you told me he was volatile, that he made you feel like a child."

I regretted the previous lies, and the new lies, and all the small connecting lies in between. I regretted bringing it up. It would have been better to say nothing. I'd made a mess of things, trying to make her feel better, trying to force her to stop worrying about me. I should have let her worry. She was wearing me down with her constant questions and concerns, and I was still no closer to finding a way to make her stop.

CHAPTER 4

iana cornered Fallon and me in the break room, our tiny team of three women, all that was left of Fly Higher, for the time being. There was no one to make coffee since James had insisted on taking full control of that task.

Diana certainly wasn't going to do it because there was no question it was not the CEO's role. Fallon didn't think it should fall to her as the office administrator. That was too much expectation of menial work, treating her as if she was less important because her job was clerical. I wasn't inclined to do it because I was rarely inclined to do anything when I could just as easily stop for a drink at a coffee shop and not have to deal with the mess of dumping out soggy grounds, cleaning the metal filter, and washing the carafe.

As a result, there was often no coffee.

I wanted a second cup after my latte was gone, so I'd condescended to make a pot. I'd been tempted to make only enough to fill a mug, then decided that was a bad move.

Now Fallon had joined me, waiting for it to brew.

"The memorial for James is Wednesday. At Our Lady of Sorrows Catholic Church," Diana said.

Neither Fallon nor I said anything.

"We can share a cab," Diana said.

Fallon blinked twice. "I didn't really know him. I wasn't—"

"You worked with him," Diana said. "Why would you say you didn't know him?"

"We weren't friends. I didn't have any feelings for him."

"He was a colleague. You owe him your respect. We're going as a team."

"It's required?" I asked.

"Yes."

"Like, it's in our job description?" Fallon pulled the carafe off the coffee stand before it was finished. Coffee dripped onto the hot plate, sizzling and giving off a burnt smell. She filled her mug and stuck the carafe back in place.

"I'm not going to have a discussion about it," Diana said. "He was a valued colleague and we need to pay our respects to him and represent this organization. Together. It's the least we can do."

I avoided meeting Fallon's gaze. I could feel her staring at me, wanting me to argue, longing for me to tell Diana I wasn't going.

I didn't want to go. I didn't want to sit in a church, even a beautifully designed Catholic version, and I didn't want to hear all kinds of exquisite lies about a man who I thought was better off ceasing to exist. I didn't want to sit next to Diana and feel the heat of her sorrow. It might be interesting and fun to watch Fallon squirm, though. So maybe it would be worth it. And Catholic churches did have nicer architecture than the utilitarian building where I'd attended church as a child.

I wondered if there would be a coffin. I wondered if they would have it yawning open and I would have to see his smug face one last time. I wondered if Diana planned to speak.

And so we went.

Fallon wore black—black boots that went over her knees with stiletto heels and pointed toes and a skirt that showed a strip of skin an inch wide between the hem and her boots. She wore a black sweater and a black jacket and a black fascinator, which made her look like she was attending a funeral in Great Britain. Although maybe they don't wear such flamboyant boots to their funerals. I also wore black, but slightly less showy. Only slightly.

Diana wore navy blue and told us we were old fashioned for thinking we should wear black to a funeral.

"I thought it was required." Fallon folded a piece of chewing gum and stuck it into her mouth. She chewed it carefully so she didn't look like she was being crass, I suppose. Maybe she didn't think about it at all.

We filed into the church behind Diana. She walked down the side aisle and chose a pew that was only four back from the front, then walked the entire length until we were as close as possible to the center aisle. It was polite of her to leave space for those who came after us, but it made me think we might end up trapped.

I had no idea how many friends and family James had. Judging by his evening drinking in the bar where I'd begun setting my trap for him, he didn't have a vibrant social life, but I knew nothing about his weekends, or his life prior to coming to Fly Higher, so it was possible, there would be hundreds of mourners.

We settled in. Rather, Diana and I did. Fallon wriggled and twisted, complaining about the discomfort of the wooden pew, checking behind her every forty or fifty seconds to see how much the church was filling up.

While we waited, an organist played hymns that were loud enough to drown out the whispers and the shuffling and footsteps that only became evident between songs.

There was indeed a coffin. The lid was closed, which I appreciated. I doubted many people left them open anymore. Most people didn't bother with coffins at all, going straight from their deathbeds to a crematorium and back into the earth as flakes of ash, which seemed a lot cleaner to me, but also possibly a bit sudden and disorienting to those saying goodbye.

Diana had directed her attention to the mahogany box the moment we were seated, and she didn't break eye contact the entire time until the priest took his place at the top of the steps leading to the altar.

The service was traditional, with all the words and songs coming out of the books in the racks attached to the pew in front of us. I'd been to Catholic churches a few times in my life, but it had been a while, and it was always shocking to see how different it was from the experiences inside the church of my childhood where everything was unplanned. It was like attending an improv show versus an opera where every note and word is scripted.

I could see where people might find comfort in this type of ritual, hearing the same thing over and over, not having to make decisions or think very much. The words washed over you with archaic structures. Words not used in daily life that could become a mantra of sorts, lulling the brain into a state of numb acceptance that might be considered a state of peace.

Diana's face grew tight once the ritualistic part ended and friends and family members began standing and walking to the pulpit to memorialize the creep she'd thought so highly of. This time, the organ music was toned down to a soft murmur, so their footsteps on the stone floor were loud, echoing through the building, off the wooden pews and beams, striking the glass and shooting back against our eardrums like gunshots.

Like the dead at all funerals, James was transformed into a saint before our eyes. His career was filled with meaning and achievements that were mind-boggling for such a brief time on earth. His sense of humor and his concern for his fellow human beings were breathtaking. His kindness and graciousness, his philanthropy and the goodness he showed his family were without compare. He was a magnificent human specimen, larger than life, worthy of being captured in a book of mythology.

I wanted to gag on the bile swimming in my stomach at the picture of this non-existent man that was rising up before all of us. Diana looked like she wanted to break into tears or a song. She nodded vigorously and eagerly at all the speakers.

When it was over, Fallon stood and tried to squeeze her way past a few others in our pew, headed for the door, eager to escape. Diana grabbed the hem of Fallon's jacket. "Not so fast," Diana said. "We need to talk to the bereaved."

"I don't know them," Fallon said.

"That's not important. You owe them your concern and James your respect."

"I don't owe them shit," Fallon said.

Diana looked as if Fallon had slapped her face. "That is so disrespectful."

"I don't owe them."

"We're going to give them our condolences, it's the entire reason for being here."

"If you say so."

"I definitely say so."

Diana took Fallon's upper arm and guided her toward the end of the pew, where we came to a standstill. The aisle was a solid line of people, all waiting for each mourner to greet the family. It took some time to shake hands, offer kisses and hugs and remark about such tragedy—the senseless murder of a wonderful man. I planned to shake their hands and let Diana speak for me. I expected Fallon was planning the same.

CHAPTER 5

*I*t took us nearly fifteen minutes to reach the three sets of doors at the back of the sanctuary. In the vestibule, the last barrier between us and the sunshine, stood James' two sisters. They both looked so much like him, I felt the bile I'd expected to feel if I'd had to see his waxen face in the coffin. Between them was a woman I assumed was his mother, bent over as if she might not manage to keep herself erect for one more handshake beyond what she'd already offered.

About six or seven feet past one of the sisters, was a man who also bore a strong resemblance to the man I'd murdered. Judging by the distance between him and James's mother, as well as the position of the buffer daughter, I assumed there was a divorce and an unfriendly gathering together to bury their son and brother.

We dutifully shook each warm, pulpy hand. Diana hugged each family member and told them how heartbroken and angry she was, and what a loss our organization had suffered. Fallon and I stood back, and then we were swept into the sunshine by the press of people behind us.

At the bottom of the steps, Fallon immediately pulled out her phone. As I turned toward Delancey Street, eager to start walking as fast as I could toward the subway, Diana said, "Where should we go?"

"Go?" I asked.

"For drinks. For our personal eulogies."

"Really?" Fallon said. "Are you for real?"

"Your lack of respect is kind of disgusting," Diana said. "And hurtful."

"I told you, I didn't know him."

"You worked together!"

"Yeah, for what, three weeks?"

"But you don't drink," I said.

She glared at me. "James's death has gutted me. And it's really sickening to me that the *murder* of your colleague isn't more upsetting to both of you."

Fallon looked guilty. She slid her phone into her purse.

Diana stepped to the curb and hailed a cab. One pulled over so quickly I thought it might jump the curb. She opened the door. "Let's go."

I thought about suggesting the bar where I'd spent a few weeks watching James go for his nightly drinks while I solidified his habits in my mind before I set him up for his death. But that would be stupidly risky, just to please myself with the game of it. If the bartender recognized me, it wouldn't be good.

In the cab, I escaped to my phone and let Diana make the choice and give an address to the cab driver. She also busied herself on her phone during the short ride to a bar that looked nothing like a place James would have chosen.

The patio was a lush garden, more wine bar with ornate iron chairs and tables than a place to order shots with rings of alcohol burned into thick oak tables. I couldn't see James liking it at all, except that it was populated primarily by women, so maybe he would have liked it after all—an endless choice of women to scrutinize, deciding whether they suited his tastes.

We settled at a table near a wall covered with a flowering vine.

The moment she sat, Fallon sneezed. Twice. "I don't think I can sit here. I'm allergic to whatever this is." She waved her hand at the leafy, flowery wall.

"Are you sure?" Diana placed her purse on the ground near her feet and picked up the wine list.

Fallon sneezed.

Diana sighed. She pushed her chair out and stood. "I don't think we'll be able to get another table. Take my seat and hopefully you'll be far enough away."

Fallon looked annoyed, her nose already red. Diana looked equally annoyed, as if Fallon had manufactured her allergy for the sole purpose of spoiling Diana's private memorial service, and might be planning to interrupt her eulogy with violent sneezes that would shake our wine glasses right off the table, covering the rough tiled ground with shards of glass.

Diana ordered a very nice, very expensive bottle of Chardonnay and no appetizers. After the wine had been opened and poured and the server had left us alone, she raised her glass. "To James. A man with deep insight into the human soul."

Fallon sneezed.

"I'll drink to that," I said.

Diana's eyes were filled with tears and I don't think she realized I was drinking to the sneeze, not the nonsense she believed about James.

For nearly twenty minutes, Diana talked about what a wonderful man he'd been—how kind and thoughtful, how intelligent, how easy-going. There wasn't an adjective or positive attribute she didn't think defined him. She didn't ask us to say much, which was good, but she repeatedly urged us to agree with her. She didn't seem to notice how limp our voices sounded when we muttered vague words that sounded like agreements but were really nothing of the sort.

When she was finished, the bottle of wine was empty. I picked up my purse, and Fallon did the same. Diana signaled the server and ordered a second bottle of the same wine.

Speaking with a clogged nose, Fallon said, "I should eat something if I'm going to have more wine."

Diana ordered a cheese plate and a large bottle of sparkling water.

As we began the second half of our unwanted wake, she straightened her back and raised her glass as if for another toast. I wondered what fantastic words she would find to say this time.

"I'm not going to have any peace of mind until I find out who did this to him," she said.

I took a long swallow of wine.

"It makes no sense. Everyone liked him. He was a good person. I don't know how I can begin to find out, and I know the police are investigating, but I have to do something. I haven't slept since the day we heard."

"It's your grief talking," I said.

"I know. But it's also more than that."

"It seems like he got mixed up with the wrong people," I said.

"That's such a cliché. You sound like his family. They've given up. They think if the police can't find any evidence, then there's nothing to be done."

"They're probably right." Fallon reached into her purse and pulled out two tissues. She blew her nose, then gave me a miserable look.

"Someone in that hotel must know something," Diana said.

"Do you have time to investigate a murder?" I asked.

"He was a good friend. Why can't you understand that? And actually, yes. I do have time. Outside of work, I don't have a lot of commitments."

"A hobby." Fallon giggled, then blew her nose again. "I think I'm going to head out, if we're done remembering James. I can't breathe and I'm tired of blowing my nose."

"It's not a hobby," Diana said. "He was *murdered*. It's not right that someone should get away with it. I want to know why. And I want that person punished."

I nodded, as if I understood her desire to know. I did understand. I also hoped she would run into a brick wall. Fallon left, and we finished the bottle of wine. When Diana walked out of the bar, I was surprised that she didn't seem at all tipsy. For someone who never drank alcohol, she'd absorbed it like water. I hoped it wasn't because she was so fired up to find the person who murdered James. The alcohol was unable to dull the adrenaline surge.

CHAPTER 6

$\mathcal{T}$he day after James's funeral, Diana and I had our first appointment with Brie Brixton. Brie was the owner of four high-end health clubs catering to people who could afford a club that was so outrageously expensive, a weekly 90-minute massage was included in the membership fee.

Despite Diana telling her she should meet with us alone, Brie had insisted her head and body sculpting trainer, Andy, would join us for this first meeting at her flagship club. As we settled into the cab, I asked Diana, "I wonder if Brie is her real name."

"I'm sure it is."

"Is she married?"

"I have no idea. What does that have to do with anything?"

"Because it sounds like a porn star name."

"I don't want to hear that comment ever again."

"I was just thinking out loud."

"Please don't," she said.

I actually liked Brie's first name, although it did make me hungry. At the same time, it was probably an unfortunate name for someone who was hard core about people getting into optimum physical shape. I kept those thoughts quiet, as Diana had advised. I was trying to establish a smoother relationship with Diana, but so far, it wasn't working. She snapped at me no matter what I said.

Every time she corrected me or told me what to do or pointed out how difficult I was, I strained to remember what it was that had seemed to click between us when I'd first started working for Trystan. It was effortless. I remembered that I'd liked her cool, detached style. She'd seemed to appreciate that I was blunt. Now, she loathed every honest word that came out of my mouth.

It seemed almost as if she'd been brainwashed, like those people who have risen up the corporate ranks and crossed the line into executive management. Once they move into the executive arena, the words that come out of their mouths are scripted by PR experts and teams of attorneys. But we weren't in a large corporation. There were only three of us, soon to be four.

There were no attorneys. All the guidelines for our behavior and strategy came directly out of her head. So what had changed? I couldn't imagine she was going to connect with people who saw themselves as trendsetters and risk takers and mavericks if she was so over-rotated toward being perfectly polite in every possible way.

The only thing she was doing that fell outside her strict rules of business management that she seemed to be inventing, as the need arose, was her pursuit of James's killer.

Brie's lavish office took up a quarter of the fifth floor of the five-story building. The strange thing about her office was that there was nothing office-like about it at all. There was no desk, no shelves, no visible computer, and no conference table. There were two leather couches facing each other, several very comfortable-looking chairs arranged in corners with tables that were basically small oak pillars with plants on them. There was no artwork on the walls because they were papered floor to ceiling with images of people sweating. One wall depicted two women sweating as they lifted barbells, another featured women and men sweating while they ran along open trails through rough looking, hilly terrain. The third showed women sweating while sparring with boxing bags, and the fourth pictured a group of men and women wrapped in small towels, comfortably seated in a sauna, with artistic drops of water running down their bodies.

I didn't know where to look.

I don't mind sweating myself, I like exerting myself, but looking at photographs of sweaty models isn't appealing. And they were so large, so all-consuming. The effect was claustrophobic, even though the room was huge. There were no windows, and the climate was controlled to perfection. I couldn't quite figure out if I was too warm or too cool or nestled into something womb-like. That too was disconcerting.

Brie had white-blonde hair cut short and made stiff with gel. She was delicately curvy, with nicely shaped muscles. She moved with the stealth of a wild animal. As soon as she'd greeted us, the door opened, breaking off one leg of one of the women slamming her boxing glove into a red punching bag that was larger than me. A man with hair the same color as Brie's walked into the room. He was dressed identically to Brie in black shorts and a white T-shirt that said Bodies By Brie, another somewhat unfortunate slogan, I thought. His muscles bulged beneath the T-shirt.

He grinned as he charged at us, his arm extended. "Andy. Head body man." His grin spread farther across his face, if that were possible. Instead of shaking our hands, he made a fist and waited for us to do the same so he could give us a knuckle bump.

It was going to be an unusual meeting, and I was quite sure I was going to have a lot more fun than Diana.

Andy sat cross-legged on the floor, still grinning. He was starting to look almost maniacal and I could see from the corner of my eye that Diana was having a hard time focusing her attention on Brie.

"Usually," Diana said, jerking her head toward Brie, "we meet alone with our clients. Your staff won't have anything to contribute to our process."

"I'm not staff," Andy said.

"It's still a—"

"Andy does everything with me." Brie placed her hand on his shoulder.

"I created Brie's body. Doesn't she look amazing?"

She did look amazing. I couldn't argue, but we weren't there to help her body fly higher. This was about her career development. I settled back against the couch, glad of Diana's constant reminders that I was to keep silent. It was like watching my own private live comedy show.

"Guess how old she is," Andy said.

"I don't think—"

"Guess."

"I don't think that's relevant," Diana said.

"How about you?" He looked directly at me. "Want to guess?"

"She doesn't," Diana said.

"Thirty-eight," I said.

Diana glared at me. She was wrong to be annoyed that I'd taken his bait. The guy obviously wasn't going to back down and Brie was smiling with a demure little pout, clearly aching for me to low-ball him. I couldn't see that the meeting was going to move forward unless someone threw out a guess. I didn't think a number was going to undermine Diana's authority, but she wasn't happy.

"Forty-seven!" Andy said.

Brie crossed her legs.

Diana sat forward. "You look great. You wrote in your essay that you have financial goals you haven't met and you wanted to strategize about how to grow your influence in the health field without necessarily opening more clubs. Our service is about shaping your mental attitude—finding psychological roadblocks to success and helping you build self-awareness. Some of our work, as you probably saw in the questionnaires, can be really personal. The process isn't effective unless it's one-on-one. To be clear, that means without Andy."

"Andy and I are a team," Brie said.

"It's possible he might be one of your roadblocks."

Andy laughed. "If you're worried about offending me or hurting my feelings, I have a really thick skin. So say what needs to be said."

"It's not a good idea for you to be here," Diana said.

"I really want him here. He'll keep me focused."

Andy got up off the floor and sat beside Brie on the couch. He was so close to her, I wondered if they were a couple. A moment later, I realized he'd moved because he was now directly across from me. He was staring at me with unrestrained desire. I gave him a cold stare. He returned it with a slow, easy smile.

The comedy show was over and this was turning into something else, but I wasn't sure what.

CHAPTER 7

The room was silent. Andy continued gazing at me. Diana stared at Brie. I could sense Diana's discomfort, and her frantic hope that silence would help her win.

"Brie is a success because of me," Andy said. "I know what women's bodies should look like. Women don't see themselves realistically. They need a man to know what's really important. I develop their workout regimens, and coach them, show them the right techniques, and make sure they stick with it. I help them lift weights properly. I help them build bodies that are attractive to men, not to other women. That's what they really want, but the hen mentality keeps them trying to fit into the mode of what will impress other women. That's what sets Bodies By Brie apart."

"Sounds like it's bodies by Andy," I said.

"I've got this, Alexandra," Diana said.

She didn't have it at all. Andy was controlling everything, and I was pretty sure that was how the entire relationship with Brie was going to play out. Brie had given the reins to Andy and he was going to remain in charge.

I wondered if Diana even had any ideas about how she might

break this up. I'd never seen anything like this with all the quirky, entitled, unusual clients I'd met working with Trystan.

These two were like a pair of dysfunctional twins. They probably weren't related, but it was hard to tell. They looked so much alike, and the A and B game going on with their names made me wonder. But because their hairstyles and highly sculpted bodies and obviously expensive yet super casual matching clothing were trying so hard to create a stylized image, it was hard to separate that from their actual facial and other physical features.

Diana had been tough enough with me lately that I had to believe she would come up with some aggressive way of breaking their stranglehold. Brie seemed to give off an air of strong, smiling confidence. Not just physically. She also exuded an inner strength that was tangible. Was it real, or was I imagining it because of the glitzy appearance and her unwillingness to back down? Who was in charge here? Was she as strong as she looked, or did Andy have complete control of her, using her while he distracted her with nonsense and flattery? I couldn't be sure.

But she didn't give the air of a woman being controlled. She wanted him there. She seemed thrilled that he had opinions about how to sculpt women's bodies. She was proud of the fact she'd hired a man who claimed to know women better than they knew themselves.

Diana pulled her laptop out of her bag. "Usually we have a casual conversation to start, but I think I'll run through a few slides first." She didn't smile and she didn't ask if they were okay with her change of tactics. She flipped open her laptop and brought up a slide presentation I hadn't seen before.

She turned the laptop to face them, balancing it on her knees. "This is private information, so of course I can't have names attached. But I want to show you the income increases that some of our clients have had as a result of working with us."

She clicked to the second slide. "This is a man who was an investment advisor. He was earning three and a half million a year, including bonuses. After working with Fly Higher, his annual income went to four point six million the first year, and has grown approximately thirteen to eighteen percent a year since." She tapped the keyboard. "This is a podcaster who was basically only making money from affiliate marketing. After a complete consultation with Fly Higher, he began earning a hundred and forty-three thousand a year. From a podcast. I know that's pocket change for you, but he was a kid. No college degree. No backing from investors. Just a kid with plenty of opinions, an incredible sense of humor, and a lot of curiosity."

She closed the laptop and stood.

"You don't have to sell us," Brie said. "And I don't want to get into a fight over it. All I'm saying is Andy and I are a team."

Diana didn't respond. She walked to the wall with the sweating women lifting barbells. She ran her finger along the curve of one of the women's biceps. "I don't need a slide for the last person. She owns a restaurant I know you've heard of. After working with us, she earned a Michelin star and the restaurant revenue tripled in eighteen months. It takes six weeks to get a reservation there."

She returned to the couches but didn't take her seat. "We have a process that's proven. If you'd rather not work with us, we're happy to refund your money." She picked up her laptop and slid it into the bag. She zipped it closed and gave me a sharp look.

I took my cue and stood, following her to the door.

"Where are you going?" Brie asked.

"I've explained our process," Diana said. "It's very personal. It's about working one-on-one with you to uncover what's holding you back. Another person's opinions and comments will interfere. In fact, again, I would suggest that might be holding you back in itself." She grabbed the door handle.

"That's hard core," Andy said. "But Brie can certainly stand on her own two feet." As if to demonstrate, he got up from his place beside Brie. "If it's a deal-breaker that this has to be private, she can brief me later."

"That's her choice," Diana said.

He joined us at the door.

"I can see you do strength training." He winked at me. "If you want to get to the next level with a body by Brie, let me know." He pulled a business card out of his pocket, tucked it behind my belt, and opened the door.

When he was gone, Diana and I returned to the couch. Diana smiled at Brie. "I'm really excited about what we're going to accomplish together."

Brie gave her a faint smile but said nothing.

CHAPTER 8

The idea of arranging a two-night getaway for Alex at a luxury hotel had been a sudden impulse while they were eating dinner at a Mexican restaurant. Hunter had suggested it without giving it any thought. He wasn't sure what had made him say it. In all the time he'd lived in New York City, he'd never taken a girl to a hotel for a weekend, so it wasn't like the idea had simmered in the back of his mind from previous relationships.

Alex hadn't ever suggested they go away together, and in fact, she'd only stayed the entire night in his apartment twice. And maybe that was it. Spending a weekend in a hotel meant she would be with him until sunrise instead of slipping out the door in the dead of night. He wouldn't wake to cold sheets and the vague feeling that he'd dreamt the previous twelve hours.

It also meant they could get to know each other in a more in-depth way. They would do normal things. Not that a five-star hotel offered anything approaching normality, but they would do those regular things like waking up together and eating all three meals together, deciding how to spend their day. Their conversations would include the mundane, not just the heightened, semi-flirta-tious chatter that seemed to characterize a lot of their time together.

CATHRYN GRANT

And it was possible he had an ulterior motive. He would have her captive.

She would relax and talk more easily because there would be nowhere she could run to hide when she felt like the conversation was getting too personal. Or whatever her issue was.

Not that he didn't have secrets too. It wasn't that he wanted to bare his soul to her. Not yet. And maybe not ever, but it was driving him crazy that he didn't know if she had any siblings. He was aware that he was becoming mildly obsessed with the idea, but she was being so secretive about such a simple, biological fact. Her refusal to talk about her siblings sent his imagination running wild. Was she related to a notorious figure? A criminal or politician she was ashamed of? Had someone destroyed her family and left them destitute and she couldn't talk about it? What was it? He found himself thinking about it all the time and he didn't like it.

She agreed immediately to the weekend, which he was surprised to find somewhat … surprising.

All she would have to do, he said, was show up at the front desk to pick up her key card.

And so, he'd planned everything, arriving the moment the room was available to make sure the champagne he'd ordered was on ice, and the chocolate dipped strawberries were as fresh and luscious as they'd described. The vase of six red roses stood on an oval table in front of the small couch.

He was playing a game on his tablet when there was a knock on the door. He went to answer.

The bellhop stood there with a cart holding a suitcase and Alex's rather tired looking leather bag that she carried everywhere instead of a purse.

Alex walked into the room and went directly to the windows. She pulled the cord to open the sheer draperies. He watched her gazing out the window at the Hudson river, blonde hair spilling over her shoulders, a skimpy blue dress hugging her body, and dark brown ankle boots showing off her gorgeous bare legs. He turned to

32

the bellhop, who was depositing the bags near the couch. Hunter handed him a folded bill, thanked him, and waited until the door closed before moving across the room to stand behind Alex. She hadn't moved.

He slid his arms around her waist and rested his chin on her left shoulder. "You're not afraid of heights, are you?"

"No, it's great." She continued gazing at the river in the distance. After a few seconds, she turned, putting her arms around his neck. "Are you?"

"Of course not."

He kissed her, aching to fall onto the bed. She seemed inclined to follow, but then he pulled away slightly. "Do you want to put your things away? Get settled?"

"Sure. If that's the first thing on your mind." She nodded toward the champagne, then the flowers. "That's nice."

"For later. I thought we'd go for a walk. Work up an appetite for dinner."

"Okay."

He settled on the couch and watched her open her bag, pulling out shoes and clothes, which she hung carefully and deliberately in the closet. He was overcome by a strange feeling of calm domesticity. The feeling made him want to laugh because he was fairly sure Alexandra was not a very domestic woman, although she was very precise about the way she was arranging her clothes in the closet and drawers.

When she finished, they went out.

During the elevator ride to the ground floor, across the lobby and through the doors into the warm, moist air of the street, he thought about the questions he had for her. He was turning into a bore. His need for information was consuming everything. If he kept himself fixated on wanting answers to his questions, he would spoil the weekend before it even started.

He took her hand and forced himself to put them out of his mind. He would ask nothing. He would let her lead the conversation. And if she said nothing, they would walk in companionable silence.

In the end, they talked about the things they saw, and his job. Now that Pauline Herrera was no longer a client of Alexandra's company, he felt more relaxed talking about his work. Alex told him about the woman she would be photographing soon, laughing at a fitness guru named after a cheese with a deliciously high fat content. She couldn't get over that, wondering if it was branding brilliance, or something that turned people away from her health clubs in numbers that she would never realize.

CHAPTER 9

They walked up to Times Square where they wandered around, lost in the overstimulation of it all.

When they returned to the hotel, they showered, dressed for dinner, and he opened the champagne. As he poured champagne into the flutes, Alex picked up one of the strawberries and took a bite.

"Oh, this is good."

"I hope it's not too cliché," Hunter said.

"Not at all." As she took another bite, bits of chocolate crumbled and clung to her bottom lip.

He wanted to lick it for her, but resisted the urge, enjoying the sensation of watching the tip of her tongue poke out of her mouth, feeling around for the chocolate, then sweeping it inside. He handed her a glass.

"You should have a strawberry."

"After we toast."

"What are we toasting?" She held up the glass, smiling over the bubbles that fizzed off the surface as the foam settled down into the pale gold liquid.

"To living in a cocoon for the weekend," he said.

"Are we caterpillars?"

He laughed. He tapped his glass against hers.

"Cheers," she said.

They both took a sip.

"Have a strawberry," she said.

They sprawled on the couch and fed each other the remaining strawberries, sipping champagne. By the time they went to dinner, he would have rather unzipped her tight black dress and moved onto the bed.

During the appetizer course, thoughts of her siblings rose to the surface of his mind with such ferocity he wondered if there was something going wrong inside his head. Why was he so obsessed with this topic? He was behaving like a child who'd been told he couldn't have a piece of candy and now, that was all he wanted. It was so immature, so unimportant. If he pressed her about it, he risked spoiling the rest of the evening.

But the more they sipped the expensive cabernet she'd selected from the wine list, the more they tasted the appetizers and then the salad and then waited for their main course, the less he found himself able to think of anything to say. He wanted to lean his elbows on the table, grasp her forearms so she couldn't pull away or look in another direction, and demand that she tell him how many siblings she had, how old they were, where they were now, and what they did for a living. He wanted to know what kind of relationships they'd had growing up and where she fell in the family order. He wanted to know if there was jealousy on her side or theirs. He wanted to pick them apart and analyze every part of whatever she was trying to hide from him.

And the bottom line was that was the cause of his obsession. It felt like she was hiding something. She *was* hiding something. No one, ever, anywhere, refused to tell you how many siblings they had. It was the most freakishly abnormal response to a casual question he'd ever encountered.

And then he was talking without even realizing he was doing it, and it was too late. "So, are you ever going to tell me how many siblings you have? Or are you taking that secret to your grave?"

She didn't giggle at what he thought was a mildly amusing comment. She didn't smile. Not even the tiniest flicker at the corner of her lips.

Finally, she took a sip of wine. She held his gaze. The thought that he would have to hold onto her wrists to keep her attention focused on him, to keep her from dodging his question, had been ridiculous. "Why is that so important to you?"

"It's not important. I'm just curious."

"If it's not important, then let's talk about something else."

"Why are you trying so hard not to tell me? It's such a simple question." He laughed, and he knew his laugh sounded awkward, nervous. He might sound almost maniacal. Maybe she thought he was trying to get information on her family so he could hurt her in some way. What the hell was going on with her? He felt a sharp pain behind his eye. He wanted to forget about it, to let it go from his thoughts, but the more she resisted, the more he felt he had to know *why*.

The server arrived with their food—steak cooked rare for her, swordfish for him.

They began eating, and she filled the space between them with a nearly non-stop flow of words about her meal, food in general, cooking, restaurants, New York restaurants in particular, his favorite restaurants, and restaurants in other cities where she'd lived.

The only thing that eventually cleared his head and resettled him was falling into the enormous bed and forgetting conversation entirely for the rest of the night.

CHAPTER 10

On the Saturday morning of my cocooning weekend with Hunter, he'd booked a massage for me in the hotel spa. I sat in the waiting room, letting the recorded sounds of gurgling creek water and birds wash over me, breathing in the scent of something woodsy that I couldn't name. I knew if someone told me what it was I would recognize it immediately, but I couldn't come up with the kind of plant or tree or whatever it was. I tried not to think about it and just breathe.

I thought about our dinner the night before and Hunter's question out of nowhere that he needed to know about my siblings. Again. It wasn't a surprise that he was still curious, but the timing had been. The only thing I'd accomplished by not telling him was making him more curious, but I had not expected him to be thinking about it in the middle of a fabulous dinner after two glasses of champagne and giggling over chocolate covered strawberries.

He tried to be clever about the way he brought it up, but it still fell splat onto the center of our white tablecloth like a piece of blood-soaked fat sliced off a rare steak.

I'd decided not to tell him. How could I answer a question like that? Did I tell him I had three brothers and leave it at that? Then someday be faced with the lie of never having mentioned my sister? But I certainly wasn't going to talk about her yet. I hardly knew him. I didn't want to talk about her. I never had. To anyone. I still wasn't sure I ever would.

Inside my head, her existence was pure. Bringing her out into the world, discussing her with a near-stranger, might turn her into someone I didn't recognize.

He was right about one thing. It was a simple question. But the other thing was, the less I told him about my life, the less I had to lie and the fewer lies I told, the less I had to keep track of.

It was very possible I might be spending more time with Hunter than I had with any guy before this. More time meant more lies, and more lies meant lots of complications and things to keep straight, and it all made me feel a little tired. Besides, a crack in the door that allowed a trickle of information risked the start of a deluge.

It seemed simpler this way. But now, I wasn't sure. The more I refused to tell him, the more obsessed he would become. I could see it in his eyes. He was almost angry about it. I wanted to laugh. Maybe we would break up because I wouldn't tell him how many siblings I had. That would definitely be a unique letter to a relationship advice person. A monumental fight and breakup over uncounted, unnamed siblings.

The pale wood door opened and the masseuse stepped into the waiting room. "Alexandra?"

I stood.

She moved to the side and opened the door wider so I could walk past her. I spent the next ninety minutes feeling every muscle in my body reshaped into something soft and pliable. When I was finished, my body felt like a bowl of pasta. My mind had followed along with it, settling into a calm place without circling, nagging thoughts.

I wanted the masseuse to transport me to a lounge chair by the pool so I could spend the rest of the day without thinking about Hunter and his questions.

CHAPTER 11

*I*nstead of being magically transported to a poolside chair, I stepped into the waiting room and ran smack into another woman coming for a massage. Literally.

We smacked into each other because she'd just entered the outer door, and she was running.

"Oh! Oh, my god, I'm so sorry." She took a step back.

My head hurt from where our skulls had crashed into each other. My neck ached and I felt a pinch in my shoulder blade. All the lovely pasta in my muscles was gone.

"I'm sure I destroyed everything they just did for you. I'm so, so sorry. I have to book you another massage. My treat."

"You don't have to," I said.

"I do. What's your name?"

"Really. It's fine. I'm only here for a few days."

"Do you live in the city? I'll get you a gift certificate."

"It's fine." I took a few steps toward the door.

The masseuse came into the waiting room. "Jenna?"

"No. I'm—"

"I have a Jenna at eleven."

"But I'm sure I booked for eleven."

The masseuse pulled her phone out of her pocket and checked the screen. "Nope. Jenna."

"Are you sure? Not Carolina?"

"I'm sure."

"Oh, damn. I hurt you and fucked up your Zen, and I didn't even have the time right. God." She grabbed my upper arm. "Can I buy you a smoothie or coffee or a mimosa?"

"I have plans, but thanks."

"Please? I owe you."

I glanced at the clock. I looked back at Carolina. What kind of name was that? She had long, pale red hair and dark brown eyes. She was thinner than Eileen had been when I first met her. She seemed far too friendly and slightly unbalanced. Why did I want to take her up on her offer? Maybe I was still hoping for the gift certificate. The massage had been amazing. It wouldn't be awful if she insisted again on giving me a certificate.

"I know you want to have something after getting jarred like that. Let's get coffee. And a certificate. I absolutely owe you big time. You have a little bump on your forehead." She reached out a finger with burgundy nails and rubbed a spot on my forehead. "What's your name?"

"Alexandra."

"Cool name." She grabbed my wrist. "Come on. What time are your plans? You can be twenty minutes late. Everyone forgives fifteen minutes and I know you wouldn't have booked things that tightly, am I right?" Her laugh was shrill and too loud for the tiny waiting room.

I followed her out. "Don't you want to ask what time your massage is scheduled for?"

She shrugged. "I live at the hotel. I can get one any time. I'll work it out later."

"You live here? Why?"

"I can tell you all about it while we're having mimosas. Or coffee. Which one?"

"Coffee."

We walked to the lobby and took a seat at the coffee bar. I ordered an iced latte even though it wasn't advisable to drink cold liquids after a massage, although no one had ever explained why. I suppose it would have been easy to find out why, but I'd never bothered. I wanted an iced latte.

Carolina ordered a mimosa. "What are you here for?" she asked.

"A weekend escape."

"Where do you live?"

"In Manhattan."

"Most people *leave* the city for an escape."

"Do they?"

She laughed. "I guess I don't really know."

"Why do you live in a hotel?"

"My husband is an attorney. He's involved in litigation with some companies here that's been going on for two years. He's been working six days a week, sometimes seven. My son and I came so we could see at least glimpses of his ass on his way out the door."

"Shouldn't his firm pay for renting an apartment or something?"

"A lot of the meetings take place at the hotel, because it's neutral territory. And there are lots of other factors. So …" She shrugged.

"How old is your son?"

"Ten. I homeschool him while we're here."

Our drinks came, and I was glad for the interruption. Carolina had a way of talking that made me feel like I needed to take a deep breath.

"How does he make friends?" I asked.

"He takes boxing."

"At ten?"

She grinned. "Yeah. It's so cool. All these little men learning how to throw a punch. No one will ever get the upper hand with my boy. Right?"

I took a sip of my drink.

"What do you do?" she asked.

43

"I'm a photographer."

She slammed her mimosa onto the bar, and a bit splashed out. "That is so cool! I would love to do that. What do you take pictures of?"

"People."

"Like portraits? Would you do my portrait? Do you do those boudoir portraits?"

"No. I work for a company that does executive coaching. I photograph people and sometimes take video. We have experts who analyze their facial expressions. We coach them on trying to better understand themselves, to get insight into things that might be holding them back in climbing to the next level of success."

"That is so fucking fascinating." Her mouth was open as she stared at me. Her drink sat in a sticky puddle of champagne and orange juice.

I took a sip of coffee. I wondered if I was as fascinated by a woman whose main priority for her ten-year-old child was throwing a punch and always maintaining the upper hand as she was by micro-expressions. It was hard to know. She seemed far more captivated than I was, but I was pretty interested in knowing what put punching at the top of her priority list.

"What can you tell from their expressions? What if they don't want you to know what they're thinking? Don't most people pose when they're getting their picture taken, so everything is a little bit fake?"

"That's my job. To get them to forget they're being photographed."

"So, like candid shots?"

"Sort of. They know I'm there, but I talk to them until they stop thinking about the photography because they're concentrating on answering my questions."

"Wow. You are like ... I don't know, like you read people's minds or something. I wonder if you could read my mind?" She laughed. She picked up her mimosa and took a sip. She put the glass down and looked at her fingers that were slightly sticky from the spilled liquid. After gazing at them for a few seconds, she carefully licked each one.

I sipped my coffee and asked her what it was like living in a hotel.

She said it was fabulous. She was from Michigan so she was used to the cold in the winter and the muggy summers. She loved the city. She was glad to be away from her small town, her nosey neighbors. She liked the excitement. She wondered again if I could read her mind.

"I don't analyze expressions. I just take the photographs."

"But you must have learned a little about it."

"Maybe."

"What am I thinking right now?"

"That you want another mimosa."

"See! You're brilliant. I want you to take my picture."

"I just guessed. And it wasn't that hard since yours is almost gone." I finished my coffee. "I need to get going."

"Aww. Really?"

"Yes."

"But your gift certificate."

"Don't worry about it. Thanks for the coffee."

"Can I get your number?"

I didn't see the point. Although, the gift certificate. Maybe it was worth it. "Sure."

"We can have lunch."

"My job keeps me pretty busy. And I'm sure your son—"

"We'll figure out something. I have to see you again. We can be friends!"

We exchanged numbers. I gave her the number to the burner phone I'd begun using after all the problems I'd had with James. I didn't like juggling two phones, making sure I used the right one at the appropriate time, but it was better than leaving pieces of information about myself all over New York City, as I had been doing more often than I should have. We also exchanged Snapchat usernames. It was a lot of information to give someone who was likely to forget she'd promised me a free massage. At the same time, it was really no information. And it truly had been an awesome massage.

As I walked away, I wondered if I would mention this to Hunter. He would probably ask why the massage had taken two and a half hours. She also seemed like one of those people who would forget the entire encounter once she started her second mimosa.

CHAPTER 12

*A*fter a weekend of indulgence with Hunter, during which he did an excellent job of not sulking over my refusal to talk about my siblings, I decided I needed some serious weightlifting during my lunch hour. After work, I would go for a long run in the slightly, but not by much, cooler evening air. The entire week would be dedicated to burning and sweating off the alcohol and all the rich food and desserts I'd consumed.

My gym bag was over my shoulder and I was hanging up the jacket I wore inside the office when I heard Diana and an unfamiliar male voice. I turned and saw her standing in the doorway.

"Oh, you're going out?" Diana asked.

"Going to the gym for lunch."

"Do you have a minute?"

"Sure."

She stepped to the side. Behind her was a tall guy with a shaved head and frameless glasses. He smiled and nodded at me. He wore a black T-shirt, black jacket, and black slacks. "This is Ian Baker. He's our new micro-expression analyst."

I stared at him.

"This is Alexandra Mallory, our lead photographer."

I felt the deliberate choice of words—lead photographer—as if she were pinching my upper arm while she spoke. She didn't emphasize the word *lead*, but she didn't have to. The fact that there was any qualifying word before photographer was more than enough.

"Great to meet you," Ian said. "I'm looking forward to working together."

He stepped into my office and extended his hand. I shook it and felt the pull of my gym bag.

"Is there a gym close by? I need to find a place," he said.

"Within walking distance …" I paused, wondering how specifically helpful I should be.

"That's great. Good to know."

So … I had heard her correctly, as I'd known I had, but hoped I hadn't. She hadn't said he was a candidate. She'd hired him without even asking me to look at his resumé, much less interview him. Was this how little she cared about my opinion now? I wondered if this guy was also a friend of hers. Maybe she was simply done with the pretense of getting a rubber stamp on a decision she'd already made.

And now, he had ideas about joining the same gym I worked out at. I didn't like the idea of a co-worker trying to talk to me while I was using the bench press or doing squats. I didn't like the idea of a co-worker anywhere near my gym. I knew I was being petty and irrational. It wasn't as if he should be expected to leave midtown to find a gym so I could have my privacy. Part of me wanted to recommend Bodies By Brie. But she was female-only, just like Diana had decided Fly Higher was going to be.

Was this the new thing? Some weird sort of reverse misogyny? Women only everywhere you went? I was pretty sure that wasn't the answer. You aren't empowered if you have to lock yourself inside a guarded castle in order to feel empowered.

"As soon as you get back from your workout, will you connect with Ian so you can give him a more in-depth understanding of your role and help him understand better how the two of you will be working together?"

"Sure."

"I've already given him the high-level details, obviously. And we'll be talking more over lunch in a few minutes, but when you meet, you can dig into the day-to-day."

"Yes. Sure."

"Thank you." She gave me a winning, charming, friendly smile. It was a smile that reminded me of her former self, until it froze and became a caricature of that person I'd thought I knew.

Of course, she probably thought she knew me. She still thought that. And she never had, so I really wasn't one to be complaining to myself about people giving false impressions of who they were.

"I really am looking forward to working with you, Alexandra. According to Diana, you're some sort of photographic genius."

I gave him a winning smile of my own. Was this his own hyperbole, or had she truly given that impression? It made my head ache to think that she was talking one way behind my back and treating me like an existential threat to my face. Maybe I needed a vacation. "Hopefully she didn't oversell me," I said.

"That's not possible," Diana said, just a bit too quickly.

I really wanted to get to the gym. My bag, with shoes, workout clothes, shower supplies, even my own hair dryer because the ones supplied by the gym created frizzy hair for some reason I couldn't figure out, was getting heavy on my shoulder. I would be spending the first ten minutes just working out the kinks instead of doing my usual warm-up stretches. I thought about my massage. It had only been a little over forty-eight hours and I was already longing for another one. I saw now why some people made them a regular thing, as if they were addicted to someone pressing their fingers and the heels of their hands into their body until their very bones seemed to move themselves into a new, more comfortable arrangement. Like rearranging furniture.

Why weren't they moving out of my doorway? I realized Ian was talking again and I had no idea what he'd been saying. Now, he'd stopped and was looking at me with eager, hopeful eyes.

I nodded. I glanced at Diana.

No one spoke. I'd obviously missed something.

"Are you okay?" Diana asked.

"Yes, I just—"

"I think she's eager to get to her workout," Ian said. "I can understand that. After sitting at a desk all morning, probably riding the subway to work, the last thing you want to do when you're ready to get moving is stand in the office and make small talk with the new guy, right?"

I laughed. "Desk work takes its toll."

"We're animals, not designed for this," he said.

I agreed with his thinking, but I didn't want to get into a philosophical conversation. The ache in my shoulder was growing more intense. I was still trying to sort out why Diana had blatantly cut me out of the interview process, and I was being careful about what I said around her in all situations. At least when I remembered to be careful, which wasn't often enough.

"I told Diana that instead of a signing bonus, I want a standing desk. And any position I accept has to allow the freedom to leave for walks around the city whenever my muscles get twitchy. You know what I mean?"

A signing bonus? I glanced at Diana. She was looking directly at me, her face expressionless.

"I do," I said. "I should get to my workout. So we can have plenty of time to meet this afternoon."

Finally, they backed out of my doorway and allowed me to escape. My muscles and my brain felt twitchy all the way down in the elevator and all the way to the gym.

CHAPTER 13

*A*s a thank you for staying at the hotel, they'd given Hunter and me a box of truffles. I'd forgotten the box of sweets in our room because Hunter and I had decided to make delicious use of that enormous, exquisitely comfortable bed one last time, just half an hour before checkout, leaving us five minutes for a shower and then a mad scramble to shove our bags out the door.

The hotel kindly messaged Hunter that the truffles were waiting at the front desk for us to pick up.

After two magnificent dinners, breakfast in bed on Saturday before my massage, cocktails and dancing Saturday night, a lavish brunch on Sunday, and all those chocolate-covered strawberries, plus ice cream and a few other treats, I did not need a box of truffles. But I was not going to pass up a free box.

I stopped by the hotel after work to grab my treats.

When I turned away from the front desk, Carolina and a little boy dressed in pressed faded blue jeans and a button down white shirt were standing a few feet behind me.

"Alexandra!" Carolina's squeal filled the lobby and reverberated up to the ceiling of the mezzanine level. She rushed at me and threw her arms around me, squeezing me so tightly, I felt like she considered me her lover. To emphasize that sensation even further, she held on for quite a long time, pressing her body against mine, breathing in the scent of my hair. "I'm so glad I ran into you again."

I eased myself out of her arms, which was somewhat challenging. "You have my number."

"But this is so much better. And now you get to meet Ricky." She turned and grabbed the arm of the boy who was dressed to look like a tiny tech worker, even down to his stylish haircut. I half expected to see a three-day stubble on his jaw when he moved closer.

"Ricky, this is Alexandra."

"Hey," Ricky said.

"Hi." I smiled at him.

He gave me an icy stare, then his gaze dropped to my chest in a very deliberate way. I wasn't sure if I should laugh or ask his mother if she'd stated his age correctly. She'd said he was ten years old, hadn't she? He was almost as tall as his mother. She was only about five-three or -four, but still ...

"Let's get a drink," Carolina said.

I looked at Ricky.

"It's cool," he said. "We're not going to the bar. So don't get all freaked out about it. You can have a glass of wine in the restaurant. No one will lose their shit."

I stared at him. Part of me wondered if I was looking at a miniature male version of myself. Another part of me wondered if he was something else entirely. Whatever he was, it was unsettling. And Carolina was oblivious to anything being at all out of the ordinary.

It wasn't as if I spent a lot of time around children. I knew absolutely nothing about children and had no idea what the norms of behavior were, but I had been a child and it wasn't as if I'd forgotten everything.

"Don't say no. You can't say no." Carolina gave me a pleading smile.

This made me want to say no.

"I have dinner—"

"Just a quick glass of wine. You had to rush off last time and I really need some adult company. No offense, Ricky. Right?"

He shrugged.

"All day teaching math and history. Ugh. I'm brain dead."

"You're brain dead. How do you think I feel?" Ricky said.

"Come on. I'm so lonely for adult company."

Every instinct told me I should run as fast as I could from this clearly unstable woman and her very unusual son, which was not so unusual when I thought about the way she was. Thinking about running reminded me that was what I'd planned to do. Instead, I'd become fixated on a box of candy I didn't need and now I was getting sidetracked further.

CHAPTER 14

$\mathcal{I}$t was possible I'd already lost my momentum. Especially after sitting all afternoon with Ian, listening to him ask questions that didn't need asking, trying to make friends with me far too fast. Although this woman was doing the same. But she wouldn't be in New York forever. Even if her husband was there long term, it had already been two years. How much longer could his case drag on?

"Sure. I'll have a glass of wine."

"Oh, I'm so relieved. The way your face looked, I thought for sure you were going to say no."

She took my free hand and started tugging me toward the restaurant. I slid my hand out of hers and followed. She was wearing yellow high heels, a yellow dress, and a white cardigan sweater. It seemed like a wild clothing choice for teaching math and history, and whatever else was in the curriculum, to a ten-year-old, if that's what he really was. But what did I know?

We ordered two glasses of Chardonnay and I thought about Damien and how much more pleasant his company was. "I can only stay for half an hour."

"Do you have a date?"

"I have a pet that needs to be fed."

"A dog?"

"No. A cockatoo. It's not mine. I'm watching him for a friend."

"How awesome."

"It's not that awesome, Carolina," Ricky said. "Get a grip."

She ignored him. She raised her glass. "What should we drink to?"

"How about drinking to hot bitches," Ricky said.

Carolina giggled. "You're so sweet Ricky. I don't think I qualify as hot anymore, now that I'm a mom, but I appreciate the effort." She clicked her glass against mine, then clicked it against Ricky's soda glass and took a sip.

I took a sip of my wine and stared at Ricky.

He stared back at me. "What are you looking at?"

"How do you like being homeschooled?" I asked.

"Hate it."

I looked at Carolina. "Aren't you here long enough that he could be enrolled in school?"

"It didn't work out," she said.

I could guess why that might have been.

"You probably get more free time, though," I said.

"Define free time," she said.

I took another sip of wine. Why had I agreed to this? Carolina was one of the strangest people I'd ever met. I was curious about her because she was fascinating in a way that shocked me, so that was probably it. I couldn't tear myself away. I was a rubber-necker looking at a gory, bloody mess of a woman on the side of the road. Every time she opened her mouth, I was startled again.

But this kid was something else. What was she doing? It seemed as if she had no idea how to raise a child. Not that I had any better ideas about it myself. I wondered about her husband. Since he was never around, maybe he had no clue what either of them was really like. Although, how could he miss it? I'd become aware in less than four minutes.

"Your mom said you're—"

"Carolina. Her name is Carolina," Ricky said.

"She said you take boxing."

He swallowed his soda and began chewing an ice cube. "Yeah."

"I've thought about taking kick boxing," I said.

"Not the same thing."

"True."

"Maybe I should try boxing. I just never thought—"

"Boxing is not for girls. It's a man's sport," he said. "That's why I do it."

"My little man," Carolina purred.

"Some women—"

"They shouldn't. Girls get ugly when they box."

"So do men, if they really get into it."

He worked another piece of ice into his mouth and began chewing.

"Enough about Ricky," Carolina said. "I invited you for wine because I'm lonely for adult company. You should be talking to me." She reached across the table and touched the back of my hand.

I jerked my hand away.

"Why did you do that?" Her eyes were glassy with tears.

"You startled me. I wasn't expecting anyone to touch me."

"Carolina is a very touchy person," Ricky said.

"How was your day at work?" Carolina asked.

"Uneventful. We hired a new guy, so I spent time getting him oriented."

"No photography?"

"Not today."

"Do you take photographs every day?"

"No, I have to organize—"

"Sounds like a bullshit job," Ricky said.

"Shut up, Ricky. Alexandra is my friend and we're having an adult conversation."

Both of us took a sip of wine. I glanced at my phone. "I need to head out in ten minutes."

Carolina pouted. "Aww. We hardly had any time."

"Well—"

"It's because my little man was here," she said. "He's an attention whore."

Ricky grinned.

"I need to get going."

Ricky looked at me, then stuck his tongue in the glass and sucked out another cube of ice.

"We need to have a proper get-together," Carolina said. "You always have to rush off somewhere."

I finished my wine and inched my chair away from the table.

"Let's plan it now."

"I'll have to let you know," I said. "Thanks for the wine." I stood and walked away from the table, feeling both of them watching me. The intensity of the energy coming from the two of them was like a thick web, trying to draw me back toward their strange world.

I was repulsed and fascinated. I wanted to never see either of them again. At the same time, I wanted to see what their hotel room looked like and meet Carolina's husband. It was a sensation that made me feel like the sticky strands of that web were clinging to my skin with a grip I would never scrape off.

CHAPTER 15

*a*lex's refusal to tell Hunter how many siblings she had was turning into an absurdity of epic proportions. Her irrational stubbornness made him feel as if he *had* to know in the way someone had to know the identity of the person who had murdered a family member, or was driven to find out who their birth parents were.

He thought about it all the time. He'd mostly managed to shove the obsession out of his thoughts during their weekend in the hotel, but a faint tone remained at the back of his brain, like a high-pitched ringing in the ear that can plague people to the edge of madness.

There had to be something horribly wrong, something deeply shameful or frightening in her family that she refused to tell him. There was no plausible reason he could think of to withhold such basic, simple, innocuous information with such fierce determination.

One of her siblings must be in prison, or worse, a wanted criminal. But this made him even more deeply curious. He wondered when she would feel comfortable telling him. He wondered if she didn't see her relationship with him continuing long term. He wondered if she'd told anyone at work, or her roommate, about her family. He wondered if she was in touch with this sibling, or siblings, if they had some kind of hold over her. Was she living in fear? Was that why she wouldn't tell him where her apartment was?

The more he thought about it, the more the questions piled on top of each other.

After a period of time of circling endlessly around thoughts like these, his mind would flip.

He was a hypocrite.

He wasn't at all ready to share his secrets with her, so what was his problem? And he wasn't even sure he *ever* wanted to reveal his entire life to another person. Was that even required? Married people, if that's where he thought he and Alexandra might end up some day, or couples living together indefinitely, permanently, whatever, acted as if they revealed every single piece of their lives to the other person. That's what they said. That's what they implied. But was that the truth?

It might be inevitable over time. The more hours you were together, the more time you spent talking, the more you learned. Small, unexpected nuggets of information slipped out. Eventually, all the pieces came together. But did that include the secret parts, the pieces that were deliberately withheld?

The things that are spoken by an individual are only the tip of the iceberg, as they say.

Did this mean he should stop trying to find out what she didn't want to tell him? If he stopped asking, it would be easier. If he stopped asking, she might eventually let the truth escape anyway. But would she?

Would he?

The other option was to hire a private detective to do a background check. Lots of people did when they started a serious relationship. He never had. And this was another thought that suggested he was having some partially unacknowledged long-term thoughts about this girl. He hardly knew her. It was much too soon.

But the thoughts continued to appear out of nowhere. Sometimes it felt as if every thought he had about her led in that direction.

After only a few weeks, not even a full season of the year, he was thinking of this near-stranger as someone he couldn't imagine his life without. Everything seemed dull when he considered his job and his usual forms of entertainment, and even hanging out or going places with his friends, without thinking of her as a sort of backdrop.

He needed to go for a long walk. It always cleared his head—the crowds of people weaving along the sidewalk like a huge, endless, living tapestry, constantly rewoven. It felt good to walk past towering buildings, to know you were surrounded by so many people who had the same concerns about career growth, improving your environment, enjoying their lives, finding a mate.

There it was again. He laughed out loud.

He changed into a T-shirt, loose shorts, and comfortable shoes. He shoved a Yankees hat onto his head, sunglasses onto the bridge of his nose, and his phone into his pocket. He went out and began walking without planning a destination. He just wanted to move, to feel his blood pumping. Mostly he wanted the jigsaw puzzle nature of navigating crowded sidewalks to take his thoughts off Alexandra Mallory and their possible future and her mysterious siblings.

Maybe she didn't have any siblings. But an unwillingness to share that fact was its own kind of mystery. He increased his pace and when he came to a corner instead of waiting for the light he turned right. That's how this would go. He wouldn't wait for any traffic lights. He would constantly turn and see where that led him. A more complex walk that was sure to keep his mind more fully occupied.

When he checked his watch after an hour, he'd walked three and a half miles around the West Village, to Washington Square Park, to the river, and back. He was sweating and far calmer than he had been.

He stopped for a slice of pizza and ate it while walking home, although he would have preferred it with a beer. But if he waited, he'd be eating cold pizza.

At home, he flopped on the couch, twisted the cap off a beer, and took a long swallow. There were three messages from Alex. He'd seen them flash across his watch while he was walking, but decided to wait. He was almost afraid to look.

The messages were innocuous. She wanted to know if he felt like watching a movie. He did. If he wanted to get pizza. He wouldn't mind a few more slices. And she wanted to know if she could come over in thirty minutes. That window had now shrunk to less than ten minutes.

He turned on the shower and thought about the plans for the evening. It sounded good. He would let go of all that nonsense about her refusal to answer a simple question. He was the one making a big deal out of it. Maybe she was a little creeped out by his aggressive questioning. She hadn't felt like talking about her family, and he'd turned it into a federal investigation. Maybe she felt smothered, a little concerned about why he was so upset about it. Maybe she saw his obsession as a red flag. He laughed and finished showering.

Combing his hair, staring into the mirror, he remembered her equally probing question into his life—*What's the worst thing you've ever done?*

Maybe that should be more concerning than the fact that she wouldn't tell him about her siblings. Maybe instead of trying so hard to get inside her head, he should be more careful about paying attention to what he was saying to her. He seemed to lose control of his senses when she was around. He often said things without thinking.

Every minute since that morning she'd been standing outside his office building at sunrise, all dressed up and waiting to be asked out to breakfast, she'd kept him slightly off balance.

He'd wondered before, and now it came rushing back at him— was all his attention on the wrong thing? Maybe someone knew more about him than he realized. She'd come on so strong and so mysterious with such unusual behavior because she was trying to trap him into something.

He flicked off the bathroom light. Maybe, he should just take everything at face value and stop over-analyzing. He should just make sure there were enough cold beers in the fridge and order the pizza.

CHAPTER 16

*D*iana had come with me to Matt Shera's final photography session. Even though she'd decided we were now focused exclusively on female clients, she'd promised him she would finish coaching him on his desire to become the minister of a mega church.

She was not backing down on her drive to only pursue and accept female clients, but I was also not backing down on looking for opportunities to argue with her.

I hoped one would come today, and for that reason, I was being polite and friendly despite the clear insult to my professionalism. The reason she was going with me to photograph him was to *make sure things didn't go sideways* as they had when I met with him the last time.

The only reason things had *gone sideways* at Matt's previous photography session was because Stephanie had been oozing all over him. I'd flirted with him for the sole purpose of making her squirm. Yes, I'd made Reverend Shera uncomfortable. But in the end, he'd taken that as part of his coaching, because I'd managed to twist his embarrassment into an insight that exposed a key weakness. Much like a clown twisting a long balloon into an animal, I'd made him believe it showed he was vulnerable to women coming on to him, which would be more prevalent in a mega church. He needed to address that before he would experience the confidence and freedom to grow.

He loved me for that insight. He thought I was brilliant.

Diana had agreed my assessment was remarkable. But she had not liked my method for getting there, refusing to see the part Stephanie had played in instigating it.

As a result, we were seated in an Uber, riding to the Bronx Zoo. Matt had chosen a zoo for his photographs because he'd had a terrifying experience at a zoo as a child. In his pre-assessment work, he'd determined that he had a lot of fears, but he didn't like admitting to them. He believed admitting to fear made him look like he didn't have the unshakable faith expected of a man in his position.

So we were off to the zoo.

He hadn't told us what his terrifying experience was. He said it still scared him enough he couldn't talk about it. But Diana had pushed him to choose a location that evoked fear, and he'd been fearless enough to name the zoo. I had to admire him for that. I'd expected him to choose precarious heights, or maybe jumping out of an airplane. I'd thought it might be fun to go skydiving and take photographs on the way down, although that probably required lessons and special equipment.

I thought about bringing up the female-clients-only issue in the Uber since we had a thirty-five-minute drive because of the traffic, but I decided that would start us out on a sour note. I would bide my time.

We bought our tickets and entered the zoo. Diana received a text from Matt that he was waiting by the primate section.

It was a hot afternoon, but there was a pleasant enough breeze. I'd worn a hat to keep the sun off my face and out of my eyes when I looked through the camera lens. Diana had nothing on her head and her forehead was glistening with sweat before we reached the primates.

Matt wore khaki shorts, a white T-shirt, and white tennis shoes. His sunglasses looked expensive, as did his haircut. My first thought was that he already had that slick look of a superstar preacher from a church with thousands of members.

CHAPTER 17

$\mathcal{W}$e all shook hands and said our hellos. I took my camera out of the backpack I used when I was shooting at outdoor locations. I shoved the lens cap into my pocket and snapped a photograph of Matt just to check the lighting.

"Where should we start?" Diana asked.

"Right here," Matt said.

"Tell us what happened," Diana said.

This was why I hadn't wanted her to come. If she talked to him, it would be no different from when Stephanie was tagging along. The intimacy created when a client forgot there was a camera between us and was speaking only to me would be destroyed. "It's better if—"

Diana interrupted—"Should we start walking around?"

I sighed. It was going to be her show. She was truly beating me into submission. There was no discussion with her at all anymore. There was definitely no arguing. All I could do was listen to whatever questions she chose to ask and hope for the best. How she could gush over my insight from the previous photo session and try to take charge now, how she could gush to Ian that I was a *photographic genius*, and take over, made no sense. She might as well just snap pictures on her phone if this was how things were going to evolve.

We walked past a cage of the tiniest little creatures imaginable. They peered at us with delicate faces, then squealed and grabbed ropes to swing themselves away, flying toward the back of the enclosure.

"It's going to sound really stupid," Matt said. "I never talk about it, but I have nightmares about it even now. I wake sweating." He laughed, his voice shaking slightly. He wiped sweat off his upper lip. "I was only four, so I'm sure that's part of it. My brother ..."

As he turned, I took several pictures of his face. He looked ill. I wondered what Ian would make of it. Or if Diana was going to handle the analysis herself so she could move Matt through the process and out the door as quickly as possible.

"I was standing in front of the apes' enclosure. I turned around because my parents wanted a picture of my brother and me in front of two juvenile apes that were tussling. My dad said they looked just like my brother and me when we were fighting. We stood with our backs to the cage ..." Matt took several strides away from the cage, leaving about five or six feet between himself and the thick wire fencing. "I can't stand that close to them while I'm telling you." His voice trembled.

I took several pictures.

Diana nodded. She looked concerned and interested. For a moment, I thought she would put her hand on his arm to soothe him. I sure hoped not. She would spoil everything, but she was moving closer with a look of near-despair on her face.

"Keep going," I said, my voice louder than necessary, hoping to break her out of whatever she was intending.

"The ... one of the apes ..." He sucked in his breath, then the words rushed out so fast it sounded as if he'd had twelve cups of coffee. "He stuck his fingers through the opening and pinched my arm and he wouldn't let go. I started screaming. My brother was laughing and he didn't do anything to help me. He jumped away from me, which got the ape riled up, and he started hooting and pinching harder. I was crying. It hurt so much, and I was scared out of my mind. I was just a little kid. I didn't know if he could get out or pull me into the cage and he had his mouth wide open and I saw all those huge teeth. I was afraid he was going to tear me up and eat me like he'd been tearing up the food the animal keepers were throwing in the cage. My dad tried to pull me away and the apes all started shrieking and people were running over and taking pictures and there was a big crowd, which of course scared all the apes in the surrounding cages." He stopped suddenly.

I took several pictures. His face had grown bright red. The color was so dark it looked like he might have a stroke. I wasn't sure if that was the sign of a stroke, but it was the darkest red I'd ever seen someone's skin turn simply from telling an upsetting story, almost as if his entire face had been bruised. His eyes were filled with tears.

"That's a horrifying story," Diana said. "It's one of those child-hood events that your logic tells you will never be repeated, yet it stays rooted deep inside and is transformed into other fears."

Matt nodded.

"We can talk about it more in our private sessions." She glanced at me. "I hope you took enough photographs while he was talking."

"I think so." I hadn't taken many, but the ones I had were power-ful. I had no doubt they would do the job. Besides, the story itself was plenty. I wondered why we'd had to drive all the way to the Bronx to hear the story. It seemed like a lot of effort, but maybe he wouldn't have become so passionate about it if he wasn't standing right there, with the sounds of the primates all around us in the zoo where it had actually happened.

Diana suggested I walk around by myself for a while. She and Matt would continue exploring his story alone and we would all meet by the front gate in forty-five minutes. I wandered away, headed toward the elephants. I found a bench and spent the rest of the time basking in the sun, watching them lumber around their space.

On the way back to the office, Diana focused all her attention on her phone, reading email and typing long responses, her fingers flying across the screen without ever seeming to hesitate. As we got closer to the office, I wondered if she would provide a chance to point out to her how helpful she'd been to Matt, planting a seed of doubt about turning her back on offering our services to men.

We were five blocks from the office when she put her phone into her purse.

"That went well," I said.

"Yes. I'm really curious to see the photographs."

"He bared his soul to you."

She looked at me, startled.

"Are you surprised?"

"That doesn't sound like something you'd normally say."

"Isn't that how you'd say it?" I asked.

She laughed. "Some people might."

"Sometimes, men feel more comfortable doing that with women."

"Maybe."

"Are you sure you're not leaving money on the table by cutting them out of our business model?"

"I'm sure."

"But—"

"Focus. We can't be all things to all people."

"I just think—"

"Focus is critical to success. It's not up for discussion. Or argument."

I sighed.

She didn't say anything else.

She was pleased with the pictures. I knew she would be. I also knew I'd now be working in a world where half the opportunity for meeting interesting people had been sliced cleanly off.

CHAPTER 18

 ortland, Oregon

* * *

The two boys that lived in the house behind ours got a treehouse the summer after I turned nine. Their father and grandfather built it, starting on the last weekend of June. By the middle of July, they had a house that was sturdy enough and large enough to hold four kids.

Jimmy was nine and in my class at school. John was four and needed help from his dad to climb the ladder up to the treehouse. When he got there, he sat down and hugged his legs and pressed his face into his knees. His father had to climb the ladder and carry him down.

It was decided that John probably wouldn't be using the tree-house until the next summer. That meant Jimmy had it all to himself. And that meant the minute his grandpa went home, I walked into their yard and told Jimmy we should play together more often because our houses were so close.

I told him playing with a girl could be fun because I was a good climber and I could ride my bike as fast as he could. He didn't believe me. I asked Jake to draw chalk lines in the street. He brought out the stopwatch he'd gotten for Christmas and we had three races. I won two. At first Jimmy sulked that I beat him, but the next day, he asked if I wanted to see his treehouse. He told me to bring snacks.

While my mother was doing her bible study homework in the living room, I tiptoed into the kitchen with a shoebox. I filled it with a bag of cheddar cheese fish crackers, six peanut butter cookies, and two boxes of raisins. I hurried out of the kitchen, across our back porch and to the end of our yard. Then I went down the slope and through the wooded area that separated the two yards.

Jimmy was sitting in his treehouse. He came halfway down the ladder. I handed the shoebox to him. He reached up and placed it inside the doorway to the treehouse and climbed back up. I followed.

The walls were unpainted wood. The roof was angled slightly so we could only stand up on one side, and the windows were plain square openings. Jimmy's grandpa had showed him how to sand the edges and said that was his job, but Jimmy got tired of it, so the edges were a little rough in some areas.

"Are you ever going to paint it?" I asked.

"My mom doesn't want paint on the tree, so I don't know. Maybe."

"I could help."

"What snacks did you bring?"

I opened the box. He grabbed two cookies and started eating one.

I grabbed one and took a large bite. We chewed in companionable silence until we'd both eaten two cookies. "What do you usually do up here?" I asked.

"Watch people."

"What people?"

"The people next door." He stood and went to one of the windows.

71

I joined him and saw that we could see past the smaller trees and shrubs into the yards on both sides of his house. We couldn't see the backyard of my house at all.

"What else do you do?"

"My mom said I could read books up here."

"That would be cool."

"Yeah." He grabbed the bag of fish crackers and opened it.

As we nibbled fish crackers, we stared out at the backyard of the house on the left side of Jimmy's. They had two separate gardens. One was a vegetable garden. The other garden was surrounded by a brick wall with a wood gate. The neighbors didn't have any kids and the woman that lived there had a pottery studio in the back corner of their yard. She made clay pots on a wheel, but she also made small clay animals, glazed them with bright colors, and arranged them inside the brick-walled garden. She'd built small wood houses for the animals and created a village for them with plants and winding pathways.

Because of the five-foot tall brick wall, most kids in the neighborhood assumed it was just another garden.

"It's not fair that big wall is around the animal town," Jimmy said.

"Why?" I bit the tail off a fish cracker.

"It's for kids. But no kids are allowed."

"I wish I brought something to drink."

"Why didn't you?"

"I had to sneak this food out of the kitchen. My mom would have noticed if I took juice boxes."

He nodded as if I was surprisingly wise to have realized the risk of taking something that might be noticed.

"We should take some of the animals for the treehouse," Jimmy said.

"Why?"

"Because."

"But because *why*?"

"For fun. We can watch her look for them. It'll be funny. And we'll know they're up here where we can play with them and she'll think they just disappeared. But we'll be playing with them."

I moved to the window on the opposite side of the treehouse and looked into the other neighbor's backyard. It was nothing but grass and shrubs and flowers. I stared at the ground, waiting for something exciting to happen. Maybe a gopher would poke its head out of a hole. Grown-ups were always complaining about gophers, always trying to kill them. I liked watching them. They were so nervous and so fast. They stuck their heads out and the minute they saw someone looking at them they disappeared as if another gopher brother or sister had grabbed their back legs and yanked them down into the hole.

No gophers appeared, but a large black dog walked down the back steps and out to the middle of the lawn. That was why there were no gophers in that yard. The dog sat down and scratched his ear.

"What are you looking at?" Jimmy asked.

"Watching that dog."

"It's just sitting there. It's boring. Let's throw something so it will bark," he said.

"I can't throw that far."

He sat down and ate the last cookie that was his, as if we were going to split them evenly. I assumed we would, but after hearing that he wanted to steal the clay animals, I wasn't sure. Maybe he liked to make his own rules about what was fair. I hadn't ever played with him until he got the treehouse, so I wasn't sure what to expect.

When the cookie was gone, he stood again. "I'll climb down and run over and get two of the animals. You stand guard and yell if someone comes out of the house."

"What will you do if you're inside the wall when I yell? You won't have time to get out."

"She's probably in the pottery shed anyway. She goes in there all afternoon most of the time. Yelling at me is just in *case* she comes out. It probably won't happen."

"I have to think about it."

"You're boring," he said.

"You're boring. Don't you have other toys?"

"I want to play with those animals."

Playing with them in the little town the neighbor woman had set up could be fun. But carrying them up to the treehouse and playing with them on a bare wood floor seemed like it would get boring pretty fast.

"If you want to," I said. "I'll watch. But if she comes out, even if I yell, I don't think you'll have time to escape."

"She probably won't come out."

He climbed down the ladder. I stood by the window, waiting to see what would happen. Wondering if I would yell, or if it would be less boring to see what would happen if she caught him inside the brick wall.

CHAPTER 19

 ew York

* * *

Diana was so eager to get Reverend Shera out of her hair, she'd reviewed all his pictures the evening of our trip to the zoo. She arranged to meet with him, and me, which was not her usual process, two days later. We met in his church office.

Diana and I sat in two armchairs from the 1980s, the cushions worn thin from what must have been thousands of people who had sat across from him. I wondered what they'd talked about. I wondered if they'd left thinking god was on their side, or out to get them. I wondered if Reverend Shera believed he'd helped them. I wondered what Diana was thinking.

Matt had turned his computer sideways so we could display the photographs and all of us could see them at once. Beside the large computer on the cluttered desk was Diana's laptop, displaying a summary of the results from Matt's personality tests and answers to the essay questions.

Diana started with the photographs I'd taken in the session with Stephanie, but hadn't included the ones where he'd become embarrassed. Those had already been discussed and she told me before we walked through the front doors of the church that she wanted this done efficiently.

While she talked to him about his personality profile and his desire to build a phenomenally large church, I tuned out. I'd never participated in these meetings before, and I wasn't sure why she'd dragged me along. Maybe she thought he wouldn't open up as much in front of two people and that would speed things along. I really had no idea, but since it wasn't my role to talk, I couldn't see the point of listening to the conversation.

Instead I stared at the walls surrounding us. Three of the four walls had floor-to-ceiling bookcases. Every single shelf was filled with books. A few of them closest to his desk were sets of research books with faux-leather, or maybe real leather bindings, the titles printed in gold. I couldn't read the titles from where I sat, but each set had ten to twenty volumes. The rest of the shelves held a mix of paperback and hardcover books. Some titles were familiar from the shelves of my parents' home. Some I recognized from the bookcases of the ministers at Pure Truth Tabernacle. Some I'd never seen before.

It surprised me that the same books filled his shelves when he was twenty years younger, maybe more, than the minister I'd grown up with. It also surprised me because he didn't seem like such a fanatic as the members and leaders of the church where they'd tried to pound doctrine into my head.

Was it possible to read those same books and come out a different person on the other end?

I wanted to ask Matt, but Diana would not appreciate the interruption.

And then I heard my name.

I gave Diana a confident smile, hoping she would give me a hint about what she'd just said about me.

"It's as if the spirit of god is directing her," Matt said.

I whipped my head around to face him. What had Diana said to elicit that comment? I glanced at her from the corner of my eye. She was smiling at me, transformed back, for a moment, into the woman I'd known before.

Diana laughed. "I wouldn't go that far. And I doubt that's how Alexandra sees it."

"Definitely not," I said.

"But she does have a unique skill in capturing people with their masks off," Diana said. "I'm stunned every single time. It's almost as if she can see inside their minds."

This was a surprise. She was gushing compliments at me after weeks of telling me in every way she could that I was the most diffi-cult, stubborn, irritating person in New York City. She was making my head spin.

"The story you told us captured everything you're feeling with absolute perfection. But what I see in these photographs, and that's the magic that Alexandra possesses, is that the experience you had was about more than the fear of the ape hurting you. It was the betrayal you felt from your brother."

Tears filled Matt's eyes. Diana reached into her bag and pulled out a packet of tissues. She handed it to him. He thanked her as the tears spilled over. I wondered if he was used to the tears coming from the person sitting on the opposite side of his desk. I wondered if he was uncomfortable, crying in front of two women he hardly knew.

He pulled out a tissue and wiped his eyes. "In my nightmares, I'm terrified of being hurt."

"Yes, but dreams are symbolic. You know that."

He nodded.

"I think your fear is the betrayal. The one person you thought you could trust abandoned you into the hands, literally, of this crea-ture that could have really damaged you. Instead of helping you get away. You felt utterly alone and vulnerable. That's the ultimate fear.

Until that moment in your life, you'd always felt your family was there for you. And in that moment, you realized you couldn't count on your brother. You weren't even sure of his love."

That was a lot to get out of an ape trying to pinch a kid, and a brother, who was a kid himself, laughing at something that was probably both funny and a little scary for him at the same time. Maybe it was a good thing I didn't sit in on these coaching sessions with Diana. I wondered if she always got into dream interpretation, or if this was more evidence of her trying to rush Matt out the door.

She went on to talk about how any kind of fear, and yes, there was still the fear of what that animal might have done to him, can be limiting. She explained that success comes from taking risks and if he was unconsciously protecting himself in multiple areas, that self-protection, that barrier of fear, was also a barrier to the risks he needed to take. And ultimately, would build a wall that would prevent his success.

He needed to dismantle that fear brick by brick.

When he asked how he should go about doing that, she said she was going to refer him to a few therapists who could help. He could choose the one with whom he clicked the best. She said the kind of help he needed was beyond the scope of what Fly Higher was set up for.

He looked surprised.

"I thought—"

"Don't look at this as a disappointment." She gave him a cool, tight smile. "To provide a bridge to therapy, Fly Higher will pay for the first three sessions."

And with her use of the word—*we*—I knew why I was there. I was the buffer to her skipping out on finishing the job. She was so eager to be rid of male clients, she was giving him a skimpy consultation and passing him off to someone else.

"It's not that I'm disappointed, I just—"

"I think your fears are very deep, Matt. I know that probably goes against how you perceive yourself, based on your religious beliefs. But it's clear in the photographs. And I think a therapist is a better solution for you. If the bridging payments aren't enough, we're happy to give you a refund of twenty-five percent." She closed her laptop.

He didn't argue any further. Maybe he was afraid to.

CHAPTER 20

*N*ow it had become a game. Hunter couldn't stop thinking about it, but he wasn't going to try. Instead of pushing her and making her defensive and worried about his obsession, he would get her to tell him about her siblings before she tricked him into telling him something he didn't want to. All he needed was vodka and vermouth and lots of olives.

She was crazy about the things. She was so infatuated with the tiny fruits, he wondered if she only drank martinis because she liked the vodka-soaked olives.

To entice her further, he stopped by Bloomingdale's after work and bought two of the most exquisite martini glasses he could find. They had longer-than-average stems, so slender they looked like the bones of a small bird. He also bought a shaker since he didn't have one. He wasn't an expert with martinis, so he watched several YouTube videos and searched for a few recipes. Then he made two practice drinks before she came over.

Consuming three martinis would surely dissolve the resistance she'd built inside her head. She would forget what she was saying, she would trip herself up. She would talk too much and the truth would come sliding out. He was absolutely confident.

He'd bought two steaks, two potatoes that he planned to bake and serve with all the fixings, and a grocery bag full of greens for a salad. He'd insisted she bring clothes and plan to spend the *entire* night.

That was the one part of his game he was uncertain about. Until he opened his apartment door, he wouldn't know if she'd agreed to sleep there or not. Sure, she'd said yes in a text message, but it would not surprise him at all to see her standing in his doorway wearing workout clothes, announcing she was leaving right after dinner. She might just as easily show up in a cocktail dress, suggesting they go out dancing instead.

First, he planned to lead her to the bedroom, slowly remove her clothes, and ease her onto the bed while the notes of a jazz playlist he'd started earlier filled the bedroom. By the time the evening was over, she would be too drunk to do anything but collapse into sleep, if things went as he'd envisioned.

He would be only moderately tipsy and in victorious possession of detailed information about her siblings. Or the confident knowledge that she had none.

When he did open the door, he wondered if she heard his sigh of relief. She was wearing flip-flops, shorts, a tank top with multiple thin straps running over her shoulders and across her back. When she moved to pick up her overnight bag, he saw there was a large birdcage with a blue cloth cover beside her. How did she manage it? The scenario he'd played out in his mind evaporated, even though she'd clearly followed through on her agreement to spend the night.

"I brought Damien," she said. "I hope you don't mind."

He stared at the rectangular cage. The cloth moved slightly, and he heard scratching inside.

"Aren't you going to invite me in?"

"Why did you bring your friend's bird? I don't think it's a good idea ... what if he makes a lot of noise? This building is old and sound carries more than you—"

"I don't have a choice. I can't leave him alone overnight. So if you want me to stay …" She stared at him, then glanced to the side, almost as if she were thinking of leaving if he didn't immediately agree to welcome the enormous bird.

"Why can't you leave him alone overnight?"

"Are you going to let us in? He could get anxious sitting here with the cover on, hearing us talking and not knowing who you are."

"A neurotic cockatoo?"

"He's not neurotic. How would you feel if you were blindfolded and two people were talking about you, one of them a total stranger?"

"He's a bird, Alex."

"A very smart bird." She grabbed the handle of the cage and picked it up.

He backed away from the door as she started forward, a buried instinct telling him the bird might be agitated from being covered and could reach a sharp claw through the rather widely spaced wires of the cage, making a grab for him.

Once they were inside with the door closed, she pulled the cover off. The bird was impressive. It eyed him with a look that could only be described as disapproval. He wondered if this would disrupt his plan for the evening. It didn't have to, but for some reason, it made him feel less like he was playing a game in which he was setting the rules.

Always with her. It always turned into this. And she didn't even seem to be trying. It just happened. She hadn't known what he was planning.

"Why can't he stay in your apartment? Won't your roommate feed him for one night?"

"It's complicated."

"What does he eat? Seeds? A little fruit?"

"His diet isn't complicated. The situation is complicated."

"Is she afraid of him?"

"No, I don't trust her boyfriend."

He wasn't sure what to do with that. Was she worried this guy would hurt the bird? Why was she staying there if the guy was so scary she couldn't leave a pet overnight without fearing for his life, or whatever it was she was worried about. But that seemed to be what she was implying.

"Do you think he'd hurt the bird?"

"I don't know what he'd do. But Damien is my responsibility, and besides, he's fun. You'll like him."

"He was fine when we stayed at the Equinox for the weekend."

"I know. But he was really quiet for a day or two after that weekend. It's just better if I don't leave him there overnight when I'm not around."

Chardonnay time!

Hunter laughed.

"I told you."

Dangerous woman!

"Who does that refer to?" Hunter asked. "His owner? Or you?"

She smiled.

CHAPTER 21

*A*lexandra moved away from the cage, walked slowly toward him, and slid her arms around his waist. She started kissing him, and a few minutes later, she was pulling him onto the couch. Again, not what he'd planned, but oh well.

Chardonnay time!

The bird's voice was loud and insistent. Almost as if he knew what he was saying, or didn't like that he was being ignored and wanted to disrupt what they were doing.

Hunter pulled away from her. "I'll put your bag in the bedroom. You can feed him so he'll stop talking. Then we can pick this up." He bit her earlobe gently, catching her earring and filling his mouth with a bitter taste.

"He comes out of his cage to eat, so I need to supervise. And it doesn't stop him from talking. He likes to talk."

"He comes out? In an unfamiliar environment?"

"We'll see, but I have to at least offer him the chance."

"You treat this bird like a human being."

"He deserves it."

"If you say so." Hunter took her bag to the bedroom. When he returned, the cage door was open, and the bird was standing in the doorway, looking around the room as if he were trying to decide if it was up to his standards.

Finally, the bird deigned to step out of the cage. He trotted around the living room, eating seeds and nuggets she'd hidden for him, pausing to nibble off a plate of cut up mango. The whole thing took almost an hour.

Hunter's desire had waned somewhat by the time they were finished watching the bird, but still he led her into his bedroom and slipped the straps of her top off her shoulders.

Dangerous woman!

"If you put the cover on, will he shut up?"

"No."

He sighed and closed the bedroom door. The next hour was punctuated by pointless and pithy comments from the bird, increasingly louder, as if he was pissed off that he'd been abandoned in an unfamiliar room.

By the time they got out of bed, it was dusk. He made two martinis, started dinner, and turned on the baseball game. Alex took her martini onto the fire escape and by the time the meal was ready, her drink was gone, his had been poured down the drain, and he'd grown used to the bird's staccato chatter.

"It's so hot out, I thought we'd stick to martinis instead of wine. Icy cold," he said as he filled the shaker with ice.

"It only stays cold if you drink it fast."

He laughed. "Are you good with that?"

She glanced at their dinner plates—the juicy steak and the split open potatoes. "Sure."

Drink it fast!

Hunter laughed. "It's funny to hear what phrases he zeroes in on, but doesn't it get old after a while?"

"No. It seems like he's talking to me sometimes. And he has his quiet moments."

"Good to know."

They ate dinner. She suggested a movie and he suggested

another martini. She hesitated a moment over that, but then agreed. "Are you trying to get me drunk?"

Her smile told him she was feeling the vodka. It was more relaxed, lingered a while, and after a moment, she seemed to forget why she was smiling, but continued anyway.

He didn't want to lie to her. Not saying things, and outright lying, were very different. He wished she hadn't asked. "I know you like martinis." His words sounded limp, but it was the truth.

They settled on the couch, cuddling in the center. Thankfully, she'd covered the bird cage after announcing it was Damien's bedtime. Hunter still felt as if the bird might be listening to them. She'd managed to convince him the creature had intelligence far beyond the norm and deserved to be treated with the respect and consideration, and possibly the concern, of a human being. He laughed to himself. Maybe, even though this was only his second drink, the alcohol was going more quickly than usual to his head. Hot, muggy weather did that sometimes. He really should have a glass of water, but he didn't want to break the mood.

"Let's not watch a movie," he said. "Let's just talk."

She laughed. "Sure. Talking is always fun. That's what they do half the time in movies anyway." She giggled longer than usual. "What should we talk about? I can tell you all about the zoo, or we can try to figure out why Diana doesn't want to offer coaching to men. Or we could talk about Damien's vocabulary. Or ..." She took a sip of her drink and her eyes seemed to glaze over slightly. He wasn't sure if she was thinking of something she didn't want to say or was suddenly aware she was on the way to getting smashed.

This was not going to be as easy as he'd fantasized. And thinking it would be easy, even after three martinis, had indeed been a fantasy. Any way he approached it, she was likely to clam up. She wasn't that drunk, and he didn't think she'd want a fourth martini.

She took another sip of her drink.

Maybe she *would* consider a fourth. "Do you want another one?"

She giggled. "I just might." She ate the last olive. "If I can have eleven olives."

There was a barely noticeable slur to her words. He'd never heard that before.

She did have a fourth, and he asked her if she missed Portland, which didn't seem to bother her. To seem less obvious, he asked about her favorite city she'd lived in. So far, it was New York. He asked if she ever went back to Portland for the holidays.

"I know what you're doing, Hunter."

He felt a groan deep inside, but he managed to keep it silent.

"You're trying to work your way around to finding out about my siblings. Fine. I have a brother. He is absolutely fabulous. His name is Eric and he would do anything for me. He's been the hero of my life since I was little and he never said no to me. He's smart and funny. He's nice. Everyone says so. He taught me lots of things like how to climb a tree and ride a bike. He has a fabulous career and an amazing family. I hardly ever get to see him but we keep in touch. He's a fantastic athlete and he was the star of the basketball team and he got straight A's in high school and played golf in college."

She continued on like this in a dreamy voice that sounded slightly unlike her. He wasn't sure if it was the alcohol or because everything she was saying was complete and utter bullshit.

CHAPTER 22

*T*he day after I spent the night at Hunter's and he tried to trick me into telling him about my siblings, I was sitting in Central Park drinking a latte instead of going for a run, which had been my plan when I got up and dressed in spandex and running shoes. But on my jog-walk to the park, I smelled coffee and I felt a little tired and a little soaked with vodka and vermouth and I decided lifting weights later that day, with air conditioning, was a better option.

I looked up from my phone and saw Carolina. It shocked me because as small as the different neighborhoods of New York City can seem, I rarely saw someone I knew.

She was sitting on a bench about twenty feet from me, just past a curve in the path. A man with black hair dressed in a charcoal gray suit stood facing her. She was yelling at him. They were far enough away that I couldn't make out what she was saying, but I could hear her voice. Joggers and dog walkers, couples and families with strollers were veering a wide path around them as they passed by.

Her head was tilted up, the tendons of her neck stretched as she talked a mile a minute. He stood there, looking down at her, the expression on his face concealed by the shadows of the trees.

I wondered if she was yelling about his work schedule, their monster of a son, or something else. Although, from the little bits I'd seen, she wasn't doing anything to reshape the monster into someone more appealing.

The man took a step away from her. He looked at his watch.

"We're not done!" she shouted.

I took a sip of my drink, wondering if she was completely unaware of everyone staring at her, or she didn't care. I wondered about him. He didn't seem all that bothered either. Maybe he was used to it.

Her voice dropped again, sucking her words with it, words continuing to spill out non-stop. He remained speechless. After a few minutes, she stood. She kissed his cheek, took his hand, and they started walking away from where I was sitting. I stared in utter, disbelieving fascination. I knew I didn't understand marriage, but this was entirely new to me.

She seemed so upset, and yet the moment she stood, she walked away with him as if none of it had happened. Was it some sort of game between them? Had he whispered something that made all of her raw, furious feelings dissolve, but I hadn't seen his lips move? Was there another signal he'd given to make everything okay between them?

I slurped down the rest of my latte, mildly regretting not following them. I tossed the cup into the trash and jogged back to my apartment, figuring a short run dodging pedestrians, pausing only for traffic lights, was better than nothing.

Inside my apartment, Damien was busy scratching at something in the bottom of his cage, so I didn't greet him as I normally did. I turned immediately into the hallway and saw that my bedroom door was partially open. I moved quietly toward it and rested my fingers lightly on the handle. I opened the door slowly.

Ned was standing beside my bed. He was holding one of my pillows, clutching it to his side like a child holds a stuffed toy. The top drawer of the nightstand was open and he was peering inside, fingering something, which I could only assume was the jewelry I sometimes tossed in there when I was too lazy to put it where it belonged.

"Get out of my room." My voice was as loud as I could make it without shouting, without it carrying into the living room and frightening Damien.

Ned jerked around to face me, slamming his leg into the open drawer. "Ow, shit." He dropped my pillow onto the floor.

"Out."

"I was … Eileen couldn't find—"

"Don't feed me a pathetic lie. Eileen didn't *anything*. You have no right to be in here."

"I'm sorry, I—"

"No you're not. Why are you still standing there? I told you to get out." My voice was a normal volume now, perfectly calm as I wondered how long it would take me to get a locksmith to come out to put a deadbolt lock on the door. And what it would cost on a Saturday.

He started toward me. I didn't move out of his way, forcing him to squeeze past me as he walked through the doorway. I could feel him trying his best not to make contact, but it was impossible because of where I was standing.

"Sorry, didn't mean to touch you. I can't … if you would move …"

"I told you to leave, and it's taking you an awfully long time and you're doing way too much talking."

"Can you calm down?"

"I'm calm."

"You seem pretty angry."

"Actually, not as much as I should be. I'm just aware that I've been proven right."

"About what?"

"You."

"What about me?"

I smiled.

"I wasn't going through your things. I wasn't snooping. I—"

"You were in my room, which is all I need to mention. But you were also looking through my drawer. You were hugging my pillow." I made a disgusted face.

"I wasn't hugging it."

I laughed. "Fantasizing? I wonder what Eileen would think of that?" I put my finger on my chin as if I were contemplating a profound question.

"It wasn't like that. Don't be a little bitch."

"Is that what I am?"

"Don't make this into a big deal. Eileen misplaced her necklace and I thought it might—"

"You thought I stole it?"

"No. I thought you might have picked it up with your things when you were straightening the apartment or something like that."

"How stupid do you think I am, Ned?"

He took several steps away from me.

"Where is Eileen?"

"She's running errands."

"And you decided to investigate." I walked to my bed and bent over it, sniffing the comforter. "I hope you didn't do anything on my bed."

"Oh God, come on. Why are you doing this?"

"You were in my room. I don't know what you were doing. All you've told me so far is a lie that's so limp a nine-year-old could come up with something more compelling. So yes, I'm thinking of all the possibilities."

"You're just trying to make me look bad. You want to upset Eileen because you're pissed and you want me to get in trouble with her."

"Why would I want that?"

"For whatever reason, you don't want her to be in a relationship with me. Why you think her love life is any of your business is beyond me."

"I don't think it's my business."

"Then why are you trying to break us up?"

I laughed. "I'm not trying to break you up. I have better things to do, a lot more interesting things."

"I'm sure you do. If you weren't so secretive about those things, maybe we would all get along. You've hurt her a lot, you know. She thought you two were friends, but you're emotionally unavailable. Cold."

"This isn't about me. It's about you trespassing into my bedroom and getting your skin cells and sweat all over my pillow. It's about you violating my space."

He took a few more steps back, bumping into the wall on the opposite side of the hallway.

From the living room, I heard Damien's sharp tone. *Dangerous woman!*

I appreciated Damien's input. It was well-timed, although it didn't make me smile as it usually did. It made me wish I could let Ned see that side of me right that minute.

"You're turning this into a much bigger deal than it needs to be," he said.

"You're minimizing it. So there we are—a classic *he said, she said.*"

He groaned.

"I would tell you to do my laundry, but I don't think that would make me feel any better, so I'll have to make some extra time in my day for that."

"Poor you," he said. "You're overreacting."

"You're pushing your luck."

"Not really. It's not as if you won't be running to Eileen to tell her what a big, bad, creepy guy I am."

"What you did is definitely creepy."

"I was just—"

"Stop."

"Should we just say I made a very bad mistake and you've been able to give me a nice tongue lashing, which I'm sure you've been wanting to do for a long time. So now we're even?"

"Not even close."

Dangerous woman! Delicious mango! Drink it fast!

I stepped into my bedroom and closed the door. I was disgusted knowing his hands had been on my furniture, my bedding, and things I might not even know about. Had he been in the bathroom? Had he slid his hands inside my clothing drawers and touched my tops and lingerie? Had he opened the closet and run his fingers over everything hanging there?

The bigger question was, what was he after? Was there something specific he was looking for, or was he just curious and hoping to stumble across something unexpected?

I took out my phone and opened up a search window, looking for locksmiths.

I hadn't decided what I would say to Eileen. It didn't really matter. She would be worried I was upset, she would be angry with Ned, but it would be fleeting. Right away, she would beg me to forgive him.

At least I could be confident knowing there was absolutely nothing in my room that would tell him anything about my life except that I liked nice clothes and shoes and that I had a lot of makeup.

CHAPTER 23

J must have been the luckiest girl alive because I found a locksmith who would come to our apartment and install a lock that afternoon.

Ned had left the apartment. I don't know what emergency lie he texted to Eileen, but I would find out when she returned from her errands.

While the locksmith's drill whined in my ears, I sat in the armchair that was wedged in the corner of my room between the bed and dresser. I texted Hunter and asked if he wanted to go to a museum the following weekend. He answered immediately that he did, meaning he wasn't annoyed with me for telling a story about Eric that I hoped left him wondering whether it was made up. Maybe he'd finally decided to relax about how many historical details we handed off to each other.

I hadn't relaxed at all. I still had an inexplicable desire to tell him everything about my life. Most of the things I'd said about Eric were true, but I knew he hadn't believed me. That's what's so funny about people. They're so certain of their own perceptions, that even when you tell the truth, sometimes they think you're lying. Of course, I'm the same. Maybe Ned really was in my room looking for something that belonged to Eileen. At first. But he should have looked in the other rooms of the apartment and stopped there. He should have asked permission. And in his case, I seriously doubted he was telling the truth.

A text popped up from Tess.

It's a done deal. I'm a vintner.

After replying with four laughing emojis, I wrote: *A vintner or a property owner with a lot of grapes that you have no clue how to turn into drinkable wine?*

Tess: *We'll figure it out. There are people who know how to do everything.*

This was followed by thirty-seven photographs. And they weren't grouped. She sent each one individually. There were pictures of grapevines and a tasting room, huge metal holding tanks and oak barrels. There were photographs of a beautiful Mediterranean house that couldn't really be called a house. A villa, maybe. Or an estate. She sent pictures of an enormous sweeping staircase rising from the entryway to a second-floor landing that ran around the entryway. There were photographs of the kitchen, a formal dining room, a living room, entertainment room, a study, a library, an office, and five or six bedrooms. I lost count. Maybe seven. There was a swimming pool on a terrace that looked out over the Napa Valley.

It was stunning and I had a sudden, overwhelming desire for open space, for fresh-smelling air, for quiet that wasn't the vacuum-sealed quiet of our apartment at night when all the windows were closed to shut out the traffic sounds that carried on until four in the morning. I had an urgent longing for more space of my own, for privacy.

By the time I was finished commenting on her photographs, I had a shiny new deadbolt lock above the handle on my bedroom door.

When Eileen found out about the lock, which was the moment she came home, because I told her, she was beside herself. She fretted that it would violate the lease. I told her I didn't care. I no longer felt safe in my own bedroom. She cried when I said that, telling me Ned was the sweetest, kindest man she'd ever known.

I said he couldn't be trusted.

"Please don't say that."

"You don't think that's an outrageous violation of my space, and my peace of mind?"

"He's my boyfriend. He's not a stranger."

"He is to me."

"How can you say that?"

"I hardly know him. And that's beside the point. He doesn't belong in there. He didn't ask permission."

"Well, he—"

"Don't make excuses. I don't want more lies."

"I asked him to look for my necklace."

I laughed. "He told you his story so you could back him up?"

"It's the truth. Please believe me. He didn't mean to upset you."

"Is that what he told you to say? Do either of you have any boundaries?"

"We share an apartment. You're welcome in my bedroom. I wouldn't be upset if you needed to look for something."

"You should be."

"I don't want to fight," she said. "I don't want you to hate him."

"I don't hate him. I don't trust him. And he doesn't belong in my bedroom. But now, I don't have to think about it happening again."

"Why couldn't you just ask him not to go in there again? A lock is so … it's so …"

"I shouldn't have to ask."

"I honestly did ask him to help me find—"

"Did he tell you he was hugging my pillow?"

She stared at me. "Hugging your pillow? He was in your bed?"

"He was standing next to it, hugging my pillow, looking in my drawer. If you don't think that's creepy and weird and a total violation, then I can't explain it to you."

"I'm really sorry. I hope you'll forgive him."

"I have a lock. And I want you to get the key back from him."

"What k—oh, the apartment key? Why?"

"We never agreed to it."

"I didn't think you'd mind. He's my boyfriend and I trust him totally. Just like I trust you. And if you trust Hunter and want him to have a key, you can—"

"That's not how things work. Are we just going to start handing out keys to everyone we *trust*?"

"Our boyfriends aren't everyone. Just two people."

"No. It's our apartment. We pay the rent. We are the only ones who should have keys."

"But he's here all the time and sometimes he gets here before I do and there's nowhere for him to wait."

"He can wait in the lobby."

Her lips quivered, and she turned away for a moment. "I told him to go into your room, okay? I trust him with my life. He's not going to do anything to hurt me or you. Not ever. I wish you could see that."

"He shouldn't have a key. We should agree on those things together."

"We didn't agree to have the bird stay here."

Damien chose that moment to shout—*Chardonnay time!*

I thought about her name on the lease. I thought about her investment in nearly all the furnishings. I didn't have a lot of leverage. I did have a lock on my bedroom door. It was time to move Damien into the bedroom with me. It was also time to ask Tess how much longer he'd be staying. Especially now that she'd purchased her estate. But for a while, I could manage to sleep with him in my room. He would be safer, and I would be safe.

And just to be one-hundred percent sure, I would install a security camera in my bedroom to keep an eye on Damien when I wasn't around, because locks can be picked.

CHAPTER 24

$\mathcal{M}$y first photo session with Brie would be in one of her private training rooms. She was rarely in her office and it wasn't reflective of her work, she'd said. That had been pretty obvious by the fact there was nothing office-like about the large room without a computer or phone or anything suggesting it was a place of business.

I entered the training room through a heavy door with no windows, which was unusual for a workout room. The moment I stepped inside, I realized why. It was like entering another world.

The walls were painted lavender with a sparkly coating. The effect, rather than looking like a nightclub, which was my first thought, was quite soothing after I'd stood there for a moment. The music coming into the room through unseen speakers was a series of gentle tones woven with nature sounds. It felt like I was standing in the middle of a forest, the sounds were falling like mist out of the ceiling. The speakers must have been hidden by the fabric draped across the ceiling, shimmering like water—lavender, green, and blue. It was all very soothing and not what I'd ever seen in a weight room, but surprisingly invigorating at the same time.

There were racks of free weights and several benches with

barbells as well as platforms for doing steps, exercise balls, pilates equipment, and yoga mats and bolsters.

I placed my camera bag on a table near the door and took out my phone. Our appointment was for ten and it was now several minutes past, but I remained alone in the tranquil atmosphere. Seeing all that top-of-the-line equipment, feeling the environment wash over me, filled me with a desire to start working out.

It was another ten minutes before Brie arrived. Andy was with her, opening the door and ushering her into the room, closing it firmly behind them. He was carrying two white water bottles with Bodies By Brie written on them in script. He touched her shoulder, and she turned. He held one of the bottles to her lips.

She tipped her head back and he squeezed water into her mouth.

I wanted to laugh. I also wished I'd had my camera ready, although it was not at all the kind of photograph I was after.

"The photographs need to be taken with Brie alone." My voice carried smoothly across the room without my having to raise it, even though it was a good-sized space.

"We're a team, remember?" Andy said.

"Diana made it clear," I said.

Andy patted the white bag hanging from his shoulder. "I need to touch up Brie's makeup during the photoshoot."

"She doesn't need her makeup touched up. That's not what this is about."

Brie laughed. "I need to look good. My image is—"

"The photos aren't for public use. Diana explained that."

"Oh, Alexandra. How naïve are you? Don't ever assume any photograph of you will remain private. How can you not know that at your age?" Brie laughed as if it were the funniest thing she'd heard in a long time.

"I'm aware," I said. "But you have a contract with us and it states the photos are protected. These aren't messages you're sending to a guy who could turn ugly after a breakup."

I began taking my camera out of the bag. Diana would want me to refuse to proceed until he left. In fact, she would want me to pack up my camera and walk out the door. But she was already busy getting rid of male clients. If she started getting rid of women who wanted to set their own rules, who would be next on the list? Soon, there would be no clients left for us. If Andy showed up when Diana had her consultations with Brie, that was her problem to deal with then.

I could handle him. I could get Brie to relax and forget about her surroundings, whether Andy was there or not. I was absolutely confident.

With the telephoto lens in place, I turned suddenly and snapped multiple shots of Brie, capturing her from the shoulders up, cutting Andy out of the frame.

"I wasn't expecting that," she said.

"That's the idea. Do you remember what Diana explained about this session?"

"Yes."

"I'll be talking to your about your business and your goals. I'll take photographs when you don't expect it in order to capture your micro-expressions that reflect—"

"I get it. I said she explained it."

I snapped several more pictures.

"Let's get you some CBD, sweetie," Andy said. "You sound tense. And a little shoulder rub." He put down the water bottles, let the bag slide off his shoulder, and pulled a small plastic container out of the bag. Brie opened her mouth like a puppy waiting for a treat. Andy placed a CBD gummy on her tongue. She chewed it and swallowed. He moved behind her and rubbed her trapezius muscle while she rolled her head from side to back to the other side. When he was finished with the massage, he ran his finger down the back of her neck to the edge of her top that scooped low between her shoulder blades.

I considered asking her what that was about. Hearing the question might provide a very telling micro- expression.

CHAPTER 25

$\mathcal{W}$hile Andy and Brie looked like they might start peeling each other's clothes off, I changed lenses and walked across the room. "You need to move away, so I can get pictures of Brie alone."

"Sure. You're the boss." Andy took a small step away from her.

"Why did you go into the fitness business?" I asked.

"She loves helping people. She loves seeing people transform their—"

"This is about Brie," I said. "I'm talking to her. You need to move away so she can forget you're here."

Brie pursed her lips and made kissing sounds at Andy. "I never forget Andy's here. He's my lifeblood."

I took a few shots, although I would probably have to delete them unless I could explain to Diana why Brie would be doing that. Or maybe I would simply tell Diana the truth.

I lowered the camera. "I know you think you understand what we're trying to accomplish, but I don't understand what *you're* trying to accomplish. If you want to uncover what's holding you back, and you hired Fly Higher to help you with that, why don't you want to follow our process? You're not going to get anything valuable out of this if I don't get some photographs where you're not thinking about the camera and Andy."

"But he's my soul."

Andy must have taken that as some kind of directive, because he rushed to her side. He stroked her cheek.

"Do I need more color?" she asked.

"You look perfect," he cooed.

She smiled

He touched her breastbone and ran his finger down to the edge of her leotard top to the center of her breasts.

I took a few steps away from them. I decided to ignore them. Maybe if they got their playacting, or whatever they were up to, out of their systems, I could finish my job.

As I watched, Andy moved around Brie. He blew gently at her hair, but it was as stiff with gel as it had been the first time, so not a single hair changed position. He ran his finger along the arch of one eyebrow, then took his hand away. A moment later, he was dragging three fingers down her bare arm. She wriggled and smiled at him.

I wanted to laugh. Instead, I walked to the table where I'd left my camera bag. It really wasn't worth it.

"Where are you going?" Brie cried.

"I explained what I'm here to do, you don't seem interested."

"You're supposed to take my picture."

"I can't do that if Andy is hovering around you. I can't do that if he's going to interrupt our conversation. You're utterly self-conscious. I won't be able to get a single useable image."

"Then you're not very good."

"I am, but he has to get away from you, and he can't talk."

"You think well of yourself," Andy said.

"I'm just stating the facts. I wouldn't have this job, we wouldn't have clients like Brie, Fly Higher couldn't charge the fees it does and wouldn't have the reputation it has if I wasn't good at this. All of that speaks for itself." I settled my camera into the bag.

"Please don't go. Andy will be a good boy, right Andy?"

"Yes. I will." He licked her cheek.

Did this woman, this couple, whatever they were, really run several extremely successful fitness centers?

"Come back," Brie said. "I want to do it. We'll follow the rules. I didn't know there would be so many rules. We just wanted to have fun. And get some cute, fun pics."

I removed my camera from the bag, thinking that in some ways, these people were a little like me. They were having fun with me and I was trying to do a job. The thought made me want to laugh. I bit down gently on my tongue and walked back to where Brie was standing, looking like a chastened child.

I raised the camera. "When you were a little girl, what did you dream of being when you grew up?" I asked.

She told me she wanted to be a female superhero. I snapped a stream of photos while she talked about the make-believe games she'd played as a child.

We talked about fitness and good health and what it felt like to be strong. With that, she began to relax. She asked me questions about lifting weights and I knew she'd forgotten the camera and her makeup, and even, possibly, Andy.

I almost had too, and then, I felt him.

I sensed the heat of his body directly behind me. He was so close I could hear him breathing. Before I could turn, before I could open my mouth and tell him to move away, I felt his hand on the back of my neck.

"Don't touch me," I said.

"You have a beautiful neck," he said.

"Get your hand off my neck."

It was the wrong thing to say, because immediately I felt his hand on the small of my back. I whirled around, holding the camera in front of me near my rib cage. The lens smacked the bone of his forearm, but he was a muscular guy and it didn't seem to cause him a lot of pain.

"Yeow," he said. "Good defensive move."

"Don't touch me again."

He smiled.

"I expect a response," I said.

"Yes, ma'am."

Without turning back to Brie, I said. "I have all the photos we need."

"Don't be mad," Andy said.

"Yeah, please don't be upset," Brie said. "He's a touchy-feely guy."

"Not with me."

"He's sorry," Brie said.

"Sorry," Andy said.

I was already at the table, placing my camera in the bag. I felt like I was packing up to leave the psych ward at Bellevue. These two were either performance artists or disturbed in a very unusual way. I couldn't even describe to myself what was going on with them. I had no idea what I was going to tell Diana. Or Ian. I wondered what he would make of the photographs.

When I left, I realized the room didn't feel tranquil at all. It felt more like it had been designed to mesmerize its occupants.

CHAPTER 26

*W*hen I reviewed the photos of Brie, they were excellent. So I didn't tell Diana anything about the bizarre interactions between Brie and Andy. I uploaded the photos to the workspace and sent a message to Ian, telling him they were ready for his expert analysis.

It was just as well that I hadn't told Diana about the disturbing battle of wills and words I'd been through because there was a fifty-fifty chance she wouldn't have believed it was really that extreme, even though she'd witnessed their behavior herself. She might have accused me of exaggerating or become irritated that I hadn't called her in to take charge. Or something else I couldn't even imagine. It was impossible to know with her lately.

I did know that it probably wouldn't have gone in my favor, because less than an hour after I'd uploaded the photos, she was in my office.

"I haven't seen the resumés for the new photographer," she said.

"I—"

"They're long past due."

"Since we only have female clients, I don't think the schedule will be unmanageable, so I—"

"We're hiring another photographer. I want them by the end of the day or you won't be going to any more photography sessions."

"Who will take the photographs?"

"I'll hire someone from a temp agency."

"I don't think that would—"

"The end of the day."

She turned and walked out, closing my door behind her.

It looked like I was being shut in my office to hunt down resumés.

I had no idea where to start, so I went to the starting place for everything. Google. I found a place where freelance photographers posted their resumés. After searching through their profiles for nearly an hour, complaining to myself that Diana should hire a free-lancer as needed when there was an overload of clients, rather than hiring a person who was going to want work all the time, who was going to fight me for every job, who was going to interfere in the flow, who was surely going to restrain my freedom, I decided I'd stalled long enough. She'd been harassing me about this for too long. She wasn't going to change her mind.

It turned out the same site had a contact name and would provide a curated search for a small fee. I sent a message with an *Urgent* subject line. Luckily for me, I heard back forty-five minutes later. The guy who responded sent me twenty resumés for photographers in New York City.

I spent the rest of the afternoon scrolling through page after page of kudos and elaborate descriptions of the work these photographers had done. They all sounded as if they knew how to operate a camera. Good for them. They'd all taken classes. Some had studied photography in depth. Some had done a lot of portrait work. Some had college degrees in art with a concentration in photography. Some had years of experience. They had it all.

I had no doubt they could all take incredible photographs—of food, scenery, weddings, department store displays, glassware, children, pets, couples in love, architecture, you name it.

There wasn't a single thing on any of those resumés that told me any of those individuals had a clue how to get inside someone's head and make them reveal things they might not want to. Not that I'd done such a stellar job with that when I was photographing Brie, but the superhero thing had been a bit of a win. I was pretty sure Ian was going to find some juicy insights there. I think she'd been caught off guard by that question and answered without thinking. I'd seen a slight flush in her forehead at the time. Not that I was a micro-expression expert.

How could I look at these people who were adept with lighting and portraits, eliciting relaxed smiles and getting animals to sit still, and know that they had the slightest clue about how to manipulate people the way I could? It was something I was born with. Something I did without thinking about it a fair bit of the time. It was something that I hadn't known would make me successful in this highly unique, incredibly well-paying job.

My former colleague, James, if you could call him a colleague, which I would not, since that implies we had mutual respect, was appalled that I had no experience for the job. But the job was invented by Trystan, and I turned it into something unique and valuable to him by the sheer force of who I am.

Diana adopted that and saw that it worked. The problem was, she didn't appreciate the facets of me that made it work.

Trystan also had tried to force me into having a supporting team. In some ways, his stubborn push for a backup photographer had led to his death. It wasn't a direct line, but it could be argued that he wouldn't be dead if he hadn't yielded to Stephanie's demand to be a photographer.

As far as I could tell from looking at resumés, none of the photographers would work. The only way I could identify someone who had the slightest chance of working in a productive way along-side me would be to meet that person and recognize that spark in them, then find out if they were interested in photography. Not the other way around. That was the point Diana was missing. That was how Trystan found me. Photography was the furthest thing from his mind when he asked if I was interested in working for him.

But Diana wanted resumés by the end of the day. And I wanted to go home.

I printed out all the resumés belonging to men. I spread them out on the floor of my office in a large circle. After digging around the bottom of my bag for several minutes, I found a pen. I placed it in the center of the circle, closed my eyes, and spun it. I picked the resumé it pointed to. I tightened the circle formed by the remaining sheets of paper and spun the pen again. I did this three more times.

When I was finished, I shredded the other resumés. I studied the documents that my lint-covered pen had chosen, and picked out a trait for each one that I would tell Diana was my reason for selecting them. I jotted my reasons down in my notes app on my phone so I could refresh my memory later, just in case my email wasn't easily accessible.

When everything was organized, I attached the digital files to an email, wrote a short note telling her why I'd chosen each one, and sent it to Diana. I locked the computer screen and left the office.

Walking out of the building into the warm summer evening, I was almost looking forward to interviewing the candidates. It no longer seemed like something that might destroy the fun I had with my job. I was curious to see how it would all play out.

CHAPTER 27

 *ortland, Oregon*

* * *

Standing at the window of the treehouse watching Jimmy creep across the backyard made me want to laugh. He looked like a nervous squirrel, jerking his head side-to-side, looking to see if anyone besides me could see him. I'm not sure who he thought was paying attention. He was still in his own backyard. I thought about shouting, just to scare him, but I decided to wait and see what he would do.

When he reached the edge of his own yard, where a strip of dirt was planted with flowers, he stopped and looked back at me. He gave me a thumbs up. Was I supposed to clap for him because he'd managed to sneak all the way across his own backyard? I raised my hands in a dramatic shrug, and he whirled around as if he thought that meant someone had seen him. He looked up at me again and I put my thumb up.

Now, he was in the neighbor's yard, tiptoeing across the grass, moving around the brick wall toward the wood gate. I wondered if it was locked. I wondered if it wasn't locked, if he would be able to reach the latch. He hadn't thought about any of those things, he was so anxious to get his hands on those clay animals.

I didn't see what the big deal was. We had lots of toy animals at our house. Sure, these were pretty because of the bright colors, but they looked like something my mom would put on a shelf. Especially without the miniature town the neighbor had set up. That was what made them interesting. Did Jimmy think that eventually he was going to steal every building in the tiny village and set it up inside his treehouse? Even that wouldn't be as much fun because she'd arranged the little houses so they had their own tiny gardens and plants like miniature trees. There were even a few bowls nestled into the ground with dirt and clover around them to look like ponds.

The more I looked at it, the more I wanted to play inside the brick wall.

I'd thought the treehouse would be more fun than it was turning out to be. Maybe the problem wasn't the treehouse. Maybe the problem was Jimmy.

Now he was at the gate. He reached for the latch, but it was a few inches above his fingertips. He looked around anxiously. He ran to the back of the house and grabbed a bucket that was sitting by the hose. He carried it back to the gate and turned it upside down. He stood on it to unlatch the gate, then slipped into the garden.

Inside, he seemed to forget all about getting caught because he took his time, inspecting all the little houses and sticking his fingers into the pond water. One by one, he picked up the animals, turning them around in his hands.

I glanced at the pottery shed. I wanted the woman to come out. I wanted to see if she would notice the partially opened gate.

I think Jimmy realized at the same time I did that he could only safely carry two animals at a time back to the treehouse. Besides, he would have to stop and put them down, latch the gate, and replace the bucket.

He managed to do all of that and a few minutes later, he was back at the bottom of the ladder.

"Come down and get these."

"You wanted them, you should bring them up."

"I can't hold them while I'm climbing."

"You should have thought of that." I sounded like my father. He was always saying, *you should have thought of that*.

"Please."

I sighed and went to the ladder. I climbed partway down and took the first animal—a bear painted red. I climbed back up and placed it in the center of the floor. Jimmy climbed up after me carrying the orange cat and put it beside the bear.

"Now what?" I asked.

"We need more animals. You go get some."

"No."

"Scaredy cat," Jimmy said.

"I'm not scared."

"Then go get some."

"I don't want them. They aren't going to be any fun up here without the little houses."

"They will be if we have more. And we can use the shoebox for a house."

"It's too small. Let's just play with these two."

"I want more."

I sighed.

The whole routine was repeated, with Jimmy climbing down, tiptoeing next door, getting the bucket, and opening the gate. This time, I saw the shed door open.

Was she coming out? Jimmy was right by the gate, ready to leave with two more animals. It was the worst time for her to come out of the shed. I held my breath. Should I shout right away, or wait until I saw her? Maybe she had only opened the door for fresh air.

While I was arguing with myself, Jimmy came out, closed the gate, and returned to the treehouse.

We played with the animals for a while, but just as I'd thought would happen, we got bored really fast. Jimmy didn't want to admit it, since stealing them was his idea, so he kept trying to invent new games. Each one was more boring than the one before.

Finally, he admitted he was bored. The only exciting part for him had been stealing them.

"Are you taking them back now?" I asked.

"Nope."

"Why not?"

"I want to keep them."

"What for?"

"That was a lot of work."

I laughed. "It wasn't work."

"I had to be careful, like a spy."

"You aren't a spy."

"What if I got caught? I'd get grounded. Or no TV. Or extra chores."

"So you were scared."

"I was not," he said.

"You need to take them back. When she notices they're missing, she'll probably guess it was you and tell your parents."

"Why would she think it was me?"

"She'll guess it was a kid. And you're the closest kid."

"I'm keeping them for a little while. I've never seen her go in there."

"If you get caught, you better not blame me."

"I won't get caught."

"If you do, you better not blame—"

"I heard you."

I knew he would blame me. He might not say I did it, but I knew he would mention my name. "Have you stolen stuff before?"

"This isn't stealing," he said.

"Why not?"

"Because I'll put them back after a while. And they weren't in her house, or locked up. If people just leave stuff sitting around, they can't be surprised if someone takes it. That's what my dad said when my brother's bike was stolen."

It sounded like something my father might say. But I knew my father would not think that meant I should take things that were left lying around. And he would probably do worse than not let me watch TV, since I didn't get to watch much TV anyway, and I already had a lot of chores.

If Jimmy got caught, I would get blamed, one way or another. I was sure about that.

CHAPTER 28

$\mathcal{N}$ew York

* * *

Alexandra had suggested they meet at the Museum of Natural History right when it opened so they could beat the crowds, at least for the first hour or so. Hunter found her waiting for him when he walked up to the entrance at ten minutes to nine.

She wanted to start with the Extinct and Endangered exhibit, featuring macro photography of insects in peril. It was a good suggestion because it wasn't one of the permanent exhibitions and he'd never seen it.

She paid the entrance fee, and they went inside.

For three hours, they talked about nothing but what they read on the informational cards and signs and what they saw inside glass cases. She was utterly absorbed. He felt light and unencumbered by questions about what she might be hiding from him.

It made him recognize, again, that he'd been too combative. But the moment he relaxed into that thought, he found himself circling back to the belief that he could not move forward until he figured out why she was being so obstinate. If she just wanted to have sex, then that was a different kind of relationship. He supposed that would be alright, but it seemed like she wanted more than that, so what was the deal? He was certain that *he* wanted more.

Maybe she was a total control freak. If that was the case, it might be better to make a quick exit. That's why this thing with her dodging such a simple question needed to be resolved. At the same time, he didn't want to turn it into an ultimatum. For that reason, he'd decided to try again. Something kinder and more natural. With his previous attempts he'd ratcheted it up too far, shoving her into a corner.

Instead, he would talk more about his own brother and see what came of it. Maybe a little self-exposure would help her relax. If there was a serious problem, she was afraid of admitting to something that she found horrifically embarrassing, he had to find a way to put her at ease. The problem, was he and his brother got along fairly well now, so he'd had to think a long time about how to accomplish that.

He felt like he was playing at being a therapist, which he didn't like.

When they were finished at the museum—insects followed by the gemstone exhibit—they walked three blocks to a place that served fancy, expensive burgers and a huge variety of IPA beers. Both of them were famished from all the standing and walking around, absorbing knowledge. Besides, since a considerable amount of the information about insects and other bugs had focused on the nourishment of their fragile bodies, both of them had found themselves thinking a lot about food after several hours of reading about the constant search for it.

They sat in a booth with walls that made it feel like a small room. He felt they could sit there all afternoon, their own private place. Maybe they would.

They ordered, then sipped their beers and talked about the exhibits. As the conversation wound down, he took a deep breath.

"When you were talking about Eric, it sounded like you have an ideal relationship. No fights or falling out," he said.

"Again? Really?"

"I'm not asking about him. It just made me think about my brother. Zach. Because for a long time, it wasn't that way for us."

"What way?"

"You seem really close. There were some bad times for Zach and me."

She ate a French fry.

"He was a little shit, to be honest."

She laughed. "I wonder what he says about you."

"When you meet him, you can ask."

"I'll do that."

"He ratted me out to my parents all the time. He spied on me when I had girls over. He hid my homework, and I got marked down for not doing it."

"Did you get him back?"

"Sometimes. I tried. But I was supposed to set the example. Usually I would end up in trouble if I did something to get back at him."

"Hm." She took a sip of her beer.

"By the time I left for college, I wanted to get as far away from him as I could."

"I can see that."

"We didn't start speaking to each other until he graduated from college. So it was over six years. Plus all the growing-up years, I mostly hated him."

She nodded.

"And my parents gave me crap about it all the time. *Call your brother. Have you talked to your brother? When are you going to see your brother? He looks up to you, why aren't you spending more time with your brother? You should go to your brother's game ...* They never let up."

"That's annoying."

"Yeah." He wanted another beer. He wanted the conversation to end. This was going nowhere. She appeared only mildly interested. She seemed almost completely lacking in empathy, and she hadn't said a word to suggest she had any similar experiences.

He'd made a mistake. Her brother was a hero to her because he was older. If anything like that had happened with her brother, she would have been the one who felt neglected. Besides, the dynamic might be completely different with a brother and sister.

"I guess you think my younger brother was right," he said. "You would have felt terrible if your older brother ignored you for ten years. Maybe you did all kinds of stuff to harass him."

"No, I don't remember doing anything like that."

"Was it just the two of you?"

She smiled. "Very clever."

He picked up his beer and took a long swallow. He put it back on the table, perhaps with too much force. "Alex. Please tell me why this is such an issue. In case it's not obvious, I like you a lot. If there's something you're embarrassed about that you don't want me to know, just tell me that. If there's something about your family that's a secret, if one of your siblings is well-known, and not in a good way, I'll respect that if you don't want me to know right now. But just tell me why this is such a secret. I don't get it."

"There's no secret."

"Obviously there is. I asked you a simple question weeks ago. And you're acting like I want to know your medical or psychiatric history. It's almost funny if it wasn't so weird."

"Why is it weird?"

"Because it's the simplest, most mundane, trivial question one human being can ask another, and you're acting like I want to read your private diary."

"Do you?"

"No." That was a blatant lie. He realized it as soon as he said it. Of course he would. He would love to get inside her head, to crawl behind those beautiful eyes and underneath that thick hair, soft as silk despite the fact that she colored it. He wanted to peel back her scalp and look inside her brain and see the neurons firing.

"You're making such a big deal out of this," she said. "That's what's weird. I just don't feel like talking about my family and you can't shut up about it."

"Because it's a normal topic of conversation between two people getting to know each other."

"Why do we have to be normal?"

"We don't, I guess. But—"

"Then let's talk about something else." She picked up two French fries and stuffed them into her mouth.

"Fine. No more family. But you have to realize that it makes me think there's something serious that you're keeping from me. It makes me speculate that you could be related to someone dangerous, and it's concerning that it might affect me."

She laughed. "Seriously?"

"Yes."

"That's the biggest leap I've ever heard."

"Is it?"

She nodded. "I'm going to get another beer. This is getting interesting. Do you want another one?"

He nodded. He watched her walk to the bar and stand with one hip cocked while she waited for the bartender. She leaned forward while she spoke to him, then waited for him to grab the beers. She pulled some cash out of the back pocket of her jeans and handed over a bill. When she had the change, she returned to their booth and placed the bottles on the table, pushing the empty ones to the edge.

She slid into her seat. "So you think I'm related to a notorious embezzler? Or someone in the mafia?"

"Or maybe a serial killer," he said.

She stared at him. "You have a wild imagination."

"Or maybe it's someone famous. And you're sworn to secrecy."

She laughed. "That sounds more fun. I'm living with a roommate in a decent, but not awesome apartment, but what you don't know is that I'm related to a fabulously successful pop star. I could be living in a penthouse and taking a limo everywhere."

He shoved the last of his fries into his mouth. She was never going to tell him. He chewed quickly, swallowed, and washed the fries down with fresh, cold beer. "Is Eric even real?"

She laughed. "Absolutely."

He wasn't sure if he believed her. It was almost easier not to. "The things you said sounded slightly made up."

"Why would I lie about that?"

He took another sip of beer and changed the subject to some of the more unusual bugs they'd seen at the museum. He asked what interested her the most. She said she wondered why creatures that were essential to the health of the planet were dying out and those that were destructive seemed to thrive. It seemed like the overarching ecosystem lacked some intelligence on that front.

It would be simpler to let the subject of her siblings die. It didn't really matter. What does an extended family have to do with a couple's relationship? How often do families get together over the years? And maybe, if it came to that, one family was enough. If she didn't want him to know about hers, did it even matter?

But he knew he would not let it go. He was simply regrouping to figure out a way to bust through that smiling, alluring, evasive facade. *The truth is out there.* His dad had said that all the time when Hunter was growing up. He wondered if Alexandra had any family stories like that.

CHAPTER 29

*H*unter and I were naked in bed, eating potato chips and onion dip, drinking beer and watching a movie when my phone buzzed with a text. I grabbed my work phone to see if it was from Diana. I still hadn't heard from her about the resumés. She'd been in meetings all day Friday, but I'd expected at least a response saying thanks.

There was no text on my work phone. I dug around in my bag for my burner phone. It was a Snapchat message from Carolina.

I need a favor. Call me asap.

It seemed a favor to ask me to call, so that was two favors, since I was sure the favor she was referring to was not the call. It was Saturday night. What favor could she possibly need from a near stranger? I put the phone back on the floor and reached for a chip. I scooped up some dip and ate it. I thanked Hunter for pausing the movie, paused longer while I finished the chip and kissed him.

My phone buzzed a second time, sounding like a large bee was trapped under the bed.

"Are you going to deal with that? Or turn it off?" he asked.

The phone buzzed again. It was a difficult decision. I didn't want to leave the comfortable bed, the movie, the chips and beer. I definitely didn't want to leave Hunter. I didn't want to do a favor for anyone this evening. I rarely wanted to do favors, period.

But I was curious. I'm never good at quieting that voice that needs to know. And I couldn't get the fight I'd witnessed between Carolina and her husband out of my mind. I was unbearably curious to know what was going on between the two of them and what was happening with that strange, obnoxious child of theirs. I wondered if she was in trouble. "I should check." I put my beer on the nightstand.

Hunter got up and pulled on his jeans. He went into the kitchen, where I heard the refrigerator door open. I realized he was glad of the interruption. Potato chips and dip, no matter how hearty the party-size bag was, would not satisfy us all night.

I grabbed my skirt and top off the floor, pulled them on, and looked at Carolina's messages filling up on the locked screen.

In order, they told me …

She needed a favor. I should call her.

She needed a *big favor*. Would I please call her as soon as possible.

It was *really important* that I call her as soon as I got the message. She would *make it worth my while*.

That last one really piqued my curiosity. I called her.

She answered before the phone rang. "Oh, finally. I know this is completely nuts-oh, but could you watch Ricky for me? Jordan needs me to go to a cocktail thing with him and I'm completely stranded. I thought about taking Ricky, but it really is so inappropriate, don't you think?"

I moved the phone away from my ear and stared at it.

No one in my entire life, well, my entire adult life, had ever asked me to babysit their child. I suppose I'd been babysitting Damien for weeks, but a human child? I wanted to laugh. She must be out of her mind.

"I don't even know you," I said.

"Yes you do."

"I've talked to you twice. I've only met your son—"

"I'm so glad you didn't say no right out of the gate."

"No," I said.

She laughed. "But that wasn't your first response."

"That's because I'm stunned. Why would you even ask me? I'm a total stranger. I could be an ax murderer for all you know."

She laughed. "Everyone says that."

"Do they?" I didn't think many people said that. I wasn't sure anyone said that. "Why would you trust a stranger with your son? You've lived here for years. Don't you have any—"

"No one else is available."

"The hotel has childcare services. They all do."

"That won't work."

"Why not?"

"It just won't. Ricky won't have it."

"I can't. You'll have to figure out something else. I don't ... I'm not a good person to take care of a child."

"He's not really a child."

Hunter came into the room carrying a tray with two huge sandwiches on it. I felt my stomach rumble softly. He smiled and placed the tray on the bed. He settled back where he'd been, picked up half a sandwich and took a large bite.

"I can't help you," I said. "I hope you find someone."

"Wait! Don't hang up. I have to go to this thing. Jordan is counting on me."

"Ricky seems old enough to stay by himself anyway. I need to go." As I moved the phone away and reached for half a sandwich, her voice came through at a much higher pitch and volume. "Don't hang up! I'll pay you five thousand dollars. He can't stay alone. He needs supervision."

"Five thousand dollars for what?" Hunter took another bite of his sandwich. He chewed slowly, staring at me with his eyebrows raised slightly.

"That's insane," I said.

"I told you I'm desperate. It's only for a few hours. You can hang out in our hotel room. Well, Ricky's. His room is adjoining to our suite. It's nothing. He'll watch TV. I just can't leave him alone."

"What will he do if you leave him alone? He seems quite mature for his age. Almost adult-like."

"That's the problem."

I laughed.

"Five thousand dollars for what?" Hunter asked.

"Is someone with you?" Carolina asked.

"Yes."

"I'll give you two minutes to work things out. I know it's super last minute. Just call me back. Promise? Two minutes. Five thousand dollars. You can't say no. And I need to leave in forty minutes." She hung up.

I dropped the phone onto the bed and picked up half a sandwich. Turkey and cheese with a single slice of roast beef added. I took a bite.

"Five thousand dollars for what?"

"This woman I met after I had the massage when we had our luxury weekend. She has this really weird ten-year-old kid who apparently can't be left alone, and for whatever reason is a pariah to the hotel childcare staff. She wants me to watch him while she goes to a cocktail party with her husband. They're living at the hotel while he's working on some long legal case. I said no, and she offered me five grand."

"Can I go with you?" He got out of bed, turned off the TV, and picked up the second half of his sandwich, taking a bite as he looked around for his phone.

"Are you serious?"

"Are you seriously considering saying no?"

"I'm not really a kid-oriented person."

"So what? He's ten. It's not like you have to play Candy Land with him. Five grand? Come on! Call her back, eat your sandwich, and let's go."

"I'm not sure it's good to get sucked into whatever is going on with her. She's a little unbalanced. And the kid is weird."

"You've met him?"

"He acts like an adult. He stared at me like he wanted to unbutton my top. And I saw her and her husband in Central Park having a very intense fight."

Hunter shrugged. He had his phone now. He was holding his sandwich with one hand, still eating, using his thumb to tap his phone. "I'm ordering an Uber. I don't care about their marital problems. And even better, I'll be with you if the kid is creepy. Tell her it's non-negotiable that I'm coming. Call her."

I was a little surprised that Hunter was so eager for the cash. He did really well running PR at the Herrera Modeling Agency. I'd never heard him say a word about wishing he had more money, about craving money, or anything whatsoever about money. Now, he was acting like someone was giving away tickets to the World Series. "Why are you so hot to do this?"

"It's the easiest money I've ever heard of. Hang out in a posh hotel, watch some kid watch TV while we play on our phones and walk away with money for a weekend trip. What's not to like? Were you that into the movie?"

I laughed. I called Carolina and told her I would do her the favor and that Hunter was coming with me. She said that was great. She couldn't wait to meet him. I wasn't sure I liked how eager she sounded.

CHAPTER 30

*W*e knocked on the door of Ricky's hotel room ten minutes before Carolina had said she had to leave.

Carolina was wearing a silver cocktail dress that clung to her thin body. The heels on her silver sandals were so high, I wasn't sure I would be able to manage them, and I had a lot of experience with dangerously high heels. Her face was beautifully made up and enhanced with silvery glitter.

She invited us inside. Jordan was nowhere to be seen.

"The TV has parental controls. So does his tablet." She gestured toward the brand new looking iPad on the table.

It was unsettling seeing a posh room obviously lived in full-time by a ten-year-old. The table, desk, couch and other furniture were all formal and obviously meant for guests with expensive tastes. The clothes and a few toys and books and board games tossed around looked like they'd been misplaced.

Like his father, Ricky was nowhere to be seen. The bathroom door was open, so I knew he wasn't in there.

"This is Hunter," I said.

Carolina nodded at Hunter, but said nothing, which was strange after her eagerness when I'd said he was coming with me.

"Where's Ricky?" I asked.

"I'll get him. I wanted to know if you have any questions. So we can talk without him hearing."

"What are the rules?" Hunter asked.

She turned away from Hunter, putting her attention solely on me. "He can watch TV, use his iPad, order whatever he'd like from room service."

"Anything at all?" I asked.

"Not alcohol, obviously."

"No limits on sweets, or quantities or anything?" Hunter asked.

Still keeping her attention focused on me, she said, "Use your judgement. As you know," she gave me a look that almost seemed like a warning, "He's a precocious child."

I nodded.

"Don't let him get the best of you."

"Not to worry," Hunter said.

"You can message me if things get out of hand," she said. "But I should be back by midnight at the absolute latest."

"Out of hand?" I asked. "What kinds of things are you expecting might happen?"

She laughed. She put her hand to her ear and adjusted the hook on the cluster of crystals hanging off her lobes. "Oh, you know boys. Right?" Now, she acknowledged Hunter's presence, giving him an elaborate wink.

"He won't expect to go out, will he?" I asked.

"He's not allowed to go out at night."

"He knows that?"

"He should."

"*Should?*"

She shrugged.

It flitted through my mind that the five thousand dollars might be inadequate for what we were facing. "Where do Hunter and I go when it's his bedtime?"

"He can stay up until I'm back."

"Okay. I guess that's—"

"It's fine. Don't worry."

"I'm not worried, I just—"

"You look worried."

I wasn't worried. I did wonder if she would have a problem with any techniques I devised to control her obviously willful son.

"It will be fine. It's only a few hours." She gave me a smile that was a disturbing blend of threatening and grateful. Then, she left the room. She returned a moment later with Ricky trudging behind her.

He gave me a leering gaze. I glared at him, but he didn't back down. He was wearing red sweatpants and a black T-shirt. His feet were bare.

Carolina wrapped her arms around his shoulders, gave him a lingering kiss on his forehead, which he didn't pull away from, then swept out the door without another word.

I wished we'd asked for the five thousand before she left because I suddenly wondered if we would ever see it. I pulled out my phone and sent a message to Hunter telling him I gave us a fifty-fifty chance of getting the cash. He replied with a thumbs up.

"Don't be messaging about me," Ricky said.

"We're not," Hunter said.

"Bullshit."

"Watch your language," Hunter said.

Ricky laughed, then went to the coffee table and picked up the remote. He turned on the TV and flipped to a car racing channel. He flopped on the couch.

If we did get the money, it might be an easy win.

CHAPTER 31

*W*atching over Ricky Scott turned out to be a no-brainer, as Hunter said. Hunter and I played games on our phones and ordered French fries and soda from room service. We watched Ricky watch cars race around tracks, then boxing, then cars race around tracks. We watched him eat a burger and fries, ice-cream, another burger, a slice of pizza, followed by more ice cream.

Ricky shot surly looks at us whenever he could, made his own room service calls, and switched channels to the point that it gave me a headache. He always landed back at the car racing or boxing.

Carolina arrived back at the room earlier than promised, just before eleven-thirty. Her husband wasn't with her. She paid us five thousand dollars in cash, right in front of Ricky. I wondered what a child would think, knowing he was so valuable that his mother would pay that kind of money to make sure he was supervised while watching TV. Or, that he was so difficult she couldn't find anyone to watch him unless she bribed them with a ridiculous sum of cash.

Feeling like we had money to burn, we took a cab back to Hunter's place. He wanted me to stay, but I needed to check on Damien, who now lived locked inside my bedroom. I needed to pin Tess down on when she was coming to get him. He seemed fine, but I assumed he must be getting antsy. When Ned wasn't around, I took him into the living room, and I made sure he could look out the windows, but he needed to move out of that apartment.

When I opened my apartment door, one of the living room lamps was on. Ned was sitting on the couch, staring at the door as if he'd been waiting for me, like a parent waiting for a teenager who had broken curfew. "Where were you?" he asked, doubling down on the impression.

"None of your business." I closed the door and headed toward my bedroom.

"I'm trying to be friendly and that's how you answer?"

"It didn't sound friendly."

"That's your interpretation, because you're so combative."

I rounded the corner and inserted my new key into the deadbolt on my bedroom door.

Suddenly, he was standing right beside me. "I was talking to you."

"I'm tired. Good night."

"Why are you being so rude? It's important to Eileen that we get along. Surely you understand that? Don't you realize how it hurts her when there's conflict between us?"

"I'm not the one causing conflict."

"It takes two. And you're the one who's being rude, who put a lock on your door."

"You were trespassing in my room."

"I told you I was—"

"I don't want to hear it, Ned." I opened my door and stepped inside.

He moved fast, putting his hand around the doorframe, then placing his foot so the door wouldn't close.

"Move."

"Say, please."

"What is wrong with you? Don't you realize you're making things worse?"

"I want to know what's up with you," he said.

"Nothing. I'm tired and I want to go to sleep. Get out of my room."

"Or what?"

I flicked on the light.

Chardonnay time!

I went to Damien's cage. I put the cloth over it to tell him it was time for sleep. He was probably confused because the room had been dark, then he was woken by the splash of light and our slightly raised voices.

"Your room stinks because of that bird."

It didn't. I cleaned his cage meticulously and aired my room out every evening. It was perhaps musty from the gravel at the bottom of his cage. "Then get out."

"Why won't you tell me where you were? It's very disturbing that you can't answer a simple, friendly question like that."

"Because it's none of your business."

"Why are you so obstinate?"

"I'm not. You're intrusive. I'm not your possession, or whatever it is you think I am, just because I happen to be roommates with your girlfriend."

"Freeloading off my girlfriend, if you ask me."

"I didn't ask you."

"I should tell her that's what I think you're doing," he said.

"Go ahead. Now get out of my room."

"Things can't continue like this," he said.

"Like what?" I went to the door. If he didn't move soon, I would kick his foot out of the way and slam the door on his fingers.

"You sneaking around and lying and picking fights with me."

I shoved my foot against his. He moved his easily, then took his hand away from the doorframe, clearly seeing I wasn't going to back down and realizing that maybe Eileen wouldn't like this.

"I'm just trying to—"

I shut the door in his face.

I locked it and leaned against it. I was trapped in my own bedroom.

Chardonnay time!

I agreed with Damien about the Chardonnay. But now, leaving my room meant seeing Ned, who was probably still lurking in the living room, or possibly right outside my door. I pressed my ear against the door, wondering if I would be able to hear him if he was standing there. I heard nothing.

I moved away from the door. I went into the bathroom and washed my face. I stared into the mirror. The thought of spending the night locked in my room was suddenly unbearable. But I didn't want to go back to Hunter's now. It was almost one-thirty in the morning.

I brushed my hair into a ponytail, changed into leggings and a long top and tennis shoes. I threw some clothes and toiletries into a bag, along with a plastic container of food for Damien. I slung my messenger bag and duffel bag over my shoulder. I poked the handle of Damien's cage through the opening in the cloth, picked up the cage, and went out of my room. The living room was dark, but I didn't change my mind.

I left the apartment and ordered an Uber. At first, the driver did not want to allow Damien in the back seat of his car. I showed him the cage door was secure. I assured him Damien wouldn't create a lot of noise.

Luckily for me, Damien was so disoriented by now, that he kept his mouth shut. When I peeked under the cover, he let me know his state of mind with his crown feathers—pointed straight up. He stared at me with his black, penetrating eyes, barely moving.

I gave the driver the name of a boutique hotel, and when he pulled up at the curb, I tipped him double what I usually did and gave him a stellar rating. He didn't seem all that appreciative when I let him know what I'd done, so it was wasted effort. It's not as if I'd ever get that driver again, but I didn't want him giving me a negative rating.

At the front desk, it took more than a demo of the lock on the cage door and a bird that was temporarily keeping his mouth shut. I had to use more of my freshly earned cash, half of which I'd already shared with Hunter, to persuade them to let Damien spend the night. It didn't seem right, since at this point, the night was mostly over and I had no plans to stay past breakfast.

Damien was starting to weigh me down. I liked having him around, but I couldn't go on taking care of him. I had my hands full taking care of myself and all the murders I was trying to keep unsolved. I set an alert on my phone to message Tess in the morning and ask her when she was planning to come get him. She had her estate now. Damien deserved a nice home, a place where he wasn't under threat from a guy who couldn't even remember what breed he was.

By the time I was in my room, pulling off my shoes, and collapsing onto the bed, I realized I'd been compelled to leave because my apartment no longer felt like it belonged to me. Slowly, Ned was becoming more of a fixture, and he seemed to take that to mean he had the right to dictate the rules, to inquire into the details of my life in some decades-old, misguided attempt to protect his lovely lady from whatever he thought I was going to do.

He was right to be worried about me, but he should have been concerned about his own safety, not hers.

I just couldn't stay there, knowing he was in the other room, knowing he believed he had the right to not only prowl around my room when I wasn't there, but now, force his way into it. Eileen and I needed to have a serious discussion.

Or maybe, I just needed to start apartment hunting.

132

CHAPTER 32

*E*ven though we were supposed to be finished with Matt Shera, I was reviewing his photographs because I thought Diana owed him a final report before she handed him off to a therapist like she was passing a football. She didn't seem at all concerned he might just as easily pass on his experience to others and damage our reputation. Maybe she figured a preacher in a modest-sized church didn't know any women who were trying to climb the skyscrapers of New York to dizzying success, so there was no damage that could be done.

Still, I thought that at some point, she would realize her mistake and want to invite the other half of the human race back into our sphere of influence. If nothing else, I thought she might eventually want the power that came with having a name recognized everywhere for helping people achieve the success they craved, not just among women.

A flicker of movement outside my open office door caught the corner of my eye.

I looked up and saw Fallon standing just beyond the doorway, staring at me, waiting for me to notice her red top, red pants, and red high-heeled sandals. It was difficult not to. I was surprised I hadn't seen her the moment she appeared. It made me squirm to wonder how long she'd been watching me. Was I that caught up in Matt's expressions of terror over a bunch of caged primates? Or was I too lost in my irritated thoughts at Diana's impossible-to-understand decision making process?

"I have some resumés for you to look at," Fallon said.

"Resumés?"

"Do you have a minute?"

I nodded.

She walked into my office and sat across from me. She placed a green folder on my desk and flipped it open. There were several sheets of paper, all with the bullet points and boxes and bold lines calling out the highlights of a career.

"Resumés for what?" I asked.

"The new photographer."

"I've already seen them. I'm the one who—"

"These are new."

"New from what?"

"Diana asked me to do some research. I found seven candidates, and she wanted me to review them with you."

I stared at the folder. I looked up at Fallon, who was looking directly at me. She probably had no idea what was going on with the photography position. But she also had no idea how to select a candidate for a photographer. Yet, she'd been appointed to do exactly that.

"Where did you find them? Did Diana ask you to talk to a recruiter?"

"Yes."

"Did she send you any other resumés?"

"No. Was she supposed to?"

"Not necessarily."

"I'm supposed to do the phone screening for these. Diana said you would go over them with me and help me come up with questions to ask." Her neutral gaze shifted slightly, turning somewhat defiant. "I'm not really sure why. It's kind of obvious. A phone screen."

"What would you ask?"

"How they got into photography. What they like about it, what sets them apart. Why they think they'd be a good fit with our organization. I'd tell them what we do, tell them about our clients and what they expect, and ask if they have any questions. Listen to see if there are any red flags."

"It sounds like you have it covered."

"But Diana said I should get your input." She pushed the folder toward me. The edge of the folder caught on my keyboard and the loose sheets of paper continued moving toward me as if they had a will of their own.

I picked up the top resumé. It belonged to a woman named Sandra Kirk. She was a graduate student at NYU. She'd studied art and was now getting a second degree, concentrating in photography.

"What did you think of this one?" I asked.

"Who is that?"

"Sandra."

"It doesn't look like she's photographed people much."

"I wonder why the recruiter gave you her name?"

Fallon shrugged. "I figured she might get cut in the phone screen. When I ask what sets her apart, if she doesn't say something about how she gets people to relax in front of a camera, she's not the best choice."

I was starting to think Fallon understood my job better than Diana did. Of course, Diana may not have reviewed any of these. Maybe the recruiter had missed the point.

"I don't think you need my help." I gave her a conspiratorial smile. "You sound like you have it all figured out."

"Don't be patronizing."

"I'm serious."

"Okay. Well, Diana said we should go through them, so we should. She'll ask me about it."

"Fine." I flipped through each resumé, asking Fallon what she thought, offering my comments. I didn't have a single thing to add to her first opinion for any of them, but she hardly seemed to notice that. She was very intent on pleasing Diana.

It was perplexing to me because she didn't strike me as a person who worried a lot about what anyone thought of her. But she was constantly trying to make sure she was doing what Diana wanted and curious about what might impress Diana … except for attending a colleague's funeral. Maybe it was all a show to keep things smooth in her job, to keep her moving forward to the next step she had planned for her career. She was definitely a woman with a plan.

As I talked about each candidate, Fallon tapped notes into her phone. I wondered if she would really use them. I also wondered what had happened to the resumés I'd sent Diana. Was the email sitting unread in her in-box? Had she discarded it because she was irritated with my all-male list?

There were at least three candidates that I'd sent who were far better than this stack of mostly graduate students who were studying art, or who had traveled to photograph people around the world, showing a variety of cultures, or sporting events, or themes about the human condition they believed needed attention.

Beneath all those questions was the realization that before I knew it, someone would be breathing down my neck. Another person would be standing beside or behind me, taking photographs, creating chaos every time I met with a client. And then, they would be sprouting wings and taking on clients of their own.

I supposed that didn't really matter. It wasn't as if I needed or wanted to work sixty hours a week. I definitely did not want that.

I was starting to think I had no idea what I wanted.

CHAPTER 33

*F*allon spent over an hour in my office. After she left, I took an early lunch. There was no time for the subway with all I wanted to do, so I took an Uber back to my apartment, grabbed my workout clothes, and took another Uber to the gym. At the rate I was going, I would burn through my half of the five thousand dollars before I even saw Hunter again.

I did an extra intense workout, pushing Fallon and her resumés and her eagerness to please Diana, and especially Diana herself, with her strange ideas and her desire to wrap me in tissue paper and place me inside a tiny box, out of my mind.

I did four sets on the bench press, burning my muscles until I couldn't complete the final set. I lay on the bench with my legs splayed, my feet planted firmly on the floor, my eyes closed. I felt a trickle of sweat run down the side of my face, making its way to my neck where it settled and soaked back into my skin. Or maybe it dripped onto the bench, I wasn't really sure.

When I opened my eyes, a woman was standing over me.

"Are you finished?"

"Yes." I sat up and moved off the bench.

She stepped in front of me and made a show of wiping down the bench.

I went into the locker room and took a long, hot shower. I stopped for a few tacos and returned to the office. I ate at my desk, staring at my computer screen.

The messaging app was open in front of me. As soon as I finished eating, I planned to type a message to Diana telling her I wanted a short meeting, but as I chewed the final bite and gulped down the rest of my water, I heard voices in the hallway. One was male, and it wasn't Ian.

I crumpled the wrappers from my tacos and stuffed them into the bag.

When I opened the door, I peered around the doorframe to get a good view of our tiny lobby. Matt Shera was there, talking to Diana. He saw me and waved. Diana turned.

"I wanted to drop by just to say thanks and let you know the outcome of my work with you," Matt said.

"Should we go into the conference room?" Diana started down the hallway, and he followed.

"You'll be coming too, won't you?" He asked as he passed my doorway.

Diana kept walking. "I don't think—"

He interrupted her. "I wanted to speak to both of you."

I crossed the hall and tossed my trash. "Would you like coffee, Matt?"

Diana tried again. "I don't—"

"That would be great, thanks," Matt said.

Diana forced a smile at me. "Sure. Thanks."

I filled two mugs and carried them to the conference room, placing one in front of each of them. I twisted the mini-blinds to bring in more sunlight, then returned to the break room to fill a mug for myself, wondering who had made the fresh pot. Maybe Ian had taken up James's role of keeping fresh coffee brewing.

When we were settled at the conference table, Matt gave us both a charming, grateful smile. He took a sip of coffee, put his mug on the table, then placed one hand on either side of it. "Well, I have to tell you, I am so impressed, and so grateful for what you've done for me."

Diana gave him a cautious smile.

"After our last meeting, I felt shoved aside, to be honest. So I spent quite a lot of time in prayer over the matter."

I took a sip of coffee and settled into my chair, determined to keep my mouth shut. I felt Diana's gaze on me.

"I didn't feel right about getting part of my fee returned, because I know a lot of work was put into the photography, and I know you've been through some rough times here. The violence … the loss of life."

"That's not an issue," Diana said. "We're professionals."

"It was still a blow."

"We're not a charity," she said. "We didn't complete your coaching and we need to make it right."

"But a lot of effort was put into the photography, the micro-expression analysis, the tests and the scoring. The coaching sessions we did have. Anyway, as I said, I spent a lot of time praying over it."

Neither of us spoke. He took another sip of coffee.

"First, Alexandra's insight when she put me in such an uncomfortable position by sitting on my lap during our first photography session, showing me in such a visceral way my discomfort with women and my vulnerability to that kind of thing … my vulnerability to all kinds of people with impure motives—not just sexual, but financial, the desire to manipulate me in many ways. That was so valuable I can't thank you enough."

I gave him a polite, professional smile. "I'm glad it was—"

"Very unorthodox," Diana said. "But it's good you got something out of it."

"And what you uncovered when I told you the story of my experience with my family … I realized I don't need therapy. That's not to say I never will, or that I don't believe in or value therapy. I just feel that what you've helped me see with so much clarity, I have a profound awareness of my weak areas. The growth I've experienced has been life-changing. Just with a few simple exercises. It's phenomenal." He gave us both smiles that looked like he wanted to jump up and hug us instead.

"I'm so pleased to hear that," Diana said.

I nodded. I picked up my coffee and took a few sips. I did not know what to say because I was fairly certain she wouldn't like anything I said. I wanted to save what little tolerance she had toward me for my conversation about the photographer. I smiled over my coffee.

He pushed his chair away from the table. "Really, that's all I had to say. Thank you for the coffee." He stood. "You're a remarkable organization, and what you're doing here is fascinating." He looked at Diana. "You and Alexandra make a phenomenal team. It's unfortunate that Stephanie was so troubled, and so sad to hear about her death. It's such a tragedy that Trystan was caught in her misery." His eyes were glassy with tears. "But the good that came out of it is that the two of you are absolutely phenomenal, as I said. I'd be honored to give any kind of testimonial for Fly Higher, if that's useful." He looked at me and smiled.

He stepped around the table and held out his hand to me. I shook it, and he did the same to Diana. "No need to see me out. Again, thank you so much."

When he was gone. Both Diana and I seemed to be glued to our chairs. A few minutes of silence passed, then Diana cleared her throat. "That was unexpected."

I nodded.

Diana stood. She picked up her mug and Matt's.

"I talked to Fallon about the resumés," I said.

"Good." She started toward the door.

"Did you already do pre-screening on the resumés I sent you last week?" I asked.

She turned and leaned against the doorframe. "I wanted to work with a recruiter, not just grab random people off an internet site."

"They weren't random."

She gave me a knowing look.

"Well, it's good knowing we're a phenomenal team, isn't it?" I said.

"Yes." The smile she gave me looked genuine.

"Even working with a man."

Her smile hardened. She left the conference room without responding.

After she was gone, I closed the blinds. I sat at the table and finished my coffee. I tried to think whether there might be a way to chisel through the armor she'd built around herself. Probably not. Just like there was no way to avoid the second photographer, who was coming at me like a meteor.

At least she hadn't speculated any further about James's weird and inexplicable murder. At least not to me.

CHAPTER 34

*A*lexandra and Hunter were walking through Central Park licking ice cream piled precariously on top of sugar cones. He'd asked her where she wanted to go for a getaway with their windfall from the bizarre childcare experience.

She'd gone quiet for several minutes and he thought she was considering the options, or perhaps recalling the blank, almost lifeless eyes of that strange kid. The only time those eyes seemed to have a spark of life was when he was looking at Alex as if he wanted to peel the clothes off her body.

He did not recall having such specific thoughts when he was ten, but maybe his memory was murky. Overall, Ricky exhibited the behavior and mindset of a kid in his mid teens.

"In New York, or somewhere exotic?" he asked.

"Well, I might have spent some of mine," Alex said.

"Yeah? Did you buy a new wardrobe?"

She laughed. "Not quite that much. I had to take a few extra cabs and Uber rides. And I spent that night in a hotel. After we babysat."

He stopped walking. "Why?"

She kept going.

"Alex. Wait." He hurried to catch up. He licked his chocolate ice cream furiously as drips that had been unattended for several minutes began to cascade down all sides. "Why did you go to a hotel?"

"My roommate's boyfriend."

"What happened? Are you ..." He was confused. He didn't even know what question to ask. Had the guy attacked her? What the hell was going on? Why would she go to a hotel at one in the morning?

"It's complicated."

"That's not an answer. What happened?"

"He was bothering me."

"Bothering you how? Did he—?"

"He wanted to know where I'd been all evening and—"

"You're kidding, right? You went to a hotel because he wanted to know where you'd been?"

"Yes."

"Why?"

"Then he tried to get into my room."

"What?"

"He stuck his foot in my doorway and he wouldn't move it so I couldn't close the door." She licked her cone, then took a bite of the coffee ice cream.

"That's really aggressive."

"Yes."

"Why did you feel the need to go to a hotel? Where was your roommate?"

"I couldn't sleep in the same building with him."

He slowed his pace, licking his cone methodically, trying to think. "Did he try to hurt you? Did he touch you?"

"No."

"Then why?"

"I didn't want to be around him."

All his promises to himself that he would take a break from harassing her about her family dissolved in an instant. There must be something horrific in her background to make her behave like that. No sane person moved out of their apartment at one in the morning because they were annoyed. "Are you sure you're telling me the whole story? He didn't try to attack you or grab you or anything like that?"

"No. I would have punched him."

"That's good. But why did you feel like you had to leave for the night? I don't understand."

She took another bite of her ice cream. It made his teeth ache, watching her sink hers into that dense ball of frozen coffee flavored cream and sugar. He shivered without thinking about it.

"How can you be cold when it's eighty-three degrees?"

"Just a chill," he said.

She continued walking, licking and taking bites of her ice cream. She would be down to the cone, while his continued to drip on so many sides he was having trouble keeping up, in the same way he was having trouble keeping up with the pace she was walking, and with her rationale for leaving her apartment. He couldn't fathom spending a few hundred dollars for half a night in a hotel just because someone was annoying. If he did that, he'd be leaving his apartment every time the people above him vacuumed at eleven at night, or the Chihuahua two doors down barked on summer evenings when all the windows were open and it sounded as if the dog were sitting on his living room couch. The guy must have done something worse than she was admitting.

"Let's sit down for a minute." He veered sharply to the left and flopped onto a bench.

She turned back and sat beside him. They continued devouring their ice creams in silence for several minutes.

"It's my money, although it was great that you came along to watch over Ricky. So I'm not sure why you're annoyed by how I spend it. Maybe it seems wasteful to you, but it was worth every penny."

"I couldn't care less what you do with the money. All of it belongs to you. I'm not really sure why you split it with me."

She grinned, her lips dark from the cold.

"I can't understand why something that sounds irritating and infuriating, but which you claim wasn't at all dangerous, was enough to force you out of your apartment. Did you take the bird with you?"

"Of course."

"The hotel didn't have a problem with that?"

"I sweetened the deal."

"I'm sure you did."

What might have happened in her life that such an innocuous question caused her to run for safety in the middle of the night? Was it something from when she was a small child? Or had there been a bad relationship when she was an adult? It was impossible to know. She'd been equally unwilling to tell him anything on either topic. If she'd been with an abusive guy, he didn't have a clue. If her family had dark secrets, or she'd had to escape something terrible in the middle of the night, he didn't know that either. But her behavior suggested something traumatic. Didn't it? Or was she just really picky and short-tempered and easily upset?

He couldn't believe it was that. He'd never seen her get upset about anything. The frustrations that irritated most people often appeared to roll off her back. She wasn't a worrier, as far as he could tell. The only thing that seemed to concern her most of the time was that damn bird.

"What did he ask you, exactly?"

"Why are you so interested in this?" She bit her cone.

"It doesn't make sense to me."

"Does it have to?"

"It's just so strange. Your roommate's boyfriend asks what you did, you don't want to tell him. He pushes the issue. I assume he followed you to your room, and that's when he stuck his foot in the doorway?"

"Yup."

"That sounds scary."

"It wasn't. It was irritating. And out of line."

"I agree. But it could be scary."

"I'm not afraid of him, I just want him out of my face."

"Okay. And because of that, you felt like you had to leave your apartment? Don't you hear how strange that sounds when I say it? It's *your* apartment. You shouldn't feel forced—"

"I didn't feel as if I *had* to leave. I wanted to. I didn't want to breathe the same air as him."

He laughed.

"Good. I'm glad you think it's funny. Now let's talk about something else."

"It's funny in the most uncomfortable way."

He finished the rest of his ice cream. This conversation was going nowhere. But he was absolutely certain she had some kind of trauma in her past. Someone had made her feel afraid in her own home and although she wouldn't admit she was afraid, she was. This creep had stuck his foot in her door. That was a threatening, aggressive move, no matter how much she wanted to downplay it.

"I'm glad you had a good night's sleep," he said.

"It was awesome. I slept until after nine."

"What happened when you went home?"

"Nothing."

"Have you talked to him since?"

"Yes."

"Did he apologize?"

She laughed. "He's not the apologizing kind, but neither am I, so I think we understand each other on that front."

He had no idea what to say to that. He knew for sure that she was probably scared and didn't want to admit it, although he couldn't figure out why.

CHAPTER 35

$\mathcal{T}$he following evening I was scheduled to photograph Brie at a nightclub. It had been her idea. Diana didn't like it and didn't think it was going to add any value to uncovering her roadblocks. She was concerned I wouldn't be able to get close enough, that the photographs would be too dark for Ian to analyze accurately. She'd spent an hour on the phone arguing with Brie about the location. Brie refused to consider any of Diana's more appropriate suggestions.

Brie thought it was critical that she show off how much her workout regime toned her body so that she looked good in a skimpy dress, dancing her heart out.

Diana had explained that she was completely missing the point, which seemed to be Brie's default position.

But part of the photography process was to take pictures of the client in their natural environment. Because that was prominently featured in our materials, Brie had fixated on it and wouldn't back down. Normally, Diana left that selection wide open for the client, after making recommendations to prompt their thinking such as photographs or video of them working with their own clients, speaking at events, or doing something active related to their professional life.

Brie had finally managed to wear Diana down, persuading her that part of what motivated her clients was the idea of transforming their body into one in which they felt completely at home, losing all sense of self-consciousness because they were so confident that they were fit and looked good in every outfit and from every angle. She told her clients that going to clubs would be so much fun once they became lifetime members of Bodies By Brie—they would never feel awkward or self-conscious on the dance floor again.

The irony of this was that Brie's behavior, although not insecure in any way, was highly self-conscious. She gave the impression she was constantly performing, always aware and thinking about how her face looked, how her hair was styled, concerned about how she sat and stood and walked across a room. I'd only met her twice, and I knew that thoughts of what impression her body was giving to those around her preoccupied her to the point that I wondered how she had space in her head for running a business.

That preoccupation was what I hoped to capture in her photographs.

It was likely the dancing would work out just fine, as long as I could get close enough to compensate for the poor lighting. I doubted the other dancers would appreciate a woman with a large camera crowding them while they tried to lose themselves to the beat, but I was looking forward to seeing how it all played out.

I arrived at the club fifteen minutes early to get a sense of the space, check out the crowd, and find a place to stash my camera bag. I was wearing a black dress and flat sandals. My hair was in a ponytail. The only thing clubby about my appearance was my makeup.

Inside the club, the music was thumping, and colored lights were circling the dance floor. It was already packed. It flitted across my mind that possibly, Diana had been right. It would be easier to take photos with my phone. I would cause less chaos as I jockeyed for a position close to Brie, but a phone camera wouldn't give the precision and detail provided by my SLR.

First, I went to the bar. I ordered a vodka tonic to smooth the way, then asked the bartender if I could stash my camera bag with him. He stared at me as if I were the ten thousandth needy woman asking to keep her purse safe behind the bar.

"I'm photographing a client," I said. "She'll be dancing and I can't be dragging the bag around with me. The camera's cumbersome enough." I placed a ten-dollar bill on the bar as a tip.

He rolled his eyes. "You should have thought of that earlier. You need an assistant." He left the ten lying on the bar, turning away to make another drink.

"Please. Can't I get this one tiny favor?"

At first, I thought he hadn't heard my raised voice above the music. Then, without turning back, he said, "Why don't you do *me* one tiny favor? Do you know how many girls want me to help with this or that? I'm not a babysitter. I'm not a bodyguard. I'm not your daddy."

"I never thought you were." I picked up the ten. I took another sip of my drink, placed it on the bar, and headed toward the restrooms. Maybe I could find a place to hide the camera bag.

The restrooms were nicer than most in clubs of this type, but not nice enough that the small anteroom with mirrors and counters for touching up makeup had cabinets or any possible place to hide my bag. There wasn't an attendant either, not that a restroom attendant would be any more willing to help me.

I returned to the bar. It was more crowded now, even though I'd been gone less than five minutes. The dancing seemed more frenzied. Nearly everyone appeared to be under thirty-five and I wondered at Brie's choice. Did she think she fit in with this crowd? Did she think she would blend in and be seen as someone just tipping into her thirties? But nothing about that woman was easy to figure out, so I wasn't sure why I was wasting brain cells trying to guess what she might be thinking.

I walked around the perimeter of the room, looking for a place by the bench seat that ran along the back wall. There was nothing. It was now ten past eight, the time I was supposed to meet Brie. I hadn't seen her. There was no doubt her white-blonde hair would stand out beneath the red and blue lights.

Half an hour before I'd arrived, I'd messaged her a reminder that Andy was absolutely not invited. I'd explained to her that it would be a chance for her and I to have some fun, to dance, to talk as much as the thumping electronic music would allow. As I stood there, wondering if she'd changed her mind, the music was working its way into my bones. I was tempted to let myself get pulled onto the dance floor to get some energy out of my own body, but I resisted.

There was a curved staircase about fifteen feet from the entrance. It led to a lounge area filled with low tables, comfortable chairs, and couches. There was an open railing to give a clear view of the dance floor below.

I walked up the first few steps and scanned the room, looking for Brie.

She wasn't there. I thought about heading back to the restrooms, but it seemed unlikely she would have come in and gone there immediately. I pulled out my phone again and sent her a message.

Where are you? I'm on the stairs near the front doors.

After several seconds, there was no answer. I slipped the phone into my tiny purse and moved aside for someone to climb the stairs.

As I looked up toward the lounge area, a hand closed around my wrist.

CHAPTER 36

I turned to see Andy staring up at me. He grinned.

"You're not supposed to be here." I said, raising my voice to be heard above the music.

"Yet, here I am."

"Where's Brie?"

He shrugged.

"You need to leave. I made it clear. Diana's made it clear. I don't know how else to get it through your thick skull." I moved down the stairs to the main floor. I put the strap for my camera bag over my head so I didn't have to keep tugging it into place. "Have you heard from Brie?"

"Not in the past five minutes," he said.

"Did she mention if she was running late?"

"No."

Between Ned and Andy, I'd had my fill the past few weeks of men who flat-out refused to listen. It wasn't a new thing, but the cluster-effect was getting to be too much.

I pulled out my phone. Still no message. I typed another one.

Are you coming or not?

I waited. There was no reply.

"Did she say if she was coming or not? Or are you here to tell me she changed her mind?" Every instinct I had was telling me she wasn't coming. Even if she was, if he was going to refuse to leave, there was no point.

"I'm here to dance. Come on." He put his hand on the back of my neck and pulled me toward him.

I ducked out from under his arm. "Don't touch me again."

"It's a club. Everyone is dancing and having fun. You need to let your hair down." He reached for my ponytail and with a deftness I didn't think would be possible for him, for most men, he grabbed my ponytail holder and slid it out of my hair.

I turned and started walking toward the door. Brie would have to reschedule. It was at least thirty minutes past eight by now.

As I pushed through the crowd, Andy reappeared beside me. Without warning, his arm was around my shoulders, pulling me toward him as if we were a couple. Before I could slip under that bulging bicep, he'd curled it closer so his arm folded around my neck, his forearm rested across my collarbone, and his hand was down the front of my dress, reaching for my breast.

Regretting my decision not to wear high heels, I turned toward him as much as the tight pinch of his arm would allow and stomped on the arch of his foot. He winced, but didn't let go.

The music was so loud, there was so much pushing and pulsing among the press of people that I didn't think shouting would do anything to attract attention. I wasn't even sure I wanted that. I never like attracting attention.

As his fingers continued to work their way around my breast, I worked my own fingers into my tiny purse and found my tube of lip gloss. I slipped it out and curled my fist around it as I leaned into him. I took the lip gloss and stabbed it into his hip bone, just above his belt.

I felt him double-up and he pulled his arm off me. "What the fuck was that?" he shouted.

"Exactly." I stabbed the lip gloss case into his hip bone again and he stumbled away from me. He gasped slightly. "You bitch."

I headed to the doors, shoved one of them open, slamming it into a guy who had just grabbed the outside handle.

"Whoa, slow down, babe. You need to chill *out.*"

I let the door fall closed. I walked quickly toward the corner, raising my arm sharply toward a cab that was letting out a group of three guys. I climbed into the back and one of them closed the door for me.

As the cab pulled away from the curb, I messaged Brie.

We need to do your photos. Message me. And if you bring Andy again, or tell him where we're meeting, there won't be any more photos.

I took a screenshot. I was about to send it to Diana, but decided to wait.

CHAPTER 37

*I*nstead of responding to my message telling me she was
ready to come get Damien any day now, Tess asked me to
keep him for another ten days—*Until escrow closes, for sure.*

I didn't mind. I liked his company. I liked hearing what he chose
to say at any given moment in time. I liked hearing how he chose to
respond to the things I said. But I didn't like being responsible for
him. I didn't like that I had to keep him away from Ned and I didn't
like that I couldn't go anywhere overnight without bringing him
along. That was not something I could keep doing indefinitely. But
she'd said ten days, so I set an alert on my phone for nine days, gave
Damien extra mango, and asked him what he thought about Ned.

Chardonnay time! Chardonnay time! Chardonnay time!

The fact that he said it three times suggested that he knew Ned
might drive anyone to drink. We both wanted Ned out of our hair,
or feathers, whichever applied.

I hadn't messaged Diana about the Andy and Brie situation.
Neither had I heard from Brie. I had so many questions, I could
hardly keep them straight in my own mind. Had Brie sent Andy to
meet me? Had she planned to show up later? Did she show up after I
left and had he still been at the club? What had he told her? Why

hadn't she responded to my messages? The more questions I asked, the more questions they spawned.

I wasn't even sure what I wanted to tell Diana. It wouldn't surprise me if she somehow twisted it around to make it a failure on my part for not getting control of the situation at the first photo session when Andy had been crawling all over Brie.

It was not a good idea to wait until Diana asked me how it went, but it also wasn't a conversation I was looking forward to having. Sometimes, complicated conversations are entertaining, sometimes, they're just too … complicated.

To clear my head, if that were possible, I decided to have a hearty breakfast. I chose a diner that was a little tired, old without being retro, but had the best bacon and fabulous, unpretentious coffee.

I settled into a booth, placed my phone on the table, and ordered. Before my mind could begin circling through its list of questions for the fifth, or fiftieth, time, I looked up to see a familiar looking man open the door and step inside. For half a second, I couldn't place him, but I was certain I should know his name.

He turned away from me, searching for a table, then faced my direction again as he headed toward the counter. And then I knew—Carolina's husband. Jordan.

In that flash of recognition, my questions about Brie and Andy, my speculation about what I would say to Diana, my thoughts about Ned, my lingering memories of Hunter's obsession with my so-called weird choice to stay in a hotel rather than breathe the same oxygen as Ned, all evaporated. I wanted to talk to that guy.

I signaled my server. She'd seen me enough times that we were on a *how-have-you-been-what's-new* basis, so she zipped right over to see what I needed. "I think I'll move to the counter."

"Sure thing." She grabbed my coffee cup and saucer and led the way.

I pointed to the empty seat one space away from Carolina's husband.

I settled on the stool, placed my phone far enough to my left that it encroached on the empty space between us, then looked up long enough that he felt my gaze. He glanced over and I smiled. He returned the smile. I was in. I took a calming sip of coffee.

Where to begin?

My food came, and I picked up a slice of bacon. I took a bite. As I chewed, his food was delivered. The same breakfast as mine.

"Their bacon is the absolute best, isn't it?" I said.

He picked up a slice. "Totally agree."

I didn't have time to dance my way slowly into a conversation, so I charged ahead. "I know your wife. She and I met in the spa at your hotel. I'm Alexandra. I took care of Ricky during your cocktail party the other night."

He turned to face me. His eyes narrowed slightly. "I've never seen you. How do you—"

"I saw you and Carolina in Central Park a week or so ago."

He looked away.

I took a bite of eggs, then some toast, then ate some bacon while he digested all the information I'd given him.

He began eating his breakfast. "Central Park. So you saw us fighting."

"Yes."

"That was—"

"You don't have to explain."

"I wasn't going to."

He ate a slice of bacon. "She asked you to watch Ricky after bumping into you in the spa?"

"We had coffee that day. And I met her another time. I met Ricky too, so I guess she felt comfortable with me."

"I see."

He didn't seem thrilled that I knew so much about his family when he'd never seen me in his life.

"How do you like living in a hotel? It sounds kind of relaxing. Nothing to worry about in terms of the business of living."

"It's not good for Ricky, though."

"Kids adapt, don't they? He's like Eloise."

He stared at me.

"The children's story about the girl who lives at the Plaza Hotel."

"Never heard of it."

"It sounds glamorous, living in a five-star hotel."

He laughed. "It might sound that way, but it's not. If you're traveling, sure. But staying in one place, for two years now, working all the time. Definitely not. And Ricky…" He picked up his orange juice and took several gulps that emptied half the glass.

"But he's getting a good education at least. I've heard homeschooled kids are usually ahead of the curve." I'd heard parents say that when I was growing up, people at our church who homeschooled their kids. I had no idea if it was true.

"I don't like it." He began eating faster now.

I wanted to keep him talking. Was that what the fight had been about? Yet it had resolved so quickly.

"How much longer will your case keep you in New York?"

"Probably six months. Maybe five. Shouldn't be more than six, though."

"Well, they do say kids are resilient, so I'm sure he'll be fine."

"He's not fine, though, is he?"

I took a sip of coffee. I ate my last slice of bacon. I nibbled on my toast, waiting. I was a little surprised he'd been so forthcoming.

"You've met him. He's …"

When he didn't finish, I filled in the gaps to encourage more talking. "I haven't been around a lot of kids, so I can't say for sure. But he seems … mature for his age."

He laughed. "It's not funny, but that's a magnificently diplomatic way to put it."

I smiled and took another sip of coffee.

He pushed his plate away and leaned his elbow on the counter. "You're Carolina's friend, so maybe it's a mistake to say this to you, but you seem easy to talk to."

"We're not friends."

"Everyone is her friend."

"Not me. She wants to be but ..." I shook my head slightly.

He laughed again. "She thinks Ricky is doing fine. Thriving, actually."

"I'm sure that's hard when you don't agree on how to raise your child. But it probably happens a lot. I guess you'll figure it out."

"We aren't figuring it out." He sighed. "Once we get back home, I'll start looking into some kind of boarding school. It will be an epic battle with her to send him away, but at this point, it's the only hope for him. If it's not too late." He drank his coffee. He looked suddenly ill. "I shouldn't have said any of that. I'd really appreciate you not mentioning this to her."

"Absolutely. I doubt I'll see her again." I wondered what I didn't know about this kid. Maybe I'd only seen the tip of the iceberg.

"You're a good listener." He pulled out his wallet and dropped two twenties on the counter. "Breakfast is on me."

"You don't need to—"

"My pleasure. Nice to meet you." He slid off the stool and headed toward the door. A moment later he was outside, and then he'd disappeared from view without looking back.

It was interesting talking to him, and I'd learned a few things, but I wasn't sure my curiosity had been satisfied at all, just shifted in a different direction. I picked up my phone. It had blown up with messages.

There were three from Diana, one from Hunter, one from Andy, and one from Brie.

Diana: *What happened last night?*

Diana: *What time are you coming in?*

Diana: *Call me!*

Hunter: *Want to go to a club Friday night?*

Brie: *Andy's sorry. You need to give him a second chance.*

Andy: *Soooorrrrrryyyy. I'll be good.*

I texted Diana that I would be at the office in twenty minutes. I sent her the screenshot of my message to Brie from the night before.

Diana was waiting for me in the lobby. She hustled me down the hallway to her office and closed the door. "What the hell happened?"

I sat in one of the chairs facing her desk. Instead of taking her usual seat behind her desk, she pulled over another chair and angled it to face me.

"Did you talk to Brie? Or Andy?" I asked.

"Brie called. She said you might be upset. She said she couldn't make it last night and—"

"Why couldn't she make it? I texted her several times and never got an answer."

"She didn't say. She was more concerned about you, after she received your text. Can you explain what's going on?"

"Andy showed up."

She frowned.

"He was there at the first photo session."

Her frown deepened.

"I could hardly peel him off her, but managed to get some decent shots, enough that will be useful. After I shut him up, I got her mind off him and the camera. Briefly."

She nodded. "And?"

"He showed up last night. He grabbed my hair, groped me, stuck his hand down my dress."

Her eyes bulged wide. "What did you do?"

"I stabbed my lip gloss tube into his hip bone a few times."

Her lips tightened as she tried to suppress a smile. "Then what?"

"I left. And sent that message to Brie."

She stood and walked to the window, where she remained for several minutes. Silence filled the office. My phone buzzed. I guessed it was probably Hunter, but I didn't look.

Finally, Diana turned to face me. "It's up to you if you want to keep her as a client."

"I'm fine with it. As I told you, as long as he's nowhere to be seen."

"We've already made that clear, but I'll try once more. And we'll choose the meeting sites."

"That sounds good."

"You handled it really well."

"Thanks."

She grinned, the first genuine smile I'd seen on her face in weeks. "I almost wish I'd been there."

I should have asked her why she'd trashed the resumés I'd provided, but since she'd smiled, since she'd liked how I handled Andy, since we seemed to be on the same page for an entire fifteen minutes, it didn't seem like the right time. The second photographer was clearly inevitable, so there really was no point. I decided to wait until the interviews started.

When I left her office, I wondered if anything between us would change. I expected things might be more pleasant, until we disagreed again. And I still disagreed with everything she was doing, so most likely, nothing had changed at all.

CHAPTER 38

*T*hat night was the first time Eileen and I were both home and awake since Ned had tried to keep me from closing my bedroom door. Even better, there was no sign of Ned.

I decided that meant it was a good night for a martini. I mixed two without asking her if she wanted one. There was also no sign that she had plans to make dinner, so I figured we'd graze through whatever was in the fridge or call for takeout.

I put the drinks on the coffee table and knocked on her bedroom door. It was several minutes before she opened it. Her face was clean and shiny, stripped of makeup. Her hair was combed back into a tight ponytail. She was wearing cut-off blue jeans and a tank top and a necklace with a large diamond teardrop that I'd never seen before.

"What's up?" she asked.

"I made martinis."

"You drink a lot of martinis," she said.

It wasn't what I'd expected her to say, but it told me everything. Ned must have given her a long story, featuring my flaws and sins and the threat I posed to her wellbeing. He still hadn't been entirely clear about that.

"So is that a no?"

She stared at me. "Are we still friends?"

"Why wouldn't we be?"

"Because Ned—"

"The drinks are getting warm. If you want to talk about Ned's issues, why don't we do it over a nice chilled martini?"

"He doesn't have issues, Alex. I don't understand why you've turned against him. He's the sweetest guy I've ever known, and it hurts me when you say things like that about him."

"I'm going to have a martini. Are you coming?" I started toward the living room. After a brief hesitation, she followed.

She sat beside me on the couch looking sulky, reminding me of Ricky. I decided not to offer a toast. This wasn't going to be a friendly, relaxing evening, despite her concern about whether or not we were friends. I took a sip of my drink.

"Ned told me what happened," she said.

"What happened?"

"That he asked what you'd been up to the other night, and you attacked him."

I laughed. I took another quick sip of my drink as the liquid slid up to the rim, a mini tsunami reacting to my laughter.

"Why do you think that's funny? You really upset him."

I put my glass on the table and pulled my legs up so I was sitting cross-legged, facing her. "Do you want to hear what actually happened?"

"Are you calling him a liar?"

"I didn't attack him, that's for sure. He's correct that I didn't tell him what I'd been up to."

"Why are you so difficult?"

I shrugged. "It was none of his business what I was doing. And I didn't attack him. Verbally or physically. Just the opposite, in fact."

"What does that mean?"

"Do you want to hear what happened or not?" I plucked the stir stick out of my drink and ate an olive.

She sighed. "What?"

I told her how the evening had unfolded.

"I can't picture Ned doing that. Are you sure you're not exaggerating?"

"Absolutely."

"That doesn't sound like him."

I shrugged.

It sounded exactly like him. Ned liked to be in control, and when he couldn't have verbal control, I didn't think he would need to take many steps to reach the point of demanding physical control. Eileen probably hadn't seen that side of him. Yet. As far as I was aware, she'd easily handed over verbal control, so he was content.

"But this is what I mean. Sometimes, you're a little argumentative. You push and push until—"

"I don't owe your boyfriend a report on where I go."

"God, Alex! It was a friendly question! You came home late, and he asked where you'd been."

"I'm not required to answer his *friendly* questions in the middle of the night. Why was he even there? Does he live here now?"

"No."

"Then why was he in our living room at one o'clock in the morning?"

"He couldn't sleep."

"Why wasn't he having insomnia at his own apartment?"

"Because he spent the night. Are you trying to tell me that's not allowed? Because you don't have that right. We can have guests."

"Yes, it's allowed. You can do whatever. I can do whatever. But in our shared space, it's a little much that he's always there, acting as if he lives here. Having a key."

"Your bird is always here."

I laughed. I was glad I wasn't holding my drink because I couldn't stop laughing. She started laughing with me, which relaxed things and made it more fun for a few minutes. But I was sure we were laughing at different things. I was laughing because she'd compared her boyfriend to a large bird. I wasn't sure why she was laughing. Perhaps she was just mimicking me, not unlike Damien himself.

"If you want your boyfriend to spend the night, I wouldn't care," she said. "And if he wanted to hang out in the living room, I wouldn't care. Actually, why haven't you in—"

"All the time? It's not a huge apartment. That's a lot of people tripping over each other."

She stood and went to the window. She pressed her face against the glass as if she wanted to cool her skin. "It's really hard to talk to you sometimes, Alex. I wish you wouldn't keep picking fights with Ned." She turned to face me. "I love him. And it means a lot to me that the two of you like each other." Her eyes filled with tears. She blinked rapidly. "Why are you doing this? Why *do* you hate him so much?"

"I don't necessarily hate him. But he's so old. I just think you can do better."

Her face turned perfectly white. She looked like all the blood had gone out of her body. She walked toward me slowly, stopping at the edge of the table. "You have no right to talk to me like that. You're not my mother. Ned is an amazing man, and that's a terrible thing to say. Age doesn't matter to me. And I'm very lucky to have him." She picked up her martini glass. She went into the kitchen. I heard her slam the glass onto the counter. I was surprised it didn't crack.

CHAPTER 39

I leaned back against the couch and closed my eyes. I shouldn't have said that. I had no idea how I was going to clean up the mess I'd just made.

The drinks and the talking were supposed to make things smoother. It was Ned's fault we were in this mess, but I still should have kept my mouth shut. No one wants someone to tell them who they should be in a relationship with. Even when they ask, they usually don't truly want to know.

Those words were going to stick there no matter what I did now to try to ease my way out of it. I opened my eyes and slid down to the floor, which was sometimes more comfortable than the outrageously expensive couch we'd chosen together and she'd paid for. I ate an olive, then took a sip of my drink, then another, feeling the alcohol run through my veins with warm comfort.

Would she believe me if I told her I hadn't meant what I'd said? Would she believe me if I told her a fantastical lie about Ned? Maybe I could tell her I was intimidated by him or something that would make her feel sympathetic toward me. I didn't want to bring up the mythical, stalking ex-boyfriend. It had worked once, but I'd gone to some trouble to un-do that lie, so spinning it in another direction didn't seem like a good idea.

I continued sipping my drink, thinking of outrageous ways to get Eileen to calm down and consider my words in a different light. Before I knew it, the glass was empty.

I went into the kitchen and mixed another drink. I had to fix this now. I couldn't let what I'd said remain in her mind or I was headed toward a showdown with Ned that would land me on a street corner with Damien in his cage, yelling at me for mango, and Ned going to Kent, demanding he reveal all the tiniest details of my relationship with the neighbor I'd murdered.

Of course, it wasn't likely to go that far, but the street corner aspect was not out of the question.

I stabbed my stir stick into the jar of olives and pulled one out. As I sucked out the pimento to give me something to concentrate on, I tried to think of a way to lure Eileen out of her room. I could turn on her favorite baking show. I could offer to open a bottle of wine, which she preferred over a martini, but we were probably long past that. I wasn't even sure whether she would speak to me if I knocked on her door.

I could bring Damien out into the hallway and try to get him to make her laugh, but he was completely unpredictable and she wasn't all that charmed by him. My last resort was to invite Ned over and see if I could manufacture a friendly dinner for the three of us. That idea quickly turned my stomach inside out.

The jar of olives was half empty.

I would knock on her door. If she didn't respond to anything I said, I would have to give myself over to the dread of an evening spent swallowing my bile and lapping up Ned's idiotic and offensive comments and pretending he was absolutely charming. When he was gone, I could tell her I'd been blinded by something or other I would come up with later, and of course she couldn't do any better. He was a gem. The finest catch I could imagine.

She could return to her fantasyland. It seemed to be what she preferred. Maybe she was more like her mother than I'd realized.

I took a sip of my fresh drink, fortified myself with two more olives, then went to her bedroom door and knocked firmly.

"Leave me alone."

At least she was speaking to me. I was optimistic. I would promise something she loved for dinner and run out to pick it up, or have it delivered. I could open that bottle of wine after all. My shoulders relaxed as my confidence grew that I wouldn't need her boyfriend in my face after all.

"I shouldn't have said what I did."

"You said what you think. I get it. I'm not surprised. I know you hate him."

"Can you come out and talk? We're both starving. I was going to order Chinese food and we could have a nice bottle of—"

The door swung open. I hadn't thought it would be so easy. She was hungrier than I was.

"I'm starving. And we should talk. Maybe this isn't going to work with us."

Good news, bad news, as the saying goes.

I poured my martini down the drain—more wasted vodka—but I needed a semi-clear head if I was going to preserve my status as Eileen's roommate for a bit longer.

We sat across from each other with a bottle of red wine between us. She drank most of it while I reminded myself of the martini I'd already consumed, taking only tiny sips from my glass.

Eileen poured out her heart, telling me how I'd let her down as a friend, how I'd hurt her to the core by saying something ugly about the love of her life, by making him uncomfortable in her home, by giving him the impression I had dark secrets, and by refusing to do anything whatsoever to try to get along with him or see his good qualities. She explained that he wasn't old and that *labeling* him *too old* was ageism and a disgusting attitude in our modern era when we had supposedly learned to accept people for who they are.

She told me she felt uncomfortable in her own home, that she respected me and I had no respect for her, using my rude and cruel comment that she could do better as proof point number one, and Damien as proof point number two.

She told me it seemed as if I didn't really want to have a roommate.

When she was finished, our plates were empty and her eyes were slightly droopy from consuming nearly three quarters of the bottle of wine in less than an hour.

"I do respect you," I said. "And that's why I said you could do better, but it was the wrong thing to say and I—"

"Don't pretend you didn't mean it."

"I'm not pretending. You're right. Ned and I don't get along. I'm a private person and he's always asking me questions and I don't agree that every question requires a response. It's like an assault."

"That's dramatic."

"Not really, if you think about it."

She sipped her wine and stared at me.

"Damien won't be here much longer. I know he hasn't helped the situation. Not everyone finds him as entertaining as I do."

"No one does."

I let that slide. I wanted to say—*Maybe you can't do better because you don't think you can*. But thanks to my clear head, I didn't. "Can we start over? And can we agree that having a pleasant conversation doesn't require answering questions I don't want to answer? That *no*, is a perfectly acceptable answer?"

"Maybe."

"I can see that you're crazy about him," I said. "And he's clearly in love with you."

That was exactly the right thing to say. A smile spread across her face like butter melting on her lips. "Do you think so?"

"Hasn't he told you?"

"Yes, but it's … reassuring, I guess, to know that it's obvious to other people."

I put my hands on my lap under the table, curling them into fists. I gave her a warm, tender smile. "It's beyond obvious. He would do anything for you. You're his queen."

Her cheeks turned red. She looked down at her wineglass, smiling to herself.

CHAPTER 40

 ortland, Oregon

* * *

The woman next door to Jimmy who made the glazed clay animals to live in her brick-walled village, was a stranger to me. I'd never seen my parents talk to her or her husband, probably because they lived on the street behind us, which was separated from our street by a wooded area.

But it was obvious from looking at that brick wall around the garden and all those little buildings and the pathways and lakes that she cared a lot about her clay animal world and would be very upset that the creatures were missing.

A man at our church had a miniature train in his basement. It ran through tunnels and over bridges and around tiny buildings and past little farms. He was an adult, but he played with it all the time and liked to have other church families over for barbecues so he could take the kids down to his basement and show them his train. The kids weren't allowed to operate the train, only he was. So I knew grownups liked toys, and they could be selfish with their toys.

I wasn't going to get in trouble for Jimmy stealing those animals, and if he got caught, I would end up in trouble. The more I thought about it, the more I knew this was exactly what would happen.

I couldn't see Jimmy's house from my bedroom window because the trees between our backyards blocked it. So I started taking my notebook with me out to the edge of the woods. From there, I could see glimpses of his house and yard. I knew how to tell time and I had my own watch that my parents had given me for my ninth birthday. Every day, I wrote down what times Jimmy was usually in the backyard and when the lights were on inside his house. After a few weeks, I knew that every Friday night, Jimmy's family got in their mini van and left as soon as his dad came home from work. They still weren't home when I was told to come inside because it was getting dark.

On a Friday night, after Jimmy had collected seven animals from the woman next door, making me be the lookout each time, I snuck over to his treehouse the minute the mini van backed out of their driveway.

I climbed the ladder, gathered up the animals in the plastic bag I'd brought with me, and carefully climbed down the ladder. I carried the animals to the edge of the yard and hid them under the bushes.

After I finished helping with the dinner dishes, when it was almost dark, I snuck back outside. The lights were on in Jimmy's neighbor's house, but no one was on the back porch. I moved slowly into their yard, keeping my eyes on the back door. I got the same bucket Jimmy had used as a step stool to unlock the gate to the animal garden.

Because I hadn't been able to see where the animals were when Jimmy took them, I had to guess where to put them back. If she noticed they'd been moved, maybe she would think they had come to life in the middle of the night. That made me giggle, so I hurried out of the garden and latched the gate.

The next day when I went over and climbed the ladder to

Jimmy's treehouse, he was standing at the top waiting for me. As I reached the top rung, I thought he might push me off the edge.

"Did you put the animals back?"

"No."

"They're gone!"

"Gone?"

"Don't look stupid," he said.

"How can they be gone?"

"Someone came up here and took them." He moved away from the edge so I could climb inside the treehouse.

"Did you bring any snacks?" I asked.

"You're the only one who knew they were here."

"How do you know that?"

"Because I do."

"But how? Anyone can climb the ladder."

He stared at me. "She wouldn't do that," he said.

I shrugged. "Your dad?"

"He would have yelled at me."

"Maybe he didn't want to be bothered."

He stared at me again, this time as if I didn't have a brain.

"I know you put them back. I can see them." He went to the window.

"Well, I didn't do it. You shouldn't accuse people of lying when you don't have proof." I'd learned a lot of things from having three older brothers, and that was one of them. You could say anything you wanted if there wasn't any proof. Someone could even *know* you'd done something, like eaten the last cookie, but if there were no crumbs on your lips and you didn't laugh or act nervous or give yourself away, if you were strong and stuck to your story, as Eric said, they couldn't be sure. They had to have proof.

"I don't need proof. You're the only one who knew they were here and now they're right back in the garden. So now you have to go get them."

"No."

"You have to or you can't play in my treehouse."

"Fine." I went to the ladder and started to climb down.

"Why did you put them back?" Now he was whining.

"I didn't."

He looked like he might cry. "I wanted to play with them."

"We can think of something else to play with. Maybe your mom did it and she didn't tell your dad so you wouldn't get in trouble."

He looked liked he was thinking about this, trying to decide if his mother would do something like that for him. "I want them back."

"Let's find something else to do."

"No. I want them back. You be the lookout." He went to the ladder.

"I'm tired of this game," I said.

"Just watch out for me." He scrambled down the ladder and ran across the yard to the bushes. Slowly, he made his way into their yard, grabbed the bucket, and entered the brick enclosure. He looked like a maniac, running around the miniature village, snatching the animals out of their happy little lives.

He was going to give himself away, leaving his footprints all over her delicate plants. I wondered if they would stretch their tiny stems and leaves back to their normal shape, erasing his footprints, or if they would leave a perfect clue for the woman to measure and go knocking on the doors up and down their street, looking for the thief.

Jimmy had gotten greedy. Instead of taking the two, maybe three animals he could carry, he began putting them inside his shirt, tucking it under to form a hammock for them. It worked while he was walking around the garden, but I could see in my head what was going to happen once he went out the gate.

He couldn't clutch his belly, swollen with ceramic creatures, while climbing on the bucket to lock the gate. But he wasn't thinking that far ahead.

Soon, he had eight animals tucked inside his shirt. He went to the gate, stepped out, and pushed it closed with one hand. Then, I saw him frown as he realized it would be hard to climb on the bucket and lock the gate. Instead, he grabbed the bucket and carried it to the side of the house, dropped it by the hose, and ran back to his own yard.

Now, he'd left a path of breadcrumbs just like Hansel and Gretel, but for someone else to follow.

He was standing at the bottom of the ladder. "Come down and help carry these up."

"No. You're stupid. They're going to catch you because you took too many, and you didn't lock the gate."

"No one will notice. Come help me."

"You should put some back."

"Come help me."

I stayed where I was.

"Do you want to play in my treehouse or not?"

I was starting to think I didn't want to play in his treehouse. I wanted my own. I was bored with his game.

"Please."

"You have to put them back."

"After we play with them."

I sighed. I climbed down the ladder and took two of the animals.

Jimmy invented a game where the animals went to war with each other. Then I was even more bored. If he just wanted to pretend they were having a war, didn't he have plastic army men, or other toy figures for that?

The ceramic animals were not fun. They didn't have arms and legs that moved. They were cute, but boring. He just wanted them because he liked stealing them. He liked knowing he wasn't supposed to have them.

When it was almost time for me to go home, I asked if he was going to put them back. He shook his head.

"You're going to get caught. You left footprints all over the garden."

He looked out the window. "I don't see any footprints."

I shrugged and climbed down the ladder. I was already trying to think of a plan to put them back.

CHAPTER 41

$\mathcal{N}$ew York

* * *

Two days! He'd spent *two days* worrying that Alex was scared of Ned, that she was living in a borderline unsafe environment, weighed down by a bird she couldn't let go of. If she was in danger and needed to escape, she would be trapped by an oversized bird in a large, awkward cage.

Now, she'd blithely told him all was going to be fine. She and Eileen had an understanding. Ned was going to give her space. There were *no worries*. And yet, she'd had a deadbolt lock installed on her bedroom door. And yet, she'd spent several hundred bucks to spend a few hours in a hotel because this creep was so disturbing. Suddenly, he'd seen her dismissal of the idea that they would ever have dinner with her roommate as something that might be more sinister than he'd realized.

But now, he wasn't sure.

Was she afraid of the guy or not?

Was she lying to him now? Had the guy threatened her?

It was impossible to know with her.

Hunter locked his apartment door. While they walked to a bistro where they had reservations at seven, he half-listened to her talk about her co-workers. He still longed to have an evening picnic in Central Park, but their standoff about that was so long ago now, it almost seemed as if it had never happened.

They took their seats at a small table with a long white cloth and too many large glasses—two enormous goblets for red wine, two champagne flutes, two large water glasses, and a globe holding a candle. If there wasn't some re-arranging, he wasn't sure where their dinner plates would go.

The restaurant was already packed, and the noise level made it difficult to have a serious conversation. It was probably a good thing. He should be happy about that. She wouldn't want another serious conversation about all the things he didn't know about her.

He was beginning to feel as if he knew absolutely nothing. He'd done a more thorough internet search than he had after first meeting her, but still found nothing. He couldn't believe there were no high school pictures. She must have made it a full-time job to avoid cameras, apparently going so far as to skip her graduation photo. She had no social media accounts. She'd mentioned college, but he found no records on that front either, so if she'd attended, she likely hadn't graduated. At least not under that name.

Was Alexandra Mallory even her real name? He'd searched the name Mallory in Portland Oregon and found so many, he didn't know where to go from there. He'd tried a social media search of the name, trying to look for others in her age bracket in the Portland area, but without any first names, it was impossible.

After they ordered, they talked about where they should go with their windfall from the evening watching that strange, creepy kid. They agreed it would be nice to go to a beach somewhere, but there wasn't enough money for something exotic. Obviously, he could pay for a nice vacation, but she wanted to dream about spending their windfall. They discussed all the places they'd like to go. By the time they were finished dreaming and eating dinner, they'd imagined a trip that would cost four times as much.

He said he would do some research and maybe they could go to one of the beaches in South Carolina.

Over desert, she showed him pictures of the winery her friend Tess had bought in the Napa Valley.

"Do you have pictures of the house where you grew up?" he asked.

She laughed. "No." She tucked her phone back into her bag.

"You know, some guys might hire a private eye if their girlfriend was as closed mouthed as you are about your past."

"That doesn't sound like a way to win a girl's affection."

"Don't you mean a girl's heart?"

She smiled. She took a bite of chocolate cake.

"It's common," he said. "Just to be sure someone isn't conning you."

"Is that what you think I'm doing?"

"I don't know what to think."

"Do you have so much money, you're concerned I might try to bilk you out of millions?"

"No. But there are other ways to con people. You can con them into going into debt, or to hooking you up with others."

"You've thought a lot about it," she said.

"Not really. I'm just thinking out loud."

"I would probably notice a private eye following me."

"Would you?"

"I'm very alert to my surroundings."

"Not the internet searches."

She ate another bite of cake. She wasn't smiling. "You sound very serious about this plan."

He laughed. "Not really. I'm just saying, sometimes I wonder if you aren't a photographer at all. Maybe you work for the CIA. Maybe you'll disappear some day and I'll never hear from you again."

"That could happen with you, too," she said.

"You know where I work."

"It could be a cover. You could still disappear. Lots of people disappear. Because they want to. Or they don't want to, but they still do." She slid her fork through the cake, cutting a clean sliver and placed it in her mouth.

"That sounds a little …" He wasn't sure what it sounded like. Unsettling. He wasn't sure where this conversation was headed. He hadn't planned for it to become something threatening, but it felt that way now, on both sides.

She finished eating her piece of cake while he stared at the dish of creme brûlée in front of him. It suddenly looked unappetizing, too gooey with custard and not very sweet. He should have ordered the cake. He shouldn't have ordered dessert at all. The meal had been filling. They'd started with several appetizers, moving on to bowls of creamy lobster bisque before the main course. He felt so full he thought his gut might burst. He put the spoon down.

"Is that what you're planning to do?" she asked.

"No. All I said was that some people might."

"But you're not some people. I thought we were getting to know each other the normal way."

"This doesn't feel very normal," he said.

"I didn't mean we're normal. Why would we want to be normal? I said that's how we're getting to know each other. Not through hiring investigators, poking through the dumpsters behind our apartment buildings. Or asking interview questions."

"Hmm." He nodded at the server and a moment later, the check was on the table. He slid his credit card inside the folder.

"We can split this," she said.

"I invited you."

"Thank you."

"You're welcome."

He wished he hadn't mentioned the investigator. He wished she would tell him what the hell was going on. He wished for a lot of things. He wasn't sure if he found her fascinating and exciting, or so exhausting that he wanted to end things right now. But he couldn't imagine going through life without her.

What was going on?

The healthiest thing to do was to drop the subject of her family, her past. He needed to stop digging for information. He needed to accept her as she was. That was the basis for a healthy relationship. But so was communication, and she didn't communicate. Not only did she not communicate easily, she *refused* to communicate. She seemed to consider it a personal challenge to hide as much about herself as she possibly could.

He needed to make up his fucking mind about how he was going to deal with her obvious need for privacy. Or whatever it was.

The check was returned, and he signed it. He pocketed his credit card and pushed his chair away from the table. He couldn't wait to escape. The room was suddenly too warm, the voices too loud, the tables too close to each other. He wanted to be outside where he could see the sky, even if he had to tip his head all the way back and gaze up between towering skyscrapers.

"Are we leaving?" she asked.

"We're finished eating. Let's go." He started walking toward the door, trusting she would follow.

When he was outside, he inhaled deeply, drinking in the sultry night air. She stood beside him, studying him with a look of concern that was unusual for her. "Are you okay?"

"Yes. Should we go for a walk?"

"Sure."

He shoved his hands into his pockets rather than taking her hand in his. He walked quickly, knowing she would keep pace, not really caring if she didn't, anxious to get his muscles working, his blood pumping.

"Did you already hire an investigator?" she asked.

"I said, no."

"That's good. I would take that as a sign you don't trust me."

He laughed.

"Why is that funny?"

"Because you don't trust me at all."

"That's not true."

He stopped and faced her. He put one hand on each of her shoulders, squeezing gently. "You've played this stupid game for weeks. You won't answer the simplest question and I don't understand it. Not telling me has turned it into a huge thing in my mind and it shouldn't be that way. I can't stop thinking about it. I don't like having these questions nagging at me. It makes me think there's something not right between us, something not right with you, to be honest."

"It sounds like you're a little obsessed."

"I'm not obsessed. Your behavior is not normal. Do you even realize that?"

She stared at him. Her eyes were wide, filled with a look of absolute transparency that he hadn't noticed before. Was this new?

"Yes, I realize that."

His hands slid off her shoulders. They started walking, and they didn't speak again until he asked her if she was tired from walking in heels and if they should get a cab. She said that would be really nice.

At his apartment, they fell into bed, clawing at each other's clothing with an intensity that felt greater than usual, greater even than the first night they'd been together. They said nothing more about her lack of normality or private investigators.

At one-forty-five, he woke from a dream where he was walking the deserted streets of New York. It was the middle of the day, but there wasn't a single pedestrian or vehicle in the streets.

Alex was gone.

CHAPTER 42

*I*t's strange how a few simple words, the most thoughtless, unimportant comment, can grow into something that threatens to take over your life, to strangle you until the breath is gone from your body. How is that possible? Even a simple yes or no can have consequences that change the course of a person's life, the course of history, if it's taken far enough.

That's how it was when I answered Ned's question without thinking—*none of your business*—four words that seemed perfectly reasonable.

It turned into a physical altercation.

That's how it was when I spoke four words to Eileen—*you could do better*—and came close to expelling myself from my luxury apartment.

With Hunter, it was the words I hadn't spoken. *I had four siblings. Now I have three.* There was no good answer, and I didn't want to explain the discrepancy. It's not that lies don't slip easily off my tongue, they do. But what was the correct answer to that question, and more importantly, would I ever want to change the answer? If I did, it would require a lot of explaining. It seemed simpler to avoid answering.

And now, I'd started a crisis that he was not going to easily recover from.

He had twisted himself into knots over words I hadn't even spoken and was imagining all sorts of wild scenarios. He was so obsessed with the topic, I wondered if he had already hired someone to investigate me. If that were the case, it made me very uncomfortable. If that were the case, I might have created a much bigger problem in my life than simply being required to talk for the first time about the death of my sister.

And, how would I know?

I very boldly told him I would notice if someone followed me. I have good instincts, a freakish awareness of what was happening around me. But did I really? Rada had managed to locate my apartment. She'd stood outside my office building and I hadn't known she was there until she told me ever-so-casually that she'd followed me. Maybe I was only aware when I had reason to be concerned about it, when I was planning to kill someone, or had just done so.

But day-to-day? Was I really watching every person who passed by, every man or woman sitting nearby in a restaurant or entering my building? Did I clock every face that I'd seen before and register its familiarity?

Absolutely not.

It was possible that Hunter had had someone following me from the first time he became upset that I wasn't being forthright with him. And it didn't even have to be a physical presence. Just as I'd fabricated a story for Eileen about an ex-boyfriend who was good with technology, there were plenty of people who could creep through the wires of the dark web and potentially find out things about me.

I'd done my best to keep myself from having a lot of online information, but as I'd gotten older, that had become more difficult. The days when I paid for everything in cash and didn't use a cell phone were long gone.

I still used a phone that belonged to my employer and I'd started using the burners for other situations. I'd only rented my own apartment once. But there were traces. I had a credit card. I'd had jobs. I had a savings account and a debit card. It's extremely difficult, if not impossible to live in a major city without those things. The people who revel in living off the grid mostly live far from civilization, as far as I know. They grow their own food and build their own homes. They don't get manicures and go to hair salons. Not that I can't use cash in those places, but I wasn't an invisible, untraceable entity.

If Hunter tried hard enough, he might eventually locate my family. If he dug deep enough, he would probably find Lexy. So why didn't I want to tell him?

I didn't want to think about it. I didn't even want to answer that question. I wanted to have fun with him and talk to him and learn more about each other, but not too much, not the things that would give him power over me.

All of it made my head ache.

I decided to go for a run. It was almost ten at night. The sidewalks were relatively empty, and if I didn't get too caught up in needing to go fast, I could enjoy an easy jog. It would fulfill a dual purpose. It would untangle the knots in my brain. At the same time, I could see if anything crept up the back of my spine and spread across my scalp, telling me that indeed, someone was watching me.

The thought that someone might have seen me when I had dinner with James, when I checked into the hotel with James, spent the night, and left alone the following day, sent a chill through my body that made me feel as if Ned had cranked the AC to a temperature designed to house a penguin rather than a cockatoo.

As I walked out the front door of our building, I looked in both directions, searching for faces I might have noticed before but paid no attention to, for someone who looked like they were loitering, someone who seemed like they didn't have anywhere in particular to go. Of the few passing by, one guy getting out of a cab, a woman

184

texting while she walked erratically toward the corner, no one jumped out as a potential P.I. After watching for a few more minutes, I turned right on West 70th and started a slow jog.

I ran until I reached Central Park, then turned. I wished I had a tiny mirror to check behind me, but it was highly unlikely someone was jogging behind me. I would have felt that. Besides, anyone who was watching me wouldn't have been prepared for me to go running at that hour of the night.

As I ran, I wondered if it might be worthwhile to hire my own investigator. Not to follow Hunter. I didn't think there was anything I needed to know about him that he wasn't eager to tell me.

I wanted someone to follow me and tell me if someone else was following me.

It seemed kind of foolish, as I thought about it, but it also seemed like the only way to know for sure. I couldn't be walking around for the next few weeks or months, looking over my shoulder everywhere I went, wondering if I was being watched.

I didn't like the thought of knowing it was even possible.

If I had been followed, if someone had noted my time with James, did Hunter know everything there was to know about me already? But if that were the case, would he be fixated on my siblings? He should have more pressing questions than what my childhood was like.

Finally, I turned the corner onto 57th and headed back toward the Hudson. I picked up my pace now. Even though it wasn't great for my joints to be running on concrete, it felt good to be running. It had been a few weeks, and the evening air made it more pleasant than the last few times when I'd sweated it out earlier in the day.

My mind eased as my stride lengthened and my feet pounded the sidewalk and my ponytail swung furiously from side to side. The music wrapped itself around my brain and my thoughts began to dissolve. I felt like I was flying into another dimension. I felt like the idea that someone could follow me was simply a figment of my imagination. I felt like Hunter knew nothing about me that I didn't want him to know.

He could worry and complain and obsess about it all he wanted. But he had to wait until I was ready to tell him about my life. That might be soon. It might be never. I really had no idea.

CHAPTER 43

$\mathcal{T}$he message from Carolina was not like her. For someone who was a near-stranger to me, it struck me as funny that I thought I could recognize a message that didn't *sound* like her usual tone. Especially since her last message to me had begun in a state of panic because she'd wanted emergency childcare.

This one was different. Cold. Without her recognizable mania.

Carolina: *We need to talk.*

It sounded like a message meant for her husband. In fact, I wondered if she'd sent it to the wrong person. I stared at the screen, wondering whether I wanted to ignore it, or suggest she'd made a mistake.

Another message popped up: *Meet me at the hotel coffee bar. 6pm.*

I was thinking about what I wanted for dinner, and it wasn't coffee. As I was getting ready to inform her of this, a third message appeared.

It's urgent. I know you're working, but I assume you can be there by six. If you can't, send me the soonest time you can get there.

I messaged her back that I had plans. My plans were to eat dinner, not drink coffee with a mildly deranged woman I hardly knew. Especially if her creepy child would be joining us.

My phone began ringing. I let it go to voicemail.

When I listened, her message definitely didn't sound like the giddy person who wanted to insert herself into my life, become girlfriends, and use me for backup childcare.

"This is important. I need to speak to you today. Either send me the earliest time you can meet or be there at six."

I called her back. She answered before the phone rang.

"I can't meet you for coffee today, or any time this week," I said.

"It's not a choice. This is a legal matter, and it involves you. I'm doing the courtesy of speaking to you before I contact law enforcement. Six o'clock." She ended the call.

I moved my phone away from my ear and stared at the screen.

Had she seen me with her husband and imagined a relationship between us? Was she going to accuse me of stealing the ridiculous amount of money she'd paid me to sit in a hotel room while her child watched TV?

It was seven minutes after six when I walked up to the coffee bar in her hotel lobby.

Carolina was sitting at a booth for two. She met my gaze, staring at me with a look that I could only describe as pure loathing as I walked slowly toward her. I slid into the booth and picked up the coffee menu.

"You don't need that, I already ordered for you."

"I want to—"

"This isn't a social event."

"That's obvious."

"My son …" Her eyes filled with tears. "My beautiful, innocent, sensitive boy told me something horrible."

I bit down on the side of my tongue when she called her child innocent. Sensitive was a laugh as well.

She dug around in her purse and pulled out a tissue. She patted around her lower eyelashes. "It's so difficult to talk about. He's so damaged and I … I'm not sure why I'm even talking to you. I should go directly to the police. But Jordan … well …" She sniffed.

She straightened her shoulders and shoved the tissue back in her bag. She leaned forward slightly, glaring at me, her eyes no longer teary.

Her resolve was interrupted as the server appeared with iced lattes. I was startled that she'd remember the type of coffee drink I preferred. Carolina glared at me as she waited for the server to leave. I gave the guy a limp smile, and he backed away slowly. "Anything else?"

"No, thanks," I said.

"Ricky admitted to me, after a lot of shame, that your boyfriend *assaulted* him."

"No he didn't."

"Ricky told me you would say that." Her voice trembled. "That's why it was so hard for him to admit what happened. He said no one would believe him. I told him you weren't like that. I said you were straightforward, but he said you would lie."

"I'm not lying. Your son is."

"You just weren't aware. Hunter went in the bathroom. He put his hand down Ricky's sweatpants and—"

"That didn't happen. Your son is making it up." I pushed my latte away from me and started sliding out of the booth.

"Stay right where you are." Her voice was a low hiss. "I'm going to the police if you don't stay put until I'm finished with what I have to say."

"What you have to say is slander. I'm not going to listen."

"My son doesn't lie."

"Apparently, he does."

"How would you know what happened in the bathroom?"

"Hunter wasn't in the bathroom. And Hunter wouldn't do that. So there's nothing I need to know about what happened in there when Ricky was by himself. What you need to find out is what is going on inside your son's head."

"He isn't a liar. It was very difficult for him to tell me this."

"He's manipulating you."

"I'm sure you're scared and disgusted and upset. I can't imagine what's going through your head. I—"

"What's going through my head is that I'm hungry and I'm done listening to this." I slid out of the booth.

"If you leave now, you will deeply regret it." Her voice was soft but hard as glass. "Sit down."

I did, wondering what she was planning and what I was going to have to do to take care of it.

CHAPTER 44

*C*arolina placed her hands on the table, her long pink nails pointed at me like daggers. "I would be terrified if I were in your position, so I understand, but my son comes first, so although I do understand, I have no sympathy for you. I won't allow you to say ugly things about Ricky. That boy is broken." She whimpered softly. "It took everything he had to tell me the truth. I had to drag it out of him, he was so scared, and *so* ashamed. It's classic. The victim feels shame when they did nothing wrong. That's what your boyfriend did to my baby."

"Where's your husband?"

"He's busy."

"What does he have to say about this story?"

"He doesn't know. Ricky was too ashamed." Her eyes filled with tears again. She blinked them back. "That hurts almost as much as the abuse. The damage that one act has done to my little man's soul, to make him feel this shame and humiliation. The degradation. It's outrageous."

"What's outrageous is that your son is telling an enormous lie and you're believing him."

"He's never lied to me. And I could tell by the way he struggled that he was telling the truth."

"He's not. I was there the entire time. Hunter and I were in the same room. He never went in the bathroom. Ricky used the bathroom once, and Hunter was right beside me. This story is bullshit."

She gasped.

"I want to know what you're going to do," she said.

"I'm not doing anything."

"You need to go with us to the police to make sure that justice is done."

I laughed. "Justice will be you explaining to your son the difference between fact and fiction and the consequences of a colossal lie."

"I thought you were my friend. Women should be united when it comes to damage done to children."

"It's an outright lie. How many times do I have to say that?" I pulled out my phone. "I'll call Hunter and he can tell you himself."

She pressed her hand over her mouth, shaking her head from side to side so fast, her earrings swung wildly, hitting the back of her hand. She moved her hand away. "Don't you dare."

"I'm leaving." Once again, I slid toward the end of the seat.

Her hand shot across the table, and she grabbed my forearm.

"If you leave, I'm going straight to the police to file a report."

"They won't believe you," I said.

"They'll listen to what Ricky has to say. They know truth when they hear it. They'll talk to your boyfriend. And you."

"And we'll tell them it's a lie."

"They'll believe my son. He's completely credible. They'll see the terror in his eyes. Their instinct will tell them it's the truth."

Still perched at the end of the bench, I turned slightly. "What do you want from me?"

"First, I want the money back."

I laughed. "Of course you do."

"I'm not going to *pay* you to assault my child."

I needed to get away from her. I needed to think about how I was going to work my way out of this. She had me by the throat in one sense. I didn't want any interaction with the police, on any matter. It was one thing to answer a few questions after someone was murdered when I had my story correctly organized. I didn't want some free-for-all with a neurotic, possibly mentally unstable woman, and her very disturbed son.

Maybe her husband didn't like the idea of her spending five grand for a babysitter. I should just give it back, because maybe that was all she wanted. But I couldn't be sure. Somehow, it felt like she might want something more, although I couldn't imagine what. And giving the money back felt like an admission of guilt.

I wondered if she was making the entire thing up herself, if her weirdly adult little boy had concocted it alone, or if it was an idea they'd worked on together. A mother-son homeschool project.

"What else do you want?"

"I want justice, of course. I want that man punished for what he did to my little boy!"

"Then why are you talking to me?"

"Because I thought you were on my team! I thought we were *friends*. I had no idea you would defend that creep and believe him over a child. You just assume he's innocent. It's disgusting. I can't believe what I'm hearing come out of your mouth."

"I can't believe you're swallowing a lie without bothering to check it out."

She glared at me. Both our lattes sat in the center of the table, both glasses filled to the top with creamy tan liquid and melting ice.

"What are you going to do?" she asked.

"I need to think."

"You need to return the money."

"I want to talk to your husband. And your son."

"Leave my husband out of this. And there's no way I'm going to let you torment and humiliate Ricky. So you can forget that idea."

I stood and picked up my bag.

"Fine. I'll give you time to talk to that boyfriend. I want to meet tomorrow and you can give me the money. Got it?"

"That's not possible. I have a job."

"I want to hear from you tomorrow."

"We'll see." I walked out of the coffee bar, pausing in the lobby to consider whether I should take the elevator to Ricky's room. I could knock and see if he answered. But did I really want to involve myself in their weirdness more than necessary?

I left, indulging in a cab ride home to my apartment. I used some of the cash from Carolina to pay for the cab.

CHAPTER 45

*D*iana had arranged for me to meet Brie at The Metropolitan Museum of Art. We would spend our time in the Charles Engelhard Court of the American wing. Brie could indulge her need for the theatrical by posing with statues, some of the male figures with physiques that would call attention to her well-developed muscles. She could also admire and pose by the gilded Diana statue, which seemed fitting.

Diana had also chosen the space because the museum was so very public that if Andy dared to show up, any difficulties would be such a breach of the usual atmosphere it would create a scene that even he and Brie might be uncomfortable with. I wondered if Diana had underestimated them on that point, but I agreed with the rest of the plan. It might provide just enough of the ego focus Brie seemed to crave that she might be able to give herself over to my camera.

When I arrived at the Museum, Brie was standing near the entrance. She smiled at me, but said nothing. She wore all white— Capri-length leggings, a white T-shirt, and white and gold gladiator sandals. She would fit right in with the statues.

We went inside and I took out my camera. I told her to walk around and enjoy the art. I would stay at a discreet distance and take photographs. After a while, we would talk and I would do more close-up work. She didn't know I would also be taking close-ups of her eyes and mouth while she was lost in her own thoughts, studying the artwork.

I snapped about thirty photographs while she walked slowly, and surprisingly thoughtfully, around the open space. Sunlight streamed through the glass panels that formed the ceiling. The space was filling quickly, even on a weekday morning. It was still the middle of summer and the city was swarming with tourists.

After twenty minutes or so, I walked over to where Brie was sitting on the bench that wrapped around the fountain, dipping her fingertips into the water.

"Is it freeing to spend time away from Andy?" I asked.

"I feel absolutely free with Andy."

"He seems overbearing."

"You don't understand him at all."

"I don't want to understand him."

"Isn't that your job?"

"No. You're our client."

"He's an integral part of my business. To be honest, I'm having second thoughts about working with you. The way you've treated him is so disrespectful."

"Did you forget that he assaulted me?"

She rolled her eyes. "You were in a nightclub."

"Being in a nightclub is not an invitation to assault."

"That word gets thrown around too easily."

"Does it?"

"Yes. Besides, he said he was sorry."

"So he does recognize that he assaulted me?"

"He said he was sorry you got so offended. He thought you were there to have a good time."

I decided this line of questions was not going to lead to useful photographs, although I'd taken a few closeups of the angry set to her jaw while we'd been talking. "Why is he integral to your business?"

"He keeps me inspired. Twenty-four-seven. He's my motivation. He affirms my attractiveness. I wouldn't have this body if it weren't for him."

"But you own the gyms. It's your name on the buildings, your vision."

"My vision would be empty without Andy."

"Then why do you want to understand roadblocks to expanding your vision? Maybe he should be the one looking for that."

"If I do, he will."

"What if he's holding you down?"

The look on her face was an exquisite mixture of horror and despair. I took seven or eight shots. Luckily, her features were frozen long enough for me to get that many. I wondered what Ian would make of her expressions. I imagined that each shot likely revealed a different nuance, even though I wasn't aware of any changes.

At the same time, I didn't think Ian's insight was needed. She couldn't function without Andy, and suggesting he was a dead weight was so upsetting to her. She probably felt as if I was suggesting she cut off one of her arms. She continued to stare at me in shock. I lowered the camera and stared back at her, waiting to see if she would argue with me.

She folded her arms across her ribs, curving her shoulders slightly. "Why are you so critical of him? You don't—"

"This isn't about me."

"I don't like you saying he's holding me down. That's so insulting."

"You're fabulously successful, and you want to do more. But you can't seem to breathe without Andy telling you when to exhale. You don't think that's a little strange? And unusual for someone with your accomplishments?"

"We're *partners*."

CATHRYN GRANT

"I get that. But It's Bodies By *Brie*, not asses by Andy."

She glared at me. "That was so crude."

I took her picture.

"Stop taking my picture."

"That's why I'm here. That's what we're both here for."

"They aren't going to be flattering."

"As I've explained over and over, they aren't supposed to be. These are for the team to analyze your micro-expressions to uncover some of your unexpressed emotions. Emotions and mind-sets that could be holding you back."

"It sounds like you've already decided that Andy is the one doing that."

"I didn't say that. I said, *what if* he is? It was just a question. Something for you to think about."

"No, it wasn't. It was an attack."

I took her picture.

"Stop doing that."

"The fact that you think it was an attack says something, because it definitely was not."

"You're trying to twist things around."

"I'm trying to catch you off guard. I'm trying to capture the expressions on your face in moments when you aren't posing for the camera."

"By provoking me?"

"Sometimes, maybe."

"I don't like it."

"But it works."

"I want you to stop."

"Sure." I snapped a few pictures.

"I asked you to stop." She put her hands across her face.

"We're probably done for now. We'll have one more session and then Diana will put together a report with the results from our micro-expression expert."

"Yeah."

I put my camera in the bag, and we walked toward the exit. Brie paused every few steps to admire the statues, acting almost as if I wasn't there. After a few minutes, I began to wonder if she planned to stay and enjoy the museum. Maybe I should just leave. It wasn't as if we were sharing a cab. I had no more obligation to her.

"I'm glad this worked out." I extended my hand. "I'll see you—"

"Are you leaving?" She looked around, tipping her head slightly, as if she were looking for someone, as if she expected someone to emerge from behind one of the statues.

"Yes. We're finished, and it seems like you want to enjoy the museum for a while."

"Don't leave me."

"I should—"

"Can't you stay for a while? What do you have to do?"

"I have other clients and work that—"

"Are you doing them right now? Right this minute?"

"No."

"Then you can stay." She hooked her arm through mine.

I tried to pull away from her. "I don't want to."

"You have to."

"No, I don't."

"I can't be alone."

I laughed.

"Don't laugh at me!"

"I thought you were teasing. Why can't you be alone? It's the middle of the day, we're in a—"

"I'm never alone. I've never been alone. And Andy... He's always there. He rode in the cab with me so I wouldn't be alone, but he can't come back until noon." She pulled her phone out to check the time. She looked at me a moment later, her smile fragile and ready to slip off her face.

"You're never alone?"

"No."

"That's not possible. Even in the bathroom, or—"

"He's right outside the door. And he's with me in the shower, and he tucks me in at night and sleeps in my room."

I wasn't sure whether to laugh or run for the exit as fast as I could. She was giving me the creeps and half of me didn't believe her.

"Are you serious?"

She stared at me. She blinked once. "Why would you ask that?"

"How long have you known him?"

"Since I was thirteen."

"But you were alone before you met him, right?"

She shook her head. "I don't like to be alone. It's scary."

"Doesn't that drive you crazy after a while?"

"No. He comforts me. I need him. I don't understand why you're taking him away from me."

"I'm not taking him away. But healthy adult women don't—"

"Are you a doctor or a shrink or something?"

"Of course not."

"Then how do you know what's healthy?"

"I just don't think it's normal to spend every waking minute of your life with another person. I don't know if it's the best idea to let him control every part of your business."

"He's not controlling anything. I told you what he does. He's my muse. My soul. He inspires me. He created my body. You make it sound like a bad thing, like something perverted, and it's not that at all."

"Then how can it be Bodies By Brie?"

"Because he creates me, and I create other bodies."

She was giving me a headache. It almost seemed as if she didn't believe she existed, as if she were some kind of funnel for Andy, for whatever sort of magic she believed he possessed. Whether that was simply his weight-lifting and nutrition regimen, or something mystical that she thought he had, wasn't clear.

I wanted to send Diana a dozen red roses and wish her good luck sorting out this mess.

One more photography session and I was done.

Brie and I were on the sidewalk outside the museum now. I looked across the street and saw Andy sitting in the back of a cab. He was leaning out the window, leering at me. He gave me a thumbs up.

Without saying goodbye to Brie, I turned and began walking up Fifth Avenue.

CHAPTER 46

*H*unter stared at Alex, thinking he must have heard her incorrectly. He'd told her he couldn't hang out that morning because he really needed to clean the apartment and she'd offered to help. When he'd explained that he didn't mean putting away clutter, that he had to scrub the bathroom floor and shower, the cooktop and oven, she'd said, I'll take the bathroom.

"You'll take the bathroom?"

"Sure. I love cleaning."

"No one loves cleaning."

"Not true."

"You …" He took her hand in his and studied her fingers. They were slender, the nails oval shaped, filed smooth and slightly long, painted cranberry red. "Aren't you worried about your fingernails?"

"Don't you have gloves?"

"Maybe."

"If you don't, I'll run out and get some." She slid out of bed. "Show me your supplies."

"Are you serious?" Who loved cleaning with such delight that she leaped out of bed on a Saturday morning, eager to inventory cleaning supplies. He started laughing. "Is this a game?"

"No. I really enjoy cleaning. It's very satisfying."

"If you say so."

"I can see the results of my work. I like knowing it's perfect."

"This apartment is old, I doubt it will ever be perfectly clean, if there even is such a thing."

"I'll get it as close as I can."

She dressed in a pair of his old running shorts and a T-shirt, tying the hem up around her waist. After she fed Damien, she put her hair in a bun on the top of her head, and informed him she was ready to work. It turned out he had a brand new pair of rubber gloves that she removed from the package and slid onto her hands. She was disappointed that he didn't have a bucket in the apartment, but said she'd manage without one, she'd done it before.

It was difficult scrubbing the oven racks, wiping down the stove, cleaning the knobs in a dishpan of sudsy water. He wanted to go into the bathroom to see what she was up to, but she'd closed the door and said she preferred working alone.

He couldn't imagine relishing cleaning the apartment, even less, someone else's apartment, but he admired the pleasure she seemed to find in it. He could hear water running on and off, and the sound of the scrub brush handle bumping against porcelain as she worked her way around the tiny room.

When she was finished, she ushered him into the bathroom. He was stunned. The room literally sparkled. It looked cleaner than the day he'd moved in.

"How did you do this?"

"People don't get things clean because they get bored and quit. I like doing it, so I take my time, and it gets clean. That's all." She stripped off the gloves. "Should we use your clean shower?"

"I'm not finished with the kitchen."

"I'll do it. You can watch."

He had no objection to that. He turned one of the chairs with the back to the table and watched her move methodically around the room, scrubbing the corners of the counters, working at stains in the bottom of the sink, polishing the faucet. She acted as if the place belonged to her.

It was fascinating and kind of exciting at the same time. The longer she worked, the more anxious he became for her to finish. He wanted to pull her naked into the glistening shower. He wanted to be next to her, feeling her movements. At the same time, sitting across the room, watching her work in silence, he was mesmerized. He felt he could sit there forever.

After a long time under the steaming shower water, soaping each other, then making love, they dressed and went out for lunch. They decided on sushi. After all that work, he would have preferred something heartier, but he wasn't going to object when she'd just devoted half her Saturday to scrubbing his apartment.

They sat at the counter and ate, talking mostly about the food.

Just as he put the last California roll into his mouth, she said, "I have three brothers—Eric, Jake, and Tom. All the stuff I told you about Eric was true. They're all older than me. We get along fine, and that's about it."

He gasped slightly, fearing for a moment he was going to choke. He'd been totally unprepared for the sudden burst of information, was confused by the timing, and now unable to chew the seaweed quickly enough to get control of the thing. He moved it around in his mouth, trying to get a solid bite, wanting desperately to say something, but battling the roll to the point that he thought about spitting it out. Then, he wanted to laugh at the absurdity of the situation. He chewed it quickly and took a sip of tea.

Then, he found himself without anything to say. How did he respond? *Thanks for telling me?* That was laughable. *Good to know? Awesome?*

"None of them are ax murderers," she said.

"That's a relief."

"I thought you'd be glad to hear it." She sprinkled soy sauce on her rice and scooped some into her mouth with chopsticks.

"What took so long?" he asked.

"You overreacted."

"I don't think I did."

"You definitely did."

He shouldn't argue. She'd told him. Why was he arguing?

"Well, I'm glad you get along." It sounded limp, but there was nothing else to say.

A few minutes later, they paid and left the restaurant. He wanted to know whether her brothers lived nearby, how often she saw them, and what they did for a living. Were the others married? Kids? But he'd learned his lesson.

He was also desperately curious to know if there was some bizarre connection between her furious cleaning of his apartment and the sudden outburst of top secret information. Did cleaning bring back memories that made her open up? Was there some family history involved with cleaning? That thought made laughter well up inside him and he had to turn to the side so she didn't see him trying to control his expression.

She was the most fascinating, confusing, interesting, annoying, mesmerizing, charming person he'd ever met. Once in a while, but rarely, he wanted her to go away and leave him alone. Other times, he felt like he couldn't fall asleep because she wasn't beside him in bed. He couldn't enjoy a meal because she wasn't seated across from him.

Right that minute, he wanted to ask her to move into his apartment. He couldn't imagine that would go well. She might take it as a desire to have someone on hand to clean for him. And there was that bird. But the more he was with her, the more he hated saying goodbye. And he really hated it when he woke and found the bed empty beside him. He never expected her to stay over, but it was still a shock. He'd asked her to wake him. She always gave a vague answer that made him know she wouldn't.

He'd tried giving his subconscious little hints that he would wake when he felt the bed move, when he heard footsteps in the hallway, when he sensed movement. But they didn't work.

It was probably too soon. There was also the irritating part. If she was there all the time, he might find himself desperate for time alone.

CHAPTER 47

I don't really know why I told Hunter about my brothers. The timing seemed right. And not telling him had become too complicated. With all the other complications multiplying in my life, I didn't need to create some of my own. He had no reason to think I was neglecting to tell him about my sister, no reason to think I might have another sibling that I was keeping to myself.

And that's exactly what I wanted to continue doing—keeping Lexy to myself.

If that required a complicated explanation in the future, I would deal with it then. Maybe it never would. For now, everything seemed easier.

Besides, I needed Hunter fully in my corner, on my team, whatever cliché I wanted to use as I tried to figure out how to disarm Carolina and her creepy kid. I was still trying to decide if I believed Ricky had actually made this accusation or she was inventing the story herself. It was equally plausible either way, and I didn't want to bet on either one.

I'd thought about getting her husband involved, but I had no way to contact him, so unless I took a page from Rada's playbook and lurked outside the hotel for a day and half the night, waiting to pounce the moment I saw him, I was stuck. Leaving a message at the front desk was impossibly risky because she might find out about it, and anything that upset her right now would make the situation worse.

I had no plans to mention anything about it to Hunter. I spent some time trying to guess how he might react and got nowhere. I knew he wouldn't take it sitting down, but that was as far as I got. Would he agreeably go to the police and fight a game of who was more credible? Would he demand a showdown alone with Ricky? Would he hire a lawyer? I wasn't sure. Maybe he would laugh it off and tell her to go ahead and report it, confident the police would have one conversation with the kid and know immediately he was troubled and completely lacking credibility.

It would be an interesting conversation to have with him, but I never would.

Because the end of the game had begun to suggest itself in my dreams, or I assumed it was in my dreams, because I woke in the morning, thinking about whether Carolina's days on the earth might be limited.

I called her and suggested we meet at a bar in Chelsea. I didn't want to go anywhere near her hotel. She asked if I had the cash I owed her. I assured her I had it. I smiled at my phone, amused that she thought I owed her anything. The debt was wholly on her side now that a casual encounter in a spa had turned first into a weird kind of obsession, then reversed into harassment and games, and I now saw was most likely a well-planned con.

Had this been her plan from the start? Was this some elaborate con that was set-up by deliberately crashing into me that morning when she had no appointment for a massage?

It was impossible to know. Everything about her said she was impulsive, but I couldn't be sure. Ricky seemed too young to have thought of this scheme on his own. Maybe they *had* plotted it together. It could be she'd baited us with the ridiculous amount of cash for an easy childcare job and would now reel us in and suck us for a much larger sum.

That made the most sense, but I didn't want to go into it assuming anything.

I decided that, until I could find out more, I would dress and behave in a way that suggested I was meek, that gave the impression she had all the power.

Leaning over the bathroom sink, I cut my hair into thick bangs to give myself a more innocent appearance. I'm not sure why I thought bangs did that, but the moment I turned the blow dryer on them and fluffed them out, I knew it was the right choice. I put on a hint of mascara and a touch of liner at the corners of my eyes to give them more of a wide-eyed look.

I pulled half my hair back with a large clip and put nude gloss on my lips.

I was already wearing jeans and pink Converse tennis shoes, a white T-shirt and single pearl hanging from a gold chain with matching earrings.

Pushing it even further, I changed my usual messenger bag for a delicate purse that held only a credit card and my phone, my apartment key and the lip gloss. I fed Damien and went out, texting Eileen from the elevator rather than knocking on her bedroom door to say goodbye.

Walking into the bar, I felt a few people staring at me. I expected I might get carded since I looked out of place and possibly too young to be there, although maybe I was kidding myself. It wasn't as if I was under thirty and easily passing for a teenager anymore. Still, I definitely didn't look my age.

I found a table near the windows and ordered a glass of white zinfandel. It wouldn't be enjoyable, but it added to the image, and it would also ensure I drank it slowly.

CHAPTER 48

*C*arolina was twenty minutes late. There was still wine in my glass, but I'd polished off two glasses of water and had already used the restroom once. For several minutes, I wondered if she wouldn't show up at all. Maybe she'd lost her nerve.

Then she slid in across from me.

"Why'd you cut your hair?"

"I needed a change."

"You look really different."

"I know."

"Are you up to something?"

I ran my fingers through my thick bangs. "Why would you think that?"

"It just seems strange. This is really important and serious and I don't understand why now is the time you chose to change your hairstyle."

"What do you want to drink?"

"I'll have champagne." She turned and signaled the server who came and took her order, which was very specific and involved a discussion about what they offered by the glass and a mild argument about why they wouldn't pop open a bottle of the one she really wanted.

"Are you celebrating something?" I asked. "Did Ricky tell you he lied and you're so relieved he isn't damaged after all?"

"I like champagne. I'd like my money. And then we can discuss what's next."

"I gave half to Hunter and I need to get it back from him."

"You told me you had it."

"I do, I just didn't bring it."

She narrowed her eyes. "Do you think this is some kind of game?"

I did, but I said nothing.

"Why did you give half to that evil man you brought into my son's life?"

"You asked us to watch your son. And we did it together. It seemed the fair thing to do."

"You should have gotten the money back when you told him we know what he did."

"I haven't talked to him about it."

"Why not? You should have been in his face the minute I told you." Her champagne arrived, and she took a sip.

"I needed time to think about it."

"What's there to think about?"

I remembered I wanted to seem meek. I wondered how I was doing. Probably not that well. "You really shocked me and I ... it took time to process."

She leaned back in her chair and folded her arms. "And have you processed it?"

"I think it would really help if I can talk to Ricky."

"No."

"Why not?"

"Because I told you. He's damaged. Seeing you would traumatize him further. Absolutely not."

"But it would help me know how to approach Hunter if I heard the story from Ricky first. If I heard it myself."

"No way."

"I feel sort of trapped. To be honest, I'm a little afraid to tell Hunter."

Her eyes widened. She looked almost excited. "Why are you afraid?"

"I don't know what he'll do. He might … I just don't know what will happen. If I can hear how Ricky is feeling, it might help me know what to say."

"I think we should all just go to the police and they can arrest him. Or …"

"Or, what?"

She sighed. "I don't know. I don't know how to handle this, to be honest. He's so upset. He won't even talk to me. He won't do his homework. He doesn't want to go to his boxing class." She began crying. She picked up her glass and took a long swallow of champagne. She coughed slightly. "This is so awful. Nothing like this has ever happened. I've done everything to keep him safe, to give him the best life. And now …" Tears were running down her face. "How can you be with someone so awful? How could you not know what he's like?"

"It really would be better if I talk to Ricky. Since I've never seen this part of Hunter, it's the best way to get me on Ricky's side, to help me know what to say."

She put her hands over her face. I wondered how long her game was going to continue. Now I was certain she was going to demand money. If her son had actually reported an assault and she believed him, she would have already gone to the police. She wouldn't be sitting in a bar sipping champagne. With her hands still covering her face, she spoke in a low, ominous tone. "You shouldn't need to talk to him to be on his side. You should be on his side because an atrocity was committed against him. You need to make it right."

"Why are you talking to me and not Hunter?"

She lowered her hands. "I'm afraid of him! I don't want to face him without the police there by my side! Surely you can understand that!"

Did she somehow sense my aversion to the police? I wanted to tell her to go ahead and call the police, but that was a risk I wouldn't take and I couldn't help wondering if she sensed that. It was the one bluff I never wanted to call. But I did want to talk to Ricky. "Then what do you want from me?"

"I want the money back, and I need that monster to pay for Ricky's therapy. I can't tell Jordan. He would kill your boyfriend. I assume I should call him your ex-boyfriend now. I sure hope so. Otherwise, I will take Ricky to the police to report this. It's the only way to fix it. I prefer to see that creep punished, but I don't want to see Ricky suffer through a trial. And then Jordan would find out."

I nodded. "That makes sense."

I finished my third glass of water. I placed two twenties on the table. "I'll get the rest of the money you paid us. And I guess you'll tell me what therapy will cost?"

She smiled, then adjusted her expression, managing to form a smile that was grieving, tender, and defeated. "I'll have to do some research. To find the most competent person, do some interviews, and find out how many years it will take. It might be challenging also because they're required to report, so I'll need to find someone who will be willing to use discretion. That will require some convincing."

"I can imagine," I said. "I do have one favor. I know I'm not in a position to ask, but …" I looked around nervously. "Can we meet in your hotel room next time? I feel really uncomfortable talking about this in public. And also, handing over the cash. You know. It's… for your safety as well. Don't you think?"

She nodded, her eyes widening as they rolled slightly toward the bar. "I didn't think of that." She picked up her glass and angled it to the side, watching the bubbles. She straightened it, took a sip, and looked at me. "I knew you and I were true friends. I knew you would see how awful this was, that you would choose me and my feelings as a mother over that creepy guy you used to be with."

I nodded. I held my eyes open, waiting for them to get watery from not blinking. After a few seconds, they complied.

She looked ecstatic at my show of emotion.

CHAPTER 49

$\mathcal{E}$ ileen informed me she was hosting a small dinner party. Not the two of us. Just her. And it wasn't something she was thinking about, she'd already chosen a date and issued the invites. This was mine.

"We've been here for ages and haven't entertained at all. With other people around, it will give you and Ned some perfect neutral territory to get on better terms again."

"If you say so."

"Actually, I don't say so. It was his idea." She grinned. "He said I'm a fabulous cook and we should do more things with friends and I haven't shown off how beautifully I've decorated the apartment."

Now I understood. "Sounds good."

"You'll make sure the bird stays quiet?"

"He usually is."

"Sometimes he starts shouting his little phrases."

"If there's music and people are talking, you won't hear him. How many people are invited?"

"Eight, including Ned and me. And Hunter is one of the guests, obviously."

"I don't think so."

"Aww. Why not? I want to meet him. So does Ned."

"I'm not ready for that."

"For what?"

"For socializing as a couple."

"That's kind of … how can you not be ready? You stay over there all the time. You've been seeing him for, what? Two months? Longer?"

"I don't want to invite him."

She heaved an enormous sigh, as if I'd just refused to attend myself, or insisted that Damien sit at the table with us, eating mango and talking about Chardonnay and dangerous women.

"I'm really disappointed," she said.

"Don't be. You should focus on your party. And pleasing the man you love." I smiled. "What are you serving?"

She began describing the food, a five-course meal with everything from chilled cucumber soup to tiramisu. She planned champagne with the appetizer, white wine with the soup and salad, and a nice cabernet with the main course.

"It sounds like a lot of work."

"Don't worry. You know I love cooking. I'm not expecting you to do anything. Just be here at seven like our other guests."

I didn't like the way she phrased that at all. Clearly this was a party thrown by her and Ned as a couple, as if the apartment were their home. Maybe I truly was a guest. Maybe they were planning to ease me out the door with smiles and good food. Maybe that's how she had *worked things out* with Ned.

Two days before the party, she asked me if I could take Damien to Hunter's apartment. She didn't trust that he wouldn't start shouting so loudly that their guests would be disturbed. They might freak out. I said that if the voice of a cockatoo made them freak out, they might not be emotionally stable adults. She said it was the unexpected nature of it. I told her that all she needed to do was explain up front that he might make his presence known. That way, it wouldn't be unexpected.

She said they would all want to traipse into my bedroom to meet him. I suggested I could bring him out. She sighed, looked worried, and begged me to do something to make sure he stayed quiet. I said I would do my best.

The morning of the dinner party, she told me to stay in my room in the hours leading up to the meal so they could prepare the food and set the table. She wanted me to walk in as a guest, not to be wandering around offering to help.

I assured her it wasn't a problem. She reminded me again to keep Damien quiet. I said nothing.

For the occasion, I piled my hair on top of my head and made up my eyes with lots of dark shadow and thick liner. I considered adding extra lashes, but decided not to because I didn't want to spend time removing them before I went over to Hunter's, which was my plan after dinner. He knew nothing about the party, so showing up with inch-long lashes would create too much of a conversation piece.

I wore a fitted, off-the-shoulder black dress and black heels. I wore a gold chain on one wrist and a silver chain on the other. As I admired myself in the mirror, I wondered if I would ever have gems on my wrists and fingers, dangling from my ears and circling my throat. I didn't want a lot of them, but for evenings like this, one or two might be nice.

I reminded myself that less is more, covered Damien's cage so he would think it was time for sleep, which he seemed agreeable to, then sat in the chair in the corner of my room and looked at TikTok while I waited for seven p.m. to arrive.

When I opened my bedroom door, the music playing in the living room grew louder. It smelled heavenly, and I realized I was looking forward to the evening. It was fun meeting new people, and as long as Ned didn't take over the conversation, I imagined it would be entertaining. That, and Eileen was definitely an excellent cook.

The table had pale gray placemats, their matching napkins draped across our simple white plates. There were two wineglasses at every place, and a row of pillar candles down the center that made everything sparkle.

Ned glided over to me. "You look stunning."

"Thank you."

He took my elbow. "Let me introduce you."

I slid my elbow out of his grip, knowing that nothing had changed, and gave him a chilly smile.

He introduced me to a couple who looked to be about his age, both of whom were instructors at NYU, and two men in their forties who did something in technology that I didn't catch, because they immediately turned the conversation to politics.

"None of that." Ned shook his finger at them. "Just good times tonight. No one wants to go home with a headache."

I wondered about the three couples, and what they'd done about the fact that I'd refused to let them include Hunter. Surely they hadn't planned a blind date for me. The thought hadn't crossed my mind until that minute.

I took the glass of champagne Eileen was holding out to me.

The couple who worked in technology also sipped from their glasses.

"Oh, you should have waited." Ned gave us a mocking frown. "We wanted to have a toast after all the guests arrived."

The three of us clutched our glasses, smiling at each other.

Nothing was at *all* different. I wasn't sure why I'd imagined it might be. The problem wasn't the way Ned behaved toward me at all, the problem was the way he behaved.

The buzzer announced the final guest was in the lobby. Eileen pressed the button to grant access and several minutes later, there was a knock on the door.

"Why don't you answer it, Alexandra," Ned suggested.

"That's silly," Eileen said. "We're the hosts." She walked to the door and opened it, stepping to the side.

Standing in the doorway, immediately recognizable after months of not having seen him, was Kent, with his shaved head polished to a sheen. He wore a black T-shirt and a black suit, the clothes cut to subtly show his well-developed shoulders and chest muscles.

CHAPTER 50

I looked across the room with a cool smile, wondering if Eileen knew who Kent was. If she did, was she setting me up as well, or was it just Ned?

My next thought was to consider whether I should leave immediately or let things play out. Of course, an immediate departure would make Ned think he'd won, but it would also keep him from gathering ammunition, or at least believing he'd gathered ammunition.

Staying might also make him think he'd won, because he might believe I was trapped and too afraid to confront him or make a scene in front of Eileen.

It was possible Ned had actually learned something about me from Kent. It was possible Kent had come to believe I had something to do with the way Rafe had vanished so suddenly. But if he did, wouldn't he have gone to the police? And no matter what he believed, or thought he knew, there was no evidence. I was confident about that. He'd seen nothing. Even if he'd talked to Victoria, he knew nothing.

The only risk was in my own mind. The only risk was my own tongue.

Unless Ned had something else in mind.

I walked slowly toward the entryway, shifting my champagne glass to my left hand. "Kent. What a surprise." I held out my hand, pleased with my self-restraint. I'd been about to gush that I didn't know he was friends with Eileen, or Ned. But of course I did. Ned had already told me about their chance encounter.

This was all I needed to do. I needed to remember Kent's approach to life—minimalist. The fewer words I said, the better. And for that reason, I would not only count the words I allowed to slip across my tongue, I needed to count the sips of alcohol that ran down my throat.

Instead of taking my hand, Kent slid his arm around my waist and gave me half a hug, jostling my glass of champagne. He kissed my cheek. "It's great to see you."

He sounded genuinely pleased. Then I wondered if he also was aware of Ned's game. Perhaps not. I could imagine that Ned fancied himself the ringmaster, the manipulator of a fantastic game of cat and mouse. He was going to end up snipping off his own tail.

Eileen was walking around with a tray of olive tapenade on paper-thin slices of toast. I took one and ate it.

"I can see why you moved out of our building," Kent said. "This place is nice."

"Isn't it?"

"Although I never pictured you with a roommate."

I smiled.

"How did you two meet?"

"I used to work with Eileen's mother."

He nodded. "Oh, right. The one who—"

"Yes."

I asked him about his job, and he asked about mine. I asked if he was seeing anyone. He was, so at least any ridiculous plan to set us up had not been part of Ned's agenda. Eileen passed by with a tray that now contained a small strip of prosciutto wrapped around a sliver of melon. I took one of those and ate it. I hadn't sipped my champagne following the toast. Kent's glass was half empty.

I asked who was living in my old apartment and he told me about three actors sharing the one-bedroom apartment to save money on rent, and the social media influencer who had moved into Victoria and Rafe's apartment. I asked him what the actors were performing in and he managed to fill the rest of the time with stories about their auditions. They were very sociable, and he'd spent a lot of time hanging out in their crowded, rather funky apartment.

When we were seated at the table, the conversation turned more general and I wondered when Ned was going to shine his spotlight on me. I wondered how their other guests would feel when they learned they were the supporting cast for his vendetta instead of guests at a dinner party.

I could see the evening might turn out to be a disappointing mess for everyone.

We were halfway into Eileen's chicken piccata when there was a lull in the conversation.

Ned placed his hand firmly on Kent's forearm. "Speaking of people who disappear from our lives, Kent has an interesting story to tell."

Kent looked at him, lowering his brow slightly.

"Your day-trading neighbors," Ned prompted.

"Yeah." Kent looked at me. "I don't think—"

"It's fascinating. You should tell the story."

"There's not a lot to tell," Kent said.

I cut a small piece of chicken and placed it in my mouth. It was absolutely delicious. I chewed it slowly. I raised my wineglass toward Eileen. "Superb."

She smiled.

"Trying to change the subject, Alexandra?" Ned asked.

"Not at all. What was the subject?"

"Your old neighbors. Tell everyone how strange that was, Kent."

Looking as if he wanted to leave the table, and possibly the apartment, never a guy who liked the spotlight on him, Kent cleared his throat. He took a sip of water. "The guy was found dead in a hotel room. Then his wife took off. She left everything behind. The landlord had to clean the place out."

"Ooh," said Danny, one of the tech guys. "She killed him because he traded the wrong stock."

"Or she wanted all the cash," said Leo, one of the NYU instructors.

Ned chuckled. "Kent didn't tell you the interesting part."

"I don't think—"

"She can take it. Nothing ruffles Alexandra. In fact, it might be fun to see her blush. I've never seen this woman blush." He looked right at me, his expression slightly leering.

I wasn't sure if he wanted to threaten me or simply watch me squirm. If it was the latter, he was never going to be satisfied.

Ned raised his voice. "What's interesting to me, is right after that, Alexandra here took off just as suddenly. At least that's how Kent sees it, right, buddy?"

"I didn't really... I was just thinking out loud. I didn't want to discuss it in public," Kent said. "Let's talk about something else."

Now, everyone had put down their utensils and was staring at me and Kent. Everyone but Eileen, who was staring at the food getting cold on their plates.

"I just think it's interesting that Alexandra suddenly has enough cash to move to an upscale apartment here. Is it from blackmail, because she knows something about the lovers' quarrel turned to murder? Or someone running afoul of the SEC, another route to blackmail? Or, skimming off a percentage for herself? There are several possibilities."

"Ned!"

Ned looked at Eileen.

"Let's enjoy our dinner and discuss something of interest to all our guests," she said.

"We were talking about—"

She cut him off. "Leo, are you still planning that trip to Greece this fall? I keep telling myself I want to travel more, and then I get so caught up in all the things to do in New York. Give us all the details."

Leo launched into his itinerary. Eileen had definitely picked the right person to change the subject. The specifics of dates and hotels, landmarks and tours, woven with historical information turned everyone back to their food since there was little room for any real conversation.

I decided I would hold out until the bitter end of the dinner, but something had to be done about Ned. He was not giving up, he was doubling down. So would I. But my usual method of resolving problems was not an option right now. I needed a different solution.

CHAPTER 51

 *ortland, Oregon*

* * *

The problem with Jimmy's treehouse was that I wanted to possess it. Just as much as he wanted those ceramic animals. But I couldn't sneak into his yard when no one was watching, take it apart piece by piece, and re-build it in my own backyard like he seemed to want to do with the animal village.

I'd asked my mother if we could have a treehouse. She said ask your father.

Knowing the answer would be that treehouses aren't for girls, I asked my father anyway. He said, "Your brothers are too old for a treehouse."

At night, when I was supposed to be repeating my weekly bible verse before sleep so that I would be able to recite it perfectly at dinner on Saturday, the dress rehearsal for Sunday school, I thought about how I could get Jimmy kicked out of his own treehouse.

His brother wasn't interested and if Jimmy was grounded, I could play in there by myself.

The next time I was in the treehouse with him, I told him to set up the ceramic animals. I pointed out that he only had eight. Leaning out the window, I counted out loud. "There are eight more animals. If you had all of them, you could make houses for them and have your own town up here where no one could see it."

"You'd have to be the lookout and you said you won't do it anymore."

"I changed my mind," I said.

"Why?"

"Because girls always change their minds."

"Yeah. I heard that."

I smiled. "Go get some boxes first. And paint and scissors, to make the houses. We need tape, too. And does your mom have sewing stuff?"

"What for?"

"For decoration. If we want a really cool village for them. It won't be as good as hers, but it will be really nice."

He nodded.

"Go get that stuff."

"Okay." He stood. "You need to help me carry it."

"Use a shopping bag. I'll watch over the animals while you're gone."

He squinted at me, his eyes doubtful.

I wondered if I was suddenly too excited about the animals. He seemed to notice that something was different about me. "I promise I'll keep them safe," I said.

He climbed down the ladder, and I returned to the window. I stared into the neighbors' backyard and tried to think about what I could do to make sure Jimmy was caught in the act. Maybe if he broke one...

I wasn't sure what they would do. I *was* sure the lady next door loved her animals and wanted to keep them safe since she had that brick wall and a gate that latched. They didn't have any children and most people that didn't have children didn't like to have children touching their things. I knew this from people on our street who got very upset when kids stepped on their grass or picked their flowers. People with kids were happy to have children pick their flowers or run across the lawn.

I had to get her on my side. I climbed down the ladder and walked into her yard. I went to the pottery shed and knocked on the door. She opened it right away.

She smiled, then looked over my head, maybe expecting to see my mother. "What can I do for you, sweetheart?"

"The boy next door is stealing the clay animals from your brick garden."

"Who are you?"

"I live on the other side." I waved my arm toward the trees. "But I thought you would want to know."

"What's your name?"

"Alexandra."

"I'm MaryAnne." She stepped out and took my hand. "You're a beautiful little girl, Alexandra. And very brave for knocking on a stranger's door. And for being honest. Telling the truth is hard."

I didn't think it was that hard, but grownups didn't like children arguing with them. "Let's go look at the world of magical creatures."

"Is that what you call it?"

"Yes. It's for my grandchildren. They only visit once a year because they live in England. Have you heard of that?"

"Yes."

"So you're beautiful and smart."

I smiled.

She unlatched the gate, and we went inside. I knew I was winning. Jimmy would have to give the animals back and Mary-Anne would know that I told the truth. No matter what Jimmy said about me.

When she saw the missing animals, she let go of my hand. She put both her hands over her mouth and let out a tiny sound like a cat meowing. "Why would he do this?"

"He thinks they're cool."

"But they don't belong to him."

I nodded.

"Does he know they're fragile? They'll break if he drops one. Where did he put them?" She looked around, as if she thought they might be hidden in the garden.

"In his treehouse."

She turned toward Jimmy's backyard, looking up at the enormous tree, the branches stretching close to the side of her own yard. Most of the treehouse was covered by leaves. We could see one corner of the roof, a piece of the wall, and the window where I'd stood watch when Jimmy stole her animals.

"Why?"

"He just likes them."

"But why would he steal them? I would have let him look at them, if he'd asked."

"I watched him take them. He wanted me to be the lookout." Since she admired honesty, I decided I would tell her the whole story. Besides, if Jimmy mentioned that part, it was better if she knew. I was the one she trusted. I hoped she would think he forced me into it. And that's exactly what she decided to think.

"That's terrible." She put her hand on my head and stroked my hair. "You remind me of my oldest granddaughter. She loves these animals. Both my granddaughters will be visiting at the end of the summer. Maybe you can meet them."

I nodded. I wondered if her granddaughters would want to play in the treehouse.

"Thank you for telling me. I'll speak to Jimmy's parents. I know his mother."

I smiled.

"You're such a sweet girl. So honest."

We walked out of the garden. She paused for a few minutes, looking toward the treehouse.

"Will you bring them back?"

I nodded.

"Thank you, sweetheart."

I gave her an obedient smile.

"If you'd like to choose one to keep, it would make me happy."

"It's okay. I want your granddaughters to play with them."

"I really want you to have one."

"It's fine," I said.

She stroked my hair again. "You have a good heart."

I crossed the yard and climbed the ladder to the treehouse. From the window, I looked out. MaryAnne was watching me. I waved at her and she waved back. I picked up the bear and carried it down. One by one, I returned all the animals.

Jimmy never came back outside that day, because as soon as the animals were safe in their walled garden, MaryAnne walked between the two houses toward the front yard of Jimmy's house.

For the next two weeks, I didn't see Jimmy or his brother.

I went into his treehouse every day and no one noticed. I took my own toys and played up there, inventing whatever games I wanted. I looked out the window at the animals in the brick garden.

At the end of the summer, I met MaryAnne's granddaughters from England. I liked their accents, and I played in the brick garden with them one time. I never played with Jimmy or his brother again, but that was fine because after that summer, I was tired of the treehouse.

CHAPTER 52

$\mathcal{N}$*ew York*

* * *

Because Andy was such a problem, we were taking the unprecedented step of reviewing Brie's photographs at the Fly Higher offices instead of on her territory. Also, because Andy had proven himself to be a man who didn't listen and couldn't be bothered to follow our guidelines, and Brie was a woman unlikely to stand up to him, and not necessarily interested in standing up to him, Diana had told the security staff that Andy was not welcome in the building.

I wondered what would happen when he challenged them. It wasn't as if we had a restraining order, and Andy did not respond to the word no.

When I mentioned this to Diana, she said she didn't think it would be a problem.

Diana never thought things would be problems because she expected situations to unfold according to her liking. Of course, I always hoped for the same, but I also expected people to do as they pleased. Diana seemed to believe the sheer force of her desire and her expectation of good behavior would magically influence the circumstances around her.

When the guy at the reception desk called to say Brie had arrived for her three o'clock appointment but she was accompanied by the man we'd said wasn't to be admitted, Diana was upset.

"I don't want a scene in the lobby. It will make us look bad," she said.

I agreed. "Maybe we should cancel the contract with Brie."

"Not yet. Now it's become a point of pride for me. She needs our help, don't you think?"

"But she doesn't want it. She can't cope without him. And if she won't tell him to back off, there's nothing we can do."

"I don't think she would still be making an effort to work with us if she didn't want our insight and support. I'm not ready to give up." Diana leaned against the doorframe of her office. She closed her eyes and pinched the bridge of her nose with her index finger and thumb. "There has to be a solution I'm not seeing."

I could think of a solution, but with a guy like Andy, even my solution might be difficult to implement. He would be challenging to manipulate, unruly and unpredictable. I wasn't sure how I would even get him to a place where I could be rid of him. And I wasn't sure I would peel him away from Brie's side long enough to be rid of him. "I'll go down and talk to him."

"After what happened? That's not a good idea," she said.

"It's not a problem. I'll send Brie up here and you can get started."

Diana was still talking, telling me it wasn't a good idea as I walked out the door.

Downstairs in our large, open lobby, filled with the voices of people having impromptu meetings and making plans for after-work drinks, Brie was frowning at the receptionist, speaking to him in a confident, somewhat too-loud voice.

"It's insulting to have him treated like a criminal," she said. "Andy co-manages one of the premier health brands in the city." She thrust her chest forward. "Bodies By Brie. You've heard of us, I'm sure."

The receptionist ignored her advertising. "This is what I was told."

"Hi, Brie." I extended my hand. She ignored it.

"Look who's here," Andy said. "All must be forgiven."

"Diana was really clear—"

"We're a team," Brie said. "Andy is my muse. He literally *created* my body and I don't know why I have to keep explaining that."

"If you want coaching from Fly Higher, you come as an individual," I said. "Solo. That's it. So you can go up now, alone, or we're done." I smiled.

"Is that what Diana said?"

Andy made a growling sound. "Ooh. The lady has fangs."

"You can go up now. I'll see Andy out. Or you can both leave. Your call."

"It's so disrespectful," Brie said.

"We've already talked about this. It's getting tiresome." I glanced at the clock behind the desk. "You have thirty seconds."

Andy did a weird shimmy. "A threat? Will the police arrive with guns drawn if Brie doesn't get into the elevator before the second hand hits the twelve?"

I said nothing.

Brie gave Andy a helpless look.

Andy looked at me. He moved closer, gazing directly into my eyes. I stared back at him, unblinking. After half a second, he took a step back. "Hey, Brie. Maybe this is a girls' afternoon, a women helping women thing. I'll leave you to it. You can tell me all about it. *Allll*, about it. Tonight. During your massage. Okay, sweets?"

She gave him a sad puppy look. "They don't *get* us. How will it help me reach for the stars if they don't *get* us?"

He shrugged. "Maybe you'll pick up a few crumbs you can use. It's a lotta cash for crumbs, but ya' never know." He turned and walked toward the doors.

CHAPTER 53

*B*rie and I took the elevator to our floor. She didn't speak to me.

We sat in the conference room. Fallon brought us coffee and a box of cookies she'd picked up from a bakery that she began arranging on a plate.

Diana displayed the bulleted summary of Ian's micro-expression analysis on the screen beside four photographs of Brie—two from the day at her gym and two from the Metropolitan Museum of Art.

"Our analyst has pointed out something very clear," Diana said. "Andy is suffocating you. Without him, you seem to hardly believe you exist."

"Not true," Brie said.

"You're paying a lot for our expertise," Diana said. "Please hear me out."

"You can't look at a picture and know something like that. You don't know Andy at all. You don't understand what he's done for me. He made me—my body *and* my ambition, and my business. He formed who I am."

"If that's the case, why did you come to us?" Diana asked.

"Because I want to do more."

"And he can't do that for you?"

"He thought it was a good idea for me to learn more about myself. He said I was getting a little boring."

"He's sucked the life out of you," Diana said. "You don't seem to have any independent thoughts, or any self-esteem."

"Yes, I do. I look amazing. My workout centers are incredibly successful. All my members are ecstatic. Our attrition rate is almost non-existent."

Diana brought up the next slide. "Here are more photographs from the museum. If I go through these quickly, in chronological order from when they were taken ..." she clicked through the images rapidly, all of them showing tight close-ups of Brie's face. "Your increasing anxiety is so clear we didn't even need our expert to speak to it. Alex saw it. The longer you were separated from Andy, the more uncomfortable you were, the more upset. In these last few, you appear lost, as if you're unsure of where you are."

Brie folded her arms across her chest. She glared at me as if my camera had betrayed her. It had. That was the goal.

"I don't know what kind of relationship you have with Andy," Diana said, "if he's your lover, or just a business partner, a longtime friend, a roommate, a mentor—"

"He's—"

"I don't need to know. In fact, I don't want to know. I'm telling you, if you don't find a way to construct strong boundaries in that relationship, you won't achieve anything more. In fact, you might eventually find yourself unable to function without him. If you haven't reached that point already."

Brie laughed. She grabbed the edge of the table, pinching it until her fingertips were drained of blood, almost the same color as her white nail polish. "I function just fine without him." She squeezed harder, bending the tips of her nails toward the table so it looked as if she might claw it. "This isn't at all helpful."

"It's the truth. You paid us for the hard truths."

"I'd be nothing without him."

"Is that what you honestly believe? Do you think you wouldn't exist as a human being without Andy? Would your business never have come into being without him? That makes you nothing but a company logo or spokesperson."

"I'm Brie! I'm the Brie in Bodies By Brie!"

"What does that mean to you? To your clients? To Andy?" Diana asked.

Brie glared at her, fingers still pinching the table, her pupils like pinpricks, even though the light in the room wasn't overly bright.

I was starting to feel as if I was in a cult that worked to provoke an existential crisis in its devotees. Was this Diana's normal methodology? Was she trying to unravel Brie's sense of herself on purpose? Did she have any idea what she was doing? It was possible that Brie might have some kind of breakdown right in front of us. How would Diana handle that? Call the police to have her taken for an involuntary commitment to the psychiatric ward at the nearest hospital?

Then I wondered about Andy. Most likely, he hadn't gone far. That wasn't how these two operated. I was absolutely certain he was just outside the main doors, waiting.

I wanted to excuse myself. I wanted the meeting to be over. Reviewing a client's photographs had never been like this. Usually our clients nodded, made comments and thanked us for the insights into their previously unnoticed areas of weakness.

They didn't raise their voices in panic, as if they were terrified someone was trying to strip away their identity.

"Should we take a break?" Diana asked.

"What for?" Brie asked.

"You seem very upset."

"Because you're not helping. You attacked Andy, and now you're attacking me."

"What did you expect to achieve, working with us?"

"I wrote all that down, why are you asking me?" Brie let go of the table and shoved her chair back violently.

"I want to hear you say it now. I wonder if you can put it into a few simple statements off the top of your head. When you wrote that, you had time to think about what you wanted to say."

Brie rolled her eyes. "I want to expand. I want to make a bigger name for myself."

"Okay. That's good. And that aligns with what you said at the outset. Now if you could expand on—"

"Of course it *aligns*, because I wrote it! What is all this? I'm beginning to realize you don't really know what you're doing. That this is all just bullshit." She stood.

"Please sit down."

"This isn't helping me."

"We haven't even started. I need you to approach our process with an open mind. I need you to consider whether Andy might be holding you back. Can you consider asking yourself that question?"

"Okay. Done." Brie grabbed her purse. "I want a refund."

"That's not possible," Diana said.

"I'll put it in writing. And you can be sure I'll tell anyone who asks that this is a useless service. I can't believe you're trying to undermine the core of who I am and what makes Bodies By Brie what it is. You have no right. And if I don't get my refund, Andy will have something to say about that." She stalked out of the room, looking as if she would punch anyone who got in her way between our conference room and the moment she reunited with Andy.

Diana closed her laptop.

"Are you giving her a refund?" I asked.

"No."

"Do you think she'll cause trouble?"

Diana shrugged.

"Do you think she has a right to a partial?" I asked.

"Not after he assaulted you." She stood.

In that moment between her standing and my next breath, I thought that things might return to a calmer state between us. I thought the tension had finally dissolved.

"Layla Lipman, James's sister, is coming to pick up his things from his office next Tuesday. Make sure you're here between eleven and twelve."

After she was gone, I had the uneasy sensation that she'd told me that simply because she didn't want me to feel the tension had dissolved. But I might have been imagining it.

CHAPTER 54

*A*sking to meet in Carolina's hotel room might bring me face-to-face with Ricky. I hoped to find out if the lie was his idea alone, owned completely by his mother, or something they'd worked on together in order to extort money from me. I just couldn't figure out why they needed money.

Jordan's position allowed them to live indefinitely in a five-star hotel. Carolina wore designer clothes. Her son took classes at an expensive gym. Everything about her suggested she didn't have to con a woman she ran into at the spa. Or had she identified me as a mark before that? Since the law firm was covering their expenses, maybe the designer close stressed their budget. Maybe their home was modest, their lifestyle in Michigan more scaled down. Maybe this was unfamiliar luxury that she'd now tasted and wanted more of.

Or, maybe Jordan wasn't as easy-going as he'd seemed. Maybe he was one of those with a pleasant smile and a perfect social demeanor that was entirely fabricated. Maybe Carolina was hysterical and unpredictable and living on the border of a fantasy world with a creepy and strange son because her husband was a monster.

Only a conversation alone with Ricky, an attempt to get past his weird, leering, sometimes little kid, sometimes twenty-five-year-old man behavior, would answer those questions. I wasn't certain I would be able to get him alone, or get any answers, but the hotel room was the most likely place where I could attempt to make any of that happen. And for that reason, I'd shown up half an hour early.

I knocked on the door and Ricky opened it.

I smiled. I couldn't have asked for a better way to start the evening, which was supposed to involve a glass of wine with Carolina before I continued on my way home, before she and Ricky met Jordan for a rare, *treasured*, as she'd said in a gooey voice, family dinner.

Ricky leaned against the doorframe, sliding his hand up, so his arm was straight above, as if he thought it might make him look taller, or more in control of the situation. "It's the pedo's girlfriend," he said.

"It's the pathological liar."

He lowered his arm. "What do you want?" His voice was a growl.

"Your mother invited me over for a glass of wine."

"She didn't mention it to me."

"Go ask her."

"She's not here."

As I'd hoped. "I'll come in and wait."

"I don't believe you. Why would she invite you over here? We're in a legal battle with you and the pedo."

"Why don't you and I talk?"

"Are you wearing a wire?"

I laughed. "Let me in." I moved closer to the doorway.

"Let me check."

"For a wire? No." I slid between him and the doorframe.

He grabbed my forearm, but I kept going, dragging him after me. His boxing lessons must not have given him much strength. Or maybe his bravado had never been challenged until now.

"If you think you're going to trap me into saying something you can use against me, you're not very smart," he said.

239

"And you are?" I sat on the couch and crossed my legs. "When is your mother coming back?"

"I don't know. She didn't tell me you were coming."

"Surprise."

"I can call security."

"Go ahead. But I'd like to have a little chat with you. Aren't you curious to hear what I have to say?"

"No."

"Why did you lie about Hunter?"

"It's not a lie."

I looked at him, waiting for him to wilt and admit what he was doing. But even though he had a weak grip, he was stronger in this way and I should have known that from what I'd witnessed the few times I'd been around him. "Why didn't you tell your father about it?" I asked.

"My mom doesn't want to upset him."

"What do you think your father would do?"

"Go to the police. Or kill your boyfriend."

"Has your dad killed people before?"

"No."

"Then why do you think he would kill someone now?"

"Because this is really bad."

I nodded. "Is it the worst thing that's ever happened to you?"

He looked away from me. "Yeah."

Liar.

I heard a key card in the lock. I wasn't too disappointed. I'd already learned more than I'd hoped for, although I hadn't learned if the shakedown was her idea or his. Most likely hers. Maybe the idea for the story had come from him. It didn't really matter.

The door opened. "Oh." Carolina looked at me, then Ricky, then back at me. "You're early."

"Ricky was nice enough to let me in so I didn't have to hang around in the hallway where a security guard might get too curious about what I was up to."

She gave Ricky a disapproving glance.

"Should we all talk about what we're going to do?" I asked.

"There's nothing to talk about. You were supposed to bring... " Carolina glanced at Ricky.

"I wanted to talk—"

"I hope you realize I'm serious here," she said. "The entire reason I agreed to allow you into our rooms was so you could return what you owe in a private setting."

"So, you and Ricky share a room?"

Her face turned dark red. I wasn't sure if it was anger or embarrassment. "Of course not. I'm in his room because this is where we do his lessons. We have adjoining rooms, but my husband is working right now. He can't be disturbed. Not that our arrangement is any of your business whatsoever."

I uncrossed my legs, stretched them out, and put my feet on the coffee table. I leaned back as if I planned to stay for a while.

"I don't want her here," Ricky said, a distinct whine in his voice.

"I know, sweetie." Carolina patted his knee.

"Why did you tell her she could come here? I don't feel safe."

I laughed. "You don't feel safe? I thought Hunter was the one you were worried about."

"It's not a joke!" Ricky said.

"I need to hear about your therapy," I said.

"I don't have that worked out yet," Carolina said.

"Still calling around to see who will give him therapy without reporting what they're required to report?"

"I don't want to discuss it with you. Did you bring it or not?"

"I have half. Almost. I told you I needed to speak to Hunter and it would—"

"What do you mean, almost half?"

"I spent some of it." I smiled.

"Surely you can make up the difference. With your fancy photography job."

It was funny how her fascination with my work had turned sour.

Had she been setting me up from the moment we met? Or had it come to her later, at the same time as the babysitting gig, or after that? When she realized how stupid she'd been to pay someone that much money to make sure her troubled son didn't create chaos when she wasn't around. What was it like to be raising a kid that she couldn't leave alone? A kid that, perhaps, she couldn't even trust to send to school so she had to teach him herself?

At what point would she become afraid of him herself?

"Do you and Ricky ever fight?"

"What does that have to do with anything?"

"Just curious. You seem very close for a mother and son. And really, any relationship with that much togetherness—living in such a small group of rooms, being his mother and his teacher—I would think it might be a situation that would cause more than the usual parent-child disagreements."

"Ricky is a good boy."

"We get along fine," Ricky said.

"You're a little old to be with mommy all the time," I said.

"Don't be ugly." Carolina stood. "We've talked long enough. Where's the money?"

"I thought we were having a glass of wine?"

"Do you even have the money?"

I reached into my bag and pulled out half the wad of cash she'd given me so recently. I hated parting with it. Free money is always nice, and it had been fun having some extra to spend.

She placed her phone on the table, and I handed the cash to her.

She thumbed the bills, moving her lips as she counted. I wondered how good she was at teaching math to her son if she couldn't calculate the total amount in a stack of large denomination bills without moving her lips while she did the counting.

"You're missing eight hundred dollars," she said.

I held out my hand. "Let me count it again. Why don't you get a bottle of wine?"

"I know how to count!"

"Let me just double-check and I'll Venmo the rest."

She handed the money back to me, pacified for a moment.

"You could Venmo me his half too, surely he's good for it," she said.

"Just get the wine."

She went into the other room. I handed the cash to Ricky. "Why don't you count it, then she'll trust the number."

His eyes lit up as if I'd handed him his own cell phone. He grabbed the cash and began counting, separating it into piles on the coffee table.

While he was busy with his math project, I picked up Carolina's cell phone and powered it down. After a few seconds, I powered it on again, then placed it on the table where she'd left it and settled back on the couch.

Carolina returned with two glasses containing skimpy pours of wine. She handed one to me and took a sip from the other glass.

"It's one-thousand-seven hundred dollars," Ricky announced.

"You let him count it?"

I picked up my wineglass and stood. I took a few steps away from the couch and positioned myself slightly behind Carolina. "I let him count it so you would believe the number," I said. "Anyway, I Venmo'd you the difference."

She picked up her phone. She tapped the screen angrily when the display for entering her passcode appeared. "That's weird," she muttered. She entered her passcode. It wasn't as simplistic as I'd expected from her, but close—121212—so easy to pick it out looking over her shoulder.

"There's no update from you."

"I sent it."

"Well, it's not here."

"Maybe it takes a few minutes."

"It shouldn't." She put her phone on the table. "Never mind. I would rather have cash anyway."

Of course she would. She didn't want Jordan to know.

"Since I don't have Hunter's share anyway, I'll give it to you all at once. I guess you'll have to wait."

"I don't *have* to wait. You and your *ex*-boyfriend are in a lot of trouble."

"I'm not in any trouble. Ricky hasn't accused me of assaulting him."

"You were an accomplice."

"That's not what he said."

"You were there," she said.

"An accomplice is someone who helps commit a crime. I didn't help anything. I watched Ricky watch TV."

"You gave that man access to my son. I asked you to provide childcare because I trusted you and you brought a strange man, a *pedophile*, into our home."

"You met Hunter. You didn't say a word about not wanting him there."

She picked up Ricky's stacks of cash, grabbed her purse from the end of the couch, and stuffed the bills inside. "You're still in trouble. When are you bringing the rest?"

"When will you know the cost for therapy that you're expecting Hunter to pay?"

"Soon."

"That's when I'll bring the rest." I went to the door. "It was so nice talking to you, Ricky. I hope we can talk again soon."

"Don't play games with him," Carolina said.

I smiled and went out. I walked to the elevator wondering exactly what I was going to do now that I had access to her phone. I was absolutely confident an idea would come to me.

CHAPTER 55

$\mathcal{O}$n Friday, I told Hunter I would pick up Thai food. We could eat at his apartment and binge something on TV. What I really wanted was to spend the entire weekend at his place. But despite my heavy-duty lock and the security camera, I still didn't like leaving Damien alone overnight in the apartment I shared with Eileen.

After Ned had whipped Kent out of his virtual back pocket and presented him to me at the dinner party, spoiling Eileen's fun while hoping to make me squirm, all in one outrageous act of manipulation, I wanted to be as far as I could from that guy.

Eileen and I hadn't talked about the dinner, beyond me telling her the food was amazing.

I hadn't seen Ned at all, and I hadn't heard from Kent. I'd wondered if I might, and I still wondered about that, even though it had been a week. Kent was the brooding type, maybe a little like me. He might suddenly appear outside my building, or even outside my apartment door because Ned had buzzed him up, wanting to ask me a question that had been nagging at him. I hoped not. I hoped he'd moved on. At the same time, I'd had the distinct impression that the only reason Kent was giving any thought to our old neighbors at all was because Ned had been feeding him leading questions, based on nothing but far-too-lucky guesses. Still, I couldn't be sure.

I ordered the Thai food from my desk and left work. I walked slowly along East 53rd, feeling the warm summer air on my face. I was glad I'd dressed casually in comfortable sandals that showed off my fresh, plum-colored pedicure, a plum T-shirt, and denim skirt.

As I walked, I moved easily, weaving among the people coming at me who didn't always choose to travel in a smooth flow. They were more like a school of fish, darting this way and that, stopping to read restaurant menus, turning abruptly toward the curb to hail cabs, and stopping to check their phones.

I arrived at the Thai restaurant six minutes before my order was scheduled for pickup. I'd thought about Ubering to Hunter's so the food wouldn't get cold, but it was such perfect weather, warm enough that everything felt calm and peaceful. I sat on a chair and flipped through the free newspaper. I dropped it back onto the table and watched the people coming in for dinner. Once my order was ready, I paid and walked outside. As I adjusted my grip on the bag, a sudden movement caught the corner of my eye. I glanced to my left just as a man lunged into a restaurant two doors down as if he were sick and in desperate need of a place to sit or a restroom.

I turned and started walking. It was only ten blocks to Hunter's. If I kept a steady pace, the food would stay warm. They packed it well and it wasn't as if frigid air surrounded the paper bag.

I stopped for a traffic light. I felt the pedestrians behind me stop as suddenly as I had and my mind flashed back to the man lunging into the restaurant. I wondered what had been wrong with him. There was something strange about it, something that had made me look, but I couldn't figure out what. Obviously, it wasn't something I saw every day, but there seemed to be more to it.

I glanced behind me. It seemed as if the crowd jostled against each other more roughly than usual.

When I turned back, the light flashed green, and I stepped into the street. I walked quickly with a slightly uneasy feeling now. I was overcome by the sensation that I was being followed. I wasn't sure if it was because of that man lunging so awkwardly into the restaurant. It might have been my sudden awareness that I was more vulnerable than I should have been in my light summer clothes, weighed down by a bag of food, or Hunter's half-teasing suggestion that he could hire a private investigator to learn more about me.

I thought about Carolina and her determination to extort money from me. I thought about James and Rafe and the other men I'd killed in New York. All of them had been cleanly taken care of, but no one is perfect.

I didn't like the direction my thoughts were taking, searching my memory for mistakes I knew weren't there. I'd wanted to enjoy the early evening light and the summer air, the streets and the press of people and the hundreds, thousands of stranger's faces and voices flowing past me.

I turned onto West 11th, not the most direct route, but the best way to ease my mind just in case someone was following. I was about five blocks from Hunter's place.

It was just now twilight. *No one* was following me. My imagination was being overactive. It wasn't as if Kent had suddenly grown an interest in potential financial crimes, and that seemed to be Ned's mindset. It was a line of thinking I should have been pleased with. And it wasn't as if Carolina wanted to hurt me physically. She wanted to drain as much cash as she could out of me. Maybe Jordan saw that she was unbalanced and kept her on a tight allowance. No one was trying to find out what had happened to the men I'd killed, with the exception of Diana and her concern for James. But she wasn't devoting all her time to it. She was upset. That was all.

No one was following me, ready to uncover my darkest secrets.

No one was mingling with the crowd, lunging into restaurants when they thought I might catch sight of them. What would they even be planning? They couldn't grab me off a busy street at this time of day. Where would they take me? I suppose someone could slide a long knife between my ribs and lose himself, or herself, in the crowd quickly enough. They would be gone before my body collapsed onto the pavement and the blood began to flow.

But I still couldn't shake the feeling there was someone back there, tracking every step, turning each corner I did, crossing every street I crossed. But now, I'd turned it around in my mind so many times, I had no idea if it was my excessive thinking along those lines giving me that feeling, or if it was my hyper-alert sixth sense telling me something truly wasn't right.

CHAPTER 56

*A*gain, my thoughts turned to the man who had lunged into the restaurant.

I was now only a block from Hunter's apartment. If someone was watching me, tracking where I went. I didn't want them to know where Hunter lived. I also didn't want our dinner to get cold.

I stopped in the middle of the sidewalk.

A woman nearly crashed into me. She glared at me. She pushed her sunglasses against the bridge of her nose. "Watch where you're going."

She had it backwards, but I simply smiled.

She frowned, then must have realized it was getting dark. She pulled off her glasses, stepped around me, and continued on. Now, my caution had risen to such a level, I couldn't help wondering if she might be some sort of decoy sent to distract me.

I turned slowly. All around me, people hurried toward their destinations, hardly noticing I was rooted to the center of the sidewalk like a misplaced lamppost.

Moving toward the building on my right, I shoved my hand inside the paper bag. The food containers were still warm, so that was good. I looped the strings of the takeout bag over my arm and my messenger bag over my head so the strap was across my body.

A few feet to my right was an opening between two buildings. I moved into the enclosure and stood there, watching the passersby, wondering if the person following me had seen me stop suddenly, then move into my hiding place. *If* there was a person following me. I mostly thought it was all in my imagination, brought about by too many people causing too much disruption in my life and by over-thinking everything.

Then, I saw Ned walk by, looking slightly lost.

So. All the thoughts trying to assure myself I was imagining things had been the erroneous ones. My gut had been right from the moment I sensed something unusual. Looking at his clothes, I was certain he was the man I'd seen lunge into the restaurant. It had been an awkward, amateur effort to avoid being seen. And in his ridiculous effort to escape being spotted, he'd attracted my atten-tion and remained in my thoughts until my awareness of his pres-ence became oppressive. I wanted to laugh, but then, he would have looked directly at me.

For now, I wanted to see what he would do. And, of course, I wanted to follow him.

That also meant cold food. But that's what microwaves were for, even if it meant the texture of the spring rolls wouldn't be very nice.

Ned took a few more steps forward, then paused. He turned in a complete circle, scanning the opposite side of the street to see if I'd somehow managed to dart through the congested traffic to the opposite side. He retraced his steps until I lost sight of him. I remained where I was, confident he would turn again and proceed in the direction I'd been going when he lost sight of me.

Sure enough, a few minutes later, he passed by again. This time, I thought there was a definite chance he would glance to the side and notice me pressed against the wall of the alcove, but he didn't. He had assumed I'd suddenly changed course, not that I'd noticed his clumsy presence and hidden myself from him.

He disappeared from view, and I waited. After an appropriate length of time, I stepped out onto the sidewalk. Ned was at the next corner, looking up and down East 13th Street. He jerked his head from side-to-side frantically, as if he'd lost a child and was afraid they might run out into traffic. Then, he turned slowly, but didn't see me since there were now quite a few people between us.

The light changed to green and he trudged across the street, still moving his head as if there were a crick in his neck. He reached the opposite sidewalk and continued at a much slower pace, obviously aware that he had no idea where he was going and continuing in any direction was futile. Finally, he stopped.

I caught up to him.

"Looking for someone?"

His face flushed. "Alex. You're the last person I expected to—"

I laughed. "I watched you following me, so I think I'm the first person you expected to see."

His flush deepened to a red so dark I thought he might have a heart attack, although I wasn't really sure if people turned red before having heart attacks. Maybe they grew pale. I'd never witnessed one.

"Why were you following me?" I asked.

"I wasn't following you. I was—"

"You were following me. I saw your stupid move into the restaurant when you thought I might catch you."

It didn't seem possible, but his color deepened again.

"Just tell me." I lifted my arm with the bag of Thai food hanging off it. "My dinner is getting cold, so hurry up."

"Delivering food to the mysterious boyfriend?"

"None of your business."

He grinned.

"Why are you following me? It's creepy and I don't like it."

"As I keep trying to explain, I'm looking out for Eileen. There are a lot of unanswered questions about you. I don't trust you."

"Clearly."

"For example, I don't know if this boyfriend is even real."

"Why does that matter?"

"Because if you've invented a boyfriend, I'm curious about why you would do that. It makes you a liar, and it makes you seem unstable."

"You wouldn't get your question answered by following me. And following me is one step from stalking. So, you should be careful."

"Careful of what?" he asked.

"That you don't get yourself into trouble."

"What kind of trouble?"

"I might need to get a restraining order. If I have a stalker."

"I'm not a stalker," he said.

"I think you have the potential."

"Is that a threat?"

"Does it feel like a threat?"

"I can never tell with you. There's something very unusual about you. And you sleep in the same apartment with my girlfriend. She's vulnerable," he said.

"She's not."

"I don't mean overall, I mean with you in the apartment. And now, that dangerous bird."

I laughed. "Well, my dinner is definitely getting cold and you've delayed me long enough." I gave him a little wave. "I better not see you anywhere nearby again tonight. Or ever."

"All I wanted was to see if this boyfriend is a figment of your imagination."

"I guess you'll have to keep wondering. I'll wait while you head back to Eileen's apartment. Or yours."

He turned and began walking away. I waited until he disappeared from sight. Then, I continued farther, all the way to Greenwich Street, circling back to Hunter's place on Charles.

The food was still unexpectedly warm when we scooped it onto our plates.

CHAPTER 57

J left Hunter's apartment earlier than usual that night. I couldn't sleep. His body was warm and relaxed, sprawled beside me. A contented expression, splashed by moonlight, lay across his face. But inside me, every muscle was like the thick, nearly inflexible springs of an old-fashioned sofa. My neck was tight, the tendons like steel rods refusing to let my head sink into the pillow.

Pulling on my clothes felt like trying to force fabric over the stiff body of a department store mannequin. I sent a message to Hunter as I always did when I left because he was never awake.

I met the Uber in front of his building and barely noticed the ride home.

Inside my apartment, I wondered if Ned was in Eileen's bedroom. I'd imagined I would feel his presence like the stink of garlic that's no longer aromatic hours after a meal has been cooked. But I couldn't tell.

Placing my bag outside my bedroom door, I took off my sandals. I walked quietly along the hallway to Eileen's bedroom and stood outside the door. I heard nothing, not even the sound of Eileen's breathing. I didn't think I would hear something as soft as a woman's breath, but I'd thought I might hear him grunt, might be aware of the heaviness of his weight as he shifted in her bed. It was utterly silent. So quiet, I wondered if they'd spent the night at his place. Was he truly that concerned about me that he'd whisked her out of there?

It flashed through my mind that he could have killed her and then himself. The two corpses might be lying side-by-side in her bed and I wouldn't know until morning. Even then, I wouldn't know right away. How long until I knocked on her door? How long until I messaged her? How long without a response until I called the police?

But he adored her, or so he said. So she believed. She wasn't dead. It was my imagination again, always busy with something new. It was my unrelenting desire to see him dead that had my mind running in that direction.

I tiptoed back to my room, unlocked the door, and went inside.

I washed my face, brushed my hair and teeth, and collapsed into bed. Damien murmured in a low voice—*Dangerous woman.*

I wondered if he was awake. His voice was so soft, the tone so unlike his usual raucous pitch, he almost sounded drunk. If I hadn't had the lock on the door, I would have lifted the cover off his cage to be sure Ned hadn't done something to hurt him.

Turning onto my side, I tried to force my eyes closed, but they refused. I stared into the darkness and imagined myself setting a trap for Ned. It was out of the question, of course. But I couldn't stop thinking about it.

It would be tricky. Luring him to a hotel with the promise of sex was unlikely to work, although it wasn't completely implausible. A man was a man. Given the right circumstances and a little alcohol... Still, he claimed to be in love with Eileen, so I doubted he would fall easily into that bottomless pit.

Our building didn't provide roof access for tenants, so I didn't have an easy opportunity to push him to his death. I did not know where he lived or what his apartment building was like, so that didn't provide me with any ideas for manipulating him into a vulnerable position.

I turned onto my other side. I could try to set up a situation where we were on a subway platform in the desolate hours after midnight. I would push him into the path of an oncoming train, but that was messy and had the potential of dragging other people into his death. It would be gruesome and it didn't seem fair to the people on the train, not only delaying their arrival home, but forcing them to live with the memory of an event they hadn't invited. It came with too many risks, although imagining the scene was entertaining for a few minutes.

I turned onto my back and again tried to close my eyes, but they weren't interested in following my wishes.

I'd always avoided knives because I was so repulsed by the sight of blood, by the mess of it all, by seeing that thick, red fluid that belonged inside the body, forever hidden from view. I didn't like the clean-up involved, and the risk of a connection to the person who died when part of them ended up on my body, in my fingernails, tiny droplets in places I wasn't even aware of. I supposed if someone became skilled with a very good quality knife there might be a way to do it somewhat cleanly, but I wasn't interested in learning that skill.

For the same reason, a gun was absolutely out of the question.

People could be poisoned, but that left a body to dispose of, and I surely didn't want Ned's corpse in my apartment. I was sure Eileen would feel the same way, and with far greater passion than I did.

I could try some kind of drug overdose, but for a man who didn't use drugs, that would be tricky. Of course, no one knows another person's secrets. But even if they could believe he was secretly using drugs, the facts would speak for themselves and disprove it. And again—the body in my apartment would have to be dealt with.

Unless I could get him to invite me to his place.

Finally, my eyes agreed to close themselves.

I tried to imagine ways that I might get him to invite me to his apartment. Nothing came immediately to my mind. Maybe I was finally getting tired. So I entertained myself with the kind of fantasy that takes leaps of logic. A fantasy in which I'd already purchased the drugs, was already sitting on his living room couch, had already mixed martinis for both of us, was engaging him in one of his combative conversations, and then ... my mind stalled. I would have to get him to pass out without the assistance of another drug before shooting a deadly dose of heroin or fentanyl into his veins. And the fact that he had no needle tracks would make that look suspicious.

A few minutes later, with all my improbable ideas discarded around me on the bed, I drifted to sleep.

CHAPTER 58

$\mathcal{A}$t seven-thirty on Saturday morning, my phone buzzed with an incoming video call from Tess. Groggy from dreams of Ned's body covered in blood, our living room carpet and couch soaked with his blood, the walls splattered with the stuff, Eileen screaming at me with blood splashed on her face, I tapped to answer. I needed something to wipe my brain clean. I would have preferred coffee before talking to her, but removing all that blood from my memory was more important.

She smiled at me, her face perfectly made up.

She was sitting outside in a garden strung with fairy lights, sipping coffee. It was still dark, and she wore a fleece jacket and leather gloves.

"Why are you awake at four-thirty in the morning?" I sat up, plumping the pillows behind me.

Delicious mango!

Tess raised her voice, calling out, "Hi, Damien!"

Dangerous woman!

The cover was still over his cage, but he was clearly awake and ready for breakfast. I was too. I could feel the dream fading. I threw off the covers and slid out of bed, holding the phone with one hand as I ran my fingers through my hair.

"Did I wake you? I wanted to catch you before you went out," she said.

"I had a hard time falling asleep."

"Is everything alright?"

"Yes. What got you up at four-thirty?"

"I'm ready for Damien to come home."

"And you had to tell me that right this minute? You couldn't message me?"

"I have a favor."

"You always have a favor."

"Do I?"

"Quite often." I walked to the kitchen. It was empty and dark, the coffee pot washed clean and sparkling from the day before. I filled it with fresh grounds and water and started it brewing. I opened the fridge and found a slice of pizza wrapped in plastic. I unwrapped it and took a bite.

"Did you just eat cold pizza?" Tess asked.

"Yes."

She shuddered.

"You should try it." I grabbed the container with fruit I'd cut up for Damien.

"No thanks."

"What's the favor?" I carried the pizza and fruit back to my room.

"I would feel a lot better if you came with him."

I laughed as I pulled the cover off his cage.

Dangerous woman!

It wasn't clear if he meant me or Tess. I put the fruit in his cage and sat on the edge of the bed, nibbling on the pizza slice.

Delicious mango!

"I can't go with him. He rides in the cargo section."

"You'd be on the same flight. He would know you were there."

I stared at her.

"What?" she asked.

I rolled my eyes.

"You don't know what he knows. He's a very smart bird," she said.

"I'm aware of that. But I'm not going to explain how ridiculous that is."

"Okay, *I* would feel better. Knowing someone was with him the whole time, looking after him."

"I wouldn't be able to do anything to look after him. You know that."

"It's psychological."

"It's psychologically unbalanced."

"Don't you want to see my winery?"

"If you want me to see your winery, why didn't you just invite me to see your winery?"

"Because I want you to come now. To bring Damien, to keep him company."

I took a large bite of pizza. I put the phone on the bed and went to Damien's cage. The fruit was already gone. He lowered his crown and cocked his head to the side. *Smart bird.*

"Yes, you're a smart bird."

"Where did you go?" Tess's voice was muffled by my comforter.

I didn't want to keep listening to her argue about something that was pure fantasy. I wondered if she really believed I would be keeping Damien company. I wondered if it really made her feel better, thinking there was a person on the plane with him. What did it matter? Did she think I would somehow keep him safe? Prevent the plane from crashing? Keep him from getting anxious or squawking the entire time? I wondered what that part of the plane was like where animals were transported. I couldn't imagine the noise, the smell. It seemed a little unfair that humans moved their pets across the country and around the world for their own convenience. But Damien had made two trips halfway around the globe and he didn't seem at all traumatized. A flight across the country would be nothing for him.

I took another bite of pizza, then picked up the phone.

"Did you think about it?" Tess asked.

"No."

"Will you? I know I could fly out and get him, but it's kind of a headache to make two trips back-to-back like that."

"Wouldn't I be doing the same?"

"You would have a week or two or even a month with me in between."

"I have work."

"You get vacation time."

Diana would probably replace me if I were gone for a month. But I did get vacation time.

"I can see you're thinking about it."

"You could take vacation time here just as easily," I said.

"I was just there. And I have a winery to run."

"You're already producing wine? You have grapes to harvest?" I laughed. "How does that all work, anyway?"

"When you visit, I'll tell you all about our plans. But there's already a whole team in place."

"You bought them with the winery?"

"Not exactly."

I ate more pizza.

Delicious mango! Smart bird!

"It's not a great time for me to be away from work," I said.

"There's never a great time to take off. With any job. You just do it."

"Probably true."

"Not probably, it's the absolute truth. And you can help me with wedding stuff."

"So now you're trying to talk me out of coming to visit?"

She laughed. "I won't bore you. Just the fun stuff. Like cake tasting and picking wine and champagne. Buying shoes."

I could smell the coffee. I left the pizza crust on the plate and carried it out of my room, holding the phone in front of me as I walked. In the kitchen, I dumped the crust in the trash and filled a mug with coffee. I returned to my bedroom and closed the door. There was still no evidence that Eileen or Ned were even in the apartment.

"Please think about it," Tess said. "Promise?"

"I don't make promises."

"Think about it. I really want him to come home. And I'm sure he's sick of being cooped up in that cage. And I'm sure you're tired of being tied down."

That was true. And there was Ned.

"Call me back. Or text me. I'll pay for your flight. First class."

She was desperate to provide a traveling companion for Damien. Even though he wouldn't have company at all. But a first class flight and a vacation at a winery sounded nice. Cake tasting and champagne and shoe shopping were always welcome. I wondered what she would say if I invited Hunter? I also wondered if it might be a good time for a bit of space between Hunter and me.

CHAPTER 59

*a*fter being followed by my roommate's boyfriend, I couldn't make up my mind whether this was a red flag telling me the man was creepy, outrageously nosey, not unlike me, or downright dangerous. Of course, that had been the question for quite a while. I wondered if all the things I sensed about him were alarming only to me, or if Eileen had any awareness whatsoever that there might be something troubling about him.

He'd stood her up. He'd made her obviously uncomfortable several times, joking and teasing that I might sneak into their bedroom to watch them having sex. That had clearly upset her, yet she seemed to have put it out of her mind entirely.

I needed to do a better job of finding out what she was thinking.

She was a stunningly beautiful woman. She was charming, intelligent, interesting, and pleasant to be around. How did a successful model and an accomplished cook end up with a guy who treated her like a child, dismissed her concerns, and seemed increasingly predatory?

Was there something deeply flawed in her from being raised by a woman who had tried to make her a tool for the god she'd created in her own imagination? Was Eileen damaged from spending her life trying to watch over and protect her mother's deeply sensitive feelings? Had her relationship with Jim utterly destroyed her and the recovery she'd displayed been superficial?

I didn't get it.

And even if that was it, why *this* guy? Why this creepy, awkward, controlling, condescending, tedious guy?

This time, though, I wouldn't attack him quite so viciously. I would pour on the syrup and look for a way to get him out of my life by getting him out of hers. Because I definitely needed him out of my life.

I didn't think he was even close to guessing that I was a killer, but he was too curious.

I wanted to share an apartment with Eileen because she was a fun person, without Ned. And she offered me the opportunity to live in a gorgeous, spacious, comfortable apartment. I did not want to remain locked in a bedroom while Ned sprawled all over her expensive furniture and ate her gourmet meals, prepared from the groceries that I helped pay for.

I suggested we needed a girls' night. Of course, she was thrilled.

On the way home from work, I stopped by a game store and bought Monopoly. It was a game I'd played with my brothers, even though my father hadn't liked it. He didn't think it taught the right values. My mother argued it did because it taught children about saving their money and being careful in their spending choices. She thought it helped children learn you had to pay rent and exercise caution with your investments.

I always won when I played Monopoly with my brothers. Every single time. I'm not sure why. I didn't cheat, although they sometimes accused me of it. Maybe I was just lucky. Maybe I had a knack for picking the right properties in the right order, for not getting too many houses and hotels too quickly and running short on cash. For whatever reason, I won. It made me wonder why I didn't have the same knack for acquiring cash as quickly in real life, watching the piles of money grow.

Playing a game would make it seem more casual when I started picking Eileen's brain about her love for Ned. At least that was my theory. Maybe she would see through me. But it seemed like a worthwhile distraction and a way to keep her from thinking I was pinning her to a wall and grilling her. Especially after the last go-around.

I'd told her I would bring home dinner, which was my second stop. I ordered carnitas burritos filled with everything, loads of tortilla chips, two containers of guacamole to be sure we didn't run out, and salsa. We already had plenty of beer in the fridge. She didn't like to drink a lot of beer because of the calories, obviously, but I thought I could talk her into one night of not thinking about that.

I was wrong.

CHAPTER 60

*E*ileen took one look at the burritos and beer and recoiled as if I were serving liver and cyanide-laced Kool-aid.

"I have a really important photoshoot in two days. I can't eat burritos and drink beer. I'll look like a blimp," she said.

"You've never looked anything like a blimp in your life," I said. "It's good for your body to have variety. And it's good for your mind to have a carb overload sometimes. Good for the serotonin. Good for your mood, for relaxing and having a good time with a friend. Stop thinking about being perfect for once."

"I can't. You know that."

"You can. It's not as if the food bulges out the minute you eat it. You're not a snake swallowing a possum."

She didn't laugh. "I shouldn't. If I—"

"You're slipping back to fanaticism," I said. "It's not healthy. This is really important. We need to relax and not think about work or the future or anything at all. Just for one night. A game and really good food. You won't regret it. I promise."

She sighed.

"Go set up the game," I said. "I'll put the food on plates. And we can spend two hours at the gym tomorrow. Followed by a sauna. Does that make you feel better?"

She finally agreed. I was starving. I wanted my burrito and a beer, and I couldn't imagine going through life without relishing my food. I got it that she was judged, every inch of her body inspected, but I also didn't get why she didn't focus on the math of it and spend more time at the gym. Or something.

How could she love cooking if she was constantly thinking about every morsel and whether it was going to destroy her career? She did love it though—her career *and* the cooking. Maybe she should change careers and become a chef.

We settled on the living room floor, our food on the coffee table, which allowed plenty of space for the game board as well as our plates and drinks. I'd decided to leave the tortilla chips for later.

She rolled the dice, and we began making our way around the board, pausing to take bites of our burritos. I imagined that I was enjoying it more than she was. We talked mostly about the property and our plans to become magnates. I sipped more beer than she did. She was the banker, doling out cash with her long, delicate fingers, her pale gold nail polish shimmering under the track lighting that we'd dimmed for the evening.

"I wonder what's the most money anyone has ever made in Monopoly?" I asked as I rolled the dice, thrilled to see the eleven I'd been hoping for.

"Good question," Eileen said. "We should Google that."

Neither of us did.

"Do you feel like you have enough with the money Jim left you? Enough to feel secure?"

Her face turned slightly pink. "I don't like to talk … I don't think about it that way."

"I just wondered. Do you fee like you *have* to work? Or do you ever think about quitting, doing something different?"

"I love modeling."

"That's good."

Her skin continued to turn brighter shades of pink. I waited for her to say more, but she suddenly seemed overly interested in arranging her property, organizing the money in the bank, and taking tiny bites of her burrito.

After a while, it was clear she wasn't going to say more.

"This is fun," I said. "I can't remember the last time I played a board game. Maybe since I was in college."

"Neither can I."

She didn't add any context, and I wondered if I'd made her think of her mother. Then I wondered if her mother ever played board games. Maybe she hadn't played a game since she was in elementary school.

"You and Ned don't play games with friends?"

"No."

That was a dead end. I tried to think of a way to work him back in again. "Are most of his friends his age, or a mix?"

"Don't start on that, please."

"I was just curious. Just making conversation."

"A mix."

"That's good."

"I wasn't trying to say anything. I know you love him. I get that now."

"I do."

"And he clearly loves you. A lot." I'd learned that was a winning phrase.

She smiled and rolled the dice.

"When did you realize you were falling in love with him?"

"It's hard to remember now."

"How do you even know you're in love?"

She picked up her marker and looked at me, holding the silver top hat in mid air. "You've never been in love?"

"Not that I'm aware of."

"Are you serious?"

"Yes."

"That's so sad."

"Why?"

"Because love is everything."

I took a sip of beer. "Move your marker."

"Don't you think it is? Don't you want to be in love? Don't you love Hunter? I thought you did. Or you were starting to ..."

"That's a lot of questions," I said.

She moved her marker and bought Marvin Gardens.

I didn't want her to worry about me being in love. I wanted her to explain how she knew that she was. But maybe her shock at my lack of love would get her there. Eventually. If she was concerned enough about me. "How did you know you loved him?"

"I just did."

"That's not very helpful."

"It's not something you can explain. Don't you have feelings for Hunter?"

"It's confusing." I took another sip of beer and rolled the dice. In more ways than one. "What is it about Ned that you love?"

"I've already told you this, haven't I?"

"Tell me again."

"He's kind."

"Lots of men are kind."

"I like being with him. I enjoy his company more than anyone else I know."

"Even mine?" I gave her a wicked grin.

She smiled. "Yes. He's funny and—"

"He is? I guess I haven't seen that side of him. He seems grouchy."

"Don't, please."

I paid the rent I owed her and nudged the dice in her direction. "What else?"

"He's just ... there's nothing I don't like about him."

"Do you think he's the one?"

"Yes."

"I don't understand how you know that. How many guys have you—"

"That doesn't matter. He's just—"

"Do you worry about him dying and leaving you alone?"

"I don't think about that."

"Why not?"

"When you love someone, that's all that matters. People can't help who they fall in love with. It's not something they can explain. You're making it like a science project. Trying to pick it all apart. You can't do that. Maybe that's why you've never fallen in love."

"Maybe."

I didn't think I was going to win. I would have to be satisfied with winning the game. And I did, just like with my brothers. I'd been so confident I could find a way to chip through the concrete wall that surrounded her, but it was built out of her idea of love being magical and mysterious, and whatever feelings she had for Ned that fit into that mysterious belief. There was no way to break through that.

She couldn't see anything wrong in him and if I said anything that even tiptoed in that direction, she shut me down. That was my own fault for attacking him, maybe. Or maybe not. I suppose loving someone means you aren't going to listen to a single word against them.

I wasn't going to be rid of him by convincing her he was a mistake. She was hanging on to him and refused to let go and there was nothing I could do about it. I could hope for an early natural death, but he wasn't *that* old.

CHAPTER 61

*U*sually, when Hunter wanted something to the point that he couldn't get it out of his mind, finding himself driven to the point where it was all he thought about, the fulfillment of that desire caused the need to fade. When Alex told him she had three brothers, he'd assumed that would be the end of his fixation. He'd expected to wake the following morning laughing at his reflection in the mirror that this simple piece of information, a facet of her life that had almost nothing to do with their relationship, would disappear from his thoughts as if it had never been there.

Instead, it erupted into a thousand more questions, like the spread of a poison ivy rash across his skin. He'd been exposed to the stuff when he was twelve, and at first, the tiny red patch was nothing. Then, it crept up his arms, across his back, and leaped to his legs, where it grew like it was setting up colonies and outposts around the globe.

He wanted to know more about her family. He wanted to hear the stories and experiences of her childhood. He wanted to know about her friends and what her elementary school years had been like. He wanted tales from vacations and family dinners and holidays.

Had she kept a diary like a lot of girls did? What games did she like? Had she played sports, been a good student, gotten into trouble? Who was her first boyfriend? When was her first kiss? Everything. He wanted everything.

The thing was, he couldn't understand why he needed this dossier of information, because he sure as hell did not want to give her that level of detail about his own life. Maybe he needed to know if he could trust her with his own stories? He wasn't sure. Maybe because she was so different from any girl ... woman ... he'd ever known, he wanted to understand why. Maybe because he thought she was too good to be true, and he wanted to find out if there was some telling experience that would show him it was all a magic trick.

Sometimes, he felt like she'd cast a spell on him. He didn't believe in that sort of thing. Not at all, but that's what it felt like.

He'd decided, at the risk of pissing her off big time, that he needed to shake things up between them. He had to figure out why there was this weird power dynamic in which he felt like she was running the show, as if she were some female Oz standing in plain view. To shake things up, he was going to lure her to a picnic in the park.

Knowing her, it was entirely possible she would decide to end their relationship over it.

But he had to do something. Relationships should be balanced, and he needed to balance it sooner rather than later.

He got it that women had been on the low end of the scale for eons, but that didn't mean things needed to do a one-eighty. Balance. He liked balance, and he was pretty sure most women preferred it.

His plan was to wait outside her building after work. He would carry his backpack instead of his usual computer bag. Before going to meet her, he would stop at the deli, order sandwiches, grab a few bags of chips, and some beers he could shove into insulated holders.

When she came out of work, startled to see him, he would suggest they walk to the park and sit for a while.

Just outside the deli, he sent the message. He figured the less time she had to change her mind, the better.

Hunter: *I'm near your building. Want to walk to the park?*

It was nearly five minutes before she replied.

Alex: *Ok ... ???*

He didn't respond. He ordered two roast beef sandwiches with everything, grabbed two beers a few rows back to be sure they were icy cold, and the chips.

He texted when he was outside the building. In less than four minutes, she came walking out the door. He felt a wash of relief when he saw she was wearing flat black shoes and a black skirt with a yellow sleeveless top. She'd taken off her jacket and hung it over her bag.

She walked up to him and gave him a long kiss. She stepped away, scooped her hair into a ponytail, tied it with an elastic strap, and took his hand. "This is fun. Like high school."

He felt she was taunting him. Was that an invitation to ask her about high school? Probably not. It was a casual comment. God, he needed to get a grip. He laughed, half a beat too late, and they started walking.

They talked about his day and hers. His had involved writing press releases and herding the social media team to follow the plan for the agency's participation in the upcoming fall show. Hers involved a strategy meeting with her boss to figure out how to manage the most bizarre client he could imagine—a woman who claimed to own a series of fitness centers but who seemed to be a puppet for a guy who wanted to run everything with her as the public face. They both sounded like a couple of freaks to him. But the whole business model for Alex's company sounded a bit fringe. It shouldn't have surprised him they had clients who were outside the mainstream, even though his own boss had been one of those clients and seemed to think their work was brilliant.

They reached the 59th Street side of Central Park and began walking along the path, slowing their pace to enjoy the lush trees and vegetation.

Alex told him about the cockatoo's owner and that the bird would be headed back to California soon.

"Let's sit by the pond," he said.

"I thought we were taking a walk."

"I like looking at the water. It's calming."

She shrugged. "It is, but I thought we were walking."

"We can sit for a few minutes."

"Okay."

They sat on a bench and he lifted the backpack straps off his shoulders. He placed it on the ground, trying to decide how to approach his transition to the food. It was going to be abrupt no matter what he did, so he might as well plunge in before she became impatient and decided she wanted to start walking again.

He unzipped the pack. "Want a beer?"

She laughed. "You brought beer?"

"In case we got thirsty. Which I am. Are you?"

"I won't say no."

He pulled out the beers, twisted off the caps, and handed a beer to her. They clicked the necks together and drank.

"You think of everything." She kissed his jaw.

"Since you like that, I also thought of sandwiches." He reached into the bag.

She put the bottle to her lips but didn't drink. She kept it there for a moment, then finally tipped her head back and took a small sip. She lowered the bottle. "Okay. So, an ambush."

"I don't think it's an ambush."

"Then what is it?"

"An ambush is when someone waits in hiding to attack you."

"The beers and sandwiches were definitely waiting in hiding."

He laughed. "Fair enough. Come on. There aren't any ants on the bench."

"They'll come when they smell the food."

"I don't think so. Not right away."

"If you drop crumbs."

"I try to be neat."

"You *are* a tidy person. That's why I like you."

He laughed as he handed a sandwich to her. "Aren't you hungry?"

She looked at it as if the thing might blow up in her face.

"It's roast beef. With everything. I guarantee this deli is one of the best in the city."

She took the sandwich, unwrapped it, and bit into it. She smiled. "It's delicious." She sipped her beer and gazed at the water.

They ate in silence, and she seemed content, but he was not.

Questions hammered his brain as if an invisible mining crew worked overtime trying to chisel its way out of his skull. His obsession with knowing all about her made zero sense. He was sabotaging himself. If she did start talking, the natural result would be to ask him questions of her own. And then what? Was he prepared to bare all? Absolutely not. In fact, he wasn't sure he would ever want to tell her about all the dark corners of his life. He hadn't told a soul about some of his more disturbing experiences. Of course, she didn't know that. And talking about your family had nothing to do with that. If you had something you didn't want to talk about, you simply avoided mentioning it. Another person would never even know that thing existed. You could talk yourself blue in the face and they would never have a clue.

Why was he doing this to her? Why the hell couldn't he just let it go?

He wrapped up the trash and stuffed it into the paper bag. He put his arm across her shoulders. "Did you have bad experiences with family picnics or something?"

"Not every opinion and preference is rooted in some childhood trauma."

"Are you sure?"

She didn't respond. She finished her beer and stood. "Let's finish our walk."

A door opened, a door slammed closed. He should have been happy about the picnic and left it at that.

CHAPTER 62

*I*t was amusing that Hunter tricked me into having a picnic. I really didn't care. I think he was happy that I ate my sandwich and drank my beer and let him enjoy eating in the park. It was actually nice. I still had no interest in tossing a blanket on the ground and hanging out for hours with food spread around me, a buffet for ants and other uninvited insects, but the sandwiches were delicious and the beer was good.

It wasn't quite as nice that he tried to find a back door into asking about my family again. I didn't understand his fascination with the past. I'd never met a guy who had so many questions about my childhood. Why was he so interested? Maybe, someday, I would ask, but right now, there were too many other things on my mind.

The first thing I wanted to deal with was Carolina, but Ned and Andy were breathing hard down my neck. Especially Andy.

He'd texted me five times while I was eating my awesome roast beef sandwich. I hadn't noticed my phone vibrating because it had sunk to the bottom of my bag. But later, when I was at Hunter's, drinking more beer and feeling more comfortable with my shoes off, sitting on his couch while he rubbed my feet, after I'd washed them, of course, I read the messages.

Andy: *You owe Brie a refund. She's no longer interested in your bullshit.*

Andy: *I expect an answer.*

Andy: *Don't think you can ignore me and get away with it.*

Andy: *This is unprofessional.*

Andy: *Do we have to take legal action?*

As Hunter pressed his thumb into the arch of my left foot, I tried to decide whether I should take a screenshot of the messages and send them to Diana, or handle them myself. It made me curious that he was sending them to me instead of Diana. Did he think I was easier to persuade? Did he really think I was the one who made that decision? Did he believe I could convince Diana to give a refund?

None of those things were true.

I let my screen go dark.

The right thing to do was to send them to Diana. But what if I decided on a better way to deal with Andy?

It was very tempting. The world didn't need a guy like him.

But my plate was full. Very full. Overflowing, actually.

And I didn't see how I would pull it off. The logistics might work out easily enough. He was definitely easy to lure to a hotel. Or maybe I could just make an appointment for a personal training session late at night and bash him over the head with a free weight.

It wasn't my style. Could I hit him with a metal dumbbell and avoid blood? I wasn't sure. Could I press a barbell on his neck and watch him suffocate? I was strong, but he was a muscular guy who looked like he had incredible strength. He would be drugged, but still...

The idea seemed impossible, even if it was appealing to think about.

I took a sip of beer.

"What are you thinking about?" Hunter asked. "You're so quiet."

"Lifting weights."

He laughed. "We still haven't talked about how we're going to spend our childcare windfall."

"I can't think about that right now."

"Why not?"

"I've dribbled some of mine away."

"On what?"

I shrugged. I wasn't planning to tell him about Carolina's demand for the cash. He didn't need to know anything about what was going on with her. I had no idea what his solution would be, but I was certain it would be very different from mine. If I ended up needing to give her the cash, which I was almost positive I wouldn't, I would use my own.

My phone buzzed and lit up.

Andy: *I'm waiting for your answer. This isn't a complicated situation. Either confirm the refund will be processed, or you'll hear from our attorneys.*

Plural. Wasn't he fancy? A whole team of attorneys.

"Someone really wants your attention," Hunter said.

"Mmm."

If I got rid of Andy, Brie might give the police a long story about Fly Higher. She might tell them a lot about me. She would mention his assault. I could taste her anger when she'd walked out of our conference room. She seemed to feel we were ripping her psyche in half by trying to sever her connection to Andy, as if we were tearing the skin off her bones.

I opened my phone and took a screenshot of the messages. I sent them to Diana, closed my phone, and dropped it on the carpet.

"Is everything okay?" Hunter asked.

"It is now." I leaned back and closed my eyes. I was relaxed. I enjoyed tossing Andy's demands, and the weight of him, off to Diana. I would have preferred removing him from the world, but I didn't need more questions from more people, especially official people. I needed to get my life organized into a tidier situation. I needed to eliminate some of the people asking questions. I needed fewer people thinking there were things in my life that were disturbing and worth looking into.

I was pretty sure no one was seriously investigating me, but I couldn't be absolutely certain. It was hard to know when someone was being idly curious and when they were concerned to the point that they were going to cause real trouble.

It was starting to feel like a chain reaction—Ned dragging Kent back into my life, stirring up Eileen, Diana wondering about James and even Hunter with all his questions.

"You seem really tense," Hunter said.

I wasn't tense. My mind was working, and the blood was flowing quickly through my body as my brain sorted through all the people pressing too close. It wasn't a matter of tension, it was a matter of arranging my priorities and deciding what I wanted to do, deciding what risk was a risk in which I could beat the odds and which risk was more like playing roulette. Something I've never done and never would and for which I can't comprehend the appeal. "It's work," I said.

This is always the perfect answer. Everyone understands work occupying your thoughts, pulling you out of whatever situation you're in, and sending you off to chase rabbits in your mind. It's the ultimate bond of humanity in first world countries, possibly in every type of existence on the planet.

"Do you want to talk about it?" he asked.

"It's the Bodies By Brie guy. They want a refund and for some reason, he thinks I'm the one who makes that decision."

"He probably thinks you're more reasonable than Diana."

I almost fell off the couch laughing. Hunter asked me why that was so funny. I asked if he thought I was reasonable. He said I was, most of the time. Maybe he was just paving the way for more questions about my family, and he thought that would butter me up.

At home, I asked Damien, "Do you think I'm reasonable?"

Dangerous woman!

I was looking forward to being free to come and go without thinking about Damien's meals and comfort and free range time, but I would miss his conversation.

CHAPTER 63

I was photographing a woman who was the head of a 200-person law firm when the Snapchat messages started vibrating my phone like bullets. The buzzing became so insistent, the client asked if there was an emergency. I was forced to put down my camera, breaking the photographic trance. But it had already been broken when she noticed my overactive phone.

I asked her to avoid checking her email and remain standing at the window, looking out at the city. "Think about your rise to power so you can remain in the right mental space."

She gave me a curt nod, which told me she would not do as I'd asked, but would be thinking about her appointments that followed this one.

I grabbed my phone. All the messages were from Carolina.

Curiosity overwhelmed me, but I managed to tamp it down. I turned off my phone and picked up the camera. I asked Kelly to face me again so I could resume, but now I was the one who was not in the right mental space.

As I asked questions about her career, her personal life, and borderline intrusive questions about her ambitions, all I could think about was Carolina. After a while, Kelly's voice took on the same shrill quality as Carolina's. I saw Carolina's pointed nose on her face and I felt as if Carolina was in the room with us. I continued taking photographs for the next thirty minutes as we'd scheduled, hoping they captured what we needed, but knowing it was a fifty-fifty shot. Possibly less. Possibly as dismal as the odds on a roulette wheel when going for a single number.

When we were finished, I took the elevator down and walked two blocks to a bar. I ordered a martini, which I thought would make reading the deluge of messages slightly more tolerable. I managed to fend off my curiosity further until the drink arrived and I'd consumed an olive.

Finally, I opened Snapchat.

Her messages were tedious, and the drink did nothing to make them interesting or less annoying for how they'd interrupted my work.

Each one was a series of angry emojis, followed by a cell phone emoji. Assuming I wouldn't get her point, she'd added—*call me*—to each one.

Her final message said we needed to meet ASAP, and I had better not stall on my reply. She was already angry that I hadn't responded to her *request* for a phone call which was *not a good sign at all*.

I tapped in the name of the bar where I was already enjoying my second olive, my drink only one sip down from the lip of the glass.

Alex: *Feel free to join me if you can get here in the next twenty minutes.*

Carolina: *You're not calling the shots here.*

Alex: *I'm not calling shots, I'm telling you where I am since you want to meet ASAP.*

I wanted to add a winking face, but I resisted. It wasn't a good idea to pour gasoline on her fire. She had definitely moved herself to the top of my priority list.

I didn't have her five thousand dollars with me. Even if I had, I wouldn't have planned to give it to her. That was the bait for her trap. I just needed to figure out where I was going to spring it—

CATHRYN GRANT

most likely in her hotel room. But then I would need to figure out how to get Ricky out of there, which would not be easy.

My martini was gone by the time she arrived forty minutes later. I'd almost decided to leave, but was hesitating over a second drink while thoughts of Ricky swirled in my mind. A lone olive sat impaled by the stir stick in the bottom of the glass.

She eased herself onto the chair across from me. I ate my last olive. Without speaking to her, I picked up my glass, went to the bar, and ordered two martinis. Waiting for the drinks gave me a chance to observe her, although I didn't learn much because she was staring directly at me as if she expected I might drop a roofie in her glass if she looked away or even risked blinking. She wasn't wrong about that. She was just off on her timing.

When we were facing each other across the table, I gave her a cool smile. "You seemed very anxious to tell me what's on your mind," I said.

"I don't think you're taking this seriously."

"I'm taking it more seriously than you realize. I just don't get as wound up as you do. How's Ricky?"

"Like you care."

"So that means he's not doing well?"

"He's resilient."

"Who's watching him now?"

"He's at boxing."

"This late?"

"I arranged a private session for him. So you and I could talk."

"It must be difficult, never being able to leave him alone. Or having any reliable childcare. That's draining."

"We're not friends anymore, so don't try to pretend you're concerned."

"I'm not pretending anything. I said it must be difficult. Is it difficult?"

"Yes. But I love my son with all my heart and I'm going to do what's best for him, no matter what sacrifices I have to make."

282

"Has it crossed your mind at all that he might be exaggerating, or—"

"Don't you dare accuse him of lying! If you do that again, I'm leaving and going straight to the police."

"I'm curious why you didn't do that first."

She glared at me and took a sip of her drink. "Did you bring the money?"

"I still don't think it's a good idea to be handing around large amounts of cash in a public place."

"You're playing games. I thought that's why you said you could meet."

"I wanted to know how things were going with your search for a therapist."

"I'm working on it."

"Still?"

"Yes."

"I thought I would give you all the cash at once. And I'm assuming a therapist for the length of time he'll need one will require quite a lot. You really don't want to be receiving that kind of cash in a bar. Or anywhere in public. So we'll have to meet at your hotel."

She gave me a single nod.

"I don't want this to drag on, so if you could get that settled quickly, it would be better."

"What did your ex-boyfriend have to say for himself?"

"He didn't—"

"Stop. I told you I won't tolerate you calling him a liar! That creep you were with tried to emasculate my son. This is how things are now. This is why I have to homeschool him."

"What?"

"I want my son to be a real man. I'm not going to raise him to be a girly man. Even my husband, sad to say, has been brainwashed by the cult of feminism. And it's all lies. That's why we're all so unhappy."

"Who's unhappy?"

"Every single lady I know. Us girls want men. Real men. We want men who will take charge. Men who know how to protect their women. That's why Ricky's in boxing, not some lame sport like soccer or whatever."

"Soccer is a demanding sport. It requires a lot of skill and physical—"

"Stop interrupting me. You're brainwashed too. Most people are. But deep inside, it's not what we want. We want men. It's in our DNA. We want men who take charge. Men who tell us to shut the fuck up and sit down. Men who aren't afraid to make the tough calls. That's what we want, and that's why we're all so miserable."

"I'm not."

"Then you're lying to yourself. Men are being turned into metrosexuals. Half girl, half man. And they're not happy either. It's all over the place. Men are meant to be in charge, to be the leaders. To be the head of the family. Ladies want men who don't take lip. Otherwise we complain and bitch and moan all day long. Spouting opinions all over the internet."

"Isn't that what you're doing?"

"I'm just letting you know how brainwashed you are. How everyone is. And I won't raise my boy to be like that. Some very lucky girl is going to thank me with all her heart one day. And your ex-boyfriend tried to destroy him."

"My boyfriend didn't do anything. Ricky is playing you. Or else this ..." I forced myself to stop. It wasn't an argument I should be having. I was going in the wrong direction. I should let her complain and spout her opinions with all the vitriol she could muster.

Then I needed to figure out how I was going to get her alone and remove her from Ricky's life so she wasn't able to raise that kid to be a monster who believed the misogyny she'd internalized from whatever underbelly of the internet she'd been crawling around. Or maybe she'd grown up hearing and observing those beliefs, and it had seeped into her bones from birth.

Getting rid of Ricky didn't seem fair. He was ten years old. Surely it wasn't too late for him. Was he already set in stone? It was hard to know. After talking to his father, it seemed like he had a chance.

I let her go on until my glass was empty, and my olives were gone.

Then I told her she absolutely needed to find a therapist who believed what she did, which I hoped she would be able to do quickly. But it didn't matter. The therapist was made up. She just wanted the cash, and I wasn't really sure why she was stalling.

But now, I was almost certain this was not Ricky's idea. It had been in her mind the day she crashed into me, eagerly demanding we become friends.

CHAPTER 64

*W*hen I returned to the apartment I was calm, with vodka in my veins and a decision in my mind.

I unlocked the door and stepped inside to find Ned sprawled on the couch.

He glared at me. "Hello, Alexandra. We need to have a chat."

"Not now. I have things to do."

"Like feed that damn bird? It's been squawking like a maniac locked on the top floor of an asylum. I thought you said—"

"Among other things."

"First, a chat." He patted the couch. "Come sit down."

"I said, no."

"Eileen told me something very disturbing about you. It wasn't a surprise. It was exactly what I expected, but I had hoped I was wrong."

I went to the fridge and grabbed cut-up fruit for Damien. I was starving after the two martinis. I should have stopped for some takeout. I moved around containers of leftovers and found a foil-wrapped baked potato. That wouldn't be too awful eaten cold. I could sprinkle some salt on it. Anything to get into my room and

THE WOMAN IN THE HOTEL

away from Ned as quickly as possible. This situation was out of control, if I was rummaging for cold food and racing toward my room like a gopher diving into her tunnel.

Piling the fruit container, the potato, a fork, a paper napkin, and the salt shaker onto a plate, I started toward the hallway.

"Eileen told me you were asking about her inheritance."

I kept walking.

"Four million dollars, Alexandra. That's a lot of money. Now I know you've had that on your mind since the day you moved in here. In fact, I expect that money is the entire reason you're living here."

He was trying to provoke me and if I said a single word to him, I was allowing it.

"Eileen has given me permission to call the building manager about that bird if you don't come talk to me right now."

I paused outside my bedroom door. Where was Eileen? Why was he here and she was not? She wasn't in her bedroom. The hallway going to her room had been dark, and I hadn't noticed any light under her door.

Was he telling the truth? I couldn't imagine her saying that, but at the same time, she thought the guy was her knight in shining armor. Had he somehow persuaded her to allow all of this? I still couldn't picture her agreeing to it, but it was strange that she wasn't home at this time of the evening and he was sitting in our living room as if the apartment belonged to him, a half-empty wineglass on the table, a half-empty bottle of red beside it.

I unlocked my door, went into my bedroom, and gave Damien his food.

Damn bird!

I strode back into the living room and stood in front of the coffee table. I was close enough to where he was sitting that he was forced to tip his head back slightly to look up at me. He appeared uncomfortable.

287

"Why have you been saying *damn bird* to Damien?"

"The devil's spawn?"

"I don't appreciate you teaching him to say that."

"I didn't teach him anything. He mimics."

"You stand outside my door and shout at him?"

"When have you ever heard me shout?"

"Stay away from my room."

"You act as if this place is yours," he said.

"Half of it is."

"Not the furniture."

"What do you want, Ned? Eileen likes me. I don't think it's making her happy that you dislike me so intensely."

"Do you feel badly that I don't like you?"

"I don't care what you think of me," I said.

"Doubtful. But I never said I didn't like you. I actually find you fascinating. I just want to understand what your game is."

"I don't have a game."

"Eileen mentioned you were playing monopoly. A strange choice for two adult women."

"What's your point?"

"Eileen has a lot of money. Are you playing a long game, thinking there's a way to siphon that off her at some point?"

"No."

He laughed. He picked up his wineglass and took a sip. "I wouldn't expect you to answer that truthfully."

"What do you want?"

"Why were you asking her questions about her inheritance, while playing a board game about money, of all things? It seems … concerning."

I laughed. "I'm hungry so I'm going to—"

"You enjoy a lot of things thanks to Eileen." He raised his wineglass, turning it slightly to catch the light. "Very nice wines, delicious meals. Beautiful furniture and artwork." He swept his arm to indicate the living and dining areas. "What do you bring to the table?"

"I don't have to explain our agreement to you."

"Why were you asking her about her inheritance? It's none of your business."

I wondered what she'd told him. I hadn't said anything about being interested in her money. All I was curious about was how she viewed it, whether she considered it enough to feel like she was secure for life, whether it ever made her think about quitting her job, or whether she thought she might find another career when she aged-out of modeling. It had nothing to do with me.

The question was, had she misunderstood, or was he twisting it because he wanted to make it into another topic for arguing with me? Had he stirred her up to the point she was afraid of me, wondering if I was after her money? She wasn't a person who hid her feelings, and didn't appear to be a very adept liar, so it was hard for me to imagine her pretending to be one thing in front of me and telling Ned something entirely different. "How on earth would I get her money, if I even wanted it?"

"Everyone wants money."

"You know that for a fact?"

"Fair enough." He splashed wine into his glass. "I should offer you some of this. You don't seem to be in a very sociable mood, but if you want some, just say so." He added a bit more to his glass and took a swig. "Anyway, it's possible there are people who don't want money. But you're not one of them."

That was true. "How would I get her money? What, specifically, are you and Eileen, so worried about?"

"Eileen is not worried. At all. And that worries me. I don't know how you would get her money. But you're clever. And you have a hold on her that I don't like. I understand it, but I don't like it. When a person has that kind of psychological advantage over someone, they can do whatever they want."

"I think you have a low opinion of the woman you love. You

don't think she can make rational decisions? You think she just blindly follows her friends without question?"

"I don't know what she'll do. But I've asked her to watch her back, and she objects to that idea, so I have to do it for her. It's not normal for a woman to want nothing but no-strings sex, and when your ex-whatever you want to call him— boy-toy, I suppose—told me that, I was even more concerned. So I'm asking you, why did you have so many questions about her money?"

"I don't have to answer any of your questions. And she didn't have to answer any of mine. We were having a casual conversation over a board game and you've turned it into something sinister. Goodnight." I returned to the kitchen. I opened the fridge and took out a beer. I found a salami log in the meat keeper. I grabbed a paring knife, a small cutting board, and went to my bedroom.

Ned called after me that he wasn't finished talking. As I unlocked my bedroom door, he shouted that the wine was delicious, and he'd never known me to pass up a nice glass of wine.

I closed my door and locked it.

I arranged my cold dinner on the plate. I changed into yoga pants and an oversized T-shirt advertising the Yankees that Trystan had given me when I first moved to New York.

Damn bird. Damien's voice was a low mutter.

I sat on the edge of the bed with my phone, one foot tucked under my other leg. I twisted off the beer cap, swallowed some beer, then looked up how to get a bird to unlearn a phrase. I couldn't find anything, but figured it might be close to how a human might change their thought patterns—repeatedly fill the space with something else.

I spoke to him in a low voice. "Chardonnay time, Damien. Chardonnay time. Pretty bird. Pretty bird. Dangerous woman."

Dangerous woman!

I smiled. I went to the dresser and cut a slice of salami. I peeled off the casing and ate it. I unwrapped the baked potato, split it open, and sprinkled salt on it. I took a bite. It wasn't bad.

I plugged my phone into the speaker, put on a Rachmaninoff play list, sat close to Damien's cage, and talked to him about nonsense. Nothing I minded Ned overhearing, since I had no doubt he was standing outside my door listening to the crinkle of the foil, the tap of my fork, and every word I spoke.

CHAPTER 65

The casual visit of James's sister to pick up his personal belongings from his office had turned into something else. Instead of what I thought would be a meet and greet while Fallon handed her a small box and Diana gushed about how unjust and awful his death was as Fallon and I nodded our condolences, we were having a catered lunch in the conference room.

Fallon told me when I arrived at what I thought was an early hour to find her already there, the conference room lights on, the table covered with a white cloth, and a vase of red roses in the center.

"What's going on?" I asked, drawn to the doorway before I'd even entered my own office.

"A lunch for Layla. James's sister."

"Why? I thought she was just stopping by for a few minutes later this morning?"

"Because we want her to know how valued he was."

The parroting quality in her tone was clear.

"That's very last-minute. I already—"

"It's required."

"Diana didn't consider we might have plans?"

"They should be canceled. Clients can be rescheduled."

I couldn't imagine anything more tedious than lunch with Layla and another monologue from Diana about how amazing James was. Well, maybe I could, but given the other options for this particular day, I couldn't.

"Does Layla know about this? Or are we ambushing her with roses and food?" I glanced at the credenza beside me. There were three bottles of white wine in coolers. Our teetotaling boss was changing her style. Or maybe she simply planned to let us drink while she waited for our tongues to loosen and she took notes.

"I don't think she knows."

"What if she—"

"I know as much as you do." Fallon smoothed the tablecloth, straightened, and looked at me with a cool, slightly disdainful expression.

"You seem to know a lot more," I said. "That there's a required lunch, for example."

"The caterers will be here at noon. Layla is coming at twelve-fifteen."

I nodded. I went into my office and shut the door. My desire for coffee had faded. There was nothing about this lunch that sounded pleasant—from eating in a conference room, to making conversation with the sister of a man I'd partially seduced and suffocated, to listening to Diana speculate fruitlessly about who might have killed him and why. I wondered if Layla would cry the entire time. She would either cry, or be filled with rage. Or possibly depressed.

I could plead a headache. Diana wouldn't believe me, of course. Even if I left with my phony complaint, the punishment she would inflict in the following days and possibly weeks wouldn't be a fair trade for the two-hour lunch.

I decided to go for the coffee after all. I wanted to get a better read on Fallon. She must know more than she was saying. At least I could figure out what she was thinking about the lunch.

The coffee was freshly brewed. I filled a mug and wandered back into the hallway. Ian's door was open, but I avoided looking in that direction. The doors to Diana's and Fallon's offices were both closed. I knocked on Fallon's.

"Entréz," she said.

I smirked and opened the door, letting my smirk slide into a sympathetic smile. "Do you need any help with the lunch?"

"The table is set up. The caterers do everything else."

"That's good." I stepped into her office and closed the door.

She winked. I took that as a welcoming sign for a bit of office gossip.

"What happens if Layla doesn't want to eat lunch with a bunch of strangers?" I asked.

"That doesn't matter. Just like us not wanting to go to his funeral didn't matter. Diana is gutted, and she wants to pull everyone else into her mourning."

"I doubt she's as gutted as his sister."

"For sure," Fallon said.

"Then what do you think is going on?"

Fallon nodded. She twisted one of her earrings. "I think she wants to compare notes."

I hadn't spent a lot of time with Diana the past few weeks. And the hours we had been together had been distorted by Andy and Brie. I'd mistakenly taken her silence about James as a bright spot, a place where my mind could stop looking for tiny leaks in my stories, a place where I didn't have to concern myself with someone digging up things that should remain buried.

I didn't like having things that I'd thought were settled resurfacing, as if they were bulbs that died off every summer, only to sprout out of nowhere after a long winter covered by frozen earth. Suddenly, sharp green spears appear in soil that's completely hostile to life, and then they're growing taller, forming shapely buds, and sprouting into blinding color.

Bulbs are the strangest and creepiest plant life I've encountered. My mother loved them, but I always found them slightly threatening—the way you thought they were shriveled and old and their lives were over, then up they came again, just when you'd forgotten where they were lurking. I think it concerned my mother that they bothered me.

"Compare notes about what we know about his life, and who might have wanted to do something so awful to him."

I looked at Fallon, who was clearly unsettled by the fact I hadn't said anything about Diana's desire to compare notes.

"Yes. I figured that's what you meant," I said.

"You didn't say anything."

"I was wondering if James's sister has any notes to compare. Maybe she's happy to let the police do their jobs."

Fallon shrugged. "Diana isn't the sort of person who lets other people be happy with their own take on things."

"True."

"I didn't even know the guy," Fallon said. "I didn't want to go to his funeral. I didn't want to go to the wine bar to talk about him, and I don't want to discuss his personal life and whatever weird or creepy people he might have known. If he did hang out with shady people, how would I even know? All of this has fuck-all to do with me."

I nodded.

"Maybe you could say something to Diana? Get me out of it? I ordered the lunch. I set up the room. But this is …" She spread her hand and studied her fingernails. Each nail was painted a different color, going through the colors of the rainbow, but they hadn't expanded and tried to find ten variations in the shades, so it went from red to purple on seven nails, then started over with a red and orange. It was irritating to look at. When she made a fist with her right hand, I was glad not to have to see them anymore.

"She's not open to my requests lately." I took a sip of coffee, suddenly aware I'd been holding the mug for several minutes and had forgotten all about it. Now, my fingers were cramping around the handle.

"Please? I'd owe you one," Fallon said.

I wasn't sure what owing me one would get me, but why not? "Okay. I'll ask. But you should have low expectations."

"You'll convince her." She grinned, relief pouring off her like sweat.

CHAPTER 66

$\mathcal{F}$ allon's enthusiasm and gratitude were premature, as I'd imagined they would be.

"Absolutely not," Diana said. "I don't care if she didn't know him. That's an even better reason for her and Ian to be there. We need a variety of perspectives. As you and Layla and I talk about the different facets of him that we knew, Fallon and Ian will notice things we might miss."

I wanted to laugh at Diana's belief in our ability to reconstruct a dead man's life. She seemed to think we were some sort of elite group of elders who had been granted uncanny wisdom to pick apart a murder investigation on which the New York police department hadn't made any progress. Only one person knew who had murdered James. Only one person understood the motive and the nature of what he'd done to end up dead in a hotel basement.

That person wasn't talking.

I wondered what Diana would expect me to say during our lunch. I hoped she didn't push too hard.

As it turned out, the lunch and the amateur investigation were more boring than they were anything else. Layla believed that James had hooked up with a sex worker, possibly refused to pay, or tried to *negotiate* her fee, and that her pimp had killed him. That, or an angry ex-boyfriend.

Even though Diana argued up one side and down the other that smothering someone after giving them a date rape drug didn't sound at all like the tactics of an angry ex, or a pimp, Layla wouldn't budge.

"He dated a lot of questionable women," she said.

"That's cruel," Diana said.

"But true," Layla said.

I could see Diana look anxious and insulted at the same time, wondering if she fell into the questionable category. I wondered how long their relationship had gone on. I wondered if Ian caught her complex expression.

"In some ways, I'm not surprised this happened," Layla said. "James had a big mouth. He said a lot of offensive things to people."

"He was always kind and supportive of me," Diana said.

"Maybe you were the exception that proves the rule," Layla said.

They talked in circles for nearly two hours. Fallon ate quickly, then tried to hide the fact that she had her phone on her lap and was messaging with someone. Diana kept asking her to pay attention, but moments later, Fallon's head would be bent again, her shoulders moving despite her effort to be subtle.

Ian kept repeating that he had nothing to offer, beyond commenting that Diana seemed right with every wild idea she threw onto the table, and Layla obviously knew James far better than any of us did.

I tried to keep quiet, but Diana wasn't going to allow that. She wanted me to recount every conversation with James that I could recall. She wanted to know what we talked about when we went out to eat. She wanted to know why we hadn't gotten along and how things had been smoothed over.

The lies grew like the bowl of discarded artichoke leaves near each of our plates. It surprised me that Fallon had ordered whole artichokes instead of a salad to go with our sandwiches, but maybe she thought eating a vegetable leaf by leaf would give us something to do while we listened to Diana lay out the case for figuring out who had murdered James Lipman.

At two o'clock, Layla looked at her watch, pushed out her chair, and stood. "Thanks for lunch. Thanks for caring so much about my brother. I hope the police figure it out, but it won't surprise me if they don't. Over 450 people are murdered in this city every year. I think they have their hands full."

As Diana was speculating again about ways to dig into James's reasons for being at the hotel that night, Layla walked out of the room. The look on Diana's face said she wanted to punch the wall. I wasn't sure if it was because she hadn't gotten any information out of Layla or because Layla wasn't on fire to find out the truth. My guess was the first—Diana wanted to be the one to figure out who had killed him. As if that would prove she'd been a good friend.

CHAPTER 67

I came into the office early the following morning. Much of the afternoon the previous day had been eaten up by Diana's post mortem of our investigative lunch. She was beyond disappointed that none of her staff, especially me, although she didn't name me, were so lacking in desire to identify and bring to justice the person who had murdered our colleague. She was nearing the point of despair, seeing how heartless we appeared to be.

Fallon had argued with her like a teenager. Ian tried to explain the irrational nature of her expectations. I explained that I was out of ideas, but she seemed to think she could squeeze a magnificent new insight out of my brain like it was a lemon she could twist on a juicer until the truth ran out like pure, tangy liquid.

As I turned into the hallway, I heard raised voices coming from behind Diana's office door. Actually, only one raised voice. A woman's.

I walked down the hall and stood outside the break room, trying to determine whether I could recognize the voice. Mostly, the woman was sobbing and hurling accusations of betrayal at Diana, so it was difficult to pin it down. At first, I wondered if it was Layla.

Had Diana pushed too hard in her quest? Had she contacted the rest of the family and upset Layla by doing this?

I moved closer, knowing it probably wouldn't make any difference. It wasn't that I couldn't hear, it was that the sobbing made most of the words inarticulate.

After a moment, there was silence, followed by Diana's calm, steady tones. Of course, that also meant I couldn't make out her words either. She talked for quite a while, then there was another round of silence.

Eventually, the other woman spoke again. The sobbing had stopped, and I recognized Brie's voice.

I made coffee and went into my office, leaving the door open. I wondered how long I would have to wait until the meeting was finished and I could find out what was going on. I supposed Brie must have come looking for her refund and Diana had said no, but then why was the meeting continuing? And what had Diana said to calm her?

The aroma of coffee wafted into the hallway. I went into the other room, filled a mug, and allowed myself to linger in the doorway, hoping to overhear something concrete. There was nothing.

It was nearly ten when Brie and Diana walked past my open door. I angled my chair toward the doorway to be sure I didn't miss Diana when she returned to her office.

A few minutes later, Diana was in my office, closing the door behind her. She pulled up a chair and sat at the side of my desk. "I probably didn't need to close the door. Habit." She laughed. "I had a long, unscheduled meeting with Brie this morning."

"To discuss her refund?"

"No. She wants to continue working with us."

"What changed?"

"Andy took off. He drained the company's cash account. She's pretty sure he's vanished. His cell phone number is inactive. Emails are undeliverable. She had a key to his apartment, but it no longer works and the building manager said he's moved out."

"Is she—?"

"She's gone to the police now to report it. She came here first. It was a strange choice, but I think it says something about what we accomplished in a short time even with a significant obstacle, don't you?"

I thought that if someone stole that much cash from me, I would report it first before trying to work on my career development.

"He told her we were trying to turn her against him. He thought we were brainwashing her, making her think she didn't need him. He was convinced the *magic* between them that made things *work* was going to be destroyed."

"That's interesting," I said.

"It sounds like he's been making comments to that effect since the day we first met them."

"He's not wrong," I said.

She laughed. "I suppose, from his perspective, it's true."

"So why has she suddenly decided she trusts us?"

"She feels utterly betrayed by him. She feels like she's in a free fall."

"But why trust us?"

"I'm not entirely sure. At this point, it might be simple desperation. On some level, she recognizes we were right in what we said about his control over her. Now he's proven it."

"Hmm."

Diana stood. "So we'll start over. She wants to do everything from scratch—her tests and written work. She believes she'll answer the questions differently, that she'll view everything about her life differently without him leaning over her shoulder."

"So, new photographs?"

"Yes."

"And she can afford it? With all her money gone?"

"It was the cash account. She has others. It will just take her time to access that money."

"She's lucky."

"She made a few good decisions. He didn't have control over everything. Although the way she talked, I'm a little surprised."

"Did she explain why she was so mesmerized by him?"

"That's a good way to put it—mesmerized. That's why she wants to do all the pre-work again. She wants to understand that herself."

It sounded like a fairy tale in reverse. Brie held captive by an evil prince and Diana the rescuing fairy godmother who had helped Brie realize her inner power rather than delivering her into the arms of a charming prince.

I couldn't understand how Diana had turned around a woman who had behaved like a cult member toward her business partner, had been trustingly naïve enough to set up her bank accounts such that he could drain one without her signature, and who just as easily came running into the arms of Fly Higher, no longer demanding a refund for being misled, suddenly viewing us as her salvation.

Maybe Diana could help her, but right now, it seemed as if Brie was leaping from the arms of one guru into the comfy nest of another. I wondered if Diana recognized that.

"She's so different from our other clients," I said.

"She is."

"Usually they come to us with some inner strength. She seems like she needs therapy."

"Not at all. I know what I'm doing."

"She could hardly speak a single sentence without him telling her what to say. He took credit for how she looked, as if he formed her muscles himself. Like she was a clay figurine."

"She's stronger than she first appears."

"Maybe."

Diana stood. "I want to thank you for your part. You made a big impression on her. Standing up to Andy the way you did, especially at the nightclub." Brie's reaction was disturbing. Did she expect that most women wouldn't have stood up to him? Would she not have stood up to him, or any man, if she'd been in my position?

It might change my situation with Diana now that she knew Brie was impressed. At the same time, Brie seemed easy to impress.

"She's eager to get started. So I've asked Fallon to schedule a photo session as soon as possible."

I nodded.

It could be interesting. Or, it could be an unsettling experience, trying to photograph a woman who had lost the controlling, driving, dynamic, personality that seemed to animate everything she did and said, who even seemed to be the creator of the vision she held for her fitness business. I wondered if I would be photographing the husk.

I also found myself curious.

I wanted to know every detail of her relationship with Andy. I wondered how they'd met, how they'd formed their connection. I wanted to know how the fitness business came into being. Had he sucked the marrow out of her first or had it been slow and steady over the years so that she didn't notice herself disappearing?

And now, *was* Brie simply filling herself with another personality in the form of Diana, as I suspected?

One minute, she'd been screaming about a refund. Even if that was prompted and fed by Andy, she had some conscious participation. But the moment he disappeared, she turned away from her large staff and came running to Diana, a person she barely knew, who was paid to tell her how to manage her life.

CHAPTER 68

$\mathcal{A}$lex had become slow to respond to Hunter's messages. When she did reply, it was often with a single word. He waited hours, sometimes half a day to get an *okay* or *maybe*. Even worse were the emojis, always open to interpretation. What did an hourglass mean in response to him asking whether she wanted to have dinner? Was she asking what time he wanted to meet?

That had been his assumption. But when he sent a proposed time, she didn't respond for two hours and then replied with *not tonight*. Was he supposed to be pleased that he'd been upgraded to two words? And what had the hourglass meant? She didn't have time? She needed time to get back to him? The time would determine whether it was *yes* or *no*?

He'd finally decided she was pissed at him. It should have been obvious sooner. She was punishing him. Or retreating. She was a private person, and he'd refused to let up with the questions. Adding to that, he'd tricked her into dinner on a park bench, and she didn't like having her wishes disrespected.

At the same time, he was confident in his ability to win her back. Not that he'd lost her. It was more a matter of reminding her about the good stuff. The only problem was he had limited access. Which reminded him again of how few details of her life she'd given him. He knew where her office was located only because he knew the name of the company from his own employer.

He had no idea where she lived. She had two cell phones, but he only had the number for her work phone.

When he'd joked about hiring a P.I., it had crossed his mind that he might lurk outside her office building and follow her home, but if she caught him, they would probably be finished.

This meant if he was to send her flowers or candy, he had to send it to her office. He had a strong feeling she wouldn't appreciate that. The way she retreated from giving information, if it truly was some bizarre heightened need for privacy, she would not want anything to do with her personal life exposed to her colleagues.

He could meet her outside the building as he had before, but now she would be guarded, expecting another ambush at the park.

The best solution was to send something that fit inside a business-looking envelope to her office.

He tapped his keyboard to open a new window on his browser. He was a genius. The only question now was, what would really surprise and charm her? Something that would make her smile, melt her resolve, and bring her rushing to his apartment without any planned date.

Closing his eyes, he tried to think of the things she liked beyond food and martinis and sex, not necessarily in that order. She was obsessed with the cockatoo, but it wasn't hers, so that didn't seem like the right road to pursue.

Clicking to a news site, he scrolled to the sports section. Distractions were helpful. If he put too much effort into coming up with an idea, he would wind up on a shopping site searching for gifts for women in their early thirties, adding unhelpful attributes like romantic or humorous, digging through ads, finding nothing but the clichéd.

Half an hour passed, and he wasn't sure he'd absorbed anything he'd read about the Yankees or pro golf, which he sometimes followed. He also hadn't accomplished any work and he hadn't a clue about what he could send to Alex to get her smiling and spilling out her crazy questions and asking where they were going to eat next.

The only ideas sliding uselessly through his brain were gift cards to restaurants or clothing stores. Not at all the kind of thing that would charm her.

Then, seemingly out of nowhere, it came to him. He laughed out loud, causing the woman across the hallway to stare at him as if he'd lost his mind, then start laughing herself because he couldn't stop and she was caught up in the uncontrollable nature of it.

He grabbed his phone and headed out, telling the receptionist he would be back in less than two hours. He went to a bar two blocks from his building that offered private rooms. He ordered a martini with three olives and paid the cover charge for one of the rooms. Inside, he pulled off his jacket and shirt. He picked up the martini, sipped the liquid so it wasn't as close to the rim, and took several selfies. He gave the most inviting look he could manage while juggling the still rather full drink and the phone.

When he thought he had a decent image, he finished the drink, probably more quickly than he should have. He walked to an office supply and shipping store, printed the photograph, purchased an envelope, and ordered a two-hour delivery to her office.

He returned to work, feeling rather smug.

Two hours and several minutes later, he received a phone call from Alex. He smiled as he answered.

* * *

* * *

* * *

They ordered Italian food for dinner and shared a bottle of wine, sitting on the living room floor instead of at the table. "It's more fun," she said.

When she unbuttoned his shirt and took it off while they were eating, he understood why.

It was only quarter to ten when Alex slithered out of his arms and began dressing.

"You're leaving already?" He sat up.

She picked up the dinner plates off the coffee table and carried them to the kitchen. He heard the water running and the sound of her washing them and standing them in the dish drainer.

When she returned to the living room, she was drying her hands on a clean towel.

"I have an early morning."

"But we're good?"

"Did you think we weren't?"

"Maybe."

She smiled. "I've been busy."

"Doing what?"

"Work. Ned."

"How are you busy with Ned?"

"It's complicated. He keeps trying to start fights. Also, I might be going to California."

"For work?"

"No. Tess is ready to have Damien come home."

"Why are you going?"

"She doesn't want him traveling alone." She laughed. "I know, but that's what she thinks. She wants to pay for my ticket. First class." She smiled.

"Nice."

"I haven't decided. I don't know if it's a good time for a vacation. Work is busy. But first class. And it would be fun to check out her winery."

He felt oddly jealous, an unfamiliar sensation. Maybe jealous was the wrong word. Like something wasn't quite right with the conversation. If she was taking a vacation, shouldn't she be inviting him? Even for a weekend trip? He could certainly pay for his own ticket, even first class. He wouldn't mind checking out a California winery. He'd never been there. He'd been up and down the East Coast, to Chicago numerous times, and a few other Midwestern cities, to parts of Europe and Asia, but never to the West Coast.

It was possible they weren't to that point yet. But there was that five thousand dollars. They'd talked about a trip, but she hadn't said anything about it in a while. He stared at her, wondering if the thought had passed through her mind.

"Why are you looking at me like that?" she asked.

"I'm not looking at you in any particular way," he said.

"You are."

He shrugged. "I don't think so."

"Is something on your mind?" she asked.

"Nope."

"Okay." She stepped around the coffee table and sat beside him on the couch. She leaned toward him and kissed him, deeply and slowly. They definitely seemed good. At the same time, they did not seem that great.

CHAPTER 69

When I was about eight years old, my parents took my brothers and me to an amusement park that offered magic shows and other acts to watch when you wanted a break from the rides. One performer was a woman who spun plates on thin sticks. She ran back and forth across the stage, spinning the plates. As one or two plates slowed, she raced to those and started them spinning again so they didn't lose momentum and fall, then rushed to tend to others that were slowing.

I stared in absolute fascination, unable to look away for even a second. At the end, she wound them all down in a methodical way that allowed her to collect the plates and stack them on a table. It was very impressive but also looked tiring.

I felt like that woman—even Hunter had begun to feel like a spinning plate that I had to keep going at full speed.

But I couldn't give him too much attention because I was dealing with Diana's anxiety and potential escalation of her questions about who might have murdered James. Ned was breathing down my neck, the taunts coming out of his mouth turning now into the fiery flames of a dragon's breath. Although Ned hadn't mentioned him again, it was still possible Kent wasn't far behind if

Ned continued to poke at him and got him thinking too hard about the shocking murder of our neighbor. The biggest problem was the possibility that Carolina's attempt to extort cash from me would turn into an actual police report that would make trouble for Hunter and me.

I might have managed her con differently, but the thought of her raising her son to be a so-called *real* man was intolerable.

I didn't have it in me to get rid of a child. No matter how despicable he was, a child, even at ten or twelve or fifteen, is still a partially formed human being. Even their bodies aren't completed, and certainly their brains still haven't taken shape. Some people would say that damage had been done, but I thought that in the hands of his father, with Carolina silenced by six feet of soil, it was possible his brain and his beliefs and everything about him could be re-shaped.

It had become clear that there was no way to end Carolina's life in her hotel room. If Ricky saw me arrive, I was doomed. He didn't know my last name, or Hunter's. He might not be able to find me right away, maybe not ever, but it was too risky. The fact that he'd seen me and knew my first name was already risk enough. She needed to leave the world under more inexplicable circumstances.

An idea was tickling at the base of my skull, but it required some work and some practices that weren't my usual habit. I hoped I was up to it.

As I'd expected when I left Hunter's apartment earlier than usual, I found Ned seated on the living room couch wearing sweatpants and a T-shirt. His feet were bare. Eileen was beside him, looking gorgeous in faded jeans and a white T-shirt, but also slightly ill. Her face was pale. There was a martini on the table and for half a second, I wondered if it was waiting for me.

Ned leaned forward, picked up the drink, and took a sip. So. The martini was a prop placed there to tease me.

"Cheers, Alex. Would you like a martini?"

"No. It's late."

"Off to your locked room as always. If I was an over-sensitive guy, I'd think you were avoiding me."

I turned toward my bedroom.

"I have some news," he said. "*We* have some news."

"Yes." Eileen's voice was so soft, I only realized she'd spoken because I'd stopped moving. "It will just take a second. I hope ..."

I took a few steps back into the living room and stood facing them. They must be engaged. I would have to find a new place. In my mind, I tossed another imaginary china plate into the air. I glanced at her hands, but her right hand was wrapped tightly around the left. Was she hiding the ring from me, waiting for a big reveal?

"I'm moving in here," Ned said. "But before you freak out, it's—"

"I'm not freaking out."

"Please don't interrupt me. I'm moving in here because as I've mentioned, I'm concerned about Eileen's safety. I don't know what your game is, and I feel the need to keep a closer eye on you."

I started laughing.

"You think it's funny?" Ned asked.

"I do."

"Why?"

I shrugged.

Eileen looked like she might start crying. "I didn't want it to be like this. But Ned really cares about me, and I trust his decisions. I don't agree, but I'm not going to argue with him."

I shrugged again. "Good night."

"We need to discuss ground rules." Ned's voice was so loud, it felt like a crack to the back of my skull.

"I think they're simple," I said. "Stay out of my room. Don't eat my food and don't drink my alcohol."

"Get rid of that bird," he said.

"Not a problem," I said.

"And you need to treat Eileen with—"

"She can speak for herself, I hope." I walked out of the room. I hadn't done such a good job not talking. I really had no idea what he thought he was going to accomplish by moving in. My best guess was he thought he would force me out. But if that was the case, why didn't he just ask her to marry him? Why didn't he just suggest to her they live together and end our arrangement? I was baffled by her acquiescence to him.

It was laughable that he thought I could manage to take her money. I suppose I could find a way to con her, but I could do that with him in the apartment as easily as I could with him not living there. If he thought I was a physical threat, then didn't it occur to him I was the same to him? If he thought I was insane, hadn't it ever crossed his mind I might have a gun locked in my bedroom?

I never would. I'd never touched one and never planned to, but he didn't know that.

Maybe he just liked fighting. He did seem to like looking for areas of disagreement and poking at them. He went out of his way to spoil Eileen's dinner party by inviting someone whose presence he'd known would shock me.

He was one of the strangest men I'd ever known, and I'd known a lot of strange men. Maybe it was a twist on that famous line from Anna Karenina—*All nice men are alike; each creepy man is creepy in his own way.*

The moment I turned the lock in my door, Damien started chattering. I put my finger to my lips and said, "Shh." I walked to his cage and leaned close. "We need to get out of here."

Dangerous woman. He said it softly, with an almost cooing tone.

There was a knock on my door.

"Yes?"

"Can we talk?" Eileen's voice was firm, confident-sounding.

"Is Ned with you?"

"No."

I wasn't sure I believed her. I stared at the locked door and tried to make up my mind.

CHAPTER 70

She knocked again. "Please, Alex. We need to talk."

"You probably should have talked to me before asking your boyfriend to move in."

"I ... please, will you open the door?"

There was a fifty-fifty chance he was standing right there. I moved up close to the door. I leaned into it, pressing my ear against the wood. I heard nothing but the sound of my own pulse thudding in my ear. I looked over at Damien. His crown was raised slightly, but he didn't seem overly alarmed.

I turned the lock and opened the door.

Eileen was standing there, her eyes wide and filled with pleading. I pulled the door wider and made room for her to come into my room. "It's late. I need to get up for work. I'm sure you do too."

"I know, but I can't sleep with things in such a mess."

"The mess is that Ned has decided to move in. So there's nothing you can say to clean it up. Unless you've told him he can't."

She walked over to Damien's cage. His crown rose, and he cocked his head to the side.

"He looks dangerous."

Dangerous woman!

"He's fine. You didn't come here to talk about him."

She turned. "I sort of did. I'm sorry Ned said he has to leave. It doesn't have to be right this—"

"I get it. I'm taking him someplace tonight."

"Where?"

"I don't think I need to tell you that."

"I just … is this going to destroy our friendship?"

I stared at her. "Why are you letting him control you? I thought we had an agreement as roommates. I don't recall discussing that other people could move in here."

"He's not moving in permanently."

"What do you want?" I asked.

"I don't want you to be mad at me."

She sounded so pathetic I wondered what had happened to her. It appeared as though the woman who had managed to get herself pulled together after being in a twisted relationship with the man who left her the four million had walked right back into an identical situation. A different guy, different issues, maybe, but she seemed to be dissolving into a helpless, cowed child right before my eyes.

"Are you mad at me?"

"I can't live with him. And it's not right that you allowed him to do this."

"I didn't have a choice. He's worried about me."

"If you believe you don't have a choice, there's something very wrong with your relationship. With him and with yourself. Why are you afraid of me?"

"I'm not. I don't … he's just …"

"I need to get going. I need to get Damien out of here. He's going back to Tess soon anyway, so unless you're here to tell me Ned isn't moving in after all, there's nothing else to talk about."

"Are you planning to move out?"

"I haven't had time to plan anything. I just need to get Damien to someplace safe."

Her eyes filled with tears. "He's safe here. And your door locks. You don't need to worry."

If what she said wasn't so absurd, I would have laughed.

"You don't have to do it tonight."

"I'm not taking him out because Ned ordered me to. I'm taking him out because I don't trust him."

She started crying. "Please don't say that. He would never hurt a living thing. You act like you think he would kill it."

I began packing Damien's bag with packets of seeds. I opened the cage door, took out his water dish, closed the door, and went to the bathroom. I emptied the water into the sink, washed it out, and used the paper towels I kept under the counter to dry it.

"Can't we talk?"

I dragged my overnight bag out of the closet and began packing my own things. I paused and ordered an Uber to arrive in fifteen minutes.

"Can I help you carry things to the lobby?"

"I can manage."

"But the cage …"

"I can handle it."

"I'll message you," she said. "What if we do something together? Saturday? Just the two of us? Would that work?"

"Sure. Now why don't you go take care of your anxious boyfriend? You don't want him to start thinking something happened to you."

"Please don't say that."

"I think it's a reasonable thing to say."

"It's just … I … can I give you a hug?"

"I'm not a—"

She lunged toward me and wrapped her arms around me. She buried her face in my hair and I could feel her tears on my neck. Luckily, she pulled away quickly and left my room without saying anything more.

I finished packing, leaving room in my suitcase for Damien's food bag.

I was standing on the curb when the Uber pulled up. Inside the cage, Damien was muttering. On the ride down in the elevator, I'd debated whether it was better to message Hunter to let him know I was coming or to simply show up. I wasn't even sure I'd packed the right clothes for work, but I would worry about that in the morning. It wouldn't be the end of the world if I showed up in jeans and the leather jacket I was wearing right now. It wasn't so cold I needed a heavy jacket, but wearing it made me feel ready for anything. As if I were wearing protective armor.

As I maneuvered the cage into the backseat of the minivan Uber I'd requested, I decided I would not text Hunter. He would ask questions that were easier to answer face-to-face.

We pulled up in front of his building. I eased the cage out of the back and dragged out my suitcase, laughing to myself as I imagined the two possible reactions from Hunter. He would either be thrilled or horrified. I didn't think there was anything in between.

When I knocked on his door, it took him several minutes before he spoke to me from the other side, asking who it was.

"Alex."

The lock turned, and the door opened.

"What's wrong?"

"Nothing huge, but Damien had to leave my apartment. Can we stay here?"

He grinned. "You don't have to ask. Although I hope he doesn't—"

"He won't. Not much. And it won't be for more than a few days. It's getting to be too much. In the morning, I'll tell Tess to book my flight. He needs to go home. I can't be dragging him all over New York."

I told him what had happened since I'd left his apartment. He looked disgusted but didn't say much. I was curious what he was thinking, but I'd told Eileen the absolute truth. I was really tired. And carrying Damien's large cage had not made me less tired.

Hunter lifted the cover off the cage.

Dangerous woman! Chardonnay time!

"I don't think so." He lowered the cover.

I wondered if Hunter was referring to the second statement or both. I went into the kitchen. Two apples and a tired-looking banana sat on the counter. I opened the refrigerator where I saw a half empty basket of strawberries. Of course there was no mango. It's not a fruit most people have hanging out in their kitchen. I grabbed two strawberries, washed them and sliced them. I put them in Damien's cage.

He took them without commenting. I filled his water dish, and we went to bed.

Despite the exhaustion I'd been proclaiming for the past few hours, I couldn't fall asleep. I could stay at Hunter's for a few days. I knew he would be happy to have me stay for longer, probably indefinitely, although I really didn't want to have a conversation about that possibility. A trip to California might be five days, maybe even ten. Possibly longer. But then what?

CHAPTER 71

*E*ileen's idea for how we might patch things up in our badly torn relationship was a ferry ride into New York Harbor and an afternoon spent climbing the stairs inside the Statue of Liberty. A friend of hers had had tickets for five months and now had a team-building event that her boss had informed her was obligatory.

I'd never been there, but I could see from looking at it that it would be a tight and claustrophobic climb to the statue's crown. I couldn't imagine why Eileen thought that would be an opportunity for a meaningful conversation, with people breathing up on us from below and their feet clanging on metal steps above our heads.

Maybe it would be one of those experiences that connects people through the sheer torture of living through the same unpleasant moments. Besides, there was only one way to repair what had happened. She knew what that was, and she was refusing to do anything about it.

However, telling her I didn't want to spend the day together wasn't a good plan either, because I still needed a place to keep my things while I figured out what was going to happen next. And there was a small chance that if I spent enough time in California, Ned might get bored and leave.

If I came home to an apartment that didn't contain him, I would be able to breathe for a few more weeks or months. It was obvious that I wasn't going to be able to live with her long-term. It had seemed like such a great idea at first. Eileen and I got along and we had a lot to talk about. Neither of us had demanded much from the other, until she started chipping away at our easy connection, wanting more and more time and attention and friendship. But even that might have been manageable.

Ned was not manageable.

Eileen had done her research. She messaged me a schedule for the day, warning that if we didn't get to Battery Park by her specified time, we might not get to enjoy what would likely be a once-in-a-lifetime opportunity. I had no doubt it was once in a lifetime because after climbing 354 19-inch steps up the equivalent of twenty stories, it was doubtful anyone would want to do it a second time. No matter how much their out-of-town visitors might beg for it.

We had to arrive early due to lines to pick up the tickets. Also built into her schedule was time to go through security. A driver's license was required, which I didn't have, so I would have to bring my passport. I wasn't thrilled about this.

On the boat ride over, Eileen and I leaned on the railing and watched the water splashing around the sides. We stared at the tiny island as we drew closer. It was almost unbelievable to see her seeming to grow larger before my eyes—the copper statue that decorated greeting cards and postcards, and was formed into tiny figurines and splashed across video montages. At times, she seemed to be everywhere, especially in New York City. But even growing up on the West Coast, I felt as if she'd been a shadowy figure in my life for as long as I could remember.

Standing at the base, climbing up inside, would be a surreal experience.

Maybe I was glad Eileen had suggested this, even if the climb would be difficult. Not the physical challenge of it, but the press of people and the closeness of the space that would prevent us from seeing out or breathing fresh air or having any hope of escaping if something wasn't to our liking.

"I'm really glad we could do this." Eileen grabbed a few strands of hair that had plastered themselves across her face and pulled them away. "And I'm glad it's cooler today. I read it can be almost twenty degrees hotter inside the statue."

"Sounds nice," I said.

"Don't be grumpy."

"I'm not."

"I hope you're not just doing this to be polite. That you really wanted to spend time with me."

"Absolutely," I said.

"I know Ned can be difficult."

"Are we going to spend the whole day talking about him?"

"No, but I want to fix things with us."

"Calling him difficult is an understatement. I hope you can see why there's a problem."

She sighed. "I can, but I just wish ..."

I didn't ask what she wished. She wished I wouldn't argue with him. She wished I would let him tell me how to live and take over our apartment and stick his nose into my life. She considered his questions friendly and all in good fun.

"I'm surprised you've never visited the Statue of Liberty before," I said. "I'm surprised Ned didn't want to go with you. Or maybe he's already seen it."

"He hasn't. We'll do it again, together."

"I'm even more surprised, shocked, actually, that he let you spend the day alone with me."

"Don't be like that."

"He's so concerned about what I might do to you that he moved into your apartment without really caring if you wanted him to. So I think he's—"

"He cares what I want."

"Yes, but he still bulldozed his way in."

"It wasn't like that."

"What was it like?"

She scooped more hair off her face and turned slightly so she was facing into the wind. "It's complicated. I can't explain it."

I turned my back to the railing and looked back at the deck where people sat and others clustered along the railing. "Maybe he followed us."

"He would never do that. Besides, you need tickets and—"

"Yes, he would. He followed me. Didn't he tell you about that?" I turned and looked directly at her.

Her dark glasses prevented me from seeing her eyes, but the fact she said nothing told me she knew, and that she was probably getting weepy. "I'm sorry. He said that was a mistake. His curiosity got the best of him. Not his curiosity, but he just … it seemed like you were lying about Hunter."

"Why would I lie about him?"

She shrugged.

"And if I did lie, what does that have to do with Ned?"

"He wants to know if you're truthful with me. It all comes back to how much he loves me. I wish you could see that. I guess since you've never been in love you don't know that feeling of wanting to look after the person you care about more than anyone in the world."

I was pretty sure that wasn't love, even though quite a few people confused it with love, but I said nothing.

I looked toward Liberty Island. "We're almost there. You should message him and let him know I didn't shove you into the water so I could collect your money."

"Alex!"

I laughed.

"It's not funny."

"You should text him, though."

There were only three things I wanted from the day. One was to see what it was like to climb up inside one of the most iconic statues in the world. The second was to enjoy a boat ride on a summer day.

The third was to get my hands on Eileen's unlocked cell phone and pluck Ned's number out of her contact list.

The first two were guaranteed. The last was going to take every manipulation skill I possessed, and possibly a bit of luck, which I never liked relying upon.

CHAPTER 72

We got off the boat and spent an hour walking around the museum, looking at photographs and reading about the history of the statue. We ate expensive sandwiches and drank bottled water before getting in line for our climb to the statue's crown.

Both of us had tiny purses to hold our phones and ID since we didn't want to lug large bags up the steps in tight quarters. I had my eye on Eileen's purse, my eyes boring through the leather as I tried to think how I would create a situation in which I could get her phone. She'd texted Ned soon after I'd suggested it and again after we ate lunch. I'd known she would. Planting the idea in her head had started her thinking about it and I could see her glancing at her phone every few minutes, wondering if he was worrying about her, wondering if he would text her first, knowing he would be pleased if she made the first move.

We'd also decided not to carry water up with us. The water with our sandwiches would be enough. "We can re-hydrate when we get back down," she said. "It will make climbing more awkward, and it's not as if stopping to sip will make much difference."

"You know what would make it even easier," I said. "How about if we get a locker and just take one purse? We can fit both phones in mine. We can take turns carrying it."

She shrugged and handed over her phone.

Now, all I needed was the perfect moment to suggest another text to Ned and smooth timing while the screen was unlocked.

I took a deep breath, gave her a confident smile, and we moved toward the entrance.

The climb can only be described as tedious.

It felt like I imagined it might to be part of a chain gang. All of us heel to toe, trudging up the stairs, mostly in silence because no one wanted to expend oxygen talking when they needed it for a 20-story climb. Every so often Eileen or I made a comment to each other, as did other groups, so there was some conversation, but it wasn't the racket of hundreds of voices all talking loudly at once, echoing off copper walls that you might expect.

There was something almost disturbing about it, locked inside that column with strangers. We were all breathing the same warm, close air, all determined to accomplish the same task, all realizing there was nothing that spectacular about it except bragging rights afterwards, and of course, the view from the crown once we arrived.

When we reached the top, Eileen gave me a hug.

I asked her if she wanted to text Ned that she'd made it and she said she wasn't sure she could get a signal from inside. I pushed her to try anyway.

She did, and when she handed the phone back to me, unlocked, I thought I was home free, but then I realized tapping into her contacts and scrolling down the list would require more time than I could do without her realizing I was snooping through her phone.

I let it go dark and slipped it into my purse.

We stood for a while marveling at the view and the realization of where we were, took our photos, and began the descent. When we reached the ground and emerged into the main building, I felt like I'd been set loose from a tunnel where I'd been held captive for hours. At no time did it feel at all like I was inside that majestic looking statue. At no time did I feel like I was doing something remarkable. I climbed tight, claustrophobic stairs, admittedly breathing harder than I should have as I neared the top because climbing steadily in the heat with little airflow is not at all like running. And then I'd turned around and walked back down.

All I could think about was Eileen's phone. I had to find a way to get Ned's number. I needed it because I had an idea lurking in my mind that would cause a little, maybe a lot of trouble for him. I slid my hand into my purse, pulled out the key to the locker and put it in my pocket.

My game for Ned wouldn't get him out of my life. It probably wouldn't end his relationship with Eileen, but it would make his life difficult for a while. And there was no way on earth he could connect it to me. He might imagine it was me. But he would never know for sure and he wouldn't be able to connect the dots.

Keeping my voice casual, I took the key out of my pocket and handed it to Eileen with a twenty-dollar bill. "Do you mind grab-bing two waters when you get your purse from the locker? I'm going to sit down for a second."

"Are you tired?"

"A little." I pulled her phone out of my purse. "You should text Ned and let him know we made it down okay."

"Give it a rest, will you? You've made your point."

"I'm trying to be respectful. I understand he's worried. It's no big deal." I held out her phone.

She sighed and sent a quick text.

Holding my thumb on the screen to keep it awake, I coughed slightly, then followed it with two more coughs. "I'm really thirsty."

"Sure. I'll be right back."

I turned and walked toward a bench that was filled with people resting their swollen feet. I leaned against the wall and tapped her contacts. I found Ned's name. He had a 212 area code so I only had to memorize the other 7 digits. I pulled out my phone, tapped them into an email to myself, and slid both phones back into my purse.

When I was finished, I realized I truly was incredibly thirsty, but I also felt a satisfied smile spread across my face. I was glad Eileen wasn't there to see it.

CHAPTER 73

J bought a new burner phone. Carolina didn't pick up when I called her. Who would? Knowing she would recognize my voice, I left a voice mail without giving my name, telling her my phone had been stolen and I'd gotten a new number for security reasons. I complained about what a headache it was to let everyone know I had a new number. I asked if she would meet me for a coffee. I told her where I would be the following afternoon if she could make it.

I had a two-hour gap between clients, which allowed me plenty of time.

My calm voice and friendly invitation, all of it sounding as if none of the threats and accusations had passed between us, must have captured her attention. Or maybe she thought I was bringing a fat envelope full of cash to a crowded coffee shop on a weekday afternoon after all. Whatever the reason, she was already seated with an oversized coffee drink when I arrived.

I gave her a tiny, frivolous finger-wave as I passed by her table, ordered my latte, then joined her, setting my cup on the table.

I spoke in a soft voice. "I wanted to tell you I have your money." I

THE WOMAN IN THE HOTEL

picked up my cup, glanced nervously at the nearby tables, and took a sip.

She was clueless enough to hold out her hand as if I would slap it onto her palm.

"Not here." I laughed softly. "How many times do I have to tell you? Are you crazy?" I lowered my voice to a whisper. "What if there's an off-duty police detective? Or just a guy who sees an easy mark? You'd be putting yourself in danger walking out of here with that much money."

"I'm assuming you have it in an envelope." She didn't bother to lower her voice much. She left her hand face-up on the table, picked up her cup with the other hand, and gulped her coffee.

"It's too risky. We can meet tonight."

"Where?"

"At a cemetery in Brooklyn."

"Brooklyn?!" She laughed. "I'm not doing that. Why are you making such a big deal out of this? Besides, I'm not going to a cemetery at night. That's creepy and weird and probably dangerous. Worse than thinking a detective is sitting around a coffee shop watching two women have coffee drinks."

"Cops love coffee."

"I'm not going to a cemetery."

"As an act of good faith, I've added ten percent interest, if you want to call it that. I know I've been stringing you along."

"Bribing me is not going to get me to a cemetery at night."

"I'm really sorry all this happened." I took a sip of coffee. "I never should have agreed to let you pay me to watch your son. That's not how friends treat each other. It was an absurd amount of money for childcare. Really, as a friend, I should have watched him for nothing."

"You're right."

"I actually think a cemetery is safer than most places. In a bar, guys would be checking you out. They would notice the money."

"How?"

"People don't hand around fat envelopes full of papers. What else would it be? You don't want someone following you. I thought of the cemetery because my mom is buried there." I blinked rapidly and looked down at my coffee. I sighed. "Anyway, no one goes to cemeteries at night. They're actually quite safe."

"I don't—"

"Do you believe in ghosts or something?"

"No."

"Then think about it. Why would someone go at night? There's some lighting, but not ideal for visiting loved ones."

She still looked slightly ill. Maybe she just didn't like the thought of being around all those buried bodies.

"It's probably the safest place for two women in the entire city at night."

She took a more cautious sip of her drink. "I suppose that makes sense. But why can't you just come to my hotel?"

"Does your husband know I'm bringing you money? Does Ricky? Because I was also thinking, even though you don't know the exact amount of his therapy, I should give you a down payment."

"How much?"

I looked around nervously.

"Why are you so worried? I didn't have the impression you're someone who worries a lot. You act like you think someone followed you. That you think someone is listening to our conversation. No one cares."

"Because we're talking about a lot of cash, and I think you should be more careful. You never know who's listening. You shouldn't assume no one cares. Some people are always alert to opportunities for crime."

She shrugged. "How much money?"

I placed my hands on the table, bending my thumb and pinkie finger, so three fingers remained pointing in her direction.

"Three thousand?"

I shook my head.

"Hundred?"

I shook my head.

"This is ridiculous," she said. "Are we playing hotter-colder like a couple of first graders?"

I moved my hand closer to her. I formed my other hand into a misshapen zero.

"Thirty *thousand*?" Her voice was far too loud. The woman at the table beside us jerked her head in our direction. She gave me a curious frown.

I relaxed my fingers and moved my hands off the table.

Carolina looked at the woman beside us, still staring at me. "I guess a cemetery would be okay." Her voice was so quiet, I barely heard what she said.

CHAPTER 74

I'd never done anything remotely like this before. The list of unknowns raced through my mind in an endless loop. The adrenaline getting my body ready for what I had to accomplish pumped through my system so fast I was concerned my hands might start shaking. My eyeballs might jitter, suggesting to Carolina that I was high.

There wasn't any question I was doing the right thing by removing Carolina from the earth. If that boy had a shred of a chance to grow up into a man who was less *real* and more realistic, he couldn't do it with his mother calling the shots. Of course, if his father left her and became Ricky's sole caregiver, that might happen, but that process would take years. Jordan would need to decide he absolutely had to get out of his marriage, followed by an epic custody battle. Even if he was given custody, Carolina would still have enormous influence.

The only chance for that kid and his father was to have Carolina out of the picture entirely. Forever.

Even then, I wasn't sure the odds were in his favor.

Had she permanently imprinted her belief system onto his

brain? Maybe not. He was a strange kid, which suggested that there was something going on behind those blue eyes that might be open to a different way of thinking. Surely he'd heard opposing views of the world, of manhood, of what women were like and what they wanted, from his father, from family friends and relatives on his father's side of the family.

But what happened after wasn't something I could do much about. I would do my part, the rest was up to his father. And to Ricky himself, obviously.

Carolina signed her death warrant when she told me that a real man should tell women to sit down and shut up. There was enough of that in the world. It wasn't useful to have her adding another to the pile.

But my usual method of seduction, sedation, and suffocation wasn't going to work.

I would have to face my revulsion at the sight of blood. That was one reason I'd chosen the cemetery. It would be dark. I wouldn't see the blood right away. When I did, it would be easy to think of it as something else, something foreign and less threatening.

For several days, I'd spent time getting familiar with the cemetery I'd chosen. I'd found the section where most of the new graves were being dug. I'd noticed there was at least one freshly dug grave every time I went, waiting overnight for an occupant to arrive the following day.

The supplies I needed weren't remarkably different from previous times. I'd purchased my heavy-duty trash bags and cleaning supplies. I'd also purchased two pairs of black leggings and two long-sleeved T-shirts, two pairs of athletic shoes, socks, and two black hoodies at a discount store. I'd bought supplies for an initial cleaning of my hands and clothing. I hoped it wouldn't be too gruesome and I could walk away without a churning, roiling stomach on top of all the adrenaline.

I also had a box of latex gloves but was undecided on whether to use them. The upside was they would keep blood and anything else from Carolina's body out of my fingernails and off my skin. The other upside was the latex would give me a firm grip. The downside was they would make my hands feel constricted. They were slightly uncomfortable. Overall, they were unfamiliar. And I had enough unfamiliar things going on that I didn't want to add more to the mix if I didn't absolutely have to. Still, the gloves were in my overstuffed backpack.

I arrived at the cemetery at ten minutes after midnight, twenty minutes before my arranged meeting time with Carolina. I went to the grave I'd chosen.

The grave was one I'd identified that morning, messaging her the names on a few surrounding headstones. I'd done my research. An unmarried forty-two-year-old man was scheduled to be buried in that spot the following day. He'd died of cancer. I would have preferred suicide, but I can't orchestrate the entire universe to my liking, and this was good enough. It was enough to confuse everyone, leaving several unanswered, and hopefully permanently unanswerable questions.

Although it sounds like a weak, implausible plan created for a sitcom, I'd studied anatomy diagrams and read quite a lot about how to most effectively stab Carolina to death. I'd never stabbed anyone before, but I had a few things in my favor. First, she wasn't expecting to be stabbed. I was far stronger than she was. As long as the first wound was disabling enough, I was certain I could complete what needed to be done. Aside from the moonlight and some solar lights along the paths that wove among the graves, I wouldn't have to see more than I wanted. Hopefully that wouldn't work against seeing what I needed to see.

I'd bought a beautiful, very expensive, incredibly sharp knife. It was a shame that after a single use, it would be wrapped in layers of plastic, sealed with duct tape, and tossed into a dumpster in Hell's Kitchen, a long way from the cemetery, but close to the small, unglamorous hotel where I'd chosen to spend the night.

This was not an evening where I could risk coming home to a barrage of questions from Eileen's boyfriend sprawled on my living room couch. And I absolutely couldn't stay with Hunter because I needed a very long, very hot, very private shower after I was finished with Carolina. I also needed a good night's sleep. I wouldn't be in the mood for conversation. Even with Damien.

CHAPTER 75

J'd gushed my gratitude to Hunter for looking after Damien while I returned to my apartment to start some preliminary packing for California. He hadn't questioned that I would be gone overnight to do this. He'd warmed to Damien to the point that he seemed pleased to spend an evening alone with him, trying to teach him a new word or two. I told him as long as the word wasn't picnic, that was fine.

When I arrived at the cemetery, I left my backpack behind a double gravestone for a husband and wife who had died within two years of each other in the late 90s. It was clean white marble and gleamed in the light of the half moon that was giving me just the amount of visibility I needed. The gravestone was almost too much reflection, standing out like a beacon in the center of the area where I was waiting.

In the pocket of my hoodie was a manilla envelope with ten thousand dollars. While Carolina was busy counting, already growing suspicious it wasn't the promised thirty-three thousand and change, I would drive the knife into her stomach just below her breastbone. It was the easiest point of entry, would cause pain and immobilize her enough that she would be unable to fight back, allowing me time for several more stabs, at least one of them lethal.

I wasn't thrilled that I had to resort to stabbing her. I preferred my usual method. It was clean. It never failed. There was very little room for something to go wrong, once I had the man in a hotel room and he was thinking about nothing but how quickly I would be taking off my clothes.

This was a hundred times more difficult. If I did this for a living, I would definitely be asking for hazard pay.

The knife was zipped inside the front of my hoodie, which I hoped wasn't too far out of reach, but I couldn't very well walk up to her holding it and it was too large for my pocket.

We had to start out as I'd promised in the coffee shop—a friendly greeting and an exchange of cash. I would offer to hold her cell-phone flashlight while she counted the bills.

I saw a figure walking along the path, headed in my direction. Immediately, I knew it was her. The way she swung her arms and hips, her thin frame, and the way she jerked her head from side to side, as if she were afraid of threats emerging from sealed graves after all.

I let her walk all the way up to the grave of the man whose name I'd given her, forcing her into a position where her back was toward me. She looked nervously around several times. I took a few deep breaths, hoping she would stop acting like a squirrel so I would be able to approach her casually without giving away that I'd been hiding.

Finally, she calmed down and I rose from behind the marble gravestone and walked toward her. I didn't speak her name until I was beside her.

Of course, her entire body convulsed, giving away her fear.

I put my hand on her shoulder. "Relax. We're fine. Did you see anyone?"

She shook her head. "No, but—"

"Of course not. I told you it's the safest place."

"I don't like seeing that open grave. It's right there!"

"Just watch your step."

"What if I fall in?"

"Why would you fall in?"

"What if you push me?"

I laughed. "Then you could call your husband to come get you. But it might be hard to explain."

"That's not funny."

"You're right." I pulled the manilla envelope out of my hoodie and handed it to her. "I know the therapy will be so much more, but it's a start."

"Yes, it will be. What your ex-boyfriend did was—"

"We don't need to go over that again." I was tired of hearing her pathetic lie. I wondered why she thought I believed her and wasn't willing to fight such an obvious game. Maybe she thought I had doubts about Hunter. I'd realized it made her slightly more willing to go along with my game because she was knocked off balance by the ease with which she was extracting money from me. She was shocked that I would so quickly turn my back on a guy who was charming and smart, not to mention so nice to look at.

Maybe she didn't find him any of those things. Maybe her head was so full of her own plans, there was no room for questions about why things were happening as they were, no space to consider that other people might have agendas of their own.

She'd already pried open the metal tabs and pulled the stack of bills halfway out of the envelope. "It's hard to count it in the dark. This doesn't look like thirty-three thousand."

"Give me your phone and I'll hold the light for you."

"Use your phone."

"It's almost dead."

She made a huffing sound, pulled the phone out of her pocket, and handed it to me. I took it in my left hand, turned on the light, and shone it toward the bills.

One at a time, she began peeling them away from the stack.

I took a few steps, moving beside her, then slightly behind.

"Don't move the light."

"I'm trying to make it more direct."

"Now I lost count." She murmured the numbers as she began counting again.

I took another step back, lifting the phone higher as I did so she would be less likely to notice my movement.

Reaching inside my hoodie, I pulled out the knife and shook off the cloth I'd used to keep the blade from nicking me. In one smooth, swift movement, I dropped the phone and drove the knife into her side.

She grunted, then cried out in pain.

I forced myself not to look around for any unexpected people taking midnight strolls among the dead, and the nearly dead. It was too late now.

I pulled out the knife, averting my eyes from the blade. I stepped quickly to my right and stabbed her again, driving the blade into her flesh as far as it would go. She made a wheezing, crying sound and collapsed on the ground. Still forcing my mind into a blank, white space, I continued stabbing her until she wasn't moving, until all I saw were her eyes, glowing almost as bright as the marble slabs in the moonlight.

The first thing I did was to find Carolina's phone that I'd tossed onto the grass. I entered her passcode and sent a message to Ned's phone.

I'm waiting at our spot. Xo

I shoved the phone into my pocket and rolled her body toward the yawning cavity a few yards from where I stood. When I reached the edge, I straightened and pushed her into the open grave. She hit the hard-packed earth six feet down with a softer thud than I would have expected.

I hurried to my backpack and pulled out trash bags and cleaning supplies. I cleaned all my exposed skin with moistened wipes, stuffing the used ones into a trash bag. Using the flashlight on my phone, I unlocked Carolina's again, and turned off the location services. I powered down the phone, wiped it with a wet wipe to remove all traces of me, and stomped on it until it was broken beyond repair. It was possible, even likely, it might still eventually be located. For that reason, it had its own trash bag and would be tossed into a dumpster far from where I planned to dispose of my bloody clothes and cleaning supplies.

I stripped off my clothes, changed into fresh ones, then wiped my hands and face again. I shone the flashlight on the wipes to be sure they were coming away free of stains. I wrapped up the trash bags, stuffed them into my backpack, shoved my arms through the straps, and began jogging, breaking into a faster run until I was out of the cemetery.

With four stops to be rid of the bag with the knife, the bag of clothes and other trash, the bag with her phone, and another bag with my destroyed burner phone minus its sim card, the darkness was fading to charcoal gray by the time I returned to my hotel.

I fell into bed exhausted, hoping my dreams in the weeks and months to come wouldn't be soaked with blood.

CHAPTER 76

*A*fter four hours of sleep, I woke and showered again. I turned my thoughts to work and the terse message Diana had sent when I told her I would be coming in late.

Team meeting at ten.

I texted back that it wasn't on my calendar. She didn't respond. She must have walked down the hallway, telling the two team members who were already in their offices about the meeting.

It wasn't like her to have a meeting that hadn't been planned a week in advance. Was this another investigative session into the unanswered questions about our former colleague's murder? I wondered if she would go so far as to haul his parents into our small suite of offices to ask about James's personal life in her determination to find out who might be lurking in the shadows. Maybe she'd contacted some of his friends. Maybe she'd persuaded his sister to return. Maybe I would walk in to a conference room overflowing with people who had known James, all eager to talk about his life, searching for clues, each with a tiny piece of information that would form a picture of his last hours on earth.

Anything was possible.

I understood why she couldn't let go of it. Having a man's body turn up in the basement of a hotel with no explanation for how it got there would drive me insane with curiosity. Anyone would be curious. Even when you're not involved, you want an explanation for situations like those.

Some, like me, are curious to the point of unnecessary risk.

I wondered if Diana was the same. Or if it was only because of how James had helped her after her mother's death that she felt compelled to figure it out. As if she owed him something.

I checked out of the hotel and dropped the second set of clothes from the night before into a trashcan in the subway station. I felt relaxed and calm, my backpack light on my shoulders.

The moment I opened the door to our lobby, I was aware of a shift in the atmosphere. There was someone new in the space. It wasn't as if I had a premonition, it was simply the presence of an unfamiliar voice and the slight suggestion of a man's cologne, which I knew Ian never wore.

I thought I'd arrived with plenty of time for the ten o'clock meeting, but the wall clock said it was three minutes past, and that was the other thing tickling my senses. All the voices seemed to be talking at once, all congested in the conference room, flowing through the open door into the hallway and out to the lobby.

I went to my office, dropped my backpack under my desk, and slipped into the break room. I filled a mug with coffee and went into the conference room.

The blinds were closed, and a slide was projected onto the screen with our Fly Higher logo—wings inside the outline of a cloud. Diana was seated at the head of the table facing the screen. Seated at Diana's right was Fallon, her laptop open in front of her. To Fallon's right was Ian, who greeted me with a large smile.

Seated with his back to me was a guy I didn't recognize, either by his build or his tone of voice.

"Have a seat, Alexandra." Diana flipped to the next slide.

Displayed on the screen was a list of our names and roles. Standing apart from the familiar names and titles of Diana, Ian,

Fallon, and myself, it was clear that this was Diana's passive-aggressive payback for all the small and large sins I'd committed since Trystan was gunned down in his office.

Dean Torres: Photographer

"I've arranged our org chart this way," Diana said, "because I want to emphasize again that I like to avoid a hierarchical structure. I don't want boxes and lines that suggest, for example, that Fallon answers to everyone else on the team, even though her role involves support for each of us. We work in a collaborative environment and I think it's important to reflect that everywhere." She turned to me in a very deliberate way. "It's unfortunate you missed the start of the meeting, Alexandra. I introduced everyone to our new photographer who will share the client workload equally with you. This is Dean Torres."

The new guy turned. He held out his hand. I shook it.

"Alexandra," he said.

"Dean," I said.

"Looking forward to learning a lot from you," he said.

"Dean is being too modest," Diana chirped.

And I do mean, *chirped*.

"He studied photography at NYU," Diana said. "He's traveled extensively and has a stunning portfolio of studio photography, location shots, and incredible candid images. He grew up with five sisters and has great sensitivity toward women. He understands their unique perspective on the world. He's won awards for his photographs of children in war zones and for his work with an international group that fights human trafficking." She gave me a smile that suggested she was overwhelmed by Dean's skill and the depth of his absolute goodness as a human being.

"I'm looking forward to seeing your work," I said as I pulled out the chair and sat down. I knew when my lines were being prompted and I knew that I had better start out well with Dean. He could prove himself one way or the other later.

Looking at him now, as I angled slightly in my chair while Diana clicked through slides and re-hashed our mission and goals and purpose, I thought he looked like he might be ex-military or a former cop. He had brown hair cut short in the style that said he got a trim every three weeks without fail. He was clean-shaven, his skin so smooth I wanted to run my finger along his jaw and ask what kind of razor he used. His eyes were brown with thick lashes and he had a nice smile, with perfectly aligned teeth that said: *I went to an orthodontist and I never once forgot to wear my retainer after my braces came off.*

He looked like he was in his late thirties. He wasn't wearing a wedding ring. I didn't think he was exceptionally tall, probably five-ten. He also had a New York accent, but it wasn't the heavy kind that you hear mimicked to the point of absurdity in movies and TV, just a pleasant reminder that he'd been born in the area.

There were three things to take away from the sudden appearance of Dean.

Diana had drawn a clear line in the sand.

I might need to look for a new job much sooner than I'd expected.

I was free to leave for a week or more, possibly a month, for a nice vacation in California.

Of course, Diana would interpret that as sulking, as unprofessional behavior. She would be extremely annoyed that Dean would be over-worked and they would continue to fall behind.

But I didn't have to tell her I was going to California. I still had a father in Portland. There was no reason I couldn't have a family situation to deal with that required my attention. She could seethe and suspect my motives and question my story, but she couldn't say no.

Diana had come to our list of new and current clients. She clicked to the next slide.

"These are the clients that need immediate attention. First on the list is Brie Brixton. Because there were so many problems there, which you're all aware of, I've assigned Dean to take over. He's been brought up to speed on everything that happened with Brie." She gave me a sharp, knowing look, and I took it that *everything* included Andy's creepy roaming hands on my body. "A fresh start, a new photographic experience, will help change that dynamic."

She went on talking about the other clients, noting which ones would be assigned to me, which ones to Dean.

It was best to wait to announce my urgently required trip to the West Coast. I would save that for a private meeting. I felt even lighter than I had when I'd put on my nearly empty backpack only an hour ago.

Enjoying the California sunshine, tasting wine, and hanging out with Tess would give my mind space to wander over the possibilities of what I might do to earn money. Hopefully, a lot more money. Taking photographs was never boring. I was utterly captivated every moment I spent peering through the lens of my camera, talking to clients, luring them out of their familiar patterns until they exposed their secrets. But I'd told Diana a hundred times I didn't want to share the job. Maybe it would be a clean line between Dean's work and mine, and it would feel the same as always. Maybe it wouldn't. But I needed time and space and distance to think.

CHAPTER 77

The moment Diana closed her laptop, Dean turned to me and asked if I wanted to join him for lunch in an hour or so. I asked him if I could take a raincheck. I gave him a big bright smile to go with my refusal, but I didn't tell him that the raincheck would be weeks away, and possibly, I would ghost him.

I followed Diana to her office and asked for five minutes. She looked smug, as if she'd expected me to come complaining.

I closed the door and sat in the chair facing her desk.

"What's the problem?" she asked. "Do you want to give me another sales pitch on how you can't possibly collaborate with another photographer? Because if that's why you're here, I'm not interested. And I expect—"

"That's not why I'm here."

She adjusted her watch, straightening the delicate gold face on her wrist, rubbing her thumb across the glass. "What is it, then?"

"It's actually really good timing that Dean is here."

"Oh?" She looked up at me, unable to hide her shock.

"I don't know if I've mentioned my father is on the West Coast … in Portland. There are some … well, some family issues I need to take care of. I was feeling terrible about telling you I need time off,

346

but now that Dean is here, and he's obviously so skilled and so competent, he can step right in without missing a step." I gave her a triumphant smile.

"I hired him because we need two photographers."

"I know. And I know there's a lot of work, but he's clearly a go-getter. And I'm sure he'll want to prove himself by working longer hours."

"I don't expect that. I don't want anyone—"

"It's ... I'm really needed."

"What's wrong?"

I folded my hands on my lap, twisting my fingers tightly around my knuckles. I looked down at them, a writhing cluster of worms. I thought about Carolina's body in the bottom of the empty grave and wondered if anyone had discovered it yet. They must have. The funeral I'd read about had been scheduled for late morning. "It's personal. I don't think I ... it's very ..." I cleared my throat softly.

She sighed. "Fine. I thought we had a better relationship than that. But I'm not going to pry. How much time do you need?"

"Three weeks."

"*Three weeks*? That's too much. Is he dying?"

"It's a big mess."

"Do you really need—"

"I don't want to have to extend things, and keep changing dates. That's the maximum. I'd rather start with that and I can let you know once I get there and assess the situation if it will be less."

She nodded. She looked relieved, obviously assuming it would be less.

Or maybe I was misreading her. Maybe she was relieved for more than one reason. I shouldn't ever assume she wasn't as calculating as I was. Behind her calm, dark eyes, her mind was churning as quickly as mine. Maybe, as she'd sat there objecting, looking directly into my eyes, she was weighing the pros and cons of having me out of the way.

Dean would have a heavy workload, but I'd been managing it.

We hadn't lost any clients or gotten so far behind it couldn't be fixed. He was full of energy and eager to get going. Maybe he was more efficient than I was with his computer work. She might already know that. Maybe he could even elicit telling photographs with less conversation, more streamlined appointments. It was possible.

Maybe she was thinking, as she tried to draw a hard line on my time off, this would allow him to settle in without any interference from me. Once I returned, I would be less difficult to deal with because Dean would be running the show. He would have great relationships with their clients, with Fallon, with Ian, and with Diana herself.

She smiled. "I hope everything turns out alright with your family. Let me know if there's anything I can do to help or support you. Anything at all."

"Absolutely," I said.

CHAPTER 78

*T*ess had arranged the promised first-class ticket for me and reserved space for Damien. Obviously, despite my talking to him about the trip to his new home, he had no clue what was coming and would be disoriented when his cage was crated up and put on a tram, wheeled to the plane, and loaded into the cargo hold.

Still, he would adapt. That's what all living creatures do. Adapt or die.

It was three-thirty when I unlocked my apartment door. I'd finished up what I needed to do, said goodbye to my colleagues, promised an extended raincheck to Dean, and taken a leisurely walk home in the afternoon sun. I would miss Manhattan. I was looking forward to open space and more sky, less humidity and more pleasant-smelling air, but I would miss the excitement. There was something about the old architecture nestled among skyscrapers, the history and museums, the theaters and bookstores and diversity and restaurants—oh the *restaurants!*—and even the unrelenting cacophony of New York that throbbed in my bones whenever I walked along the streets and avenues.

I estimated I had at least an hour, possibly ninety minutes, to finish packing before Ned showed up to start his guard duty for Eileen's physical and financial safety.

I stepped inside and shifted my bag to the opposite shoulder. I went to the kitchen and filled a glass with water. I grabbed an apple from the fridge. Taking my first bite, I started toward my bedroom. Just as my key entered the deadbolt lock on my bedroom door, I heard another door open. I turned suddenly, splashing water onto the back of my hand.

"You're home early." Ned's voice seemed to reverberate through the apartment.

I couldn't see him, but the sound came from the direction of Eileen's bedroom. I turned the key. The lock clicked. Leaving the keys hanging, I reached for the handle, but before I could open the door, Ned appeared a few feet from me.

He was naked except for a large pink bath towel wrapped around his waist. His hair was wet and there were drops of water on his face and chest, suggesting he'd dried quickly so he could rush out to startle me. Had he been planning to catch me by surprise, but I'd surprised him by coming home even earlier than expected?

He moved toward me. "Did you get fired? Or were you hoping to sneak into the apartment when no one was around?"

I opened my door and stepped into my bedroom. Juggling my bag, the glass of water, and the apple prevented me from closing it before Ned was able to move into the doorway. He was quick on his feet for a man wrapped in a bath towel.

I tossed the apple onto my bed. "Get out of the way."

"Which is it?" he asked. "Fired or sneaking around?"

"Get out of my room."

"Why are you so angry all the time?"

"I'm curious why you think that every time I ask you to treat me with even the minimum amount of respect, you interpret that as anger or upset or some other unrelated emotion."

He stepped into my bedroom.

"I want you out of my room right now."

"What are you going to do if I don't leave?"

That was a good question. I was sure I could inflict some harm, but I wasn't sure how far he would go, and he obviously outweighed me. He was easily eight or nine inches taller and although I was strong, I doubted I could win, even fully clothed.

I let the backpack slide off my shoulders and placed my glass on the dresser, just in case it came to that. I took a step toward him. "I don't know what your issue is. I'm assuming you want me out of Eileen's life entirely. If that's the case, it would be simpler if you'd just say so. But even then, she and I agreed to be roommates, and it's her call if she doesn't want to live together anymore. She likes living with me, or she did, so I'm not sure what you're trying to accomplish."

A smile spread slowly across his face. He didn't move toward me, but I could smell his shampoo and feel the heat of his breath and somehow, it felt like he had moved closer. Stepping away from him would suggest I was afraid of him. Surely he didn't think we were going to have a violent encounter over territorial rights in an apartment that was legally, more or less, half mine.

Usually I can guess with some degree of accuracy where other people were coming from, what they want from me. But with Ned, I couldn't figure it out. If he really loved Eileen, he seemed intent on upsetting her to the point of despair. If he was truly concerned I was a threat, he didn't seem to realize he was probably escalating that threat beyond his ability to control it. Nothing he did made any sense, and it was exhausting trying to figure it out. It was never clear if he just wanted to make me uncomfortable, to show me he had the upper hand, or if there was more to it.

With a flick of his wrist, he answered all my questions.

He released the towel from around his waist and I realized I should have glanced down earlier to see what he had planned.

He took a step closer. "You are so damn hot when you talk back. Don't you know that, Alexandra?"

Before I could consider what I would do, his hand was on the back of my head, pulling my face into his chest. His other hand was on my thigh, sliding up my skirt.

With that, I didn't need to think. My leg came up almost of its own volition and I slammed my knee between his legs.

He cried out and shoved me away. "God dammit." He bellowed and grabbed himself, bending over. "What the fuck! Why did you do that?"

"Get out of my room."

"You are the biggest tease I've ever met. Dancing around in your short skirts and low-cut tops. All that sassy fire. You know damn well that makes men want you. Kent told me all about you—no morals whatsoever. But I'm the one guy that you suddenly get all puritanical with?" He laughed bitterly. "I'm not buying it. I told you it's not normal for a woman to want nothing but casual sex. There's something wrong with you. No matter what I say, you never blush. Never. Do you even realize that?" He laughed harder, louder, followed by a grunt of pain.

I kicked the towel. It landed on his feet.

He didn't bend to pick it up, still holding onto himself with both hands, still hunched over. He groaned softly. "Now I'm really gonna need you to help me feel better."

I shoved him. He stumbled away from me but didn't fight back, still cupping himself, still grimacing from his injury. "You're not getting away with this. You've been teasing and tempting me, making up some guy named Hunter." He laughed until it sounded like he was bellowing. "*Hunt*-her. Very sly to pick a name like that. Trying to make me jealous. Come on, what do you want? Are you waiting for me to break up with Eileen first? Is that the hang-up?"

"You're disgusting." I put both hands on his chest and shoved him hard. He fell against the edge of the door, causing him to lose his balance. I grabbed his arm to keep him from falling, moved around to his side, and dragged him, limping and groaning and cursing, out of my room. I gave him a final shove. He crashed into the wall on the opposite side of the hallway.

I hurried back into my room, slammed the door, and locked it.

CHAPTER 79

I'd installed the security camera in my bedroom to protect Damien. I'd done it when I had the deadbolt lock placed on my door. It was an extra, somewhat extreme, mostly unnecessary layer of protection. It never crossed my mind that it would protect me, or that it would save Eileen from one of the worst mistakes of her life.

It also saved me from having to tell her the details of what happened. It saved me from a *he-said-she-said* scenario, one which Eileen might have been slow to believe. A picture is worth a thousand words, as the saying goes. Maybe that means a video is worth ten thousand words.

She cried. Then she hugged me. She cried some more. She thanked me so many times I began to feel slightly queasy and ran out of things to say in return. But she cried an enormous amount of tears before she got to the thanking part.

After that, she began begging me not to go to California. She even asked me to bring Damien back to the apartment. She said he would be good company.

Finally, I peeled her arms off my shoulders, and her words out of my ears, and her sad looks off the side of my face. "It's probably good for you to live by yourself, even if it's only for a few weeks."

"Why is that good?"

"Because you never have."

She stared at me.

"Without someone to lean on, you can figure things out," I said.

"There's nothing to figure out. I'm not going to rush out looking for a new guy today, if that's what you're thinking. I love my career. I haven't aged out. Not yet." She laughed, although it sounded as if her head was partially submerged in water with all the congestion from crying.

I shrugged. "Still. Living alone, even for just a few weeks will be good. You can clear the clutter out of your mind. The only voice in your head will be your own."

She stared at me so hard, her eyes seemed to bulge out.

"It's just a thought. Besides, you don't really have a choice. Unless you're going to invite someone to sleep on the couch while I'm gone. I'm still paying rent, so my room isn't up for grabs."

"I'm not worried about the money. But I don't want to be alone all the time. I don't like eating alone."

"Being alone is good for you. Especially after having someone infect your thoughts like he did. You need to try it. And make sure you call a locksmith. Today."

"I got the key back from him."

"Call a locksmith. Okay?"

"You really don't trust …" She nodded. "Okay."

We didn't say much more after that except the ritualistic *goodbyes* and *have a good trip* and *message me* and *send me pics* and *see you soon*.

As I rode down in the elevator, I wondered how the next few weeks would go for her. I also realized her mother had stripped her of most of her innate survival skills. I wondered if she could develop some in a few short weeks. She was a resilient person. She had lots of friends in the modeling industry, and I doubted she would be eating dinner alone every night.

By the time I left our building, I was confident my leaving was the best thing that had happened to her in a long time. Adapt or die.

CHAPTER 80

*H*unter and I went to dinner at a steak house. I didn't tell him about Ned. In fact, I didn't talk much, egging him on with questions about sports and his job, while a piece of my mind spun wildly in the background, wondering what was happening with Carolina and Jordan and Ricky.

I'd seen a news article about the discovery of her body, but that was it.

I could only assume that at some point, her cell phone records would lead them to contact Ned. He would have had an alibi in Eileen, but I wondered now how badly he'd messed that up. Still, she was a profoundly open and truthful person, so it was unlikely she'd leave him hanging, even after what he'd done to her.

Ricky was fully aware that his accusation against Hunter was a con, and a rather weak one, engineered by his mother. I was confident that all thoughts of that, as well as Hunter's name and mine, had died with her. Even if we came to mind with enough force that Ricky mentioned us to his father, or the police, all he knew were our first names.

Once Ned insisted he'd never seen nor heard of Carolina Scott, they might assume she'd texted a wrong number and would go searching for lovers rather than going through every contact on her phone. They would only have my burner number on a phone that no longer existed and a first name. It's a somewhat unusual name, but there are over fifty-nine-thousand Alexandras in the United States. The risk seemed low that they would try to locate me.

But I didn't like the loose ends. More than I'd ever had before.

I couldn't be sure if I was getting careless, or there were just so many things to think of and so many more people surrounding me that it was beginning to feel as if I were careless. I hoped that being in the open vineyards under the nearly cloudless blue skies of the Napa Valley would clear my head.

There was one thing I knew for sure. I did not want to make a habit of using a knife, no matter how polished and sharp and well-suited to the job. I still felt a visceral revulsion at the thought of encountering blood. The reality had been almost too much.

After dinner, we went back to Hunter's apartment where he made us martinis. We stood on the fire escape, leaning against the railing, sipping our drinks, and looking up at the stars. Then we went into his bedroom and it was the best ever, probably because we weren't thinking about that moment, but about all the moments that we wouldn't be together in the next few weeks.

He fell asleep in my arms, but I lay awake staring at the ceiling, thinking about the many ways things might play out with Carolina, wondering if Diana would have worked through her determination to find some way of identifying the person who murdered James, and trying to decide what I might do after my vacation.

I didn't fall asleep until after two. But with a first-class seat, I would enjoy a lovely nap on the plane

* * *

When I told Dean I'd take a rain check, they were empty words. When I told Eileen I had no plans to move out, those were truthful words because I didn't have plans to move. I also didn't have plans to stay. So maybe it should be called a half truth. A truth to buy me time.

Telling Diana I needed three weeks had been the result of closing my eyes and throwing a dart at an imaginary calendar. There was nothing about Fly Higher that made me want to return, aside from my paycheck and the chance to manipulate people with my camera. But I could find both of those things in other places.

As I was getting ready to leave, Hunter's eyes looked full of doubt. I wondered if he knew I was in the habit of saying whatever was most convenient at the time, truthful or not. But this time, I meant it. I didn't know when or how or in what way things would unfold between us, but I was not walking out of his life. I was not simply saying words to make leaving smooth and drama-free.

I kissed him again. When I pulled away, his eyes looked different, but I couldn't guess what he might be thinking. Maybe I never knew what he was thinking. Maybe I'd been wrong about the doubt as well.

"I'll be back," I said.

"I have no doubt," he said.

As I stepped out the door, Damien had the final word. *Dangerous woman.*

Hunter winked at me and closed the door softly.

ABOUT THE AUTHOR

Cathryn is the author of over thirty psychological suspense novels, including the ALEXANDRA MALLORY series featuring a sociopath you can't help but love. Readers have called the series "addictive".

The things that torment us in real life—obsession and revenge, guilt and envy and longing—are endlessly fascinating in fiction and she never grows tired of writing stories about characters struggling to overcome the worst.

Cathryn also writes ghost stories because who knows what lies beyond our senses—The Haunted Ship Trilogy and the Madison Keith series of novellas.

When she's not writing, she's usually reading, walking on the beach, or playing golf, going way out of her way to avoid hitting her ball in the sand or the water. She lives on the Central California Coast with her husband and her cat, Cleopatra.

You can get in touch with her by email, find her social media links, or sign up for her monthly newsletter at cathryngrant.com/contact. As a thank you for signing up, you'll receive a free short story about Alexandra Mallory.